Other books by the author

Raven's Realm Series
Raven's Child
Windows to the Soul
Chaos Within
Immortality
Darkness Falls

Women of Ravenwood Series
Fallen
Unspoken Oaths

Immortal series
Whispers of the Immortal
Tears of the Immortal
Soul of the Immortal
Fall of the Immortal
Echo of the Immortal

Immortality

M.J. Spickett

NORTHERN GEM
PUBLISHING

Immortality is a work of fiction. Names, characters, places, and incidents either are products of the author's imagination or are used fictitiously. Any resemblance to actual events or locales or persons, living or dead, is entirely coincidental.

Published in Canada by Northern Gem Publishing
Printed in Canada
Distributed by Ingram Worldwide
First Edition: Devine Destinies (2010)
Second Edition: KCEditions (2017)
Third Edition: Pen Knights Press (2019)
Forth Edition: Northern Gem Publishing (2024)

www.mjspickett.ca

Library and Archives Canada Cataloging in Publication
Spickett, M.J., 1976-, author
Immortality / M.J. Spickett
Issues in print and electronic formats

ISBN   978-1-998318-13-1   Paperback
ISBN   978-1-998318-14-8   Electronic Book

I. Title.

To my fans who continue to encourage me to write.

.

Author Note

MJ Spickett is a Canadian Author. Most locations within her novels focus on Canada and England, as such, words and spacing may appear differently than they would in America. For example, we often follow British English to use "U" in many of our words, for example "honor" (US) and "honour" (Canadian) or favorite (US) and favourite (Canadian). We write grey with an "e" not with an "a." My editor is also Canadian and is helping me keep to Canadian standards. As well, although it is normal in American to use a single space at the end of a sentence, Canada tends to double space. This also makes it easier to read and give an extra pause to help readers digest what they just read and better comprehend it. These are not spelling or formatting errors but simply the way we are taught to read and write.

Canadians tend to be a complicated group but that's also what makes us special.

Chapter One

1955, Talamasca
London, England

Anthony frowned at his reflection as he stepped up to the massive stain-glassed double doors of the old mansion. What was he doing here?

It had been years since he visited the Center for Paranormal Studies, otherwise known for being the meeting center for the British High Council of Magick. He still had no idea why he had allowed Henry to talk him into coming here. He had returned to England to visit his family for Christmas and was only staying three months. He had a lot planned for that time, too, none of which included traveling to London. However, it seemed the moment he stepped into Ipswich, Henry Griphan, the Police Chief from Coniston, near their cabin in the Scafell Pikes, was at his door step, begging him to go to the Center. Now, two days later, he was there. He had not even had a chance to travel to Cambridge and see his family. Instead, he had come to see a man he truly never wanted to see again. Worse than that, he had left his Guardians in Ipswich. It had been a last-minute decision, but in the end, he believed it was for the best. Anthony was not sure what he was about to face and he had no desire to endanger his children.

The old mansion had existed for several hundred years and was perhaps one of the largest in all of England. Sometime in the mid eighteen hundreds, it had been converted into an office building directed toward the British High Council of Magick and the research of all that was paranormal. There were over forty offices and nearly thirty bedrooms for those who traveled great distances to reach it. It was quite beautiful with its vast gardens, high ceilings and large archways. It reminded Anthony of his father's mansion.

"May I take your coat, sir?" an elderly man inquired. He stepped up to Anthony, one hand out expectantly. Old hazel eyes brightened at the sight of him. "Ah, Master Anthony! It's so nice to see you again. I was beginning to fear you would never return."

"Hello, Albert," Anthony said with a smile. He clasped the man's bony hand. "I can't believe they still have you working here."

"Be what I am doing. I would go nuts if I didn't work." The whitehaired, frail looking butler took Anthony's heavy trench coat and led him through the foyer. "I'm afraid your father's not here today. Your sister says he caught that blasted flu that's going around. It's that time again. Much of the country going through it, you know. Best make sure those lil' ones of yours are wrapped up warm."

"I will. Is Lord Porter here?"

"Porter. I thought—"

"It's important, Albert."

Albert became thoughtful as he led Anthony through the grand hall. He scratched his head. "The library, I believe. He said he wanted to do some research. New spells and all, I suppose. He's very busy these days. Talking about marrying this lass from France. A young Sorceress."

"Really?" It sounded odd. Porter getting married, maybe that meant the warlock would finally grow up. Perhaps that was the news that was so important.

"Shall I bring you something to drink, sir?"

He nodded. It was considerably cold outside. Snow was bond to fall within the next few days. He could taste their crispness in the air.

"Tea, please. Thank you, Albert."

Albert gave a small bow before hurrying off.

The library was huge, perhaps the most elegant and diverse in all of Britain. It held every magick book found in Europe. High Priests of the Order had traveled worldwide and had made copies of as many Grimoires as possible and brought them back here, yet there were still so many out there. Anthony's personal library was not even a quarter as large as the Council's were, yet he had many they did not. However, those were in Canada and he made a promise long ago not to bring them to his homeland.

The four-story high and five-acres square library was a labyrinth of shelves and books. It would take an entire lifetime to read each and every book, maybe even two. As a child, when Anthony's father felt it necessary for him to attend Council meetings, he had spent the winter months playing here, or would send hours on end reading as he got older. His father had been intent on him knowing as much about magick and his gifts as possible and proclaimed Anthony's gifts were stronger than his siblings were, and that he was the one to unite Eastern and Western magick. He was to be the savior of the magick realm.

The Savior.

It was why Anthony had run away after his wife had died. It was why he had abandoned their child. Both sides of his family believed he was the one to lead them into a new state of magickal being. A child of two worlds, yet belonging to neither.

He closed his eyes. Such thoughts were no longer worthy of his attention. He had come to grips with his life many years ago. He was neither British nor Spanish, he was simply Anthony Sinclair, son of Jonathan Sinclair and Helena Syffern, and he took pride in that. He had his mother's black hair—so shiny it looked blue-black—and his father's build and height, as well as his ocean blue eyes that were oddly tri-coloured and seemed to make the girls go wild. He loved his eyes best of all. No other human he had ever met had them. Only those of Faerie.

The sun shone brightly through the eastern windows as he entered the elegant library. Large green plants gathered from many countries around the world stood or hung all over, basking in the light from the huge bay windows. It gave an earthy smell that Anthony took a moment to savor. That smell was one of the few things that he had missed from his frequent visits. It gave the aura of peace and serenity.

The librarian looked up from her book and smiled sweetly at him. A Lycanthrope, he realized with a smile of his own, one of the best guards they could hire to protect the ancient texts concealed in the room. No-one…magick or otherwise, was able to take the books out of the mansion. The shape shifters made sure of it.

"Excuse me, where might I find Lord Porter?" he asked the young blonde woman.

Her eyes met his and widened slightly. His eyes always took people by surprise. The British were not used to seeing a tall Spanish man with such bright blue eyes and pale skin, nor with the ability to speak fluent English without an accent. He enjoyed their surprise.

They often thought he was full blood faery.

"Ah…" She blinked and shook her head. "He was near the rear, researching vampires of all things."

He graced her with a happy smile. "Thank you."

Vampires. Why would Duncan be studying that particular mythic creature? He silently laughed. Was he planning to join the Paranormal Squad? The High Council had their own policing system. Those abusing their gifts or any paranormal activity such as demon-rising or satanic rituals sent them into action. As children, Anthony and Duncan Porter wanted to join them and fight the demons of the world. Now that he was grown, Anthony discovered that there were better things in life than hunting monsters. That didn't mean that he didn't have his fair share to deal with in Canada.

Duncan was where Anthony expected he would find him. He was high up on a ladder, searching the top shelf. He didn't look down as Anthony approached. "I thought you weren't coming."

"Henry can be very persuasive."

The warlock nodded, his long brown-black hair pooling around his shoulders as he looked down.

His light blue eyes regarded him with a look of longing. Anthony ignored it as he studied the spine of the books across from him. He didn't want to stay too long if he could help it. Just find out what Porter wanted and go. "I hear you're getting married."

Duncan blinked, then smiled. "Yes, this spring." He descended the ladder to stand before him. "It's good to see you."

"It's been a long time."

"Since Elizabeth's—" He fell silent. "I'm sorry."

Anthony frowned. He folded his arms across his chest and leaned against the bookcase. He did not want to talk about his sister. It was hard enough now that she was gone. He had come to accept it. There was no need to open old wounds. "What do you want, Duncan?"

A soft smile crossed the younger man's lips at the sound of his first name. It had been so long since Anthony had used it, and why he did so now, he would never understand.

"To see how you were. It's been three years and even then, you've barely spoken to me."

"I wonder why."

"You know I had nothing to do with that. I was as shock as you when I heard Nathaniel had been kidnapped by that cult."

Anthony raised a brow. He didn't believe Porter, couldn't. He still couldn't understand how it had happened, why no one had seen anything. It was just too convenient. He gazed at the book in the other man's hand.

"And the reason for studying vampirism? Just coincidence?"

He held up the book with pride. "Psychic Vampires. Completely different from what happened to your angel."

Anthony grunted, his gaze traveling to the stack of books on the floor, all similar to the one Duncan held. He must have been planning to stay for a few weeks. The Missus-to-be must not like that.

"So, you begged Henry to bring me here to talk about vampires?"

You're that desperate to see me?" He shrugged. "I missed you."

Anthony laughed. "Next time come to Ravenwood." Not that he ever wanted to see Porter anywhere near his home. However, the chances of the warlock ever traveling overseas were about as unlikely as him growing wings.

"I might just do that."

"When pigs can fly. Without magick."

Porter smiled broadly. "Well since you're here, why don't we send some time getting to know each other once again?"

Anthony sighed. This was the part he had been hoping to avoid. "We're not friends any more, Duncan. You murdered my sister. You should be happy I don't kill you. All I want is for you to leave my family and I alone. Do you not understand that?"

The warlock looked away with sad eyes. It had been a spell gone wrong that caused Elizabeth Sinclair's premature death. Yet, it was a different situation when Nathaniel almost died. That had been deliberate no matter what Porter tried to tell him.

"Your father is talking about making me the next leader of the Council unless you agree to take his place. That's why I'm studying so much."

Anthony's jaw dropped. His father would never allow Duncan such a position. Not after what happened to Elizabeth and Nathaniel. It wasn't possible. It must be a trick to keep Anthony from returning to Canada. He would put nothing past his father.

As always, Duncan appeared to read his thoughts. A small frown creased his lips as he picked up his books. "He misses you, Raven. We all do. Would leading the Council be so bad?"

"It would be different if I wanted the position and was voted in, but to inherit it simply because I'm a Sinclair? It's not right."

"Anthony, you are a Sinclair and the most powerful sorcerer in your family. It's your birthright."

"It's not my birthright. Even the Oracles see that. How many wizards have challenged me for it? Including you? I've lost count. It's just as bad in Spain."

"And yet you're hiding in Canada."

Anthony shrugged. Duncan hit the nail on the head. There was no denying that hiding was exactly what he was doing. He was tired of fighting. He just wanted to be alone with what family he had. His Guardians were as much family as anyone else, perhaps even more so.

Duncan began absentmindedly flipping through his first book. "So…what's your opinion on vampires? Psychic vampires?"

Taking a deep breath, Anthony took one of the books and scanned through several of the pages. "I don't know. I never had to deal with one. Why don't you just tell me why I'm here? Is my father's trying to get you to challenge me again? Or do you want me to graciously hand you the reins to the Council? Heck, if you want them they're yours."

They'd had this argument too many times over the years. All he wanted was to get his meeting with Duncan done and over with so he could go about his day…yet, he could not shake how tired he suddenly was. His eyelids felt heavy. Stifling a yawn, he reached out with his senses to see if any foul magick was being directed toward him. Finding nothing out of the ordinary, he shrugged inwardly. The ride to London must have tired him out. Or maybe it was the subject over their conversation. Normally he liked a good vampire story, but research into psychic vampires got boring after a while. It had been his field of research as a teen. Closing his eyes, he listened to Duncan ramble on. At least Nathaniel and the others knew he might not be home for a few days. He just hoped they didn't kill each other in his absence.

"Funny thing is, Raven, most of them are completely human and have no idea what they are or doing. Sometimes they can take one's energy without ever knowing it, the poor souls."

"Uh-huh."

"There are others, like your Guardians, who know and can control it so that they only take it when desperate. However, they can only take it from someone with a much higher magick level than their own. Otherwise, they could inadvertently kill someone."

True, he had trained his Guardians how to retrieve more magick if needed, but he was the only one from which he allowed them to feed. He knew how to deal with such a loss of magick. There was no need for them to find another source until the day he died, but he had set plans into motion to protect each of his Guardians. They would not become a danger to the public after he was gone. In time, he hoped they would be able to draw their power from the elements, as most of faery-kind do.

His eyes became impossible to open as the tiredness grew. It felt like a heavy weight pushing down on him. Certainly, he couldn't be that tired in the middle of the day? It was a long ride on horseback from Ipswich to London, but he had made the trip countless times in the past without ever feeling so worn. He laughed at himself. *Maybe I'm just getting old.* He hoped Duncan got to the point soon. Falling asleep in front of his rival would not be a good thing.

Brushing back a few loose strands of ebony hair that had escaped his ponytail, he tried forcing his eyes open once more. It was no use. They refused to open. It could be a spell, yet he could sense none. Nor could he sense any hostility from Duncan.

"Others do it for the thrill, the wave of power that comes from their unsuspecting victims. I always wondered how you might react to one. If you could stop one before it was too late. I don't know if I could. I never had to yet."

"Stop the energy current," Anthony murmured.

Was that what was happening to him? Did Duncan hire a psychic vampire to attack him? It was next to impossible to sense them. If he could focus, pull himself out of the sleepiness that was enveloping him, he could close the channels, stop the flow of energy throughout him. Not having any energy meant nothing for the vampire to feed upon.

His mind was too muddy to concentrate as the cloud of sleep wrapped around him thicker.

"Raven?"

"Hmm?"

"You look tired. Do you wish to rest?"

He would have retorted, joked about Duncan's perceptiveness, but he felt as if he were falling into a deep black hole. He could feel magick now, knew Duncan was using it to keep him from falling and smacking his head against the hard wooden shelves and marble floor. He silently thanked his old rival for saving him the indignity. There were very few good things to say about Duncan Porter. This was one of them.

Large arms, definitely not Duncan's, caught him before he hit the ground. The warmth and aura finally made his eyes open. The large man was fuzzy at first and it took a moment to realize his spectacles had fallen off. Duncan carefully placed them over his eyes making the man come in clearly. Anthony smiled as Henry Griphan's large bulk came into focus. The short strawberry hair contrasted with the large muscles, police uniform and deep gray eyes that could intimidate any criminal.

"Hi, Henry," he managed with a small laugh. "I thought I'd take a nap. Libraries are nice and quiet, you know."

"I'm sure." A smile lit up the police chief's serious face as a warm hand touched Anthony's neck. It was an odd gesture for the usually distant man. Physical contact had never been one of Henry's strong points. "Are you okay? The flu has been hitting just about everyone. You look pale."

"I'm part faery, I'm always pale compared to you."

That earned him a laugh from his best friend. Anthony's eyes once again closed of their own accord. His world went black before he could apologize. Maybe it was the flu, but it wasn't very often he got sick. In fact, he could not remember catching a cold since he was a wee boy.

Henry's strong arms lifted him off the floor and he could feel himself carried out of the library. He knew the mansion like the back of his hand and just feeling the direction Henry was taking, he knew they headed for the guest rooms. He had no fear when with Henry. The large man was his most trusted friend, one of the few reasons he returned to England once a year. He could trust Henry with his life and knew that in the next he would always be safe with him. It brought a small, sleepy smile to his lips.

Who cared about psychic vampires with friends like that to care for you?

Chapter Two

Present day

Elijah Hawke ran a hand through his long black hair and smiled warmly out the van window. The English mountain air was sweet with pine and spruce, and the many forms of wildflowers growing on the side of the mountains that rose on either side of the twisting road. It was a synergy of beauty and serenity. The green contrasted the bright blue sky perfectly.

Although Eli loved Canada with a passion, he did miss England's beauty and old-world magick. He peered out of the SUV's window, giddy at the fact that he was finally returning home after nine months. A solid year if he included the time he had spent in London. The Scafell Pike Mountains were home to him. He had spent most of his life there with his grandfather and cousin, Selena, and was more than happy to finally return home. The best part was Grandpa Henry had insisted he bring his friends and *adopted* family to visit as well. It gave him a chance to show off the English splendor he had boasted to everyone.

Thankfully, it was summer break for everyone, including Nathan Hastings and Scott Dion, who were both in college and working. It had taken a lot of persuasion to get them to take the time off work. The only ones who could not make it were Daniel Dion, who was in India on a dig, and Eli's girlfriend, Melissa Corbriere, who was in Florida with her family. At least he had Alexis, Miao, Nathan, Scott, Selena and the two Familiars with him. He couldn't wait to introduce them to

Henry. He had wanted to for so long that it had become a physical pain the last two days before their flight.

Now they were almost there. Twenty minutes, a half hour tops,

but it felt like a lifetime before they would ever reach the cabin. Eli never thought he would get so homesick.

Nathan leaned against him a little to peer out his window. The ash blond-haired man was at awe. His slight-build barely weighed a thing as he tried to get a better look.

"So, this is where you grew up?" he asked. His soft brown eyes sparkled with a hint of amethyst as he stared wide-eyed at the mountains. "It looks so much like…home."

Eli smiled and he was tempted to hug him. Nathan had next to no memory of his life before awaking in Canada sixteen years ago. At least not while he was in this form. When he was in his faery form as Frost, did he remember his past? Nathan only remembered what his other personality allowed him, and that volume was slowly increasing. Either way, it had been over forty years since Nathan had been in England. That was forty years too long.

"Anthony used to bring the Guardians here almost every Christmas," Eli explained. "There's no place like England for Christmas."

Nathan beamed with warmth as he wrapped an arm around the younger man. "I remember. Papa loved the snow."

For a moment, Eli could only stare at him and then warmth filled him at the fact that Nathan did indeed remember a bit about his past. Frost was opening more and more to his human form. He smiled proudly as he turned his gaze back to the scenery.

"Eli, the Mountain Man," Miao suddenly teased. He swatted Eli's shoulder. "How did you ever get so prim and proper living up here?"

He twisted in his seat and glared at his cousin. "I'm not a *Mountain Man*, Miao. I spent every summer and Christmas with Henry since I was born. The ranch is far from what your traditional cabin is. It's practically a mansion in itself."

Miao Syffern, one of his cousins and favourite rivals, gave a smug, lopsided grin and squeezed his girlfriend. The auburn-haired woman rolled her eyes at her boyfriend's antics and elbowed him. When it came to Miao being a smartass, Alexis Dion always put him in his place. It was one of the best things about her. She didn't take guff from anyone. She was also his cousin, but one the other side of his family and shared no blood-ties with Miao, or at least not enough to be of consequence.

Nathan placed a hand on his shoulder which kept Eli from reaching over and swatting the other, although Eli was more than tempted to use magick on him.

Miao suddenly whistled, his chocolate brown eyes growing wide. "I take it back. Wow!"

Eli turned back to the front window. In the distance, the large three-story cabin came into sight. The lake below shimmered in the bright July sun like a jewel. Nathan leaned forward, holding the back of Scott's seat so he could get a better look as Selena pulled onto a private road.

There was a familiar crackle of magick as they passed through the protective shield. Raven's magick instantly recognized them as friends, not foes. The current was warm as it brushed past Eli, like a hug from an old friend. Nathan and Selena were affected in the same way, although Nathan seemed slightly confused by it.

"Protective shield. No one can get through it unless they're of Raven's blood or invited."

"Oh." He looked thoughtful as he stared at his hand, still feeling it. "It felt warm."

Eli nodded in understanding.

Alexis leaned over the back of their seat. "Eli, your home's beautiful."

He blushed slightly and rubbed the back of his head. It had been so long since he had brought friends up here. "Ah...well, thanks. Anthony and Henry began building it when they were teens. It took over eighteen years before it was completed. In the end, they had to hire a crew to finish it."

"Why?"

He laughed. "Henry had a family to care for and Anthony had the Guardians. It's hard to finish things when you have kids running wild."

"Like you're easy to care for, squirt," Selena teased, pulling into the drive. She glanced into the rearview mirror and winked at them. Her long brunette hair obscured one side of her face, she brushed it back with a smile. "At least Anthony could use his magick to discipline us.

I'm stuck grounding you, and if that doesn't work—" Her smile broadened as she petted the black cat curled up on the dashboard. The mystic cat purred sleepily, basking in the hot July sun. "I'll just get Cleo to sit on you."

In his true form, Cleo was a large panther with amazing black feathery wings. He, and the winged wolf lying next to Alexis, Sif, was his and Alexis's familiars, summoned by Anthony Sinclair to protect them. They both weighed a ton. Eli knew from personal experience. Selena was not bluffing when she said she would have Cleo sit on him. She had done it many times in the past.

Selena, like Nathan-Frost, was a faery just as Cleo and Sif once were. Even in her fey form, she was strongest at night, even more so on a full moon. She and Frost were Sidhe. Then again so was Eli, partly, at least. Nocturnal magick had been his past life's specialty and, although Anthony loved the day, it was easier to concentrate in the darkness of night. No cluttered thoughts from busy town folk as it were during the day. That had not changed in this new form and life. Eli felt at home in the dark and shadows. Well, not all shadows.

A cold chill ran up his spine as an old childhood fear washed over him. He wasn't sure why, but he was always careful in the shadows despite his love of them. Forcing those thoughts back, Eli tried to concentrate on his home welcoming. There was no need to think of silly things such as unnatural shadows or the cause of them. They were aspects of magick, or at least their users were, that he did not like. Such painful thoughts were best left at home, in Ravenwood. He came to the cabin to relax and that was exactly what he planned to do.

He stretched as they neared the end of the drive. This was going to be his best summer vacation. He was going to make sure of it. Nothing strange ever happened up here, other than the odd faerie prank that usually had little to do with Selena. Nope. This was going to be perfect.

"I don't mind. Cleo's fun to play with, and Sif only doubles it. Besides, you know Henry. *No false forms.* You'll have to..." he trailed off as Scott turned and stared at him in puzzlement. It took a moment to realize what the older man was worried about. He glanced at Nathan who had slipped into deep thought again. "Oh, damn. Nathan, I'm sorry, I wasn't thinking. Henry hasn't seen you or *Frost* in so long. Back then, you two thought as one...usually. He doesn't understand that you and Frost haven't merged back into one yet. He'll expect to see—"

"Frost." He gave a reassuring smile. "I understand."

Scott didn't seem so convinced or understanding. He stared at Nathan for an eternity, as if they were able to read each other's minds. They probably could, they were so close. Scott was clairvoyant while Frost, even in Nathan's form, was highly telepathic. Not as strong as Eli and Selena, they had been training half their lives, but he was still more than effective. The amethyst of Frost's eyes shone through Nathan's soft brown ones.

Scott gave a nod and sat back. "If you two weren't merging, I would've said no to a full two weeks. It may prove a large strain. You've never been dormant for more than twenty-four hours."

Nathan shrugged his slim shoulders. "I can handle it and Frost deserves a vacation like anyone else." Another nod.

"And it's not like before. I don't fall asleep every time Frost is in control. He lets me do as I wish and it's fun." He gave a private wink that only the two would understand.

Selena giggled while Eli rolled his eyes and looked out the side window once more. Scott and Nathan were lovers, life partners, and, although Eli would never admit this, he was jealous. Once, long ago, when he had been Anthony Sinclair, he had been lovers with Frost. Well…Nathaniel actually. The feelings were not truly his, but the remnants of his past self's and had only started after learning the truth about his former relationship with the faery. It was a memory that should never have surfaced, but did only because of a warlock with a grudge against the former couple. Since then, Eli had to come to reality about Frost's love for Scott.

He dug his fingernails into the flesh of his palms. He would not allow himself to think of Frost in such a way. Frost was one of his best friends no matter what form he was in, and he had promised himself a long time ago never to fall in love with him. Frost had made a similar promise to never hurt him, to love him as he would a brother and Eli was grateful if not a little disappointed. His emotions regarding the guardian were uncertain.

Maybe Nathan sensed this. He wrapped an arm around Eli's shoulders and leaned close. "Your hand is starting to bleed," he whispered, carefully uncurling the youth's fingers.

Eli winced slightly, but let him do it. Nathan was very discreet. No one, other than Selena, glancing through the rearview mirror, noticed what was going on.

Nathan gave a sigh as he studied the small, moon-shaped puncture wounds. They weren't deep, but did sting. Pain always eased the turmoil of emotions Frost unconsciously brought to Eli, but it seemed even his human form now brought them as well. He blushed and tried to pull his hand away only to have Nathan rub his thumb over it. It was odd. In this form, he had no true magick, but Eli could feel the faery's warmth, taste the sudden power flowing through them. He watched in fascination as he hand completely healed as if nothing had happened. His world became consumed by the unexpected magick. He didn't even notice Selena park in front of the large ranch style cabin.

"How... When..." he murmured. He held up his hand to inspect. He was not paying attention to Miao and Alexis as they bounded out of the van. It wasn't possible for Nathan to perform magick. Both personalities could not have merged so far without Eli noticing, could they? It was the only way Frost could utilize his magick in human form.

"Frost showed me."

Frost showed him? So, he hadn't noticed. "You're merging faster than I thought," he whispered. It was fantastic! It was a little surprising, but also amazing. They had waited so long for this to happen.

Scott had slipped out before them, seemingly oblivious to the closeness between them. Eli could not help but feel a pang of guilt for him. How did Scott feel about his lover merging with his true self? It often fascinated Eli how Frost was able to speak through Nathan. They were one after all, but so different at the same time. Frost must have felt the same the few times Anthony's spirit had spoken through Eli. In many ways, he had more in common with Nathan than anyone else. It made him feel close to the older man.

"You're feverish," Frost said through Nathan's lips. He cupped Eli's cheek. "Are you alright?"

Damn it, Anthony, Eli swore to the spirit of his past self buried deeply in the back of his mind. *Did you have to love him so much?*

He tried reining in his emotions and the sudden desire he felt for the unearthly being holding him. He had to pull himself back when he realized he had been inching toward his friend's full, soft lips. Mentally, he berated himself for such stupidity and suddenly wished Scott were there to distract Nathan and keep him from making a huge and painful mistake.

In either form, Frost was beautiful. His build was disarming, only standing approximately five foot seven inches, slim and very light on his feet. He did have a lot of muscle even if it didn't show. As Nathan, his hair was ash blond and he wore wire-rimmed glasses. He was very soft spoken and loved to tease Scott. As Frost, he was different. His hair was long and flowing to his feet and was as silvery white as the moon. Amethyst eyes replaced the soft amber and were far more watchful. Large snowy white wings donned his back, but were able to retract into his back when not in use. He was far more formal and had a tendency to appear cold and distant. That was an act. The true Frost always appeared in Nathan, even if they acted as two separate people.

It was hard not to love them both.

Nathan pulled back in understanding and slipped out the open door. It took a moment for Eli to catch his breath before following the other to the front door.

Scott gave Eli a funny look as he caught up with both men. Guilt rolled in Eli's stomach. The last thing he wanted was the elder Dion angry with him or mistaking his feelings for Nathan and Frost. Worse thing was Scott could read him like a book. He had to resist the urge to step back when the young man frowned. Eli immediately plastered his trademark smile on to hide his unease.

Scott shook his head and gave a smirk. "Kids! You're going to take longer than the others."

That made Eli laugh. It seemed many of the younger members of their group had crushes on Nathan at one point or another. Scott had become used to his lover getting all the extra attention. He never seemed to mind too much, at least not when it was Alexis a few years back. Maybe it was because of Anthony's and Nathaniel's past that he kept a closer eye on Eli, but at least he wasn't mad.

Selena opened the door and gestured for everyone to enter. They piled into the foyer and dropped their bags. The smell of spices filled the house. Eli took a moment to breath in the familiar aroma. This was home. Childhood memories filled his mind as he instinctively placed his bag on the first step of the front staircase.

The foyer was large, lined with paintings he had made for Henry when he was young. The walls were all wood panel and the floors were hard wood covered with a lush burgundy rug. The furniture was all very modern compared to what Eli owned back home. Still, he loved it. Henry always followed the latest trends thanks to Selena.

"Henry! We're home!" Selena called. She sat her bag next to Eli's and wrapped an arm around his waist. "Come see how big Eli got. I'm telling you, the food in Canada just keeps making him grow! He's addicted to pizza!"

An elderly man in his mid-eighties strolled into the foyer. His short, crew-cut style hair was completely gray with silvery white on the sides. Despite his age, he looked extremely young and fit, only in his mid-sixties if that. He was built like a wrestler. Tall and broad-shouldered, his only rival could be Scott, but even then, Eli was sure Henry out-did him by at least two inches.

Henry leaned against his cane and gave a smooth smile. "Selena, my love, you can wake up the dead. I'm sure there are a few ghosts who'd prefer to sleep if you don't mind." He easily picked her off her feet and gave her a large hug and kiss on the cheek. "How are you, my dear?"

"Good, Grandpa, and you?" she giggled. She gave him a tight embrace.

"Better now that you're home."

He let her go, his eyes widening as he caught sight of Eli. He hobbled past the brunette and stood, towering before him. Henry Griphan was perhaps the tallest man Eli had ever met and it was easy to feel like a little kid compared to him. He was more than three times Eli's size. Those warm gray eyes that always made him feel safe seemed a little different, as if something was missing, but it cleared away quickly as he was pulled into a crushing bear hug.

"Eli, my boy! You've grown into an incredibly handsome young man. The girls must be going crazy about you."

He let the oddness in Henry's eyes pass as surprise to how much he had grown the past year and how long his hair now was. Henry had never really liked long hair on men, but rarely voiced it because of his friendship with Anthony Sinclair decades earlier. Besides, Eli was old enough to make his own decisions, especially when it came to his hair.

The tattoo on his back was another story. Henry was likely to kill him if he ever saw it.

He wrapped his arms around the big man's neck and tightened the embrace. "I've missed you, Grandpa," he whispered. Tears prickled at the corner of his eyes. He never realized just how much he missed being hugged by the elderly man.

Setting him on the floor, the former army general and police chief studied him. "I see the man I once knew in the youth before me." He buried his hand in Eli's long, thick hair and pulled him into another embrace. "You look so much like Raven."

"Really?"

It was a question he asked every time someone said that. He knew it was true, but it was still hard to believe. Anthony had been very handsome, he was told. He could still recount every bedtime story Selena and his grandmother had ever told him as a child. Even the evidence he saw in the mirror every morning wasn't enough, nor the fact he was now an inch taller than Nathan and four inches taller than Miao. He was just as bad as the others for worshipping Raven so it was a little hard to believe he would one day look like the once great Sorcerer. They had the same blue-black hair that hung midway down their back, same ocean-blue, tri-coloured eyes, although he preferred to keep his hidden under glamour—just freaked-out some people out when they looked at his eyes—same nearsightedness where they were forced to wear glasses, even the same taste in glasses. However, Eli had yet to grow the shoulders and height. Scott had inherited that from Anthony much faster than he had, but he was getting there. Another year or two and he would match Scott and look identical to Anthony. He wasn't exactly sure if he liked that idea or not.

"Yes, but when he was your age his hair was much shorter. He didn't start growing it until he was almost twenty, after he moved to Spain."

"I decided to get a head start." Eli liked his hair long. It felt good. Henry had always tried to get Anthony to cut his, but it never happened and Eli was not going to cut his either. Although there was no way, he was going to let it get as long as Frost's. Waist-length was as long as he would let it grow.

Henry seemed to read his mind as he ruffled his long bangs. "It's your hair to do with as you please. It's nice to be able to see an old friend again." He chuckled at his surprise before almost being knocked on his rear by a hyperactive albino husky. "Sif!"

"Henry! I missed you! You missed me too, right?"

"Of course, Sif." He petted the husky's head as he had so long ago.

The animal whooped in joy and dragged a very annoyed Cleo deeper in the house before the black cat could greet his old friend.

Henry laughed, as did Eli. It was almost like old times when Anthony and his Guardians would visit for Christmas. Only one guardian had yet to greet Henry. Nathan was hanging back, unconsciously grasping Scott's hand in a death grip. There was a look in his eyes that unnerved Eli. It wasn't the response he had expected from the faery. There appeared to be fear hidden within their depths. It was definitely not a Nathan-Frost expression. It had to be the fact that he was home after all these years. Or the fact that Henry was not as young as when they last saw each other. Those were natural emotions to have, yet something was different, even in the way Henry was looking at him. An anger Eli had never seen in Henry before. Nathan flinched under the angry stare and held Scott's hand even tighter.

It took a moment for Eli to figure what the problem might be. Henry wasn't overly fond of homosexuality. He would never say it out loud, but he had that look that said if he weren't a gentleman, he would break you in two for it. There had been more than enough arguments between him and Anthony concerning Nathaniel's sexual orientation. After all, they had been lovers and Anthony would never allow harm to come to his precious angel from anyone. Maybe he thought Nathaniel had betrayed Anthony or Eli by being with Scott, but hey, that's the way life goes. He could not expect the faery, even if he was immortal, to wait forever for Anthony's return or Eli to come of age. Heck, Eli, and Frost had had that discussion often enough. When it came to Henry, you never knew what to expect. Nonetheless, it did not explain Nathan's sudden fear.

Henry's cold gray eyes softened. "Come here, boy."

It was Scott who tightened his grip on the smaller man's hand. He gave his love a questioning gaze, once again sharing their thoughts. With a reluctant nod, he let Nathan go. The moment Nathan stepped away from Scott, he was swept into a bear hug that should have crushed his small frame.

The change took place in mid-squeeze as both Nathan and Henry were bathed in a blinding flash of light. Snowy white wings flared on Nathan's back before vanishing and revealing Frost's pale form. His long silvery hair grew from Nathan's short ash blond. His white robes replaced Nathan's street clothes.

The transformation didn't faze Henry. He held the ethereal being closer. "It's been over forty years, Nathaniel. No visits, letters or even a phone call. I was sure you'd get a hold of me after meeting Eli. I've been so worried about you."

Eli sighed in relief. It wasn't Nathaniel's sex life that angered him. Then again, over forty years without communication was a good reason to be upset. Hell, he would be, too.

"I'm sorry, Henry. I...couldn't come back. There were too many memories. I needed time."

He was lying! Eli blinked in astonishment. Why? He was tempted to read the angel's mind and find out, but stopped himself. He was not the guardian's Master in this life, the Dions were and either way Frost was entitled to his privacy. He certainly didn't look comfortable hugging Henry, even if the old man seemed content to just hold him a few minutes longer to make up for all those lost years.

Henry had Frost a good foot off the ground, arms wrapped around him so tightly, it was as if he were afraid to let him go. His face was buried in the silky waves of silver hair. It looked as if he were crying, or talking very softly to the smaller man.

Scott's discomfort seemed to match Frost's. Henry looked up questioningly as the equally tall man stepped up to him. "I'm Scott Dion, Fr—that is, Nathaniel's boyfriend," he announced. He nervously stuck out his hand.

Henry let Frost slide to the ground and took Scott's hand, pumping it twice. "Your father tells me you're studying to be a doctor. He's very proud."

"A surgeon, yes." He smiled at Frost as he straightened his robes and stood next to him. "And Nathaniel is studying to be a professor of Mythology and Anthropology."

Henry was obviously surprised to hear Frost was in school, even though Selena and Eli had told him a dozen times that as Nathan, Frost attended the local community college in Ravenwood with Selena and Scott. In fact, he had just graduated at the top of his class and was enrolled in university that coming September. He was presently studying with Professor Dion to prepare for the upcoming school year. He really enjoyed working with Scott's and Alexis's father. It had taken forever for him to decide what he wanted to do and when he finally did, he was more than content. Nathan and Frost were part of the Dion family, after all, so it was nothing new to study with Daniel.

Eli felt the same. He loved visiting the Dions and being tutored by Daniel. Like Frost, he felt extremely close to the professor, but he had a very good reason. Daniel held the other half of Anthony Sinclair's spirit and was his uncle. It was because of a car accident that part of Daniel was reincarnated into Eli. It had been a near-death experience like no other. Despite their age difference, they were practically brothers, but Eli preferred to think of him as a second father as did Frost. Henry approved, which was a huge relief.

Frost was proud of his education. He smirked when Scott snaked an arm around his waist and gave him a squeeze.

"We're all very proud of him. He's been one of Dad's teacher aids for several years now."

Henry raised a brow. "Is that so? Anthony always said you'd make a good teacher."

Alexis, for all her faults, felt the tension between them as well. She glanced at Eli who could only shrug. Something wasn't right. Frowning, she stepped past Frost and Scott and made herself the center of attention. The tension rising between Scott and Henry broke instantly.

"Hi! I'm Alexis Dion and this is Miao Syffern," she said with a soft smile.

The eighteen-year-old boy gave a small bow. "Hello," he said softly.

Henry bowed as well. "Welcome to England. My home is open to you both." He smiled at Miao's surprised look.

Miao smiled. "Thank you. It's a beautiful house."

"You haven't seen the half of it," Henry joked. He turned to both Selena and Frost. "There's only one rule. I want all my Guardians in their true forms. Oh, and there is no magick in the kitchen." He gave Eli a pointed look.

Selena burst out laughing as Eli blushed and covered his face. *No, not that story*, he groaned inwardly. He had hoped Henry would not bring that up, at least not when they first walked in.

"That was eleven years ago, grandpa!" he groaned as the other teens and adults stared at him.

Frost looked at Selena in confusion as she threw an arm around Eli's shoulders and playfully rested her head against one shoulder. It wasn't much of a reach, he was only two inches taller than her, but she acted as if he were huge. "He set the kitchen on fire," she said in all cuteness.

"I was seven!"

Miao burst into laughter. "The great Raven set his kitchen on fire!" he cried.

Eli's eyes narrowed. "You're asking for it."

That only made him laugh harder. *Yep, best friends were always great to have. They always stood by you.* If it weren't for Henry's *no magick* rule, which in fact covered the whole house not just the kitchen, he would have done something to wipe that smirk off Miao's face. Maybe actually make his lips disappear.

"Yes, well it cost a fortune in repairs, so all heavy or elemental magick is done outside."

Selena saluted Henry as she transformed into her faery form. Her hair turned to a black-red and her brown eyes became a tri-coloured red, making her look like one of the goddesses of death.

"Yes sir, General Henry, sir," she giggled, as she grabbed Frost's hand and began dragging him and Scott to the stairs. "Come on, Frosty, you're got to see what I did to your room."

"Selena!"

"Hey, we only unlocked it last summer. It needed serious dusting and painting. The mattress needed to be replaced, but at least your clothes were protected. Henry bought you a new rug and..." Her words faded as she dragged the other faery to the third floor and up to the attic bedroom, to which Frost had laid claim so many years ago.

Eli smiled as they disappeared past the balcony. Selena was so excited about having Frost home. She had been talking about this day for several years now. It felt nice having the whole family back together again.

"Well, I'll show you to your rooms," Eli said, with a smile.

Grabbing his duffle bag, he smiled at his grandfather and led his two friends up stairs to their spacious guest rooms.

This was going to be the best summer vacation in history!

Chapter Three

"So, what's the deal with you and Henry?" Selena asked. She flopped on the queen size bed.

Scott dropped his bag next to the large armchair and sat down. He peered up at his tired angel as Frost took a seat on the bed next to his sister. He seemed exhausted just dealing with the old General. He was paler than usual and for Frost that was almost ghost white.

Scott could never recall Frost ever looking so translucent.

"Are you alright?"

Frost lay back on his bed, his white robes blending with the snowy white and silver covers. He draped an arm over his eyes, looking ready to pass out. "Yeah, I'm fine, just tired. Henry and I had a misunderstanding a few years back. It's nothing to concern yourselves over."

"Try forty-some years back," Selena corrected.

"Whatever."

Scott sat up a little straighter. "I'm guessing it had something to do with Raven's death?" He nodded.

Despite their love for each other, Frost was borderline obsessed with Anthony Sinclair. Anthony had brought them together to become his Guardians and somehow along the way, he and Nathaniel had become lovers.

When he died, it had broke Nathaniel's heart in two. Selena often said the day they buried Anthony they had also buried a large chunk of Nathaniel. It was the reason for the personality splitting into Frost and Nathan. It took Scott a long time help Frost move past it. The faery had slept almost forty years before awakening as Nathan. Anthony's death was still fresh in his mind, as if it had only happened yesterday.

It took even longer to convince him that Eli was not Anthony reborn, but a reincarnation, half a reincarnation to be precise, and a child.

That was well over six years ago and Eli was anything but a little boy now. It made Scott worry. The raven-haired teen looked so much like his past self and Frost, even if he denied it, was becoming more and more aware of it.

Frost nodded with a frown. "I stayed here a few weeks after Anthony died. He got drunk one night, we had a fight, I left."

Now there was a story with a lot of holes. Frost looked distraught, a complete change to how Nathan was in the van. Something had obviously happened between Nathaniel and Henry that Frost had made sure Nathan remember nothing of. It scared him.

Scott stood and moved to the bed. Straddling Frost's hips, he leaned forward and brushed his lips against his lover's. Frost purred contently under him.

"Whatever happened, it was decades ago," he growled against Frost's flushed lips. "Think anyone would mind if we took a nap? I'm tired as hell."

That worn out look turned to playful eagerness. Frost wrapped his arms around Scott and snuggled closer. His cat-like purr increased as Scott gently massaged his wing joints, a very tender and sensitive area on all the Guardians, Scott learned over the years. Add magick to the touch and the mystic creature was literally panting for more. It had been while making love to Nathan that he had learned about that particular quirk. With his wings folded within his lithe form, or in human form, it had the same effect.

Frost arched his back, pushing again the hand between his shoulder blades, in silent plea for more.

Selena groaned in longing and gave Frost a playful slap. "You know he's just doing that so he can interrogate you."

"Hmm…" Frost hummed. He gave Scott full reign of his body. He tensed for a moment before he slumped against the large man's arms. A content sigh escaped his lips as he rested his head on those broad shoulders.

Selena shook her head and slide off the bed. "Well, that was fast. I'll let you two get comfy and see you shortly, okay."

"Yep," Scott chuckled. He held his wingless angel to him and offered her a kind smile as she left the room.

Selena was cool. She was often a big tease, but also one of their biggest supporters. Scott could not help but adore her.

"Who bothers you more, Eli or Henry?" Frost asked softly after the door was shut and Selena safely out of ear shot.

He stared down at the silvery crown of hair leaning against his shoulder. The *angel* was purring so softly Scott thought he had fallen asleep, but as usual, he was only resting while unconsciously poking through his thoughts. The bond they shared had grown increasingly strong over the years to the point they always knew what the other was thinking. It was a mixed blessing.

"You're scared of Henry." It was best to deal with the most worrisome first.

A restrained sigh escaped Frost's lips. "No, not really. It's a long story, Scott. I'd rather not get into it."

"Did he hurt you?"

"Once, a long time ago."

"What did he do?"

Frost stiffened and pulled out of Scott's arms. There was an anger there Scott had never seen before. It made his dislike of the old man grow, but he didn't push the subject. The last thing he wanted was Frost retreating into his shell again. It would make their two weeks together horrible. It was Frost's vacation as well, he deserved to be happy.

Frost began unpacking Nathan's bag, neatly placing the clothes in the antique oak dresser against the far wall. The whole room was neat and orderly. Beautiful paintings decorated the white walls and long silvery white silk curtains hung over the wall length bay windows and balcony doors. The same curtains formed a canopy around Frost's bed, which was a platform of sorts instead of the tradition four-poster bed they had found in many of Raven's other homes. It was very modern compared to the others. The blankets were silvery white like the curtains, with soft blue sheets hidden underneath. Fresh, new plants decorated very corner, giving the room a round feeling. It was very Feng Shui. Eli must have asked Henry to do it. The overly white room had to be Selena's doing, but Frost tended to favour white in both the way he dressed and his decor.

"So, what about Eli?"

Frost shut the drawer and looked at him. "What about him?"

There was a restrained sigh in his voice. It was understandable. This was a normal and constant argument between them. However, this time Scott was concerned. He was sure he had a good reason, even if it was just a feeling, a very bad feeling. The past year had been very hard on him. Even though everything with Chaos and the High Council were over, it was best to keep an eye open for trouble, even if Eli was unconsciously the cause of it. Too much had happened to not worry about him.

However, there were times Scott just wanted to bug Frost for the sake of being a bug. Nathan did it to him often enough.

"He's growing up."

"Yes."

"Hair's growing like no tomorrow."

"Yes?"

"He's taller than you."

"I've noticed."

"Doesn't he remind you of anyone?"

That pushed the wrong button. Frost glared at him and Scott could not help but smile. "What happened to his hand?"

"He dug his nails into his palm," Frost answered as he returned to Nathan's bag.

"I wonder why? You two really shouldn't sit together."

"I just healed his hands."

"Hmm…and he nearly forgot himself. He almost kissed you before snapping out of it. You're lucky he's the one with Raven's memories. Imagine if it were Dad." He chuckled at Frost's horrified expression.

"Scott!"

"Yes?"

The fey groaned and rubbed his eyes tiredly. "You're a brat, you know that?"

Scott flicked out his tongue teasingly.

"Keep dreaming."

Scott became thoughtful as he leaned on his elbows. "He is cute, if a little too young."

"Scott Dion, I swear—"

"I'm kidding, I'm kidding!"

Frost sighed, leaning against the dresser. "He's just a kid and having a hard time adjusting right now. His powers have increased far more than he was prepared for. This trip may be hard on him, remember? It's one of the reasons we're here. We don't know how his powers are going to react to the eclipse."

"And still going through puberty doesn't help much."

"I would never—"

"I know, I know…but you've thought about it."

Just the way his face fell, Scott knew it was true. He wasn't angry.

Eli simply looked too much like Anthony for Frost to ignore. Nevertheless, Frost held himself in check. It was for Eli's sake more than anyone else's was. The young man was still recovering from the mental abuse a warlock had put him through that previous March. Scott knew that Frost loved him too much to even risk a relationship like that with Eli. Besides, Eli may have had a crush, but Scott knew he wasn't truly in love with Frost. It was just Anthony's feeling for Nathaniel that still existed in Eli.

"Besides, I think his eyes have been wandering to Selena a lot, lately," he finally admitted. "Since making that deal with Chaos, he's been eyeing her more than usual. I wish I knew what happened between him and the demon."

"Three guesses and the first two don't count."

Frost sighed. Yes, he could guess what happened between the two. The demon could have taken any form it wished to seduce Eli. The last one Frost would have ever imagined it using was Selena's. Eli and Selena were like family, not lovers. He simply could not wrap his mind around it.

"I don't think coming here was the best idea," Scott finally admitted.

Frost raised an elegant eyebrow. "Henry and I will get over our little fight. It's nothing with which you need to be concerned."

"No, no. It's not just that. There's something about him. Something that was not right. Did you see the way he looked at the kid?"

"No."

"Frost, no grandfather stares at their child like that."

He was obviously confused. Maybe Nathan was too busy with the flood of memories he had received before being squeezed to death by Henry. He probably didn't have a chance to get a good look at

Henry and Eli. Or maybe Scott was wrong. Perhaps it was just how much Eli had grown in the last year, or the fact that he did look so much like Anthony. They should call it the "Raven syndrome." Nonetheless, that look in Henry's eyes was eerie.

He shook his head. "Never mind, I'm just reading too much into it."

"How did he look?" There was worry in Frost's voice as if he knew something he was afraid to voice.

Surprised, Scott sat up. "Like Nathan does food if he waited too long between snacks."

"Anthony and Henry were never lovers," Frost snorted with a hint of laughter. It was a line Scott often referred to when he and Nathan had been apart for too long, as if Nathan was about to "devour him."

"No?"

"No. They were best friends since childhood. Like brothers. Henry's a little...homophobic."

Maybe that was what he saw, but somehow Scott doubted it. The feeling was all wrong for it to be brotherly love. Henry had no magick, but his feelings for Eli were strong...very strong. It wasn't hate, nor lust, but a longing so deep and unsettling that Scott wasn't sure what to make of it, but he didn't like it. A part of him screamed to take everyone home. There had to be a reason Henry wanted Eli home for the solar eclipse.

Chapter Four

Henry prepared a feast for them. A large ham and turkey with all the trimmings sat on the dining room table. Everyone was full before they even got to dessert, including Frost who rarely ate. Henry had been just as insistent that Frost join them for dinner as he did when Anthony was still alive. Both Scott and Selena tried to explain to Henry that Frost simply didn't like to eat because of his consciousness being separated between the Nathan persona and his faery form. Nathan ate more than enough to do two people anyway. However, Henry was just as stubborn as he had been in Anthony's time and announced no one was leaving the table until Frost ate at least half his meal.

It took an hour and a half before he even touched it.

Nathan whined deep inside his mind. It was an annoying noise to say the least. The food monster was always hungry. If he did not eat at least twice a day, he complained. Funny coming from a grown man, but Nathan was able to eat for an entire army at times. When he got hungry, he got hungry.

Come on, Frost, just half, Nathan begged. *We haven't eaten in hours and Henry went through all this work. It's only polite.*

He growled inwardly at the young man, keeping their psychic conversation private. *He knows I don't eat.*

Well, I do, and I'm starving!

You're always starving.

Nathan gave a growl of his own. *Fine, I'll just take control then.*

Frost groaned when he lost control of his hands. Nathan directed them to cut into the ham and then shove a piece into Frost's mouth. He hummed at the good taste and cut some more. With a sigh, Frost gave in and let Nathan have full reign of their body without changing forms.

You owe me.

Hmm...you get to sleep with Scott tonight. That's payment enough.

Scott snickered beside him, drawing his full attention. He motioned to Frost's plate, which was now more than half-empty. Blinking, Frost cursed. Nathan was definitely hungry for him to eat so much so quickly. Frost only prayed he didn't ask for seconds. That worry was pushed aside when Scott squeezed his thigh. He looked back at the smiling dark-haired man.

Let him eat and don't worry what you look like. Henry has probably seen you at your worst.

Nathan never ate like this back then.

He never had to when you ate for yourself.

Frost would have objected if it weren't true. He sighed mentally and chewed the food Nathan had shoved in his mouth. It was almost impossible to remember when exactly he had stopped eating or when he created a personality for Nathan that was separate from his own. It was so long ago. Little things like eating, drinking and so forth he left for Nathan, while he absorbed the moon's energy. The moon fed their magick while Nathan fed their body.

"Henry, can I—" Frost's eyes widened and he clamped his mouth shut when he realized Nathan was about to ask for more. Chuckles and giggles went around the table as he blushed profusely. *Not a chance, Nathan.*

I'm still hungry!

That plate was filled up and over. You can wait until dessert.

The mention of dessert shut up the little demon within him. There was a rumble in his stomach as Nathan made room for more. Smiling shyly at Henry, Frost shook his head. "Never mind."

The old man chuckled. "Eli says you're merging with Nathan once more. It'll be nice to see you back together again."

"What do you mean?" Scott asked, surprised.

Henry sat back and eyed Frost for a moment. He frowned, as if the memory wasn't very pleasant. With a sigh, he glanced at Eli. The look in his eyes made Frost squirm slightly. Something very bad had happened. Frost raked his mind to try and recall what it may have been.

"When Frost was about Eli's age, Anthony had been captured by the Egyptian Priestess you fought back in November, Dominique. Same reason, too. Anthony had the power to open dimensions. She really didn't need his blood, but when he refused to open one for her, she decided it was the best way to gain his magick. Blood lust to be blunt."

Eli visibly shivered at the memory of his own abduction. Selena wrapped an arm around him.

"Dominique could not capture Anthony—not on her own. She didn't have the power to fight him and you Guardians, so she hired an extreme telepath, one of the best in all of Europe. A very talented young man named Duncan Porter. Together they managed to separate Anthony from the Guardians and capture him. They tormented him in ways not many could understand. There were many things about Anthony she wanted, as did the warlock. All of which Anthony's Guardians felt, especially Nathaniel. Their bond was the closest. After they rescued him, Nathaniel hid all his anger and hate toward his captors behind his human form's smiling face, even if it meant lying to Anthony. Anthony had almost gotten Nathaniel back to normal when he had passed on. It sent Nathaniel further into hiding."

He smiled at Scott. "Had he not met you and your family, I fear he would've continued hiding until he found a way to do away with himself. Sometimes love can be the harshest thing for any of us to deal with. Losing that love is so much like dying."

Scott nodded in understanding. It had taken a lot of work on his part just to get Frost to show himself. Nathan almost died before that had happened. Convincing him that Scott truly wanted to be his friend as well as Nathan's had thrown the scared being for a loop. Their relationship slowly built after that.

Frost was proud to say after almost four years, he had finally made himself a part of their family. Even Daniel accepted him for what he was. Every full moon, or whenever they or Nathan asked him to come out, he would spend that day in his faery form. He actually enjoyed the time Nathan gave him to be out in the real world.

Usually, he would spend his time in the back of Nathan's mind where he could spend weeks, even months or years without rising. As long as the Dions and Ravenwood were safe, he was happy to fall into a dreamless void. He liked looking at the world through his human eyes or simply sleeping and dreaming of the past.

Now, after a very stubborn Scott had pointed out that he could not love Nathan without loving him, Frost tended to come out at least once a day for several hours. Just to shut Scott up and confess his feelings, the first thing he had done was to kiss him passionately and make love to him. To Nathan's utter delight, their relationship grew.

"I've missed his smiles," Henry continued, snapping Frost out of his daydream. "And Anthony's."

That made Eli blink in surprise and look up at him.

That look Scott had told him about returned to Henry's eyes as he turned in his seat and brushed the long wispy bangs from Eli's eyes. It was gentle, loving like any other grandfather would, but his eyes spoke volumes that even managed to spook Eli at little. It was as if he were out hunting and eyeing his prey. Eli was like a deer caught in the lights of a Mack truck. Yet neither Selena nor Cleo questioned it. Maybe this was normal for them. Frost didn't like it. Henry had no magick whatsoever. He was as normal as people came. There was no way they could be sharing some telepathic message.

It lasted only a brief moment before Henry smiled warmly and pulled back. "Eli, would you mind getting the dessert from the kitchen?"

"Sure, Grandpa."

"I'll help!" Frost practically yelled as he jumped out of his seat.

Scott stared at him with surprise that quickly turned to understanding as he gazed back at Henry. Something wasn't right here.

Following Eli in the kitchen, Frost placed a hand on his shoulder.

The young man paused before the strawberry shortcake. "What's going on? Is he always like this?"

"No," Eli answered with a shake of his head.

"Can you read his thoughts?"

His head bowed. "He asked me not to." He turned to look at Frost and for a moment, he looked much older than eighteen. "It's abuse of my powers to invade anyone's mind without their permission. Anthony never—"

"He never looked at Anthony like that."

"I know." He sighed. "He just misses Anthony like the rest of you. You've looked at me like that when you first found out who I was. It's been a year and I've grown quite a bit. You've said yourself I look more like Anthony every day."

"That's not the same."

He put on his most stubborn face meaning the conversation was over. "I won't intrude on his thoughts."

He snatched up the cake, his ebony ponytail swishing from side to side, as he headed back to the dining room. Shaking his head, Frost followed Eli with the folks and saucers. If only Eli knew just how dangerous Henry could be, he thought sadly. He had seen that look before in Henry, and it wasn't one to ignore. Scott had every right to be worried.

"You're still angry."

Not many could sneak up on Frost. His keen hearing and strong empathy gave people away long before they neared him, but as always, Henry somehow did. The old man knew how to block his thoughts and was quieter than a cat.

Henry stood next to him on the balcony overlooking the large swimming pool, a new addition since Frost had last been there. The kids had already begun their morning by jumping in the pool. Selena was running about showing off her itsy-bitsy bikini, which caused Cleo to yell at her to cover up. It was namely because Miao was blushing and Alexis slapping him every now and then for looking at the faery for too long. Scott was *trying* to not pay attention to her and Eli seemed embarrassed as well at how much skin she was showing off. They were certainly enjoying themselves.

"It's been a long time, Nat. I had hoped you had gotten over it." A firm hand fell upon his slim shoulder causing Frost to jump. "You left so suddenly I had no chance to apologize or thank you. You opened my eyes that night."

"Happy to hear."

"But you're still mad."

Frost closed his eyes. He didn't want to think about back then. "Yes."

He stiffened as Henry pulled him into an unwelcome embrace. His bare arms fell to his sides, refusing to return the hug.

"I've missed you, little one. Some things I can't fix. Others," he gazed at Eli splashing Cleo and Sif. "I can. With help."

Frost stared up at Henry in confusion. He did not like the way he was looking at Eli. The child reincarnation was truly acting his age for once, laughing and playing like any normal teenager. He was even taunting Scott for the odd gaze he would give Selena whenever she bounced to one of her favourite songs, her bikini showing far more than it should. Scott was fair play when it came to teasing and always got even. Alexis liked to help to a point. While she had Eli distracted, Scott caught him from behind and threw him in the pool. It earned him a tidal wave when Eli resurfaced and used his powers. It became an all-out water war after that.

And Henry's gaze never left Eli.

"Has he mastered his new gifts yet?"

Frost raised a brow. "He told you about Chaos?" He gave a small nod, still watching the youth.

"Some of it. Most has already dispersed back into nature."

Henry finally looked at him with skeptical eyes. "Dimensional gateways?"

"No. He's worried he may not be able to control it yet and apparently Anthony never wanted that."

"Anthony said that?" Henry shook his head. "No. Anthony would want him to master it all. You must train him."

Frost was taken back. "Cleo and Selena are his Guardians th—"

"Anthony chose you."

That was enough to anger Frost. It was Henry's answer to everything. "No, Anthony instructed me to train and protect The Dions. He does not want them to create dimensional portals and only open them when absolutely needed. I would guess the same applies to Eli."

"Anthony said—"

"Anthony is dead, Henry. He didn't know about Eli until he was on his deathbed. He told Selena to watch over him in case he became a danger, not only to himself, but everyone if his magick became too powerful. He did not want Eli to suffer and he surely did not want him tampering with alternate worlds." He sighed. The anger dispelling into resignation. "How Anthony was able to foretell Daniel's accident causing his souls to split in two will always be a mystery to me."

The old man gaped at him in astonishment. The outburst had caught him off guard and Frost was glad to prove he was not the same naive little *angel* he had manipulated so long ago.

Laughter met Frost's ears again and he turned to look down at the pool. Eli was backing away from a very soaked and not very happy Scott. Whatever the mage had done was making it hard for him to stop laughing and convince Scott the attack was meant for Miao. Not even Anthony could keep a straight face with Scott looking like a drowned rat.

Frost smirked and leaned against the rail as Henry stormed off.

"Scott, seriously, I didn't mean to hit you with the tidal wave. Miao ducked behind you. It's his fault," Eli tried to explain. He smiled innocently.

Scott only advanced on him. He had a look that was half-smile, half-growl. It was a look he usually reserved for Nathan and Frost when they were play-fighting, or when he tormented Alexis and Miao. He looked up at Frost's smirking face as if asking for permission. Frost could only widen his smile. For the first time, he wasn't afraid of Eli getting hurt. He could take care of himself and deserved to be picked on if he insisted on being a pest.

Eli's sharp blue eyes followed Scott's line of sight and gazed up at Frost. Frost gave a small wave, effectively distracting the young man as Scott made his move. Eli's eyes widened as realization dawned on him, but it was already too late. Scott grabbed him and threw him over his shoulder, spinning in circles while Eli tried to pull himself out of his arms.

"Scott, stop!" Eli laughed, not at all upset about being *tortured*. He closed his eyes tightly and held on for dear life.

Alexis climbed out of the pool and tried to help her cousin, but every time she was about to grab Eli, Scott would turn the other way. Eli must have been getting dizzy. He was still laughing, but tried to push himself up, so he wasn't hanging upside-down. Scott was obviously having too much fun.

Miao laughed, encouraged Scott further while both Alexis and Selena tried to rescue Eli. They managed to get a good hold on him and pull him away, only to have Scott shove all three into the pool.

The young intern was laughing uncontrollable until the Wind spirit, commanded by a rather angry Alexis, dragged him in as well. There was more laughter, more water fights. They all seemed to be having fun.

Frost would have joined them. He would have loved to splash around with them or simply sit on the pool's edge. He was not a good swimmer...not anymore. As much as Anthony and even Scott had tried to get him interested in again, it was one thing he could not bring himself to do. At least in a lake. He wasn't sure about a pool. He just could not shake that cold grip of death he had experienced when Elizabeth Sinclair had died. Maybe, in time, he would learn once more to enjoy the water. Nathan did, but only in a pool.

Besides, he had no doubt that his siblings would conveniently *forget* his little problem and shove him into the deep end. That just the way they were. He silently wished to be having fun with them.

Alexis dried her hair as Sif held the hair-dryer in his jaws. They had spent all morning swimming and had a blast. She always knew Eli's family was rich and Anthony had made sure he was well looked after, but she had never imagined he had a place like this. It was paradise. If only Frost would smile more. She had thought visiting Anthony's old summer home would have made her guardian happy, yet he looked more distraught than ever, and even more protective, especially toward Eli.

She wasn't jealous or even upset about it. After everything that had happened in less than a year, it was natural to be overly protective of him. They had almost lost him twice to demonic possession and those of the dark arts. Eli was still recovering. He was not the same young man she had met almost seven years ago, far from it.

In some ways, Dominique, Chaos, and Porter had been good for Eli. They had made him open his eyes and live life to the fullest, even if he had a funny way of doing it. Now he seemed so much more...alive.

She was sure there was no reason for Frost to worry. Mr. Griphan was a little odd, but obviously loved Eli and his Guardians, and Sif simply adored him. It was most likely because he got goodies without begging. She was sure her winged wolf was going to get fat one of these days, but Mr. Griphan was also very kind to her, Miao and Scott, and seemed deeply concerned about Frost.

She took the hair-dryer from Sif as a knock came from the door.

A soft smile spread across her lips as she felt Eli's warm aura. Turning off the machine, she scratched behind the great wolf's ear. "Come in, Eli. Thanks, Sif."

The door opened and Eli poked his head in. "Hey, guys. Henry says the carnival's in town. Want to go?"

Her eyes lit up. "A carnival? Cool! Did you tell Miao?"

A mischievous gleam came to his eyes telling her it was a surprise for their friend, an early birthday gift perhaps. With a nod, she swore her Familiar to secrecy and joined Eli in gathering the rest of the gang.

Everyone was ready in less than half an hour, although it took nearly fifteen minutes to drag Scott and Frost out of their room. Alexis really didn't want to know what they were up to; she could already guess just by the noise. They finally had to threaten that Selena was going to run in there with the camcorder if they didn't hurry. It made them move faster.

Once everyone was finally in the foyer and Guardians back in their domestic forms, they had to wait for Henry to get off the phone. This of course left Scott grumbling about why they had to hurry.

Curious, Alexis and Eli stepped into the kitchen to retrieve him.

"Grandpa, we're ready," Eli said, leaning against the doorframe.

Mr. Griphan raised a hand indicating for them to wait a minute. "Yes, twenty-five minutes... Great... We'll talk then." He hung up without saying goodbye. Turning to the two of them, he smiled.

"Everyone ready?"

"Yep!" Alexis chirped.

He wrapped a large beefy arm around both their shoulders and steered them back to the others. The big man towered over them and Alexis could feel the brute strength hidden in his elderly form. She hated the idea of ever making him mad. He could easily crush them.

They had to split into two groups to get everyone into town. It wasn't because they couldn't fit everyone in the SUV. No, Selena had a Porsche stashed in the garage that she wanted to show off to Scott and Nathan. The teens and the now house-pet forms of the familiars, piled into the sports van with Henry. The drive was all of twenty minutes—well at least for the teens. Selena, Scott, and Nathan made it in ten. After that, Scott swore never to let Selena drive again because of it.

Coniston was a fair size for a town, over three thousand people. The carnival was set up in the back of a schoolyard near town square. It wasn't as big as the ones back in Ravenwood but pretty cool. The markets around the carnival were so different from the ones back home. Eli was ecstatic as he led them into the park, showing them around a bit before attacking the rides.

Henry watched them run off. He sat on the bench and smoked his pipe in deep thought. It was interesting watching Eli and Selena interact with their friends. Selena was always a little hyper, but Eli was never this happy. He seemed to really love hanging out with the two other kids.

Of all the years he had known the reincarnation of his old friend, he had never seen Eli smile so much or laugh and mean it. It was a pleasant sight. He looked so much like Anthony when he was happy. With his hair growing as it was, Henry had no doubt he would be seeing Anthony once more. Selena had said as much the last time they talked before they returned to England.

Apparently, Chaos had given him advanced healing abilities and his hair was growing faster because of it. It looked good, very good…but shorts and a t-shirt? It took away from Anthony's appearance within him. If he had his sorcerer robes on, he would look right. Actually, any of Anthony's old clothes would do.

But that was not what they wanted, he reminded himself. Eli was to live his own life, not relive Anthony's.

"Every time I see him, he's grown."

Henry sucked on his pipe, then blew out a cloud of smoke as the young man sat next to him. "Sure has."

"He looks just like him."

"Yep."

He glanced at the youth dressed in black despite the heat. His long dark brown hair was almost black. He was slim built, like any other Sinclair, and was only a few years older than Eli. His deep blue eyes were not those of a nineteen-year-old. He could feel the power of them even through the dark sunglasses. Even imagined the tri-coloured irises they hid.

"You're sure he can do it? The gates are not easy to open."

The young man adjusted his glasses. "Most definitely. It's been foretold. *The Oracle will unleash the powers of Heaven and Earth. Only the power of the Lock can end the Chaos before it begins and save the Key.*"

"All due to the eclipse?" Henry shook his head. "Last eclipse we put him asleep for it. There was no danger."

"Chaos has given him a huge power boost. Asleep or not, the gates will open. If he cannot control *them*, then we are all domed…and if the power controls *him* rather than he controls *it*, he will be no worse than the Chaos demon itself. He will feed off the destruction the gates will cause. He *must* control them, and close them."

Henry gave a small smirk. "I don't think he has even opened one of his own yet. How do you plan to have him control them?"

There was a long sigh as the young man stood up. "Then he has to learn quickly or he will become the danger so many fear. Under proper supervision he will do fine."

"To you believe the prophecies? Are you sure he's the one?"

The youth's face fell for a moment as he watched Eli and his friends get on one of the rides. "I felt it from the time he was born. He's the one, Henry, otherwise I would never have staked as much on him as I have." He turned back to Henry. "His friends give him strength."

"And the other half?"

"Oh, he will come. He will come when the time is near." He began walking away. "I'm sure Eli can handle it. He's strong, Henry. He took down one of England's best warlocks. You should have more faith in him. I'll check out the situation tonight."

Henry shook his head as the young Sinclair disappeared into the crowd. The man was such a troublemaker, but Henry needed him and his magick to help prepare Eli. Only he could help Raven's reincarnation relearn some of his old powers. Time was running out.

Forcing himself up on his cane, he began searching for his other friends.

"That one, Eli! Try for that one!" Alexis cried out. She pointed at a stuffed penguin backpack. "Melissa would love that one." She bounced on Miao who was already juggling two large stuffies he had won for her.

Eli smirked. The way she was going, they will need a separate car just for their prizes. He steadied the rifle and aimed down the long barrel. This was one sport at which he excelled. Henry had been teaching him since he was very young. It was supposed to be for extra protection, but it was handier in games like this.

He was about to squeeze the trigger when a warm current brushed past him. Dizziness filled him as a familiar chill ran down his back. His eyes closed of their own accord. However, before the dizziness could swallow him whole, a voice pulled him back.

"Going for that one?"

He blinked and looked to the right. A young man a few years older than himself stood next to him, staring at the Penguin backpack. He smiled down at him with starting blue eyes. Eli opened his mouth to answer, but no words would come out. Instead, he nodded.

"It's cute. For your girlfriend?"

Eli blushed slightly. He had been dating Melissa Corbriere off and on for four months. They weren't serious, not like Alexis and Miao, just good friends keeping each other company. Many mistook them for a couple. They did have a lot in common, so were able to offer each other advice. He loved spoiling her every now and then.

"Sort of."

"My name's Michael. You're Eli, right?"

Eli paused from re-aiming the rifle. How did he know his name?

"Ah...yeah." He did look familiar. He had magick, very powerful magick, and an awfully strange aura.

"I'm a friend of your grandfather's. Actually, he's friends with my grandparents. I'm visiting them for the summer."

"Oh." That did explain some of it. Maybe his grandparents had also been friends of Anthony's. It would explain his aura and appearance. His magick felt like it came from the Sinclairs, but there was something mixed in it. It sent chills down his spine. Yet it was oddly alluring at the same time.

"Don't forget your prize for your friend."

"Eli?" Alexis asked, touching his shoulder.

He practically jumped, completely forgetting about his two friends.

"Yeah, sorry."

Re-aiming, he lined up his target. Just as he squeezed the trigger, magick exploded next to him. Reality slowed as he watched the pellet exploded from the barrel. The penguin fell from its hook before the pellet hit the marker and the buzzer rung loudly in his ear a split second later.

He blinked as the man running the game picked up the stuffy and announced the winner before handing it over to him.

"Oh…ah…thanks," he murmured. He held the black and white creature and glanced at Alexis's and Miao's confused expressions before turning to Michael. "Why?"

He smiled innocently. "You weren't focusing," he said, matter of fact. "It was nice seeing you again."

Eli stared at him as he walked off. I know you, he whispered to himself. He couldn't remember ever seeing him before, but he knew they had met once before. Shaking his head, he turned back to his friends. "Shall we try another ride?"

Miao raised a surprised brow. "Accent's back," he declared. "He spooked you with his little trick."

"No, just surprised me."

Alexis grabbed both their arms. "Well, he's gone and I want to go on the Twister!" she giggled. She pulled them toward the rides.

She didn't give either of them a chance to drop off the prizes in the SUV. She loaded them and the stuffies into the Twister car. Eli was actually thankful in the end. The stuffies cushioned them as they were twisted and thrown in every direction. Poor Miao looked as if he would be sick once the car came to a stop and they stumbled out. He was dizzy himself, his heart racing. Trying to see straight made him giddy and the three ended up holding each other until the world stopped spinning. It didn't take long for him to forget all about Michael.

For a small town it was a big carnival. Alexis made sure they went on ever ride. Twice on the ones, she really liked or almost made them sick. She seemed to enjoy seeing Eli and Miao dizzy. They lost track of the older kids. Selena was doing the same thing as Alexis, dragging Nathan and Scott to every ride and game. Henry checked up on them from time to time, but stayed with his friends at the Fiddle and Step contest. Cleo and Sif spent most of the day with him, not being able to hang out with their respected masters.

When they were done on the rides or at least taking a short break, Eli gave Miao and Alexis a tour of town. Everyone met up at an old family restaurant for dinner where Henry astonished their guests with more tales of Raven and the terrible pranks he used to pull. Eli blushed fiercely as Henry compared some of Anthony's stunts to those Eli had been pulling since he came into his magick, noting that Eli's were more creative, but not half as dangerous. By the time Henry was done telling all the *good* stories of how Eli's first tries at magick caused mishap he was forced to hide his face behind a napkin. His grandfather certainly knew how to embarrass him.

It was nearly midnight before they finally headed home and Eli was more than happy to slump against the soft leather of the passenger seat as Henry drove down the twisting highway. He slipped in and out of sleep as Cleo curled up in his lap. Miao and Alexis had fallen asleep in the seats behind him. The two cuddled together as Sif, still wide-awake, snacked on a bone that Alexis had bought for him. Eli didn't want to move when the van pulled into the garage and his grandfather urged everyone to wake up.

They walked in a daze to their rooms. It took more energy than usual just to change for bed. When he finally did, he was out like a light before either Henry or Selena could wish him goodnight.

He rolled on his side and hugged the spare pillow as he did every night, still missing the warm of his beloved Aaliyah McNeil. It felt like an eternity since he last spoke to her, almost four months actually. It had only been a few short months ago since their break up was official. She was older than him by nearly twenty years, and many, including his friends, thought of her as a pedophile. However, their relationship had never involved intercourse until four months ago. Usually, it was just hugging and kissing and the odd touching. No one truly understood the fact that most of the time he never felt eighteen. He had the memories and life experiences of a man in his late thirties. How could anyone expect him to act like an actual kid?

Even though he loved and cared for Melissa, he was not in love with her like he had been with Aaliyah. There was only one other he had ever loved as much as Aaliyah, and that, too, was because of his past life. That was Nathaniel.

He rolled over, bringing his squished pillow with him. Burying his face in another pillow, he tried to calm the tightness in his stomach thoughts of the faery also brought. He could only imagine what Scott was doing with him right that moment and it made the knot bigger.

Rolling onto his stomach, he pushed the burning desire he felt into the farthest reaches of his mind, reminding himself it was Anthony's will. Frost's happiness was all that mattered and if Scott made him happy then he will be happy for them.

The warm sense of Sinclair magick woke him hours later. He paid it no mind, at first believing it was merely Alexis searching for the bathroom in the dark. She was probably using a Glow spell to find her way. He waited for the magick to dispel before attempting to sleep once more.

As the minutes ticked by, the magick grew to the point he covered his head with a pillow and raised his metaphysical shields to block her out. Nevertheless, it echoed in his head as if the magick was fighting to get in. Maybe Alexis was sleepwalking and had no idea how loud she was projecting. He used to do that when he was young.

Alex, tone it down and go to bed, he called telepathically.

There was a murmured reply and he could feel her hugging Sif in her sleep. So, it had not been her. She was still nice and cozy in bed. He called out to the only other one with Sinclair magick, although he highly doubted Scott could project as much power as he was feeling.

The response he got from the elder Dion was anything but pleasant.

Quite poking through my head, Eli, or I'll come down there and kick your ass for it! Scott snarled, half-asleep. There was a mental yawn and the calmer version spoke. *Go to sleep, Eli.*

He was about to when he, through Scott's mind, felt Frost wrap his arms around him and gave him a sleepy kiss, his snowy wings brushing against his arms and chest.

Eli pulled back instantly. He was wide-awake now, his chest burning where the wings had made contact with Scott. His heart was racing to the point it felt like a pounding in his head. There was no way he was going to get to sleep now. Being telepathic had its downside. It wasn't as if he didn't have enough trouble dealing with his feelings for Frost, now he had to feel the beginning of their lovemaking?

He stared up at his canopy. Bloody hell, he cursed. Why couldn't he just move forward with his life without thinking about Frost? Memories from his past life pushed themselves forward. He shook his head. No, don't picture Frost naked. Don't picture him sprawled out on your bed. This bed where Anthony and Nathaniel had made love so many times…

He needed a new bed.

The magick grew stronger, but he ignored it, sure that it was only the two men the floor above him. He closed his eyes and tried his damnedest to get back to sleep. A warm caress brushed the side of his neck. It felt like a small kiss. His eyes snapped open as he felt someone brush his hair back and kiss the nape between his neck and shoulder.

He slowly turned to see who was there, but found no one. Confused, he sat up and put on his glasses. The room was empty. Getting up, he looked around. No one was there. Yet, the sense of Sinclair magick was constantly growing. It had to be Scott and Frost. Frowning, he walked back to bed. Definitely fantasizing about Frost, too much, he decided.

A spiritual presence caught his attention, as if all the Sinclair magick had manifested into a solid form. From the corner of his eye, he caught sight of the misty humanoid form. Startled, he turned and stared at it. "What the—"

It moved at an incredible speed. He barely had a chance to reach for his totem before it enveloped him. The golden charm fell back onto the nightstand as he was filled with warmth he had not felt before. All fight left him as he stood just a few feet from his bed.

Magick surrounded him far more intimately than ever before. Invisible hands caressed his body, strengthening the desire he had felt moments earlier. Lips covered his as he found himself maneuvered to his bed. It took a few moments as his nightshirt magickally opened, for him to come to his senses.

"Stop," he breathed, trying to get up. If there were something he could have grabbed, he would have as he felt a tongue tease his chest. Teeth nipped and he almost collapsed under the sensations. "Please, no."

This had to be a dream. There was no way this was actually happening. He had not invoked one of the spirits to come to him. He certainly didn't call one to make love to him.

"You want him. I can taste your lust," a familiar voice rung through his ears. He couldn't place it, but knew it spoke the truth. "I can give you release."

Eli closed his eyes and arched his back, feeling the hands move under his shirt.

"Please," he whimpered, not sure whether he wanted what the spirit offered or wanted it to leave him.

He didn't fight it as it moved along his body. Rational thought left him. His hands knotted in his sheets as he cried out, the sensations far too overwhelming.

Chapter Five

Eli's body felt stiff as he rolled onto his back. Sunlight streamed through the open curtains onto his face. Waving his hand, he used his magick to close them. Once the dark grayness took control, he attempted to get some more sleep. It was still far too early to get up yet.

As Eli tried to recall the night before, he realised that it had to have been a dream...or was it? Surely it had to be a dream...there was no way that had been real.

There had been something else.

Something created by magick.

He could clearly remember the voice whispering to him, the hands touching and lips moving over his body. Whoever or whatever it was had made love to him.

Even if it was only a dream, it had drained him. He was too tired to move. It had felt good, so very good. He just wished he knew what had caused it.

With a sigh, he opened his eyes and looked at his alarm clock. 6:15 AM. It was far too early, but he could not sleep even if his body refused to move. He might as well get up and shower.

The bathroom was another thing Henry had upgraded in the last ten years. The bathtub was larger and fitted with whirlpool jets. The shower was now separate with a stall that stood across from the tub. Both were large and meant for comfort, at least twice the size of normal ones. It was extremely elegant.

Turning on the shower, Eli jumped into the warm spray. Within ten minutes, he had finished and was drying himself off. He went back to his room, dressed, and then got clean sheets and blankets for his bed.

By the time he was done cleaning up, the rest of the house was up and buzzing. He could hear a faint argument between Scott and Alexis on who was showering first. He heard Selena's giggles before a bunch of protests echoed throughout the hall. Obviously, she had slipped into the bathroom and had brought Alexis with her. It was a good thing the tub and shower were separate or he would have worried.

Stepping into the hall, he smiled at the three young men leaning against the walls. Frost's hair was down for once. It pooled around his feet in waves of silk so soft it was hard for Eli not to run his fingers through it. He stood next to Miao and Scott as if he were just one of the guys and not the celestial being his features betrayed him to be. It was nice to see him so comfortable amongst them. Throw in a few more people and the fey would instantly revert to his cold persona and hide behind Nathan's cheery mask.

"Hey, guys!" Eli called as he approached them.

Miao raised a surprised brow. "What happened? Wake up an hour ago to shower first?"

"Of course," he lied with a big smile. "I'm surprised I was up before Frost. It usually takes an hour or two to get all that hair untangled.

Frost threw him a smile that made his heart flutter slightly. "I was occupied."

His smiled faltered. "Indeed." He bit his inner cheek as Anthony's disappointed voice escaped his lips. There were times, not as often as when he was a child, that the spirit of his past self would take him over. It had become increasingly rare as he got older and was only triggered by dangerous situations or over-active emotions that he could not handle.

Frost's eyes widened for only a moment at the sound of Anthony's voice, but he smiled warmly, nonetheless. "Henry says you'll be visiting your parents today."

"Oh?" His eyes widened. For the first time in twelve years, he had forgotten all about his parents. He had to visit them today before he forgot again. "Yeah, actually I'm going to head up now before it gets too hot. I'll see everyone after breakfast." He waved before taking off.

Henry was busy making breakfast when he ran into the kitchen. The old general glanced up as he grabbed the hedge clippers from the drawer.

"Going to cut them some roses?"

He never needed to ask when Eli grabbed the clippers who the flowers were going to be for. It was either for his parents or Aaliyah, but since his Watcher had moved off to London, it was obvious. Besides, Miao would kill him if he brought Alexis a small bouquet without reason. He still tended to get jealous for no reason.

"Yep. You should have reminded me yesterday. I completely forgot."

"Oh, I'm sure they'll forgive you." He flipped the pancakes and put on some more toast. "I would think they'd be happy to see you hanging around people your own age rather than spending the day talking to the dead." He grinned. "Use to get a little spooky, you know."

Eli grinned. "What? Standing on rooftops in the middle of night to talk to great Grandpa John scared you?"

"The old goat was always being so serious right to his death. It was all an act. At least I now know where you and Anthony got it."

A sly grin crossed Eli's lips as he took two apples from the basket. "Yep. I should only be an hour or so. I'll take Midnight with me."

"What about Cleo?"

"He's still sleeping."

"Well, be careful. I haven't been up there in a several weeks and we had a big storm not long ago."

Throwing both apples in his jacket, Eli headed for the door. "Don't worry, I will."

Rose bushes lined the property, hugging the house and driveway. Anthony's baby sister, Elizabeth, had loved roses of all varieties and with the help of his Guardians, Anthony had been convinced to plant them in her memory. It was a good thing Henry's wife, Dorothy, had loved them, too, or they would not have gotten away with planting so many.

There were thousands of other flowers in the numerous gardens from all over the world, many of which should not have been able to grow in England's wet weather. Years ago, Anthony placed a spell on the vast property long ago. Not only did it protect them, but it also enabled the foreign plants to grow healthy, no matter the temperature or weather.

Eli went to the nearest rose bush and cut two of the best flowers. Tying them together, he started up the hill to the stables. It only held three horses now compared to the huge stock of stallions that Henry once cared for back when the ranch was filled with the voices of children on a daily basis. As Henry got older, he began to downsize. His children and grandchildren had grown up, had families of their own and didn't visit as often as they used to. Henry could not possibly take care of so many on his own. Three must have been hard enough.

Eli was thankful that he had kept the last three. He loved riding horses above all forms of travel. It was something he knew came from his past life. It was one of the few times he felt completely at peace with himself. No conflicting emotions to confuse or torment him.

When he had first began spending his summers and holidays full time with Henry back when he was six, Henry had taken him and Selena to town to pick their own steeds. It seemed only natural for him to pick the pure black colt that was only a year old. Midnight's colour matched Cleo's and was just prefect. The mahogany mare Selena had picked for herself also suited her. When Henry had sold the other seven a few years later, he had made sure not to touch theirs. Eli was thankful. He loved Midnight, and like his parents, regretted not visiting his old friend sooner.

Flipping on the light, he went to Midnight's well-kept stall. The pitch-black horse was now full-grown and as beautiful as he remembered. He would never tire of Midnight. He may not be magickal like Cleo and Sif, but if he were not living in the city, he would beg Henry to let him take the steed home.

The saddle and harness hung from their usual hooks. He took them down and began putting them own the steed. "Hey, there, old friend," he cooed.

Henry had already been up there to feed them. He was always up at the crack of dawn for as long as Eli could remember. The other horses were already out pasture and he could only guess that Midnight was left behind in preparation for his trip. Henry had a way of doing that.

Pulling out one of the two apples, he held it out, palm open, for the horse to eat. Once Midnight was done, he led him outside before climbing on his back. "Let's go see Mom and Dad."

The gravesite wasn't far, only a ten-minute ride. It wasn't really big, only an acre in size and held a total of twenty graves. It was already half full, only modest size family cemetery. Despite his age, Eli had already made plans for the future. Should anything ever happen to him, he wanted Selena and Cleo to bury him there. It was where he had seen his first ghost, that day so long ago when he was forced to bury his parents. It would be his final resting place.

His parents' final resting place was not as well decorated as he would have liked. After twelve years, he still had no clue what type of statue to erect for them. Two stone angels—a male and female, who represented the family Guardians, guarded the gates. There was no need for one of them to stand guard over his parents.

He tied Midnight to the cherry tree hanging over his parents' markers. It had been his mother's favourite, but it was too late in the season to pick a small branch of cherry blossoms. He would have conjured some up, but he knew if she were alive, she would have reprimanded him for such misuse of his power, even if it were for her. So, he had to make do with the roses. Kneeling in the soft grass, he placed one on either grave.

"Hi, Mum, Dad. Sorry I took so long," he said, sitting back and folding his legs beneath him. "It's been a wild year. You would never believe what's been going on. I suppose your predictions about me finding myself in Canada have come true, Dad. I guess I was just too stubborn to realize that the first time I was there. I met the other half of my soul. You would have liked him. His name's Daniel Dion and I swear he's my complete opposite. He looks just like you, Dad, but then, I suppose that's because he's your twin. You would like him. I really wish you could have grown up with him. I'm sure you would have been great brothers. Sometimes, I think he's you."

"It's easy to see Anthony in him, despite what Frost says. You have to know what you're looking for. I know I told you about him and his family before and the Guardians, Frost and Sif, but I really enjoy spending time with them."

He pulled out the extra apple and took a bite as he organized his thoughts. There was so much to tell them, it was just hard to decide where to start. He smiled. Good news was always best.

"Believe it or not, they sort of have adopted us. Now that Dan knows what's going on and all about the Guardians and his past self, he's really accepted us. He took it better than I thought he would. He loves the idea of Frost and Scott being together. He thinks it's good for both of them. He's so cool! I hope I grow up to be at least half as good as him."

He took a moment to crunch on his apple. Talking to his deceased parents had become a habit from the moment he realized he could see spirits and interact with them. He rarely saw his parents' spirits, not since a few months after the car crash. Nan had said they had moved on, but Eli wasn't so sure. He felt them, always in the same place, always here.

Shaking that small chill that had run down his spine at such thoughts, he turned his head skyward and laid back. There was a clear blue sky that morning, not a cloud. It was one of those days he would spend playing in the grassy fields with his parents, chasing butterflies or trying to catch a slippery frog. That was a long, long time ago. When was the last time he had captured a frog? Or let himself get so dirty?

Closing his eyes, he let himself rest. It was too beautiful a day to do anything but relax. He let his mind wander back to his dream. It had felt so real. Not like the visions he usually had. They foretold the future and were usually too muddied for him to decipher right away. No, this was far too vivid to be a simple dream or vision. He folded his arms behind his head. Blue mist. He remembered seeing blue mist. What could that have been? No outside magick had entered the grounds without the will of Anthony or one of his descendants. Other than Miao and the Dion family, no other magick had come through the protective shield. It had to have been a dream.

He tried to recall what it had told him. It knew of his feelings for Frost, knew he was jealous of Scott. Worse, it knew that he had accidentally reached into Scott's mind and felt what they were doing. The voice, he knew it. It was so familiar and definitely male. That was a little disturbing. In his past life, he was bisexual, but in this life, he wasn't sure. He had nothing against it and he did have feelings for Frost, but that had been the magick. Wasn't it? He sighed. "I must be crazy."

"I've been saying that for years."

"Huh?" His eyes flew open and he stared upside down at Miao leaning over his head. He hadn't even sensed their approach. "Miao? Alexis?"

Miao shook his head with a dramatic sigh. "Laying on your folks' graves? Talk about morbid."

"It's actually very calming." He rolled over and sat up, giving his two best friends a smile.

"Nothing like the sleep of the dead, huh?"

He shrugged. "You can say that." His smile grew when he caught sight of Cleo and Sif.

Alexis knelt next to him. "Cleo says you come up here every spring on the anniversary of their death. I'm sorry you couldn't have come sooner."

"They understand. My father always said my schooling was the most important thing for me to focus on. I don't always agree, but…" he shrugged.

"Sounds like my parents," Miao muttered, sitting next to them.

"Seems like all Raven's descendants have that little flaw," Sif teased, sitting on his hunches. "I always said Tony should have lightened up more." He paused in thought. "Then again, he did have a twisted sense of humor. I think he just studied to frustrate me."

Cleo rolled his eyes. "Of course. It was all because of you."

"You and Nate liked studying with him."

"While you and Selena raided the ice box and pantry!"

The kids chuckled as the two familiars argued. Neither of them had changed, even after Raven's death. They bickered as much now as they had then.

"Well, I suppose I ought to introduce you," Eli suddenly said after receiving odd looks from the other teens. "I know, I know, it's weird, but hey, my parents so…" He held back a laugh as Miao raised a brow. "Put your hands on both markers."

"Okay."

They did as requested, Miao sitting behind Alexis so they both could reach.

"Believe it or not they can feel you." Eli licked his lips. He had never shared this with anyone, apart from Selena and Cleo. He hoped it worked. "Mum, Dad, this is Alexandria Dion and Miao Syffern of the Syffern Clan. Alexis, Miao, my Mum, and Dad."

"Ah…hi," Alexis said softly, very nervous. She suddenly blinked and looked at Eli. "They got warm!"

"I know. When I came here in the middle of winter once, they were ice cold, but the moment I began talking to them, they warmed instantly. The snow even melted around them."

Miao pulled back and turned to face him. "Are you sure you're not doing it subconsciously? Your magick may be influencing it."

He shrugged. "Maybe, but I prefer to think they know I'm here."

"Yeah, I talk to my mom all the time. Don't you ever talk to your brother, Miao?"

He looked at his girlfriend still touching the markers. His chocolate brown eyes turned to the clear sky. "I suppose."

"I miss them."

They watched as Eli lay back down. He stared up at the cloudless sky once more. His dark eyes saddened as tears threatened to spill from his eyes. "I miss my mother singing. I still remember the way she would tuck me in at night and the smell of her perfume when she held me close.

"I miss my Dad's cologne and the way his whiskers would scratch my head before he shaved. The tall tales he would tell me at night of wizards and hobbits, faeries, and elves, all those stories that turned out being true. He knew. The land is full of mythic creatures hiding from the modern world."

"I wish I could remember my mom. She was so beautiful. I know Dad and Scott miss her. Wherever Debra is…she must miss her, too, or why else would she leave us?" Alexis stretched out next to him.

"My brother died in the line of duty, defending the clan. I was very young, maybe four, but I remember his smile," Miao said softly as he lay next to Alexis and pulled her into his arms. "He was a great warrior."

Eli smiled. It was the first time any of them had talked openly about their deceased family members. It was usually a private subject, although his life had recently become an open book, thanks to Selena. She was only trying to help by explaining some of the things that had happened to them, but it was more than anyone really needed to know. He wanted to tell them when he felt the time was right. Selena had only tried to explain why he acted so odd for his age. She was only trying to help.

Alexis propped herself on her elbows and peered down at him.

"How long until Nathan and Frost merge completely?"

He blinked at the sudden change of subject. Sitting up, he frowned. Frost and Nathan had been slowly merging back into one since Frost had first awakened eighteen years ago. Both personalities lived in harmony and full knowledge of each other now, but were still separate. Frost had created Nathan…at least his personality, many years before awakening.

Eli suspected it had something to do with Daniel's near-death experience that had caused his soul to rip in half and Eli to be born. Frost had saved Daniel and kept him from fully being reincarnated into Eli. In the end, Frost was the dominate personality of the two, even if he claimed Nathan was a completely separate person.

Over the last few years, Frost's emotions were overlapping Nathan's and Nathan's did the same to Frost. The fey smiled more often and even made jokes now and then. Little things he had not done since Anthony became sick. The occasions were still limited to Scott and the odd time the teens. The best thing was that he was still ticklish in either form and Scott often bragged that he would bring Frost or Nathan to tears when he attacked those areas and nothing they did could stop him.

"Not long now. Nathan has already been dreaming of his past and has been seeing through Frost's eyes rather than sleeping." He gave her a reassuring smile. "I'm honestly surprised by how long it's taking them."

"All this because Anthony was attacked?" Miao asked, while resting his head on Alexis's hip.

"No," Sif suddenly said with an angry growl. His gray eyes stared off into nowhere. "We are immortal as long as we have a source of power to sustain us. Anthony was the first and only Sorcerer to summon and fully sustain a faery, let alone four Guardians. There were many, even a few stronger than Anthony, who were jealous of his gift to us. There were legends where if you drank the blood of an immortal you can become immortal."

"Vampires."

"Some, but not like your stories. These are different and very real."

"Someone did that to Frost?" Alexis whispered, obviously concerned for her guardian. She sat up straight and stared at her winged wolf.

Sif glanced at Eli as if unsure of the extent of Anthony's memories within him. Eli furrowed his brows, trying to recall that particular memory. Anthony hid many things from him. It was a form of protection, like Frost with Nathan, but it was frustrating as hell when he really wanted to know something. However, he was insistent and the part of him that was still Anthony sighed inwardly before providing him the knowledge he wished. He almost cried and his breath caught in his throat as the images assaulted him.

"H—he was in Nathan's form—his human form," he began, trying to control his emotions.

Anthony's rage, hurt and sorrow for what had happened filled him and it took a moment to rein in all those emotions to get a clear story.

Cleo nuzzled his neck, offering comfort and strength. The winged panther seemed more in tune to his emotions than anyone else. He accepted his friend's encouragement full heartily and allowed Anthony's spirit to overlap his as he retold the story he now wished to forget. "We had gone to the market for supplies. Selena had asked me to make her a new gown and Nathaniel was on the hunt for a new novel, one that was not already in our library. He went to his favourite shop while the rest of us looked around the market." He paused and took off his glasses to rub his weary eyes. "He was only gone five minutes, maybe ten, when his aura disappeared... just simply disappeared."

He closed his eyes. Losing Nathaniel must have nearly killed Anthony. He could feel the deceased magician shiver within him as tears threatened to overwhelm him. He must have thought the worst when Nathaniel's aura had vanished.

"Go on," Miao encouraged, holding Alexis's sudden shaken form.

"We went to the store, but no one knew where he went. We searched and searched, but could not find him. Not even a feather. I cast many spells, but whatever was shielding his aura blocked them."

"I thought Raven was the most powerful sorcerer?"

"In Canada, perhaps, but here there were many witches stronger than I." His frown deepened. "At least at that time. After a week, a ransom demand came. They could not get immortality from him so they demanded I cast the same spell that created my children upon them and they would give me back Nathaniel. I went to them and did as they asked, but I placed a time limit of a month. I had never met an evil magician until then, but after seeing what they did to my son, I have to say they were truly evil.

"I found Nathaniel in a deep narrow cave with barely enough room to sit. He was lying on the ground, hands and feet bound together. He was also gagged...and just to mess up his senses more, they had ear-plugs shoved deep in his ears." He took a deep breath, knowing the next part was hardest for Anthony. "His wings were broken and hung limply over his body. He had no idea who I was when I first touched him. Even his telepathy was shot. He screamed behind the gag, flaring his wings to a point he reopened the numerous wounds covering him. They had stripped him and cut him so many times to feed on his silver blood like a pack of vampires."

"Oh Goddess!" Alexis mewed, covering her mouth.

"When I got everything off him, he suffered sensory deprivation. Everything was too loud, too bright. His throat was so dry he could only whisper. I wrapped him in my cloak and had to force him to walk out of the cave after making his wings disappear. He practically collapsed the moment he got outside. His muscles had knotted so badly. I carried him home and had Selena, Sif, and Cleo care for him until I returned." He bowed his head in shame. "I then hunted down and killed every last one of them. All but one."

"Porter?" Miao asked.

He nodded sadly. "He's dead now. Nate doesn't need to worry anymore."

"Or you."

He smiled, Eli's personality returning fully. "No, not anymore."

"Nathan doesn't know any of this?" Alexis breathed, still in shock.

"No. Frost's form of protection, I suppose. While he's Nathan, nothing can hurt him or so the theory goes, but...soon Nathan will know everything."

"I don't think he can handle it."

"He's much stronger than you think." Standing, he offered his hands to the duo. "Come on, Henry must be wondering what's taking so long." He helped the two to their feet before saying farewell to the tombstones. Gathering Midnight's reins, he walked the steed down the long track to the cabin while he told his friends more pleasant stories of Anthony's life in England as well as his own.

"Thank God for microwaves!" Henry teased as he shoved the platter of eggs and pancakes in the economy-sized microwave. He gestured for the three teens and two animals to sit around the kitchen table.

"So how were the grounds?"

"They're beautiful, Grandpa," Alexis said enthusiastically.

"Very beautiful," Miao agreed, obviously not sure if he should really call the old man grandpa, too. Henry insisted upon it, but Miao was always a little shy about such things.

Eli sipped at his orange juice while he waited for the food. Selena had taken Scott and Frost to show off the property. They were many things that had changed in the forty years Frost had been gone and she was more than excited to show him everything. She loved the fact that her younger brothers were finally home.

Henry placed the food in front of them and sat down. "Thank you. Pietro works very hard for me."

"My cousin—our cousin," Eli explained, with a gesture to Alexis. "Where is he?"

"He's visiting his folks in Cambridge. Then I think he and his girlfriend are going to Westchester for the weekend. He should be back next week." He gave a wink. "I wanted some time to you all by myself. Pietro pulls out the jelly-beans and you disappear on me."

"Grandpa!" he gasped, trying not to choke on the juice. Of all the— "I don't go nuts over jelly-beans! Besides, I was little then."

Henry waved it off. "He has a jelly-bean fetish. So did Anthony."

"Did not! Do not!" Eli folded his arms stubbornly across his chest. "I was a kid."

"You still are." His smile broadened as Eli pouted. "That's okay. I wanted to get you three to show off your powers a little. Maybe a demonstration this afternoon? A game of tag?"

Eli stuck out his bottom lip, sulking playfully. "We're on vacation." He glanced at his friends who nodded. "Ah…sure. Why not?"

Henry clamped his shoulder. "Atta boy. Did you bring your battle uniforms?"

He shook his head. "No. I—we didn't think it would be necessary."

"Well, don't worry. I'm sure we have some here that will fit." There was a group of smiles as the other two teens agreed.

The conversation became lighthearted as Alexis gushed over the beauty of the land and hills and how much she would love to learn how to ride one of the horses. Eli promised to teach her and Miao either that evening or the next morning. There was so much he still wanted to show them and only a week and a half in which to do it.

Chapter Six

Professor Daniel Dion looked up from his studies as one of his students stepped into his tent. The young man handed him his findings on one of the relics they were studying. He gave a nod and took the report. Laying it next to the others, he continued his own research. The antique necklace reminded him of Sif, his family's familiar. It even felt like the wolf's energy. Odd. It could not have belonged to Anthony Sinclair. Not this far east of Spain. Still, it looked familiar and had magickal warmth that only made him wonder more.

There were several more pieces resembling Raven's creations, a ruby and bronze bracelet with a waning moon and small dragonflies that reminded him of Serenity. A turquoise and silver one with the waxing moon and doves, obviously Nathaniel. Then a beautiful teal and ebony head dress with images of a mighty panther engraved like the necklace of the wolf. They were made for a woman. Perhaps even Alexis herself. Maybe Raven had created them for her. He had had visions of her long before he started seeing Eli. Maybe all four Guardians were originally supposed to go to the Dions.

The question remained—what were they doing in a temple of Kali? The temple itself was thousands of years old and had only been unearthed not five months ago. They were the only ones like them among the relics and were in considerably better shape. Almost as if…

"…they were placed here," he whispered to himself. He had no clue how or why they would be placed in a country Anthony had only visited for a few short weeks before returning to Spain. That had been long before creating his Guardians. Daniel had spent much of his free time studying the deceased mage to the point that he was almost positive he knew Anthony's entire timeline before passing on, and India was not a big marker on the list.

The other thing that seemed odd was that the jewelry seemed to fit together. The groves on each piece lined up to its corresponding guardian. Blood Moon-Eclipsed Sun, Selena and Cleo, Blue Moon, Radiant Sun, Nathaniel, and Sif. The gold necklace connected to the silver bracelet that connected to the bronze bracelet, which connected to the ebony headdress, forming a unique orb. It was hard to tell which way was top, as both familiars faced one another. He studied it carefully, turning it over and over in his hands.

The teal eyes of the panther drew his attention. He rotated it until the panther was on top. The eyes were so real, as if they truly belonged to Cleotro. It was uncanny the work put into it. He brought it closer to his face, peering into those beautiful eyes.

"Now, just how did you get all the way out here?" The eyes glowed brightly at his words, completely captivating him. His eyes grew wide as the glow got brighter. He could not let go of the orb and with a gasp, found himself transported to a land he had never been to before.

The sun seemed incredibly large, far more so than normal. The moon, full and in all its glory, was moving before it, drawing its silvery face into shadow while hiding the sun's brilliance. Something tingled within Daniel. It was warm and alluring, overpowering in a way he had never felt before. Large sparkling rectangles appeared all around him as a staff appeared in his hand. Creatures shot out of the portals, some humanoid, many not. They attacked him, wrapping arms, tentacles, and what other appendages they had around him. Oddly enough, he managed to stay calm and not panic. Raven's magick circle appeared beneath his feet.

A voice, his own yet not, spoke through his mind as the circle broke in two. *Both halves must be united. The Key must not fall in the wrong hands.*

He awoke with a start as a hand fell upon his shoulder. "Wrong hands," he murmured, sitting up. He wiped his brow and looked at the young woman who had pulled him out of his trance. "Oh, Jacqueline. Sorry, I must have dozed off."

"It's alright," the redhead woman said. She held up a leather-bound book. "We found this not far from those other artifacts. It appears to be Gaelic."

"Gaelic?"

Now that was odd, especially being in India.

He took the book from her hands and dismissed her without another word. It was indeed Gaelic. Each letter was written in a rush. Not the typical calligraphy associated with the books of Raven. It was easy to tell the handwriting. Anthony had written it, most likely during the last week of his life. Many pages in the back were empty. Why Gaelic? Why an Irish text? He was used to seeing books in Latin, Spanish and English. Anthony did have a friend who was Irish. Sister Maria. Maybe he wrote it for her. They were very close and Anthony had treated her like a mother until the day of his death.

Gaelic was not one of the languages Daniel spoke, although given enough time, he was sure he could translate it. After all, being one of Anthony's present incarnations gave him an uncanny ability to pick-up languages. It's what made him a good Professor of the Occult and Anthropologist. Ancient languages were his specialty. He was willing to bet anything that the book had something to do with the strange orb sitting on his desk. Maybe it would explain the strange vision he had just had.

That was worrying him. What did it mean? There was an eclipse coming in a few days that would be seen clearly in England, but what did it have to do with Raven? And what were those portals? It made no sense. His first vision since childhood and he had no idea what it meant.

Sighing, he poured himself another cup of coffee. This was going to be a long night.

Chapter Seven

Selena stifled a giggle as she stepped into the living room with Scott and Frost. All three teenagers were passed-out on the sofa.

Both familiars slept at their feet. Placing a finger to her lips, she gestured for both men to be silent as she slipped into the study. She was back a moment later with an impressive Polaroid camera.

Taking aim, she snapped a picture. The bright flash caused Eli to furrow his brows before returning to his dreams. She couldn't hide her smirk as she brought the camera back to her eye and took another photo. The young man tried burying his face in the arm of the sofa, obviously too tired to cast a simple spell to deal with her. That meant she could easily get off another two shots before the camera melted in her hands, but she was tempted to see just how far she could push her luck with him.

"You guys want a copy?" she asked, holding up the two photos. "I'm going to get one for Daniel and Henry, too."

Frost shook his head as he took one. "Do you torment him this often?"

"Him and Cleo," she corrected. "All the time."

He glanced at Scott. "She's just as bad as you."

Scott raised a brow playfully. "Me? Would I do a thing like that?"

"Yes," murmured Miao, straightening in his seat. Alexis's head rested against his shoulder. He wrapped an arm around her waist to keep her from slipping.

"Oh, how cute!" Selena cried, snapping another picture. Seeing Alexis in one of her childhood outfits was enough to make her take a dozen pictures. It was a jumpsuit Anthony made for her when she was Alexis's age. The pants had to be tight because at the time she refused to wear anything that made her look like a boy. The pants they made today for women she didn't mind. They were very feminine. She highly doubted Anthony would have ever made her a pair of hip huggers.

The camera only flashed twice before it was yanked out of her hands by an invisible force. She growled as it was dismantled and every piece sent to a different corner of the cabin. Her tri-coloured scarlet and ruby eyes flashed at the raven-haired young man as he sat up and yawned. "Eli!"

"I was trying to sleep," he murmured, taking off his glasses to rub his eyes.

"That's what beds are for."

"I would've, but Grandpa only gave us an hour break."

It took a moment for her to realize they were all in battle attire. None of them had brought theirs from home so they were wearing the ones that had been here. Alexis had Selena's old one. Miao wore one that was now too small for Eli, maybe even one of Nathaniel's childhood ones. It was all white and hard to tell for sure. Thankfully, Miao was much smaller than Eli, even if his shoulders were slightly broader. Eli had managed to fit into one of Anthony's, even if it was still a little big. Selena made a mental note to take it in for him that night. She wasn't as good at sewing as he was, but judging by how tired he was at that moment, she highly doubted he would be up to it.

Henry must have had them training or showing off their powers for them to be dressed up, and knowing how hard Henry tended to push, there was a good reason why they were so tired. After an afternoon of training with him, she never had trouble-putting Eli to bed. The old man was very demanding.

"He's worse than Frost," Alexis whimpered. She blinked and looked up at Frost. "I promise never to complain again as long as you don't get as bad as him."

Frost only smiled and gave a nod. Usually he trained Alexis and Miao, but since they were in England, he had given them the two weeks off. It was a good thing, too. The kids would have exhausted themselves if they had to put up with Frost's training and Henry's.

Sif stretched before sitting up. "Alright, guys, an hour's almost up."

A group of groans and moans filled the large living room. Even Cleo frowned at being awakened. The wolf pounced on his panther counterpart. "Come on, Cleo, up and at'em."

Cleo growled, swatting his annoying brother in the head. "Midsummer isn't until tomorrow. Calm down."

"Just because spring's over doesn't mean you need to be all grumpy." He pushed the black cat over with his head. "We'll let the kids sleep and go play without them."

"Hmm."

"Come on!"

Cleo finally got up. "Sure, fine. Whatever shuts you up and lets Master Eli sleep."

Selena rolled her eyes. "Just call him Eli, Cleo."

He snapped his jaws at her before following Sif outside.

She could not stop herself from laughing. It was an old argument dating back to Anthony's time. Anthony never liked to be called Master nor did Eli. It was people like Anthony's father that insisted the Guardians be more formal.

"How long have you guys been training?" she asked, sliding into the seat next to Eli.

"Since noon," the youth answered, automatically turning to lean against her shoulder. She wrapped an arm around him and let him rest. Eli wasn't naturally clingy, but when he was worn out, he did like being held now and then and the powers of the Moon, which resided in both her and Frost, had a calming effect on him. It was easier for him to regain his strength, and she liked the days she could fuss over him like a child again.

"I take it they're too tired to continue?" Henry asked, stepping into the room.

"Four hours in *play mode* is a little more than they're use to," Frost said, folding his arms across his chest.

"Oh, oh," Selena murmured, wondering if the two would argue about training techniques. There was something obviously not right between the two. She wasn't sure what, but she definitely didn't like it.

"How many hours were you planning?"

"Another two." Henry also folded his arms. "You're too soft on them. When Eli was in my care, he, Selena, and Cleo would practice from dawn to dusk with no complaints."

"That was before he split his powers with Daniel and before Chaos possessed him. He's just recovering from Chaos. Alexis is nocturnal, like Eli. They're stronger at night."

"It's okay, Frost," Eli said softly, finally deciding it best to stay awake. He stayed in Selena's warm arms, still too tired to move. "I've been slacking off lately."

"No, you haven't—"

Scott wrapped his arms around the agitated fey's waist and pulled him close. "I've got an idea," he said in a soothing voice. He leaned his cheek against Frost's silvery head in a gesture for him to relax. Turning his blue eyes on Henry, he smiled. "Why not give the kids another hour or two to gather their strength and have dinner, then we'll all join in for the training session."

"Yeah!" Selena chimed in. "Well give them a real work out. They'll be so tired by the time we're done, you'll have to let them sleep-in tomorrow."

"It's better than one of them getting hurt due to exhaustion," Frost agreed. "At least we can protect them from themselves if need be."

Henry took a moment to think. He stared down at Eli who kept a pleading look on his face. The childishness of it was what made him break. All Eli ever needed to do was make a pouty face to get his grandfather to do as they asked. Ah, to be a kid again, Selena thought, giving the young man a squeeze.

"Alright, alright, don't get all cute on me. You know I can't stand that," Henry said, ruffling Eli's tousled hair. "You look too much like Anthony as is, I don't need you pulling his tricks on me."

"Thank you, Grandpa."

He waved a dismissive hand as he walked back to the kitchen. "I'll get you back later, kiddo."

Selena settled back with Eli still in her arms. His head slipped from her shoulder to her chest. She giggled as he tried to get comfortable against her breasts before dozing off once more. "What is it with guys and breasts?"

Eli murmured something non-coherent that made Scott laugh. He hugged Frost tighter. "They make good pillows."

She burst into laughter at Frost's confused look. He had never been with a woman even though he had many female friends in Nathan's form. Although he laid in Mrs. Hastings's arms many nights when Nathan was young, he still had very limited knowledge of women and all their body parts. Everything he knew must have been learned at school. Scott would have to introduce him to the rest of the world one of these days.

Adjusting Eli so he was sleeping on one breast, she began combing his tangled hair until it was manageable.

Frost was cute, adorable even, and if he weren't her brother, adopted or not, she would have easily dragged him to her room and taught him the finer points of feminine sexuality, but alas, they were siblings and he was gay.

She stared down at her sleeping charge. Eli was also at a point where he was not sure of his sexuality. He liked women. That was obvious in his relationship with Melissa Corbriere. He did eye other women, too, but he also had an attraction to Frost. It was growing to the point that Eli was having a hard time not staring at the angel-like faery or even Nathan, and it was frustrating him. No doubt, he was the one Eli had been dreaming of the night before. So far, he had been able to control himself, but she doubted it would last long unless he found another love, someone to occupy his full attention. Anthony's love for Nathaniel outweighed his more practical thinking.

She smiled up at Frost as he squeezed Scott's hands. They were a good pair. They picked up each other's thoughts easily and knew how to sooth the other's pain or anger. It was true love, an unshakeable love. So much like Anthony and Nathaniel. It was no wonder why Eli got jealous when he watched the two hug or kiss. Seeing such affection between them must have torn him up. A part of him would always long to hold Anthony's angel. That would never happen. No matter how much they teased each other, neither would cross that line.

"Well, I suppose we'll save the pub for tomorrow night," she teased with her British charm. "By the time we're done, we'll be lucky if we can make it to our rooms."

Frost sighed, completely comfortable in his love's arms. "I can't believe he conned them into training. This is their vacation."

"Henry loves watching Eli in action. We used to train all the time. He just doesn't understand the whole Chaos thing or why he gave up half his magick to Dan. All he knows is what we tell him. He wasn't there."

He just snorted in distaste.

"What's with you two?"

"Nothing."

"Nothing my foot."

Violet eyes glared at her. "Forget about it."

"Fine," she snapped, unconsciously holding Eli tighter.

Scott sighed into Frost's hair.

Stupid *angel*, always acting so cold around Henry! Just as bad as the way he used to treat the kids before Nathan's persona began slipping through. Only one he ever let close was Scott. I ought to—

"You're thinking too loud," Eli murmured, sitting up. He rubbed his eyes and glanced at the two men holding each other. "What's wrong?"

"Nothing, Eli," Scott said, letting go of Frost. He offered Eli a hand. "How about you and I help Henry set the table?"

Eli hesitated a moment, surprised by Scott's odd cheeriness toward him. He looked around as if trying to figure out what he missed, but finding nothing of dire importance, took Scott's hand and got up. It took a moment for him to find his footing, but Scott was patient and gave him a chance to yawn and wake up fully. Wrapping an arm around his shoulders, he led the smaller man to the dining room.

Frost frowned in frustration as Selena stood. "It was a long time ago. I should let it go."

She did the big sister thing and took his hand. Giving it a gentle squeeze, they went outside. The sun was still high and only a few clouds had moved in to obscure the view. "You can't move on until you've told someone what happened." They sat at the patio table for a long time in silence.

Frost stared off into the horizon, obviously trying to gather his thoughts. "I miss roaming those hills with Anthony. He used to show us all the different magickal herbs and earth spells." She gave a nod, encouraging him on.

"I came back here so I wouldn't forget. I didn't want to go back to that mansion and be alone. Sif was in that damned book and I used to carry it around wherever I went, but it wasn't like having him there with me. I may have been able to sense him, but it wasn't like he was actually with me. So, when Henry asked me to come here with him, I was grateful. I thought I could pull myself together, but it was just as bad as if I had returned to Ravenwood on my own.

"It started off fine. We laughed and talked… shared memories. He kept me busy. Unfortunately, he had to return to work and I was left alone. I missed you and Cleo and Sif, and especially Anthony. It was a physical pain after a while.

"One night, Henry was late coming home. I had mustered the strength to go to Anthony's room. Seeing everything so neat and tidy, waiting for his return, made me break down. There was a faint scent of him everywhere. I found his favourite cloak in the closet, the one he wore when dealing with the High Council, and held it."

His eyes were far away and tears were beginning to build, but he didn't seem to notice. Selena had the urge to reach over and wipe them away. They didn't seem right on his pristine face.

He suddenly looked at her and his eyes made her freeze in her seat. "I had fallen asleep on his bed, must have cried myself to sleep. Henry came back plastered, early in the morning. He found me in Anthony's room and was angry to say the least, but he said nothing at first, just let me sleep. Then..."

His eyes hardened.

"What?" she asked in shock. Henry had been the police chief at the time. Serve and protect. He would never, ever hurt one of them. "Frost..."

He shook his head. "There's something not right about him. I noticed it just before Anthony died." The hatred in his eyes had turned thoughtful. "Anthony should have got better. We were transferring magick to him constantly. His tools were sealed. You and I were the only ones drawing magick from him. However, every time Henry spent any time alone with Anthony, he got sicker."

"What are you saying?"

"Didn't you find it odd?"

"A little...but they talked for hours. Maybe he was just tired out."

He raised a brow. "This is Anthony we're talking about. Find a topic he likes, he'll talk for hours. I'll reintroduce you to Daniel in case you forgot him."

She smiled. Dan did talk a lot. It made him a good teacher. "I don't know why Anthony's magick kept slipping like it did, but I don't honestly believe Henry had anything to do with it."

"When he caught me—did what he did, I had almost passed out before he even..." His voice trailed off. "I guess I'm worried about the kids. Scott says Henry has been staring at Eli in an unusual manner. I'm sure it's nothing."

"He loves Eli like his own child. He has never raised a hand to him."

"I know, but…"

"What?"

"Has Eli ever gotten sick for no apparent reason?"

"All kids do." Seeing the seriousness in his eyes, she nodded. "Yeah, he had pneumonia shortly after we returned to England. His magick was a lot weaker. He couldn't protect himself like he use to. He was in bed for a week. Ah…once when he was really little, he had sunstroke. Henry took care of him both times."

"So…"

"It's natural. Just because Eli's a Sorcerer doesn't mean he's immune to the outside world."

"Maybe." He tried to smile. "I'm sure you're right."

Yet something in his words left a cold chill in Selena. There were other times Eli had been sick, but they had all seemed natural. She had always written it off as something he caught at school. What if it was something more? She could never believe Henry would intentionally hurt him. Something just didn't seem right.

Dinner came and went far faster than any of them wished. Frost had actually managed to skip-out of eating. He stayed outside, waiting for everyone to finish. When Eli had asked what was wrong, Selena only said Frost needed time to think. Henry had tried talking to him, but it ended in another argument.

Eli was seriously beginning to think it had been a bad idea to bring Frost back to England. There were too many bad memories. At least he was sure that was the problem. The kidnapping… All of Anthony's memories pointed to Henry and Frost being close. He could not understand why they were so wary of each other. Selena and Scott agreed it had to have been a misunderstanding between the two of them and were having trouble getting past it.

Normally, Eli would have entered Frost's mind to find out what was going on and try to help, but Scott had insisted it was something very private and if Frost wished him to know, he would tell him. Selena, surprisingly enough, had agreed wholeheartedly.

Henry was oddly silent after his talk with Frost and ate his dinner in silence. Eli could not remember the last time it had been so quiet around the dinner table. "So, what do you have planned for tomorrow?" he asked, trying to break the eerie silence.

"What do you want to do?"

That cold stare sent shivers down his spine. For a moment, he could not recognize his grandfather. "Ah…uhm…what about the market or carnival?"

"The carnival, again?"

He shrugged back in surprise. "It's only here this week and I thought you were going to the fiddler's contest."

"Not this year."

"Oh." He glanced around the table. Everyone seemed just as confused as him at Henry's sudden anger. "Did I do something wrong?"

He actually growled at the question. Leaning forward, he stared Eli in the eye. "How often do you practice your magick?" he demanded.

Surprised, he blinked. "Every Saturday night after soccer and every second Sunday."

"Saturday and the odd Sunday? No wonder your aim's off. You're one of the most powerful sorcerers in the world! Is this just a game to you?"

Eli's breath caught in his throat. "I—"

"You wear Raven's robes, but you don't respect the seriousness of your gifts."

"Henry, that's enough!" Cleo snarled, coming to Eli's defense. "We haven't allowed him to push himself. The new powers he has should come to him naturally and not be forced. If that means taking a year or two to study them, then so be it. You cannot force your will on something you do not understand. The magick realm simply doesn't work that way. Eli did not learn magick in one day. It took years, as will these new gifts."

If looks could kill, Cleo would have been a ball of fire. Eli had never seen Henry so angry. Those icy gray eyes turned back to him. "You will show me the full extent of your powers, Eli, or you will not be leaving at the end of next week."

"What? You'll actually make him stay here instead of letting him go home?" Selena demanded angrily. "You can't do that!"

"I'm still his legal guardian, Selena. If he leaves without my permission, I just have to make one call to High Council of Magick." He gave a small smirk. "And you both know I will do it."

It was no bluff, Eli knew. He had done it once already when Nan had died and Eli had refused to move to the cabin. Henry and two social workers had to half-drag him out of the manor in Ipswich when he was eleven. Selena was, in Henry's opinion, still too young to fully take care of him on her own.

"Look," Scott suddenly snapped, drawing everyone's attention to him. "The kid can put an entire city to sleep, open different dimensions and convince my father that he's family. What more do you want?"

"My grandson home with me where he belongs." Henry's eyes narrowed at the young man. "He's only opened one dimensional portal and that was to the Void using Dominique's spell. I want him to do it on his own. I know for a fact he can do it."

"Anthony was a grown man when he first did that," Sif interjected.

"He was fourteen the first time."

Eli shivered as the cold gaze found its way back to him. Something Frost said had made Henry blow up. He had never threatened him like this before. Everything he said was true, though. He should have learned to open dimensional gates by now. He was slacking off.

"I'll do it," he said softly as Sif and Cleo continued to argue in his defense.

"Eli, no," Cleo said sharply. "That takes a lot of magick. Even with what Chaos gave you, you're not as strong as Anthony was. Not by half."

"I'll work on it. Build it up again."

"Eli…"

"That's my boy," Henry said, finally smiling again. "We'll prove Nathaniel wrong. You're every bit the magician Anthony had been."

Frost doubted him? Didn't think he was as good as Anthony had been? That hurt. Had he not split his power with Daniel, he would have been stronger than Anthony by now. It was painful to think everyone still compared him to his past self, but it was to be expected. Not being good enough? That just hurt. He'd show Frost. He'd show them all. A smirk crossed his lips as he looked up at his grandfather. "Yeah. We'll show him."

He didn't even bother with dessert. Learning Frost had no faith in him was enough to make him train harder. It seemed funny competing against his past self, but there was now a need to impress the fey and he was willing to push forward even if his friends objected. However, they refused to let him do it alone.

Opening a portal was easier said than done. He absorbed and redirected his friend's attacks, hoping that combining their energies would allow him to open the fabric of space. Yet, no matter how hard he tried, he could not access the power of the Netherworld. No gates would open. Henry's disappointed eyes broke his heart. No matter how hard he tried, he simply could not do it. Maybe Chaos's magick was no more.

Levitating high above the east garden, he sighed. What was he doing wrong? Why couldn't he do it? Even without Chaos's power, he should have been able to open a portal.

Anthony had.

But he wasn't Anthony.

Sighing, he watched as the sun began to set to the west. It was going to be a hot day tomorrow if the deep red clouds were any indication. He hated practicing in the heat, but knowing Henry, that was exactly was he was going to be doing tomorrow.

The moon was glowing softly in the east. It was only a sliver, the night before the beginning of the full moon. Five days of darkness. Frost and Selena weren't going to be happy about that. Thick clouds were moving in, obscuring the bright twinkling stars, and slowly hiding the moon from his view. It was going to pour. He could feel it in the energy the air was producing. Thunder and lightning were coming.

Even the magick that the night was giving him wasn't enough to give him the strength he needed. Somehow, he had to prove himself to Frost. He just didn't know any other way. He had to open a portal.

He was too tired to care anymore. Tomorrow, he would try again. So, he couldn't open any portals, did that really matter? Even if he could, what would he do with them? If he really wanted to see into another realm, it was easy enough to open a window to view it. Besides, Anthony only used portals to trap anyone or anything seriously threatening him or his loved ones, or if there was a threat too strong for mankind to handle. Eli could count the number of times

Anthony had done so on one hand. Anthony had taken no pleasure in any of them.

Raising his arms, he let the cool night breeze soothe him. Scott had been wrong. Yes, he could put an entire city to sleep, he had been able to destroy an entire nation if he so wished, but the portal to the Void had been opened through Dominique's spell. He had only provided the last ingredient—his blood. He had never opened a dimensional door on his own. It wasn't fair! Why couldn't he do it? He was sure it was not one of the gifts he had given to Daniel. If his uncle managed to open one without the proper knowledge all hell could break loose!

No, he wouldn't let that happen. He had to find out the extent of Daniel's powers. Maybe there was a good reason why he couldn't do it.

He gasped as the air was knocked out of his lungs and he was thrown forward. Panic began pounding in his chest as the sudden attack made him lose focus. He was plummeting to the ground at a speed he knew he could not pull himself out of. Strong arms wrapped around his waist. The flapping of strong wings echoed in his ears as his descent was slowed. It all happened so fast he didn't have a chance to think as he and his savior landed rather hard on the lush grass.

Rolling over, Eli frowned at the silvery being crouched next to him. "Damn, Frost, a little warning next time."

To his surprise, Frost hissed and grabbed him, pinning him to the ground. His weight effectively kept Eli's legs down while he held his hands on either side of his head.

Don't panic, don't panic, Eli kept telling himself as he stared up at his friend in a mixture of confusion and fear. Frost would never hurt you. The horrors of the last time Frost had pinned him in such a way played in his mind. Back then, it had not really been Frost, but a warlock playing tricks with his mind. Frost was his friend. Eli trusted him with his life. "Frost?"

"What the hell are you doing?" the fey demanded angrily. "You've been drawing magick all night. Do you want to put yourself in a coma?"

"I..." Frost was so mad it was actually scary. First Henry, now Frost? Some vacation! "I was trying to open a portal."

"What?"

"Henry said—"

"Henry?"

He bit his lip and nodded. This wasn't good.

"Fuck!"

Eli blinked. Frost never swore.

"I'm going to kill him!"

"Frost—"

Those amethyst eyes glared coldly at him. "Raven doesn't want you tampering with the gates, Eli. You're not strong enough to handle that much power."

"I am, too!" he cried like a stubborn child.

Why couldn't Frost just have a little faith in him? The weight to his legs and arms increased until it was almost painful. He struggled under the slightly smaller being, but Frost had the ability to make himself extremely heavy, completely unmovable when needed. Eli was suddenly too tired to even try. They weren't enemies, no matter how upset they got. He looked up into those amazing eyes. "Frost, I'm tired. I want to go to bed. Please let me up."

Frost's eyes softened. "You're going to burn yourself out. Forget about opening portals."

Seeing the doubt in Eli's eyes, he sat back and brushed a loose lock of hair back. "Do you remember how much of a strain it was on Anthony? I'm sure Selena would panic if you passed out or slipped into a coma for a week or two. We all did when it happened to Anthony."

"Henry said he could handle it."

He shook his head. "Not always."

"But that demon in Spain—"

"That took many weeks of preparation before being set into action."

Now that he thought about it, it was true. Anthony had been working on that spell for a long time. It wasn't originally to imprison anyone. It had been a place for Anthony to escape to when the world became too much for him. It was changed when a Warlord turned demon had become too much of a threat.

What about Henry? As much as he loved England, Canada was his home now. He could not bear the thought of not returning to it. If he had to open every portal in the universe, he would do so to get there. "Whatever Henry said, forget about it. I'll deal with him," Frost said firmly. He helped Eli to a sitting position.

"You don't understand." Frost was truly stubborn. He held his wrist tightly for a moment. Eli feared he was going to yell some more, but Frost only shook his head.

"Eli, you will burn yourself out if you keep this up. You're one of my best friends and even if I'm not your guardian, I do worry about you. Believe me when I say you shouldn't do this. You will eventually hurt yourself."

Eli sighed. "I'm not a little kid, Frost. I don't need your protection. Nor do I wish it." He stood up. "You should focus on Alexis, not me."

Frost stood as well, his eyes once again cold. "Alexis is not the one pushing herself past her limits. Selena's too damn afraid of losing you to stop you. Whatever Henry said at dinner scared both her and Cleo. Alexis refuses to tell me what's going on and Scott's pissed off. He's the one who asked me to stop you."

"Scott?"

"He's worried. Said Henry won't let you go home unless you open a gateway."

"Frost..."

"Is it true?"

"Yes." He blushed slightly as Frost cupped one cheek. It felt odd looking down at him where only months ago he had been looking up. "He still thinks of himself as my guardian, that I'm only a kid. He trusts Selena, but..."

"He doesn't like you so far away." An understanding smile crossed his lips. "He misses you. You have grown much this last year and he missed it. You're not a child anymore. Besides, if he worries so much about you, he can always ask Daniel to keep an eye on you. They have become good friends. He trusts Daniel's judgment."

"I don't know. He was so angry."

"At me, not you. Come, it's getting late."

Reluctantly, he followed Frost back to the cabin and passed a slightly angry Henry. His grandfather said nothing, only giving a nod in greeting. He stifled a yawn as they approached the stairs. He was tired, so tired in fact that he wasn't sure if he could make it up the stairs. He had to pause halfway up to yawn. Frost only chuckled next to him and held his elbow.

"See, you pushed yourself too hard."

"Oh, shut up." He yawned, taking the next step.

That caused him to chuckle even more. He helped him up the stairs despite his insistence that he could do it himself. Eli appreciated the help, nonetheless. His legs felt like lead. Levitating would have been much easier, but the idea didn't occur until he began opening his bedroom door.

Frost hesitated before following him. It took a moment for Eli to figure out why. Once, long ago, the spacious room had belonged to Anthony. He was willing to bet Frost was a little nervous to see how it had changed.

Frost stepped inside and blinked in surprise. Eli only smiled as he draped his cloak over the large wingback chair on one side of his bed. Sitting on the edge, he began removing his shoes.

All Anthony's furniture still decorated the room, but there were a few more bookcases and shelves, each loaded with childhood toys, CDs, books, and computer disks. A state-of-the-art computer sat on the old oak desk. There were also more paintings and photographs, even a signed poster of a concert he had attended with his friends. Definitely, a teenager's room, Henry said, despite how clean it was. Eli loved it. It nicely combined the old with the new.

He began changing into his pajamas as Frost looked around. He didn't mind Frost being there. After all, Frost had seen him in worse conditions.

"Grandpa—Henry spoiled me quite a bit. He didn't want us using his computer so he brought Selena and I our own. Too many police files or something he didn't want us getting into." He took off his glasses and laid them on the nightstand. "He's a very private person."

"Yes."

"He doesn't mean to be so pushy. It's just the way he is." He could not believe how tired he was. An automatic action made him pull back the covers. Normally, he would untie his hair and brush it out, then braid it for the night. Selena got him into the habit after having to deal with tangles one morning. His arms felt ready to fall off and the need for sleep outweighed the need to care for his hair.

Frost covered him up as he lay down. "Don't worry about your grandfather, Eli. I'll straighten everything out."

He just yawned and gave a nod. "Goodnight, Frost."

Frost smiled softly. "Goodnight."

His eyes drifted closed as the lights went out and the door shut. Frost was right, he was pushing himself too hard.

Miao and Alexis were probably still awake and wondering why he had gone to bed so early. He would have to apologize in the morning. For now, he was just too tired to worry about entertaining them.

Sleep claimed him in a matter of minutes.

Frost knocked on Alexis's door. He waited for the young woman's answer before entering. His young Mistress sat on her bed; legs folded under her while Selena brushed her hair. She didn't seem so happy as she held her stomach. Selena only smiled at his concern.

"That time of the month," she explained.

Alexis cringed at the very mention of her period.

She always got embarrassed when such things were mentioned in front of him or Nathan, even if she had been at the ice cream parlor with Nathan and Miao the first time it had happened. With all his magickal wisdom, Frost still wasn't sure how to deal with such issues. He thanked the gods every day for Selena coming to help him. At least he had learned the basics. "Cramping?" he asked gently.

Alexis nodded.

"Would you like some tea?"

She smiled gratefully. "Yes, please."

He gave a nod. So far, this was turning out to be a wonderful vacation, he thought sarcastically. First his and Henry's feud, then Henry began to push Eli too hard and now Alexis? What next? He practically ran into Scott on the staircase. His love caught his shoulders and steadied him before he could trip.

"What's up?" the taller man asked.

"Alexis." He didn't have to say more, their shared mental link told more than either really wanted to know.

Scott grimaced at his sister's predicament. "I'll get the Advil."

Nodding, Frost hurried past him. When it came to Alexis, they had a perfect understanding. Both had a hand in raising her, Scott more than Frost.

Frost entered the kitchen and put on the kettle. Lightning flashed across the darkened sky, followed by a soft rumble of thunder. The storm was quickly approaching. It was a good thing he had dragged Eli inside when he did. The young man would have tried opening the gates regardless of the rain. He seemed so intent on making Henry happy, no matter the cost. Using such magick was exhausting for one still so young. Maybe, if he tapped into the darker recesses of his magick, those of the Netherworld, he could do it, but that was out of the question. They were trying to dispel that magick, purge it from his body. Such power was dangerous, even for someone as strong as Eli. Lord only knew what affect the eclipse would have on it.

Henry was being anything but helpful under the circumstances. Frost had expected more from Anthony's old friend. A plan of sorts. Henry did have access to things they did not—drugs, medicines, things that could render the young man in such a deep sleep that no magick could reach him. He was certain Eli would be just fine if he slept the day away. The only thing that worried him was Daniel Dion. The other half of Anthony's soul was so far away and it was his first eclipse with his new powers. Would he be affected? He had no idea.

The whistle from the kettle drew his attention. Turning the burner off, he poured the hot water into two teacups. Since Selena was caring for Alexis, it seemed only right to bring her something to drink as well. There were a few things he had learned about Alexis over the years. When it came to her menstrual cycles, she loved honey and cream in her green tea. It eased the pain in her belly.

He placed the cups with a small container of biscuits on a tray, pausing only a moment to watch as the sky opened and rain poured from the heavens.

"Is he asleep?"

He fought the urge to jump and turned to face the elderly man standing in the doorway. "Yes. You exhausted him. Why?"

"To see if he could do it." Those stone-cold gray eyes softened. "So far he can't. I suppose it's no longer within his means." He eyed the tray of tea. "Alexis's still not feeling well?"

"That time."

Henry gave a nod. "Does she have enough supplies to last her the night? We'll go to town tomorrow and get her whatever she needs."

"Thank you."

He shrugged. "She's a good kid and Eli adores her. Besides, they wanted to go to town anyway." He made himself a tea as Frost gathered the tray. "Goodnight, Nate."

Surprised by his sincerity, Frost nodded. "Goodnight."

Miao was sitting on Alexis's floor when he got back to the room. The young sorceress had pulled her knees to her chest in an attempt to ease the pain. Sif lay next to her, his large head affectionately rubbing her bare arms. Frost knew the look. She would be in too much pain to do much of anything for the next two days. He eased the tray on the small dresser and went to check Alexis. Placing a cool palm against her cheek, he gave her a dose of healing energy, enough to soothe her cramps for the coming night.

She smiled softly after a moment. "Thank you, Frost."

"Is there anything else I can get you, Alexis?"

Cradling his hand to her cheek, she shook her head. "No, thank you. I think Scott wanted you."

That caused a small chuckle from the other two Guardians.

"Jealous?" he taunted, no longer caring what any of them thought of his relationship with the Mistress' brother.

Selena smiled teasingly. "A little."

Patting Alexis's head, he gave her a gentle smile. "Go to bed soon, Alexis. Goodnight, Miao."

The youth smiled, wishing him goodnight as well. Frost left them and headed to his and Scott's room. His love was out on the balcony, watching the downpour. Lightning skirted overhead, silhouetting the young man's fine features. Frost wrapped his arms around the taller man's waist and rested his head against his broad back. Scott clasped his hands and pulled him as tight as possible. No words were needed as they stood together. Holding Scott like this was so relaxing, Frost could easily fall asleep leaning against him. It was easy to forget all their troubles while like this.

"Hmm..." Scott hummed, squeezing his hands. "There's a lot of energy tonight. Eli expended a lot of magick. The earth is still trying to absorb it all."

"You can feel it?"

"Yeah. How is he?"

"Fell asleep before hitting the pillow."

Scott's chuckle was deep. "He pushes too hard."

"Hmm..."

"He did it for you, not Henry."

"What do you mean?"

Scott finally turned around. Wrapping his arms around Frost, he kissed him lightly. "Henry said you didn't think Eli was a worthy magician. He did it to prove to you he was. To show you he's just as good as Anthony."

"He did it all for me?" He shook his head in frustration. "Eli knows I care deeply for him. He has nothing to prove to me."

"Except that he loves you."

"Scott."

"He wouldn't push himself if he didn't, even with the threat of staying here."

Frost sighed and rested his head against Scott's chest. He had always hoped Scott was exaggerating about Eli's feelings for him, but with his gifts, Scott could see things Frost could not, or refused to. He had hoped Eli had used so much magick to prove himself to Henry not him, but he had not eaten at dinner despite Nathan's cries for food, and had not heard what had transpired. It seemed all Scott's teasing was actually coming true.

Scott rested his chin against Frost's head. "How do you feel for him?"

"I love you, Scott, and only you." He could feel Scott's cheeks pulled back in a smile as the embrace tightened.

"Then we should tell him."

Pulling back, he stared up at that handsome face. "Are you sure? You and Nathan wanted to announce it when we got home so Daniel will be there."

"I'm sure Eli can keep a secret."

Frost bit his lip. It seemed too soon to tell anyone their secret. He doubted Eli would really understand either.

Eli's bedroom door opened silently. Henry peered in before stepping inside. The room was pitch-black with the exception of the odd flash of lightning through the open windows. He left the lights off, moving through the room with decades of experience. Lifting the large wingback chair, he moved it closer to the bed and sat next to his sleeping grandson.

Eli murmured softly in his sleep, hugging the one fluffy pillow as if it were a human-sized teddy bear. He flinched slightly as Henry caressed his cheek. Reaching behind him, Henry undid the young man's hair and let the velvety hair fall around his shoulders and pillow.

He still could not believe how much Eli had grown to look like Anthony. The resemblance was uncanny. He moved his hand down Eli's jaw to his throat. It would be so easy to end it all now. If he broke his neck, the demon powers developing within him would die as easy as his body.

Ocean blue eyes peered through long, thick lashes. The angelic face tilted up to him. "Grandpa?" Eli asked tiredly.

Henry moved his hand to his shoulder. He could never kill Eli. Never in a thousand years could he ever hurt him. "Go back to sleep, Eli." But he had to do something. He had a duty to his country.

"I'm sorry."

Henry raised a brow. "For what?"

"Not being able to open a portal."

His heart melted at those words. He leaned over and kissed the young man's forehead. "Don't worry about it."

In no time at all, Eli fell back to sleep. He looked so peaceful, so innocent. No, there was no way he could be possessed. Yet he could not take the chance of it being true.

Eli suddenly gasped, his eyes shooting open as he sat up. His gaze immediately went to the patio door.

"What is it?"

He followed the Eli's gaze with concern.

"Someone's here."

"Are you sure?"

Frightened eyes stared up at him. Henry tried to give a reassuring smile, but it fell short as blue mist began to seep through the patio door that was inching open. Eli reached for his magick charm, ready to defend himself. For a moment, Henry hesitated. Was what they were doing right? Was Eli as much of a threat as everyone predicted? Did they have the right to do this to him? He didn't know. He wanted to believe they were overreacting, but what if they were right and he let the world come to an end because of his compassion for the child?

He made up his mind and grabbed Eli's wrist, pulling the magickal tool out of his hand. Eli's shocked face tore at his heart, but he held the necklace out of his reach, ignoring the flow of magick pouring from it. Instead, he pulled it into himself.

The mist took on a humanoid form as it got closer to the bed.

He would watch, Henry declared to himself, and make sure Eli was not hurt in any way. He would make sure the warlock did not abuse him and keep Eli from escaping. "It's okay, Eli. Just relax."

"Grandpa, what's going on? What—who is that?"

"A friend."

Eli pulled back when the ghostly figure was in reaching distance. Henry smiled as it wrapped itself around Eli's slim form and pulled him closer. Magick filled the room, sealing it from the rest of the house.

Eli's eyes were wide with fright as the ghostly figure held him. "Henry, give me the totem!" he demanded, foregoing formalities.

He squirmed it its grasp.

Henry held the totem tightly as Eli tried to summon it.

The fight left the child as the creature moved about him. His dark eyes glazed over as if he were touched somewhere very intimate. He became eerily calm as the creature took shape. Henry was not surprised when it took on Nathaniel's form. Eli was obviously in love with the *angel* and the warlock visiting them was willing to fulfill Eli's every fantasy in order to get to the power building within and destroy it.

Henry settled back in his chair and watched as Eli slipped into a trance. He had incredible will-power for one his age. Very few magick users would have been able to penetrate his mind without being instantly shoved out. Not this warlock. No, they were tied together in a way no others had been before. For better or worse, they stuck together now.

Judging by the amount of magick they were now conducting, Henry would finally be able to feast without fear.

Cleo sniffed Eli's door. Powerful magick radiated inside. Using his own magick, he opened the door and padded in. The scent was so strong he could almost choke on it. The first thing he had to do was open the windows wider. Once done, he beat his large wings, fanning the offensive smell outside. Soon the smell left the large room and he was able to breathe once more.

The room cooled rapidly as he went to check the sleeping youth. The boy was curled up in soaked sheets. His hair was inky black as it clung to his back, neck, and cheeks. His body appeared flushed and he felt hot to the touch. Not a fever. Getting up on his hind legs, he sniffled the youth. An unusual smell was coming from his bare flesh, snowy lavender, almost like Frost but human. Definitely not Nathan or anyone else in the house. Fear and anger fought for control. Who would dare touch Eli in such a way?

Not sure what to do, Cleo hurried out of the room and raced to the attic bedroom. He did not bother knocking, knowing full well the couple would be nude and asleep. Slipping inside, he went to Frost's side of the bed and nudged his brother's head with his.

"Frost, wake up," he urged.

Slowly, the eyes opened and stared at the feline. "Cleo? What's wrong?" he whispered, trying not to wake Scott. "It's Eli. He...ah...well...I need your help."

Frost yawned, too tired to move from his love's embrace. "Why? Was he levitating again? Did he fall?"

"No, no. Nothing like that. I smelled strange magick on him."

He yawned again, not interested. "You always smell strange magick when you haven't had enough sleep. Go back to bed."

The panther shoved his muzzle into Frost's bare chest, determined to get him up. "It smelled like you, but human."

Frowning and knowing he would never get any sleep as long as the panther was panicking about Eli, Frost untangled himself from Scott. His sleeping lover was resistant and wrapped himself tighter around his smaller frame. It took a few attempts before he managed to pull himself out of bed.

Cleo waited as patiently as possible as his brother pulled on his trousers and housecoat. His long silver hair cascaded down his back and dragged behind him as he followed Cleo down the stairs to Eli's room. The smell, although not half as strong as it had been, was still over-powering. The magick was unbelievably strong. Someone had been there but Eli appeared unharmed.

"Oh, Eli," Frost murmured as he checked the youth over.

He was just as stumped as Cleo was to who or how this could have happened. It was Sinclair magick, but why had no one noticed it until now?

Frost covered Eli in a fresh blanket and instructed Cleo to spend the rest of the night with the young mage. There was nothing they could do until morning. Hopefully, Eli would have some answers.

"What's wrong?" Scott asked as Frost slipped back into bed. He wrapped his arms around his love's slim waist and drew him close. He raised a brow at the smaller man's stiffness. "Frost, you okay?"

"We have a problem."

Scott sighed. "Eli?"

There was a small nod.

Of course, Eli. It was always that little creep...eh mage. "What now?"

Surprised by the sudden response, he stared at Scott. "Someone was in his room. They..." Frost rolled over and leaned his forehead in the crook of Scott's neck. "He didn't seem hurt."

"Maybe he invited someone over. He has friends here. Maybe he has a lover?"

"He's only eighteen!"

It was such a silly argument, especially from his angel. He didn't bother reminding him just how old they were when they found their first loves.

Pulling Frost closer, he combed his fingers through the long silky strands of hair. "You're not going to be able to sleep, are you?"

"No," Frost whispered.

With an understanding smile, Scott hugged him. "Would you like me to brush your hair?"

It was the easiest way to calm his angel. It always relaxed him and Scott had found it a good form of meditation for both of them.

"I should shower first."

"I'll help," he said being cheeky.

Frost finally laughed, relaxing fully in Scott's arms. "Maybe."

"That's odd," Alexis whispered as she sat next to Miao at the breakfast table. She poured herself some apple juice and looked questioningly at Miao. "Eli's not up yet."

"Henry said he wasn't feeling well," he answered, taking a folk full of egg. "I guess he exhausted himself using so much magick. He may have been Raven, but even he needed a break now and then. Right, Sif?"

The wolf chewed his food before answering. As usual, he was making a pig out of himself. "Just as stubborn. Tony never knew when to call it quits." He chomped on a pastry while he thought about it. "He worked until he passed out half the time. Especially when he started having visions of the future Masters. Everything had to be perfect for them."

"Sounds like Eli," Alexis confirmed.

As much as she loved Eli, he did work himself too hard. The poor boy would probably sleep the morning away. It did surprise her, however, that with all his power and skill that he could not open a portal, not one-dimensional gateway. She had witnessed first-hand the ones Anthony had created many decades ago. The alternate world was amazing, unlike anything she had seen before. With all Eli's magick and Anthony's memories, he should have been able to do the same. Maybe he couldn't any more. Maybe he had given up that skill to her father.

"Well, he better wake up soon. We're supposed to go to town."

She smiled at Miao's handsome face. His chocolate brown hair and eyes were so unlike Eli's. No one would have ever thought them cousins. Miao looked a lot like Selena, only more Hispanic where one would have thought Selena came from Ireland. He wasn't exactly the most patient person she knew either.

"We can wait."

"Wait for what?" Selena asked, taking a seat across from them. She took an orange from the fruit basket. "Where is everyone?"

"Frost and Scott are outside and Eli's still asleep. Cleo's keeping an eye on him," Alexis reported.

"Oh?" The faery looked up at the ceiling. She frowned for a moment as she silently spoke to Cleo. "That is odd." She stood up, forgetting her orange and left.

"What was that about?" Miao whispered.

Sif snorted. "Apparently Eli had a very weird dream. Cleo wanted her upstairs. I guess he's having a hard time waking him up."

Selena rushed into the room. Cleo had sounded so worried. Maybe Eli was sick. Perhaps the use of so much magick had weakened his body. No, that couldn't be it. Eli had used much more than that before. A vision! It had to have been a vision. Those took a lot out of Eli. He was usually in a daze for hours, trying to figure out the meanings behind them.

She froze in her tracks when she found the young sorcerer sitting in the middle of his large bed with only a sheet wrapped around his lower half. He looked pale, exhausted, and utterly confused. His hair was matted and tangled, and smelled of sweat. His knees were pulled to his chest in a foolish attempt to protect himself. He looked about his bed in dismay.

The air was salty and instantly understanding came to Selena. Another wet dream. She sat next to him, carefully avoiding the wet and sticky sheets. "Eli, you okay, honey?"

"Someone was here," he said in such a soft voice she had to lean in close to listen. Cleo nuzzled him affectionately. "Someone very powerful."

That wasn't possible Selena wanted to shout, but Cleo nodded an affirmative. Selena's heart sank. The panther could pick up the scent where Selena was only able to detect a faint aura. Very faint. It didn't make sense. Had there also been someone there the night before?

"Raven's shield is supposed to protect us from outside magick," Eli continued, his voice far away as if he still thought it was all some horrible dream. "But I felt it…someone was here."

He looked up at Selena pleadingly. It was as if he thought she would not believe him. Brushing his hair away from his eyes, she pulled his shivering form into her arms. "Do you remember anything? What the person might have looked like? A man or woman? Did they hurt you?"

Stupid question. Whomever did this must have done something to subdue him. Eli would not simply give in to someone he did not know. Or did he know them?

He shook his head. "No, nothing. I felt Sinclair magick, then passed out. I don't remember anything except being held and…" He began chewing his lower lip in an obvious attempt to hide the rest. "I don't remember anything else."

He had felt the whole thing. Most likely had thought it all some absurd dream. That was even more frightening to Selena.

He laid his head in her lap. "I don't remember a thing."

Sighing, she wrapped the sheet around his shoulders and rubbed his arms. There was no need to push him for more information. She knew all she needed. Someone had broken through Anthony's shield. Only a Sinclair was strong enough to do that. Who amongst the Sinclairs would want to do such a thing to Eli? He wasn't hurt, but that wasn't the point. A Sinclair, someone related to Eli, had invaded his room, and violated his body. No one had the right to do that.

Eli had been through so much Selena didn't think he could take any more. She was sure of it. Why couldn't he just be left alone? His magick attracted the wrong type of attention. It always had. Anthony's family had always cared for Eli and made it their duty to make sure his magick never got out of control or fell into the wrong hands. Such power could cause such destruction that the world would tremble.

Why would one of them harm their own?

It didn't matter why. It was her job to protect him. Sinclair or no Sinclair, no one was going to harm him, even if that meant giving up her plans with Scott and Frost. They would understand.

"Hey," she said, perking up. "Why don't you spend the night with me? No one would be stupid enough to touch you if I'm with you. Cleo can come, too. We can have a great big sleepover in my room like when we were little."

He sniffled and wrapped his arms around her waist. "Are you sure?"

"Of course! What kind of guardian would I be if I didn't protect my favourite Master?"

He smiled softly. "Friend. I prefer being your friend. Both of you."

Cleo wrapped his long body around both of them, resting his head on Eli's waist. He purred contently as his master hugged him.

The engine revved as they raced through the country road. Selena glared at the road before her. Her mind raced just as fast with Eli's new problem and the secret Frost had revealed to her. Frost's fear for Eli was evident on Nathan's soft features. He had not wanted the teens left alone with Henry, not after what had happened to Eli. He was certain Henry had something to do with it. She was starting to wonder if he was right. Henry would never harm Eli, but what if he had allowed someone else to get that close to him? No. There was no way

Henry would do that. Eli was his grandson, the reincarnation of his best friend.

Scott was very diplomatically staying out of it. He sat in the backseat quietly as the music blared. His quietness was beginning to piss her off. He offered no advice and seemed as lost as they were. He wasn't even comforting Nathan, which was seriously out of character. Normally, he was the first to assure him that everything was going to be fine, calming Frost before he lost his temper.

She was losing her temper and fast. She took the next turn too sharply and sent the Porsche into a spin. It skidded to a halt just meters from the old bookstore.

"Selena, what the hell!" cried Nathan, gripping the dashboard. Amethyst eyes fought through his hazel-amber ones. "You could have flipped us!"

"I'm taking him to see a doctor. Find out exactly what happened," she barked back.

His eyes softened. "He won't go. You know that."

Rage and bitterness claimed her. "If someone was in there and assaulted him, I want to know who. Henry's police buddies can do an investigation." She clenched her teeth at the pitying look he gave her. "I won't let him be hurt anymore! I don't care if it was a Sinclair!"

Her knuckles began to turn white as she gripped the steering wheel. "I won't let anyone hurt him."

"Selena." He undid his seatbelt and embraced her. "I know."

She kept herself from crying. Strength was the only way to handle this. Too much had happened since Eli's birth to lose herself now. She would simply hold on and do her duty to the best of her ability like she always had. That was all she could do.

"You okay?" Nathan said gently after a moment. He wiped a rogue tear from her cheek.

Nodding, she pulled back. "Yeah. Thanks, Nate."

He gave one of his beautiful smiles. He eyes looked where they had stopped and frowned at the old bookstore. "Ah, Selena?"

"Yeah?"

He gestured at the bookstore with confused and fearful eyes.

"Did you have to park here?"

She stared at the bookstore in confusion before it hit her. It was the place he had been kidnapped many years ago. Frost must have panicked. Putting the car in gear, she pulled away. "Sorry."

He buckled himself in. "Frost was getting antsy…eh, uneasy."

She chuckled at his correction. Frost never got *antsy*. The *angel* was so full of himself sometimes.

"What's with the bookstore?" Scott finally asked, leaning forward as she guided the car into the market's parking lot.

"I—we…something bad happened there. Frost won't tell me," Nathan murmured.

Definitely a good thing. Frost was already irritated by just the sight of the store. Nathan did not need to remember what had happened to him back then.

"Selena, what happened?" Scott pushed, not worried.

She shook her head and parked. "Sorry, love, when Sparky's ready, he'll tell you."

"Anthony?"

She gave a small nod and turned in her seat to face her brother.

His large eyes regarded her carefully. "It's better this way as it is for Eli."

He was far more understanding than Scott. "Yeah, another week and then we're back home. What can happen between now and then?"

Both she and Scott cringed at that thought. It felt as if those words jinxed everything. There was already the mystery of Eli's late-night visitor. Someone who may next very well target Alexis and Miao. The two were new to their country and very vulnerable. Currently stronger than Eli and with Raven's powers within her as well, Alexis would be wanted. Many would try to control her. Miao was soon to be the leader of his clan. If he were kidnapped, war would surely befall the magick world. They would have to stay close to the children.

With the retractable roof down due to it being such a beautiful and hot day, Scott was able to jump out of the car once they parked in front of the drugstore. He opened Nathan's door and pulled him out and into his arms. The smaller man laughed as Scott enveloped him in his large arms. They were so adorable together, she couldn't resist. Pulling out her camera, she snapped a picture of them before they could pull apart.

"Selena!" Nathan laughed.

He actually did like having his picture taken with Scott, and Frost loved it. There were very few pictures of Nathaniel and Anthony. None of them, holding each other, nothing that proved that they had once been lovers. Nathan tucked his head under Scott's chin.

"I'm hungry. Frost didn't eat last night or this morning. He's being a grump."

Scott laughed. "I've never known someone so small who ate so much."

"It's not my fault. Blame Anthony."

Selena locked the doors and closed the roof. "Poor Nathan. Guess we'll just have to raid the fridge while we wait for Henry and the kids."

For a moment, Nathan's eyes flashed again at the mention of Henry, but quickly brightened at the concept of food. He let go of Scott so they could follow Selena to the nearest restaurant and found a window seat.

Watching her brother eat was always entertaining. He ate enough to do a small army. Sandwiches, soups, baked goods. She and Scott picked at some of it, but when Nathan was in lunch mode, very little drew his attention. Not even Frost could stop him. By the time he was halfway done, Henry had pulled up with the kids.

Alexis stepped into the restaurant, followed by the two. She plopped down next to Selena as Eli and Miao pulled up chairs. "Hate Henry's cooking that much, Nate?" she teased, plucking a muffin from the basket.

"Hey, monster, you had breakfast," Scott chastised even as Nathan nodded to her to do so. He yelped as his little sister kicked him under the table.

Nathan chuckled, finishing his third sandwich. "She's getting strong."

"Don't even need magick to kick your butt," Selena added teasingly. She wrapped an arm around the young woman's shoulders. "You do know Frost has been training her just so she can pick on you. I can see it now, an erase spell stealing all your clothes, even the ones you're wearing." She gave Nathan a wink. "The Duplicate spell making a copy of Miao."

The boy laughed at that one.

"Fertility creating a forest out of your bedroom. Oh, oh and—"

"I get the point, Selena," Scott muttered, raising a hand to stop her before she gave Alexis any bright ideas.

"And Water Sprites would never leave you alone," Eli threw in with a wicked smile.

He certainly recovered quickly, Selena thought as Eli ordered three sodas. He was even laughing now.

"You're the evil side of Raven. I hope you know that," Scott growled at him playfully.

Eli smiled even more. "But of course! And Frost and I are having an affair behind your back."

Nathan feigned guilt. "Eli! I told you never to tell him!"

"Sorry, angel."

Selena grinned. The old mocking Anthony had entered his persona. He glanced at the jukebox in the corner.

"And now I'm going to steal Alexis from Miao!" Eli announced, taking the woman's hand. He pulled her from her seat and led her to the small dance floor. Alexis picked the music, something soft and upbeat.

Scott almost choked when Eli pulled her close and they began to sway to the music. He looked from Eli to Miao and back again. "Aren't you mad?" he asked Miao in confusion.

Miao shook his head as he sipped his drink. "They think of each other as siblings. I trust Alexis." He gave the older man a smug smile. "Besides, he knows I'll kill him if he tries anything."

"Did he say anything on the drive here?" Nathan asked, offering him a blueberry muffin.

"No. He sat up front with Henry and was pretty quiet the whole ride. I think Henry's worried. Eli barely spoke to him." He glanced at his friends dancing. "What's going on?"

Nathan shook his head. "We're not sure."

He looked from Scott to Selena. Selena shook her head. It was too soon to tell him or Alexis. They had to figure it out first, then tell the kids. There was no need to scare them if it was nothing.

"So, who do you think will kill me first?" Eli inquired as Alexis rested her head on his shoulder.

He leaned his head against hers. Their magick flared around them as they melded it into one. She was very kind-hearted, letting him draw strength from her powers. He felt unusually drained, as if someone had taken his strength.

He refused to tell anyone.

He was still trying to figure out who and how someone got into his room and why he had not awakened. His body hurt in ways he could not understand. His knees still felt weak, but he could not bear the worried looks the older three kept giving him.

"Oh…I'd say Scott," Alexis giggled. She pulled him closer. "Feeling better?"

With a nod, he stepped back. "Very much so. Thank you." He bowed gracefully and kissed the back of her hand. "You're a very elegant dancer, Alexis."

She giggled more. "And you are such a charmer!" She looped arms with him and led the way back to the table. "So, today's Midsummer, huh? What's the plan for tonight?"

Eli's eyes widened. With what he had awaken to, he had completely forgotten about the Sabbath. That must have been why Henry had given in to them coming to town rather than trying to open a portal. If luck was with them, he might even let them throw a party, just like old times. That meant shopping for supplies! It would be the first Midsummer he celebrated with his friends. He wanted it to be special. He was willing to put aside all the strangeness he had awaken to just for an incredibly fun night with his friends.

"A huge party!" Selena announced Eli's thoughts. "We'll have a bonfire on the beach, go swimming, maybe even some fireworks. Eli can teach you different ways to thank the Goddess. It's not the same as in Canada, but you'll love it."

That was putting it mildly. Alexis was already bubbling with excitement. Even Miao was interested. That only made Eli more than happy to teach them. He smiled brightly and laughed as Selena went into detail. This was exactly how the celebration was supposed to be done, and he could always fix whatever she forgot. It was going to be a great night either way.

Eli and his friends left the others in the cafe and made their way through the marketplace. The girl, Alexandria Dion, he thought in distaste, stopped at a jewelry vendor booth. Eli stopped with her and looked them over while the future Syffern Clan leader leaned against the stand. Eli's face was gentle and sincere as he held an antique necklace up to her. He had a brotherly look on his face as he bought it for her. She giggled as he placed it around her neck.

They moved on and he stayed as close as he dared. He kept his presence hidden from the three mages as they moved about. His gaze never left Eli. The young man was so full of energy, far more than he had been moments ago. His eyes seemed so much brighter. Full of life. It was something he had not seen in such a long time.

Magick swirled around Eli. There was such vibrancy in one so young, yet his aura had gaps. Dark shades in it that very few could explain. There was still a darkness hidden beneath the innocence. Darkness he had not been able to rid the child of the night before. Chaos had given Eli more power than he had originally thought. He was almost as strong as Raven and far more dangerous. There was no way he could bring such power under control before the eclipse. He needed more time and a place safe and private to train the child reincarnation.

Henry was not going to be happy.

Adjusting his sunglasses, he followed the teens back to the carnival where they engrossed themselves in cotton candy and Frosties. Their laughter filled his ears as he moved closer.

"Duncan!"

He looked up to see Henry waving from his perch at the music grandstand. Fiddlers were setting up for the evening's contest. People of all ages and genders were tuning their instruments. The noise was actually soothing. Henry patted the space beside him. He sat down and took the proffered coffee his friend held out to him.

After so many years, the former police chief and army general knew exactly what he took in his coffee. He sipped it thankfully. The night with Eli had taken a lot out of him, far more than the mage he had attempted to tame. Yet, he had no time to rest. His mind and body would not allow him. It was something that had claimed him since first speaking to Eli the other day. It had never happened before.

"You look beat," Henry stated with an amused grin.

"Astral travel and holding a solid form in it can be very draining." He yawned and stared off to where he felt Eli's aura. He and his friends were on the Zipper once more. It was dizzying just scanning his aura.

"And here I thought he wore you out," the old man teased.

Duncan groaned. "That, too." He sighed and took another sip. "I can't do it. I can't cage that much power."

Henry raised a brow in surprise. "What do you mean? You're the strongest telepath in England."

He shook his head. "Was. Eli took that from me. I need more time."

"The eclipse is in four days."

"I know."

"Now what?"

He was silent, frozen by the suggestion he was about to give. Henry was temperamental, sometimes erratic, and dangerous. He had been so since Raven's death. Eli was all that kept him grounded. That was now slipping away. That had been evident the night before. This may send him over the edge. However, if they were to succeed it had to be done.

"I wish to take Eli to my home. I can slow time long enough for him to master some of his new powers. Or, if necessary, eradicate them."

"Selena won't let him. Especially if she finds out who you are."

He closed his eyes. Why was this so difficult? If he could just pose as Eli's friend, it would be so simple. He frowned. That wouldn't work either. If they sensed his true aura, it would never work. "We take him," he said after a moment.

Henry stared at him in surprise. "How?"

Standing, he took off his sunglasses and looked him squarely in the eyes. "He trusts you. I'm sure you can find a way. Tonight, after their party. I'll be there by midnight."

He didn't bother waiting for an answer. Henry would see to it. He would find a way to bring Eli to him. He knew the young man's weakness. That was the one thing he could trust about Henry—he could always convince Raven to join him.

"Wow!" Miao breathed, stopping at another booth. He picked up a ring with a fierce looking wolf engraved on it. There was a matching bracelet next to it. It looked identical to Sif. Alexis would love it. The smoky topaz eyes gave it life.

He frowned as he stared at the price tags. Sixty pounds for the set. It was slightly more than he was carrying.

"That is cool," Eli agreed, looking them both over.

"Yeah."

"What's wrong?"

He shook his head and put the ring back. "Nothing." He really wanted to buy the set as a surprise for Alexis. It was the perfect time to. She had gone to use the restroom. Hopefully, they would still have it tomorrow, but he doubted it.

Hearing Eli talking to the vender made him turn around again. His eyes widened. Eli was buying them both! "What are you doing?" he demanded. If Eli gave them to Alexis, he was going to have to kill him.

With a large, happy smile, Eli deposited both wrapped boxes in his hands. "Making Alexis happy makes you happy so think of this as a birthday present."

"I…" He blushed slightly and shook his head. "Eli, you're the weirdest guy I know."

Eli laughed. "I know you love me."

Miao punched him in the arm. "And give Alexis up for you? Not a chance."

"Trying to steal my boyfriend again, Eli?" Alexis tsked, wrapping her arms around Miao's neck. "Shame on you."

He tapped his chin thoughtfully. "He is cute," he said in a mock serious voice.

"Isn't he though?"

Miao rolled his eyes. "You two are insane. Definitely Sinclair kids."

Alexis held him tighter and kissed his cheek. "You're so sweet, but hey, so are you."

Eli laughed, matching her smile. "Come on, guys, let's finish buying the supplies."

Chapter Eight

Miao and Alexis caught on to horseback riding as if it were second nature to them. Eli was impressed to say the least, and finally decided it was time to take them to one of his favourite sacred places.

They had plenty of time before dinner would be ready and Henry had insisted he didn't need any help. It was the perfect Midsummer Day.

Far in the woods, hidden in the lushness of nature was a group of waterfalls that ran into one another and ended in a small lagoon. The foliage grew close to the water with only a small sandy beach and rocky ledges near the base of the waterfalls. It was very serene and relaxing. It was Eli's most favourite spot in all of England. It was a place of pure magick.

They sat under the poplar tree closest to the falls while their horses grazed close by.

"Eli, this is…wow…" Alexis breathed, still eyeing their surroundings. It was like a page from a fairy tale. "Anthony found this place?"

"Yes, when he was very young."

She seemed amazed. "I should have brought the camcorder. Melissa would love to see this."

"Tomorrow we'll bring it," he assured.

He bit his lip, hiding the smile that was trying to give him away. Cupping his hands in his lap, he closed his eyes and murmured an incantation. His hands closed.

Concentrating on the space within, he imagined soft, snowy feathers.

Opening his eyes, he released his new creation.

A gorgeous white dove fluttered out of his hands.

Alexis gasped in awe.

But that was not the end of the spell.

The dove flew above them, circling just above their heads before vanishing. Tiny white, pink and baby blue butterflies took its place. Thousands of them glided down from the bright green leaves of the old poplar tree.

Alexis raised her arms to embrace the mystical creatures. She giggled as they fluttered in her hair. Small pink roses formed where they touched until she wore a ring of them.

The rest slowly made their way to the ground where they turned into more flowers. An array of red, blue, and gold flowers appeared around them. Large sunflowers grew until they hung over their heads.

Miao touched one, amazed by the fact they were real. He picked it and weaved it through Alexis's hair with the others. "Impressive," he said, leaning back on his elbows.

"It's how I give thanks to the Goddess." He shrugged. "It's small, but Aaliyah… used to love it."

His voice broke slightly at the thought of his Watcher. He missed her with all his heart. He mentally shook himself. This was not the time to be thinking of her, even if she usually sat with him beneath this very poplar tree every Midsummer.

This was the first time they would not be together for the festival. "You're thinking about her."

He looked up to see Alexis smiling kindly. Her knowing emerald eyes regarded him lovingly. He had done the same many times. He appreciated it more than he could ever put in words.

"It's hard not to. Especially here."

It was hard to forget where he received his first kiss by the woman he was so sure he was in love with, despite the age difference.

Dinner was out on the patio that evening. Sif started a bonfire shortly after. Gold and red candles decorated the beach and half the yard in front of the cabin. Soft music filled the air.

Eli slipped into Anthony's ceremonial robes. It only felt right to be dressed up for the celebration. He had taught Alexis and Miao various spells that paid their respects to the ancient gods of the land. They had done very well for their first times.

Once darkness took hold of the night, Scott set off the fireworks Selena had bought and filled the night sky with wondrous colour. The night was more than Eli could have hoped for.

Around eleven, he accompanied Frost into the cabin to fetch more snacks and deposit the garbage. He retrieved the case of pop while the faery got the cake Henry had hidden from Sif in the walk-in cooler. Frost was oddly silent from the moment they entered the house. He seemed lost in thought. Maybe it was the darkness of the moon. The beginning of the New Moon always put a drain on his powers. Whenever Frost could not view his precious moon, he got antsy, but today seemed worse than usual. Placing the heavy case on the table, Eli drew in a deep breath. Bloody thing weighed a ton.

"Frost, could you carry—" he began.

"Eli, we need to talk," the brooding fey announced, placing the cake on the table as well.

Surprised, he nodded. Frost gestured for him to sit down. He did as asked, confused by the mixture of emotion playing over Frost's usually serious face. The mask of indifference had slipped away long ago. It was now easy to see the worry he had.

With a look of determination, Frost sat next to him and turned his chair so they could face one another without obstacles. "Eli, you know I care very deeply for you." Eli nodded.

"But I love Scott."

"I know, Frost. I would never—"

Frost held up a hand to silence him. Eli shut his mouth quickly and let his friend finish.

"I know you would never break us up, no matter how you feel for me." He inhaled deeply and let it out slowly. He slipped a hand in his tunic and pulled out a white gold chain with a ring on it. He held it out for Eli to see. "Scott asked me to marry him. I've accepted."

Despite himself, Eli felt his heart break for a second time. Or maybe it was what was left of Anthony. He knew he never had a chance with Frost, not with Scott in the picture, but a small part of him had hoped that he could rekindle Anthony's and Nathaniel's love. Now it was impossible. That small piece of jewelry marked Frost as Scott's forever, "Till death do they part." He groaned inwardly. It wasn't fair.

"Eli?"

Blinking back tears, he forced a smile. "That's wonderful, Frost. Congratulations."

Those piercing eyes stared at him. "You're not happy."

"Of course, I am. It's wonderful news."

"You're not good at lying when you're emotional. Neither was Anthony."

He choked back the laughter that forced its way through. "You know my biggest weakness."

A soft, understanding smile caressed Frost's lips. "I do need you to do something for me and Nathan. It's very important and you're the only one I trust you with the task."

He looked up in surprise, not understanding what it was Frost would need him to do. Alexis was his Mistress.

"It's a very big job. Two, actually. One—you can't tell anyone just yet. Two—" They locked eyes for a moment. "Would you be my best man?"

Eli was stumped and completely in shock. He didn't know what to stay. He just stared at Frost. "Best man?"

"Say yes."

"I…"

"Or nod."

"…don't…"

"Eli?"

"Ah…yeah, sure." He blinked and tried to focus. "I'll be honored, but what about Alexis?"

"As best man?" He thought about it for a moment. "Wouldn't work, but I can always talk to her."

"No, I mean…"

He smiled. "She'll be okay with it. It's not like she's going to be losing me."

It was all too much to consider at once. Eli could not bring himself to be angry nor could he be completely happy. As long as Frost was happy, he kept telling himself, but it didn't make him feel any better. Even as Frost insisted their friendship would never change, he knew it would never be the same. Scott would become even more possessive and Frost's solo visits to his home would soon cease. He didn't need to see the future to know it would happen. He kept his silence as he followed Frost back outside. No matter what, he would keep his promise.

The rest of the celebration flew by with little realization. Soon enough Henry was encouraging the younger teens inside and extinguished the flames of the fire. Eli helped blow out the candles and gather whatever food they managed not to eat.

Selena continued to complain it was too early, not even midnight. Eli was too exhausted to care. Not even about the weirdness of the night before. He made plans with his two best friends to camp out in the den to watch movies and pig out on leftovers. It let Selena off the hook of protecting him that night. What could happen if the three of them and the Familiars slept together? At first, she was troubled by the idea, but he reminded her that she had made plans with Scott and Nathan, and that those of the magick world were still partying in town. It took more convincing than normal, but she soon left with both men in tow.

Once Frost was out of the house, Eli was finally able to think. Nathaniel, Anthony's angel, was getting married. It was unbelievable. He didn't know whether he was happy or sad. He was happy Frost had found someone who loved and accepted everything about him. Scott had known the moment he saw Nathan he was not human. He had seen his true self, hidden deep inside. Even when Nathan had no idea who he truly was, Scott had cared and watched over both forms. Was that not true love? Why couldn't he just be happy for them?

He, Alexis, and Miao had thrown every pillow they could get their hands on onto the floor and were sprawled out watching the DVD of *Star Wars: Episode III*. He would have preferred to watch *Underworld* or some horror flick, but Alexis didn't like horror movies, so they had to settle for a science fiction flick. He didn't really mind. He had come to like the *Star Wars saga*. Anakin Skywalker's trial often reminded him of his own, the feeling of viewing everything as one and not always being a part of it. That's what Frost's news had left him feeling.

As much as he tried, he could not focus on the movie. Finally, tired and bored he stood up and straightened his robes. "I'm going to change for bed," he said, excusing himself. "Did either of you want anything?"

Miao shook his head and Alexis yawned, "No, thanks," before curling up in Miao's arms.

Even Alexis and Miao were happily in love. It just wasn't fair, he thought as he watched them snuggle closer. He sorely missed Aaliyah and how she used to cuddle him. He still hated himself for scaring her away. She had not called or wrote since the day they had broke up. He wasn't even sure how to get a hold of her any more. Melissa was too far away to get a hold of.

He went to the kitchen. His throat felt dry and he had the sudden urge to eat an apple. Henry was still up, working away in the kitchen. It seemed awfully late for him to still be up. Then again, he did like a good party like the next man. Rummaging through the fridge, he found himself a bright fresh apple and sat at the table. "Need any help?"

Henry smiled. "No, just about finished. Having fun?"

He shook his head.

"What's wrong?"

Oh, how he wanted to spill his heart out about Frost's engagement, but he said nothing.

"Get in an argument with Miao?"

He laughed. "No, nothing like that." Curiosity got the better of him. "Grandpa, why do you and Nathaniel argue so much? Before Anthony died the two of you—"

"Were very close." He put the last dish away and sat next to him. He straightened Eli's ruffled collar. "Many things happened after Anthony passed on, Eli. Much pain. Nate couldn't let him go and I could not continue to watch him suffer. It ended our friendship."

"What did you do?"

"Something very stupid." He gave him a one-arm hug. "It's nothing to concern yourself over."

Eli frowned. He was just as secretive as Frost. He really wished he knew what had happened. If he did, maybe he could find a way to heal both their wounds. Biting into his apple, he tried to come up with possibilities, but none made sense.

"You love him."

Blinking, he stared up at him. "I...no... It's Anthony's love for him. It will never die, even if he is gone."

Henry took his chin in his thumb and forefinger and inspected his face. "No, my little Raven, he is not gone. He lives within you." His other hand caressed his cheek, moving across his lips. "You look so much like him. Much more than last summer. Long hair suits you. With those eyes and that mouth."

Eli's eyes widened as Henry unnaturally moved closer. He came within inches of his lips before gently tugging his chin down and kissing his forehead. Eli sighed in relief. He loved Henry, but not like that. The old man pulled him close and let him rest his head against his chest. He didn't resist. It was natural to rest against his grandfather. It was relaxing and made him feel safe.

"I miss him so much at times," Henry whispered.

"I know."

Eli wrapped his arms around Henry's waist. Anthony had been his best friend. Henry always said he had died far too young. He often blamed himself, although Eli could not see how Henry could ever have saved Anthony. He had died by forces no man or modern medicine could have countered.

A trickle of magick fluttered at the edge of his senses. It grew, slowly at first, as if far away, at the edge of town. It quickly grew, filling Eli's senses. It was Sinclair magick, like the night before. Startled, Eli stared at the cellar door. For some reason, the magick was being directed to the old wine cellar. Pulling away from Henry, he went to inspect it.

"Eli?"

"Someone's here," he said, holding a hand up for him to stay where he was.

Raising his personal shields, he cautiously opened the door. The aura of magick grew, but nothing came at him. Flipping on the light, he took a step down. The magick swam around him, pushing against his shields. Dizziness gripped him, forcing him to grab the rail to keep from falling. This wasn't good. Whoever possessed such power was incredibly strong. Even with his metaphysical shields at full strength, the magick was overwhelming.

He gasped as large arms wrapped around him from behind. Before he could cry out to Henry for help, a rag clasped over his mouth and nose. A menthol solution burned his eyes as he was forced to breathe it in. The dizziness grew to a lightheaded sensation.

Panicking, Eli grabbed at the arm covering his mouth, digging his nails as deeply as possible before his arms were pinned to his sides.

Something inside him felt as if it was being pulled. A magick he normally would not unleash, but was more than willing to under the circumstances.

Where was Henry?

Was he okay?

He struggled harder.

He had to get to his grandfather. He had to protect him.

"Easy, child. Just breathe it in."

His eyes widened. It wasn't possible. Why would Henry do this to him? His grandfather would never hurt him. It had to be a lie!

Henry's grip tightened and Eli found himself lifted off his feet, making his struggles futile. "Shh…it's okay."

Henry was too strong.

Eli could not break free. Wiggling one arm free, he reached for his totem, but a sharp jab to his spine caused him to inhale sharply, breathing in a fair amount of the menthol solution. There was little else he could do. The pull of magick increased, but no power unleashed itself. It felt as if it was being pulled out of him.

Mentally, he called out to Cleo. He could feel the panther stir in his sleep. He silently pleaded for his guardian to wake up, to somehow help him, but his strength fled before he could make full contact.

His eyes felt heavy and body numb. He was no longer able to struggle let alone lift a limb.

Why was Henry doing this?

Whatever answers he had hoped for, faded away as he finally slipped into unconsciousness and went limp in Henry arms.

Henry sighed. Eli was certainly stubborn. It took much longer than he had expected for the drug to take effect. With all his struggles, Henry would have thought the child would pass out faster. Inhaling so much should have affected him more.

He waited a few seconds after Eli's body went limp before laying him on the floor. His breathing was slightly erratic from the fight, but he seemed alright. Duncan would be happy. Thank God, Selena and the others had gone out. He doubted he would have been able to pull it off if they were there.

Straightening Eli's robes, he sat back on his heels. Duncan's magick had distracted Eli enough for Henry to knock him out. Even in his sleep, he looked as if he were fighting to stay conscious.

"What happened?" Cleo gasped from the doorway. The black cat raced up to Henry and stared at his sleeping master in horror.

Surprised, Henry simply stared at him. "I—I don't know," he lied. "He sensed someone outside, then fell to the ground."

With his magick, Cleo made the back door fly open. Growling, he raced outside in search of the intruder.

Raising the gun he had concealed in the back of his pants, Henry aimed at the winged panther's rump. The silencer kept the tranquillizer from making any serious noise and waking the two sleeping teens in the den. Cleo fell with barely an uttered cry and reverted to his house cat form automatically. Satisfied he would have no more unexpected guests, Henry picked up Eli, cradling him against his chest, and retrieved Cleo.

The large black limo awaited him in the driveway. A young woman held open the back door, nodding a greeting as he handed Eli over to her passenger. He slipped in a moment later, not sparing a glance at his home or the children he was abandoning. They would be safe. Sif was still there to protect them, and Selena and Frost would return the moment they felt Eli missing. There was no need to fear for their safety.

He settled back and watched as Duncan cradled Eli's head on his lap. A broad, loving smile caressed his lips. The two could be classified as brothers. Eli's hair was darker and his Spanish features more apparent than his British heritage, but they had the same bright tricoloured blue eyes and build, even if Duncan was taller. He deposited Cleo on the empty seat next to him.

"Why bring the cat? He's just trouble," Duncan asked, toying with Eli's loose bangs. His fingers traced the line of Eli's cheek. He smoothed out the furrowed brows.

"Insurance."

"Hmm. You may be right. He is strong willed." He removed the wire-rim glasses from Eli's face. "He escaped me twice, but not this time."

His hand moved to Eli's forehead. The younger man inhaled sharply as Duncan's hand began to glow. He twisted away, fighting even in his sleep. Fastening one hand on his jaw, Duncan forced him to stay still as he cast the binding spell. Nonetheless, Eli fought him.

Sapphire eyes peered through long black lashes. He stared into the mirrored image of his eyes. For a moment, Henry thought he would recognize Duncan, but the mage said nothing. His eyes drifted closed once more and he lay silently in Duncan's arms.

The older man smiled devilishly at him. "No magick, no threat."

"That won't last long. Anthony is still stronger than you."

"Yes, but this nullifies his magick against the Sinclairs. After all, Raven would never harm family."

Henry raised a suspicious brow. Duncan happily cradled Eli. They did look right together. Just like so many years ago. A feeling of déjà vu filled him at the sight, but it was a good feeling. Almost like old times.

Nausea filled his senses as the limo passed through the fabric of time and space and entered a protective realm guarded by Duncan's magick. It was a natural effect. He never could adjust to the change in reality.

Since claiming a new body, Duncan Porter had been living outside of time. Here they would train Eli. Here they would open his mind to the rest of the world, to the power he had yet to master. Or destroy it. If that was the price of God's will then so be it.

Anything to protect England.

And maybe taste the flow of magick once again.

Chapter Nine

"Ha!" Selena cried as she got the last three balls in the holes without sinking the white ball.

She held the pool cue triumphantly at her side and held out her hand to Scott. "Twenty pounds."

Nathan burst into laughter as Selena forced his love to pay up. He sat on the ledge and took a swig of his beer. It wasn't fair really. Selena was a pool shark. One of the skills she had picked up from Henry, not Anthony. Scott was also good. He played in college during spares when he wasn't studying or working. Nathan often played with him, especially if they didn't have time for anything else. Unlike many other sports, he was not as good as his sister and was not willing to lose his money to prove otherwise. He could not help but pity his lover for falling for Selena's innocence of the game. He should have learned long ago that she may be cute, but she was also very tricky.

With a humph, Scott sat next to him. Losing to Selena always made him grumpy. He should have learned by now, but he had that Sinclair stubbornness. It made Nathan smile. So many little things about the Dions proved they were descendants of the Sinclairs...proved they were Raven's children.

Scott growled softly at his amusement. He snatched the beer from him and drank over half before Nathan could protest. He handed the half-empty mug back to him and smiled innocently. Shaking his head, Nathan jumped down and took the vacant pool cue. Selena was already racking up the balls.

"Can't expect to make any money off you, huh?" she asked, standing back.

"Nope." Leaning over the table, he took his shot, sinking three at once. "Solids," he called, since two out of three were. He lined up his next shot and managed to sink two more. Selena whistled in surprise and Scott came closer. Nathan was better at this game than he thought.

"Double or nothing he beats you!" Scott declared, slapping twenty pounds on the table.

That caused Nathan to get nervous. "Scott, no." Betting was not something he was into, it made him lose focus. The next shot went wild, sinking the wrong ball and sending another flying.

Selena caught the ball with a smirk. "Thank you, Nathan."

Scott buried his face in Nathan's ruffled hair as he pulled him from behind. "You had the shot. You could've won," he pouted. He wrapped his arms around his waist and playfully sobbed as Selena won once more. "She's taking all my money!"

"Poor baby."

Nathan laid the pool cue against the wall and intertwined his fingers with Scott's, not caring about the disgusted glares some of the onlookers gave them. He was used to it. Since he and Scott became lovers more than seven years ago, they had been called every name in the book, been in more than one fight and still managed to stay together. Let people say what they want. He didn't care anymore. He loved Scott with all his heart. If only he could wear his engagement ring and show the entire world. Telling Eli was such a weight off his and Frost's shoulders. They both felt better. However, he was worried. Eli had a bit of a crush on Frost. It hurt to see his heart break.

Scott was on the same wavelength. Selena fiddled with the jukebox and gave them some privacy. He squeezed Nathan, nibbling lightly on his ear lobe yet trying to hide it from onlookers. "He didn't take it well?"

Nathan tried not to giggle as his ear was tickled. "He was a little flustered. I asked him to be my best man. Do you mind?"

"No. It's great. He'll probably feel better if he's part of it. He really does love you, Nathan…iel."

Nathan blushed slightly as his other half also acknowledged it.

"Course he loves you," Selena chirped. She swayed to the music, humming cheerfully. "He waited all his life to meet you. He had dreams of Anthony's angel for as long as I can remember. The day you cornered him in that tree, his heart almost stopped. The moment he saw you he knew who you were. Saw Frost instantly. Poor boy was gushing for days about you. You have no idea how hard it was to keep him away from you before knowing for certain Daniel was his missing half, especially when you saved him from the Rusalki. Anthony missed you so much. He just wanted to hold you."

Nathan turned red at Selena's honesty. Scott growled softly from behind. "Don't remind me. I could've killed the little creep when I saw you holding him!"

"What?"

Selena just laughed at his confusion. Many of his memories from when he had first met Eli and Selena were still muddy. It was before Frost allowed him to see through his eyes and know what was happening in both forms.

"Dance with me?" Selena offered, holding out her hands. She pulled him out of Scott's protective arms.

He couldn't help but smile. He loved to dance where Scott would rather sit and watch everyone else. The music was much slower than Selena's normal tastes, as if she had picked it out for him.

"So, what exactly is Eli a part of?"

"Oh! Ah..." He glanced at Scott. Selena had a big mouth and everyone would know by morning if he told her. Then the secret would finally be out in the open and that tight knot that was eating at his stomach would finally be gone. "Well, we're getting married," he blurted out.

Her face lit up as bright as a Christmas tree. "Really?"

"Really."

"Oh!" she cried, hugging him so tightly he could hardly breathe. She began bouncing up and down, clasping his hands and laughing hysterically. "Goddess! My little brother getting married! Oh, oh, we need to celebrate!"

"Another round, bar keep. She's paying," Scott called to the bartender, pointing to Selena.

"Hey!"

He grinned at her. "Steal my money, pay for my drinks."

Nathan just smiled as she rested her forehead against his. Arguing was no use. Their drinks came within a few minutes as they kept dancing. He gave himself into the music, letting it take over his body. It was soothing, even Frost relaxed under it. Nathan barely felt his other self. Frost was calm and happy, so much better than he had been the past few days. Alcohol usually didn't affect him as it did humans, but tonight he was very mellow.

At the end of the song, he returned to Scott and took a long drink of his new beer. Man, he was hot and thirsty. Over half the mug was finished before he knew it. Scott just stared at him in amusement.

"What?"

"Drink casually, Nat," he warned gently.

He was feeling giddy. Slowing down was probably a good idea. Laying his drink on the table, he rummaged through his pocket and pulled out a handful of change. "I'm hungry. You guys want anything?"

"Cheezies if they have them," Selena answered immediately.

"I'm fine," Scott said.

Nathan moved past the tables, ignoring the glares, and off-handed comments about his relationship. When it came to homophobes, not much changed no matter what country he was visiting.

"Hi," he said to the middle-aged bartender. The dirty blond-haired man looked him over before nodding. "Can I get a bag of Cheezies, four slices of pizza and a big bag of Doritos?"

The man hurried about gathering the food. Nathan leaned against the bar and waited. If Frost would only eat more. He was amazed the faery had eaten at all, but it still wasn't enough. He was starving.

"Bloody faggot!" a man snarled beside him.

He kept his gaze on the food the bartender was bringing him. Best to keep his mouth shut on the issue.

"Let me guess, you're his woman?"

Biting his cheek, Nathan kept himself from retorting. Bastard was drunk. Smelled worse than just beer. Something much stronger. Whisky or tequila. Whatever it was, it stunk.

"Then again you are rather petite. Pretty thing like you, he may have got confused. Or maybe you're both doing the girl?"

"Look, pal—" He grunted as he was shoved roughly against the bar.

The man was larger than him, heavyset and obviously aroused. Nathan groaned inwardly. Funny how much those who were most against gay people were usually the first to sexually assault another man. Disgusted, he rammed his elbow into the man's gut. Frost awoke instantly. He was enraged by anyone attempting to touch his human form, but Nathan could handle it himself. Scott had been training him to defend himself and he was more than willing to prove he could. He swept his foot under his attacker and sent him to the ground. An angry snarl passed through his lips as he followed the man down, a hand on the larger man's throat and finger digging into his windpipe. Nathan had never felt such anger before, but he was sick and tired of people treating him as if he was defenseless…as if they could do whatever they wanted to him.

"Touch me…or anyone like that again…and it will be the last time," he snarled, his voice not his own.

The man stared up at him with wide, frightened eyes, and gave a small nod.

"Stay down," Nathan warned.

He slowly released him, having to flex his finger several times to make them let go. He wanted to kill this man, and he had never wanted to kill anyone before. Carefully, he stood, prepared for the man or any of his friends to retaliate. No one made a move toward him. Instead, everyone stared at him in a mixture of surprise and horror. Nathan's eyes glowed violet. Silver streaks flashed through his hair. A ripple of magick raced through him. Frost was wide-awake, but it had nothing to do with the man at his feet, nor the sudden changes.

Frost! Alexis screamed in his mind.

He stumbled back, bumping into the bar. Grabbing his head, he tried to ease the sudden throbbing between his ears. Hands grabbed him, pulling him away from the crowd. He didn't need to look up to know it was Scott.

We can't find him! Frost, where are you?

"Not so loud, Alex," he called back, speaking both aloud and through his mind to the young sorceress. He sat at their table and was handed a cold glass of water. *Calm down. What's wrong? Who can't you find?*

The girl was half-sobbing. She was undoubtedly scared. It was so late. She must have had a nightmare. It was severe enough to bring Frost fully awake. Poor kid. Her nightmares were so vivid sometimes, much harsher than a normal teen's. Maybe a vision. Hers were far more vivid than Eli's these days.

A sudden premonition knotted his stomach. Who couldn't she find? Why was she so scared? Frost's memories from the early morning hours filled him with dread. What if that person had come back?

"Selena, check on Eli," he demanded.

Surprised, she did as he ordered. Her eyes closed; her mind opened to telepathically communicate with her charge. Her brows came together in confusion. Precious seconds ticked by. She began biting her lower lip. It was all Nathan needed to know that something was not right. After a few minutes, she opened her eyes. They were wide, fearful, and utterly confused.

"I can't find him...or Cleo. I can't feel them. They're just gone. Absolutely gone."

"What do you mean *gone*?" Scott asked, still holding Nathan's hand.

Nathan stared at her in fear. "No," he whispered as understanding dawned on him. "It's as if they don't exist."

Scott broke the speed limit the whole way back to the cabin.

Selena controlled the traffic lights while they were in the town's limits. Once on the country roads, Scott had them going at just under two hundred kilometers per hour. Nathan didn't care. It wasn't fast enough. Alexis, Miao and Sif were searching for Eli and Cleo. Even Henry was missing according to Alexis. That bothered him even more. Selena had to agree it was strange, but she still refused to believe Henry had anything to do with the other two's sudden disappearance.

It was all too convenient. They go out for one night and Eli goes missing? Literally off the face of the planet? Selena had scanned all of England and found nothing. She was terrified, but managed to keep her cool as they raced back home.

Luckily, there were no police this far in the brush and they did not have to stop until they were in front of the door. Scott shut off the engine and left the keys as they jumped out of the Porsche.

Frost took over in mid-stride and pushed the front door open.

Sif stood in the foyer. His gray eyes were weary as he looked up at them. "There's no sign of them or evidence of a kidnapping."

"None?" Selena inquired as she pushed past Frost. "Where do their auras disappear?"

"Driveway. Miao's double checking." He snorted in distaste. "He thinks Eli's playing another joke on us. Eli was distraught earlier. Maybe he's hiding himself so we won't bother him."

Frost's stomach knotted more. Did his news bother the child enough that he would hide from his friends? Cleo would most likely be with him for support, but that didn't explain Henry's disappearance. It was worth checking out. He found Alexis sitting on the sofa, holding her crystals in front of her. She was talking to the spirits within them. The Wind spirit's pale-yellow form floated from the patio doors and swirled around her for a moment, then returned to her celestial form. The woman's face fell. The news was bad. Kneeling before her, Frost took her hands in his. "Windy could not find them?"

She shook her head. "A water sprite said she saw a large car this evening, but it disappeared as quickly as it came. They don't recall seeing anyone."

"We should never have left you. I'm sorry, Alexis."

She wiped away her tears and gave a weak smile. "You didn't know."

"I..." He would have apologized more, but she wrapped her arms around his neck and buried her face in his hair. "It's alright, Alexis. We'll find them."

"Miao's still searching. Can you get him? It's going to rain."

He nodded mutely.

Stupid English weather! Too damn cold. Worse than frigging Canada, Miao thought grumpily as he shone his flashlight through the dense woods. *Leave it to Eli to play a prank at this time of night. It's sadistic! If Anthony was like this in his time, I pity his poor Guardians. He best have a good excuse. If it's another one of his games, I swear I'll kill him!*

A thousand acres of land was far larger at night than during the day. Thankfully, he had found some four-wheelers in the garage. It made his search a little easier, especially climbing up that hill. He parked it at the top of the hill after visiting the graveyard. He left the headlight on so he could find it after searching the woods. He only hoped the battery didn't die while he was gone.

So far, there was no sign of his cousin. He aimed the flashlight upward and illuminated the branches above him. If anything, that was where he would find his mischievous cousin. Nonetheless, there was no hint of him. Miao's frustration was growing by the minute. Where the hell could he be?

"*Eli! Cleo!*" he yelled, praying one of them would answer.

Silence was all that came to him.

A cool wet drop fell on his upturned face, followed by another, then another.

"Great! Just great! It's raining and I'm out here searching for your damn butt! I hope you appreciate this, Hawke!" he yelled as the drizzle grew heavy until it became a full downpour.

He was soaked within moments. Growling angrily, he turned back in the direction of his four-wheeler. Stupid, blasted English weather! Does it ever stop raining?

The ground was slippery under his feet, forcing him to concentrate hard on his footing. Somewhere along the way, he became lost. Frowning, he backtracked, but everything now looked the same in the dense rain.

He was about to lose his temper.

It was too dark to see anything except the pool of light from his flashlight. He stepped a little too close to a steep edge. Before he could correct his footing, the ground gave way under him. His ankle twisted painfully, and he let out a cry as he trembled down the hill to the river below. A crack echoed in his ears and a thundering headache filled his head. His flashlight landed in the mud next to his half-submerged form. The water rushed over his body as he lost consciousness.

Despite her objections, Frost finally convinced Selena to stay and protect Alexis while he, Sif and Scott searched for Miao. They had a good idea where he was, they could see the light the four-wheeler cast from the bottom of the hill.

Scott rode the other one up while Frost and Sif flew.

He really had not expected to find Miao with the vehicle, but was a little disappointed. The forest could be very dangerous at night. Both he and Sif folded their wings within themselves as the rain grew heavy. The added weight now gone it was easier for them to maneuver.

They waited for Scott to pull up beside the abandoned four-wheeler. He climbed off and whistled at the sheer size and darkness of the woods they were about to enter. Frost glowed softly. The darkness of the moon was affecting his powers. He could not cast his glow as bright as he would any other night. Scott found another flashlight, which saved Frost from straining his magick.

Sif sniffed the ground, instantly picking up Miao's scent.

"This way," he growled, leading the way.

Miao had to have searched the entire woods. His trail went all over. He rarely got lost.

Scott was grinning like a maniac. Miao was in for some serious taunting when they found him. Scott had a major sister complex and picking on her boyfriend was not just a job, it was a hobby. After twenty minutes, Scott's grin became a worried frown, something very rare when it came to Miao.

"The rain's getting worse, Sif, hurry it up," he urged.

In fact, if it weren't for the shield surrounding them, they would have been soaked. Miao did not have such power. He was most likely drenched. It wasn't really cold, but considering the climate Miao came from, his body may not be able to handle England's weather. Being out so long was not good for him.

Nor Eli, but at least he could shield himself.

If they didn't find Miao soon, Frost would not be surprised if the young man came down sick.

The sound of rushing water caught Frost's attention. The river was not far.

Many years ago, Anthony and Henry used to go fishing there. The salmon ran at this time of year. It was one of Anthony's favourite past-times where he never used magick and just joked around like one of the guys. The slopes around the river were high and dangerous on rainy nights. How many times had Anthony warned him not to play there?

Considering how dark it was, Miao could have easily slid down the slope. With so much rain, it was common for the river to flood. Narrowing his eyes, he stared off toward the river with inhuman sight. A sliver of light pierced the black sky.

"Please no," he breathed, suddenly terrified. "The river! He's at the river."

Sif's head shot up, his muzzle muddy from sniffing the ground.

"River?" He blinked. "No way!"

Scott's faced paled at the seriousness of their voices, but Frost was now too worried to answer his unasked questions.

He began running, knowing both the rain and thick woods would only hinder his wings should he take flight. He ignored the branches and fallen logs that threatened to trip him and rip his clothes. His long hair managed to stay untangled, phasing in and out of reality.

Reaching the river's edge, he looked down.

It was utter blackness except for the pale glow of the fallen flashlight. His keen eyes saw past that to the limp figure unconscious in the water. The water was washing against Miao's chest and getting rougher by the moment.

Not waiting for the others, Frost descended the muddy hill as quickly as he could.

"Miao! Miao, wake up!" he cried, running to the young man.

He fell to his knees next to him. Mud and dirt had fallen on Miao, weighing him down. Frost cleaned him as best he could, but the rushing water made matters worse. It pulled at his legs, threatening to drag him down river. Extending his shields, he kept the rain and sliding mud away from the young man and jumped into the water. Using his dagger, he tried to cut the weeds tangling Miao's legs. The blade was ripped from his hands as a stray branch floated past.

"Frost, is he alright?" Scott bellowed as he stumbled down the slope.

Noting Miao's condition, he jumped into the water and shooed Frost back to the banks. He pulled out his hunting knife and dived under the water.

Frost sat in the water, holding Miao's limp form as his beloved worked. Sif helped, tearing the weeds and veins with his teeth. He protected Scott from the traffic of debris. Scott took a deep breath of air when he surfaced.

"They're digging into his legs," he reported. "It's going to take a while. Keep his head up. The water's rising too fast."

He glanced at the youth's face for a moment, then frowning, took Frost completely by surprise by undoing the young man's pants and sliding them off his hips.

"It'll be easier to free his legs without them," he explained before diving back under the water.

It seemed forever before Miao's body was loose enough for Frost to pull him out of the water. His legs were an awful mess with lashes and cuts from the debris that had tangled around them. A nasty bruise marked his forehead just above his left eye, but his heartbeat was strong. Nothing seemed broken.

Scott took off his coat and wrapped it around the youth. "Miao, come on, wake up."

He made no sound, nor moved.

Sighing, Scott hefted the eighteen-year-old onto Sif's back. "He'll be fine. A concussion by the looks of things. We better get him inside and into some warm clothes."

The walk back to the cabin consisted of slipping and sliding. Scott had to keep a hand on Miao's back to keep him from falling. They could not find the four-wheelers.

Sheets of rain made it impossible to see.

It was Alexis and Selena's auras that lead them to the safety of Henry's cabin.

The warmth of the house was a welcomed sense of home, far more than the day Frost had first returned to the cabin. Selena placed a sheet towel over the sofa and had Scott lay Miao on it. He was stripped, dried, and then changed into a warm jogging suit and heavy wool socks. Alexis went to him, holding him and sobbing over the ugliness of the injuries. Scott reassured her he would be alright, but she refused to leave his side. She fell asleep a few hours later, holding his hand. For once Scott wasn't disgusted by the display of affection. He settled into the big armchair and watched over the two.

In a fresh, warm pair of Nathan's jeans and sweater, Frost sat on the floor next to Scott. His head rested in his love's lap as they both watched over the two teens. He was tired. His head ached and all he wanted was to climb into bed and hold Scott, but he was not willing to let either of the two remaining teens disappear. Having Scott gently massaging his scalp eased some of the pain and coldness that was squeezing his heart.

"Selena says Henry and Eli never came back. There's no sign of them or Cleo. She can't even sense them." He closed his eyes. "Neither can I, but for her it's like being half-deaf. They form a power of three, a power base stronger than most others. Without Cleo and Eli, her power weakens. She draws power from Eli. Should anything happen…"

"She may die," Scott finished.

Frost opened his eyes to look at his young Mistress and her boyfriend. They slept so peacefully. Miao's wounds would be easy to heal in the morning when they all felt stronger. Thankfully, he was not seriously hurt when he fell. With Eli and Cleo missing, it would have shattered Alexis's heart if she had lost Miao as well.

She truly loved him.

She loved all of them, and he wasn't about to let anything happen to them. Eli and Cleo were out there somewhere. He silently promised Selena he would find their missing loved ones.

No matter the cost.

Chapter Ten

What had been mere hours in the real world had been almost a full day in and around the old Gaelic castle. Evening was beginning to set. Vast shades of purple and pink fluttered through the open windows, casting a magnificent glow upon all the metallic objects in the large bedroom. Long silk sapphire curtains adorned each window. Matching ones hung from the king-size canopy. Even the colour of the bedspread was sapphire.

The chamber was a unique mix of torture and sleep. Heavy chains hung from the top edges of the canopy at the foot of the bed. There was a matching pair at the bottom as well as a smaller set connected to the headboard, restraining their captive.

In contrast, the room was fully furnished. A wide screen television, DVD player and stereo, CDs, books, and numerous other items that would interest a teenager filled the room, taking away from the gloominess of the chains. Even a bar fridge was provided, loaded with food and drinks. All for their young guest. He was certainly being spoiled, Henry thought in distaste, but knowing Eli, he would not care nor appreciate the trouble they had gone through for him.

The change from real time to what they had gone through had yet to affect Eli or Cleo. They both slept peacefully. Cleo was on the dresser in a small cage far enough from his master that he could not interfere, while Eli slept in the large comfy bed.

Eli was adorable when in deep sleep. One hand curled around his face, the other clenching his pillow. Large cuffs imprisoned each wrist, the chain connecting to the headboard. He still wore his robes. The collar of his cape had been undone in case he twisted or turned, but Duncan had not wanted to remove it yet. He wanted Eli to look like

Anthony, as usual. It draped over Eli like a warm sheet. Although he looked comfortable, Henry was beginning to worry. The time-change was taking its toll on the youth and Henry wanted desperately to see his grandson's eyes open.

Incense filled the air. Duncan moved about the room, placing and lighting hundreds of candles, which cast the room in a warm glow. He was completely dedicated to the spell he was about to perform. Here they had far more time to train and control Eli with no fear of interference. Nevertheless, the warlock was still nervous. Dealing with Eli in person rather than through the astral realm meant he had to reveal whom he truly was, which meant gaining the mage's trust would be next to impossible.

Duncan had good reason to fear him and he was now taking the preparations he should have months ago. He was more cautious now, watching Eli as much as possible, learning everything he could before striking. He did not want to frighten Eli as he had done before. In doing so, he was recreating the mistakes he had made with Anthony and all Henry could do was laugh.

Duncan was falling in love with Eli, and in this form, it was like repeating history. They were both young again.

Blowing out the long wooden match, Duncan sat on the other side of the bed. He reached out to touch Eli's forehead, but pulled back. He stared at his shaking hand nervously, obviously still a little afraid of Eli's power. He bit his lip. His eyes became determined as he reached over and placed his palm over the younger man's head. It glowed brightly for a moment before he pulled back. They watched Eli intently for several minutes.

Eli's brows bunched together. A soft groan escaped his lips as he blinked his eyes open. Facing Henry, he did not see Duncan. Not noticing the heavy bonds at first, he simply stared tiredly at his grandfather as if waking from a bad dream.

"Grandpa?" he asked in a parched voice. He closed those brilliant sapphire orbs for a moment. When they opened, they were intense, taking in his surroundings and remembering their struggle. He stared coldly at his bonds before looking back up at him. "Why?"

The hurt look in his eyes broke Henry's heart, but he could not give in to Eli. "It was needed."

"What have you done, Henry?" Anthony's deep voice, mixed with Eli's, demanded.

Henry blinked. It had been so long since Anthony took-over Eli in such a way. Had it not been for the spirit's sudden appearance, he would have slapped Eli for such disrespect. However, Eli had little, if any, control over his past self. The anger and fear were expected, especially after awaking in such a strange room chained to a bed. The youth managed to get himself into a sitting position where he could look Henry square in the face. He noticed Duncan at that point as well.

He turned and stared at him in confusion. "Michael Sinclair? What are you doing here?" He turned back to Henry in sudden rage. "The Sinclairs kidnapped me?"

Duncan relaxed instantly now that his secret was still safe. It made his job slightly easier. To Henry's surprise, he leaned very close to Eli, a little more than polite nicety required. "In a way."

Eli stared at him in utter confusion. Duncan's closeness alarmed him. He moved back as far as the chains would allow and stared up at Henry. "Why did you do this?"

"We're here to help you, Eli. Just relax. No one will hurt you," he insisted. Tentatively, he placed a hand on his shoulder. "Michael is here to help prepare you for the eclipse. He will make sure the power Chaos gave you is under control."

"Is that true?"

Duncan nodded, moving closer. "And I will teach you how to create other worlds as Raven once did."

"No."

It was hard to tell if it was Anthony or Eli speaking. Eli shook his head. "Raven doesn't want me tampering with such things. Too many people can be hurt by such power. Too many have already."

Henry was ready to blow up. He couldn't understand how Duncan could be so calm and patient.

Duncan only smiled kindly at Eli. "Don't you want to explore other realms? See what no one else can see?"

Eli fell silent. Piquing his curiosity had always been the way to win him over. It was purely Eli who answered. "Yes, but…"

"Anthony's dead, Eli. The decision is yours and yours alone. I can help you. I can pull the magick you need to the surface. Together we can open any portal. Do and go wherever we wish. Let me show you what true power is."

"I…"

Henry sat closer. Yes, this was easier than he thought possible.

Without his Guardians and friends, he was much easier to persuade.

No Nathaniel to interfere.

"No. I promised I wouldn't."

Rage erupted inside Henry. He grabbed the collar of Eli's jacket and shook him. "I told you I wanted you to open one portal, just one! And by God, boy, you will do as I say or forfeit that power!"

"Fine! Take it! I never wanted to be the most powerful magician! Why do you think I gave half of it to Daniel Dion? Do you think I like being hunted down by every rival magick user? Do you think I like visions that wake me up screaming at night or put me in a trance during the day? Do you really think I want more power just so they can get worse? I gave up half my power so they would go away. I didn't want Chaos to increase my power. I don't want to open portals or create new worlds. I just want to be left alone. You, out of everyone, should know that."

Tears of rage dotted the corners of Eli's eyes. His words were true, Henry knew that, but he could not comprehend why anyone with such gifts would refuse to use them. He rarely used his magick in everyday practice either. It was only when he was too tired to do something himself or in training sessions like a few nights ago. It was only used when needed or to give thanks to his deities. He was so unlike Anthony in that way, but then Anthony had come from a family of magicians where Eli had only discovered his gifts at the age of six. The young man had been through much more horror than his past self had been due to it.

He let go of the young man with a soft growl and sat back. Grabbing the bottle of wine on the nightstand he poured himself a glass and drank in, trying to cool-down the anger bubbling within him. He poured another glass and handed it to his grandson. "Drink this."

Eli held it in his weighed down hands. "But…"

"Humor me."

He hesitated a moment, watching both Duncan and Henry as he brought the glass to his lips. He made a face as he drank it. The wine was bitter with a bitter aftertaste that most likely burned his throat.

Once the glass was empty, Eli began coughing. "It's horrible," he murmured. He went to hand it back to Henry only to have it refilled. "No. I already feel sick."

"It'll help you relax," Duncan said, taking the glass. He took a mouth full and smiled coyly.

"I don't want to relax. Where's Selena? Where am I?" He was startled when Duncan cupped his cheeks.

"What—" Eli yanked his head free. He struggled, using his legs to push Duncan away from him. "Get away from me!" he ordered.

"This needs to be done, Eli. Let Michael do his job," Henry advised.

"No! Get off! Stop!"

Henry watched as several small objects began shaking on the table. They trembled fiercely as Duncan got Eli's legs pinned.

"Henry, please!" Eli pleaded. "Help me!"

Standing, he patted Duncan's shoulder. "Be gentle. This isn't like the astral realm."

Duncan nodded as he summoned his magick. Henry watched from the door for a moment before he exited the room. He shut the door tightly and leaned against it. His heart raced as he listened to his grandson call for his help, his heart sinking with each cry. He prayed he was doing the right thing for Eli. His stomach churned in worry.

"Stop! Grandpa! Grandpa! No!"

He squeezed his eyes shut as something large crashed against the door. There was another muffled cry, then silence. Chuckling to himself, he strolled down the corridor. Now it was just a matter of time.

Selena gasped as a blow hit her stomach. She clenched it and fell to her bed. *Eli, where are you? What's happening?* She called through their bond, but nothing came back. The pain turned to a blinding form of pleasure before fading into the depths of her mind. It all happened so fast, only a few short seconds. It could not be what it felt like.

She rolled over and clung to her old stuffed teddy. What was that? Paper crumbled under her. Surprised, she pulled it out from under her. A small letter in Henry's messy scroll, far worse than Anthony's chicken scratch, filled the sheet. Flipping on her lamp, she read it over.

My Dearest Selena,

Eli and I have gone to visit an old friend. I hope to have his powers under control by the eclipse. Sorry I failed to discuss this with you first, but time is of the essence. I will call you in the morning and give you details.

Love, Henry

She sighed in relief. Eli was with Henry. Safe and sound. Cleo probably went to help protect him. That odd sensation was most likely from one of Eli's dreams. Everything was alright. She burst into laughter as she clenched the note to her chest. She had to tell Frost and Sif. Bouncing off the bed, she raced downstairs.

The kitchen had a dark sense to it. Something awful had happened there. Frost could feel the remains of magick course down his spine. It was cold. Frighteningly so. Closing his eyes, he opened himself to the flow of magick. He slipped back several hours.

Eli stood up from the kitchen table, leaving Henry to check out the cellar. Henry stood up as well, following the youth. Eli paused a few steps down. He seemed overwhelmed by an odd force. A white clothed flashed out of Henry's pocket. He grabbed the young man from behind, wrapping his large arms around his much smaller frame. The cloth pressed against Eli's mouth and nose. The young man struggled fiercely until he could no more. He passed out.

That was all Frost needed to see. Henry had kidnapped Eli. He didn't know why. He didn't care either. All the fears he had hoped he was overreacting to were coming true. All those looks Henry had given Eli flashed before him. His own torments returned to the surface. By all that was good, don't let him hurt that boy, he prayed, closing his eyes.

He left the kitchen, no longer able to handle the darkness it held. Sitting back beside Scott's sleeping form, he frowned. Why? Why would Henry take Eli? If he had helped raise Eli all these years, why take him like that? Why had he invited all Eli's friends to visit? If Eli had come alone, it would have been so much easier. There had to have been a reason. It didn't make sense.

Selena was going to be heartbroken. She trusted Henry with their lives and loved him dearly. She would find a reason for Henry taking Eli. Somehow, she would justify it.

Resting his head against Scott's lap, he tried to rest. Miao's wounds healed quicker than they had expected. A simple spell. Even without the power of the full moon on his side, he could heal the flesh. When Miao awoke, there would be no evidence of the fall. At least flesh was easy to heal. The mind was different.

"Frost?"

He looked up to see Selena bounce down the stairs.

"Henry has them!" she cried happily. "They're off visiting a Wicca friend."

"I know." He forced himself back to his feet and led her to another room.

"You know? Well, that's good. They're safe."

"They're anything but safe," he corrected, frowning. "Eli didn't go willingly."

"What? Frost—"

"Henry kidnapped him." Rage filled her eyes.

Her hand came across his cheek so hard Frost felt as if his head was going to be knocked off. He held his cheek as she stormed away.

"Henry would never do that!"

Sighing, he flopped onto one of the study's chairs. Finding Eli was not going to be easy if Selena was on Henry's side. They needed her to find them.

The plane over Germany could not move fast enough. Daniel sat ramrod straight in his seat. His eyes closed as he tried to make sense of the emotions that played through his mind. They were not his own. He could not recall ever feeling such a bizarre mix of fear, pain, and pleasure. It ate at his soul so perversely that it was hard to believe it was not actually happening to him. It certainly felt like it. Instinct told him the emotions were someone else's, someone he was extremely close to, but he could not comprehend who could possibly be in such pain and so much fear. It took all his willpower to keep his power from responding to the psychic onslaught.

Deep down, he knew. The half of him that was Raven could feel everything that happened to the youth. His heart cried out to the youth, prayed for him to be strong. He had no idea how to help him. It tore him up. A small trail of tears lined his cheeks.

"Oh, Eli. Fight them. You're stronger than you think," he whispered. It lasted no more than ten minutes. The pain and satanic pleasure faded away, leaving only a cold fear. He sighed, letting himself recline in his seat. He felt so worn, so weak. Whoever you are, keep your hands off my children, he mentally swore. Somehow, he knew Alexis and the others were not with Eli…rather, they were safe. That gave him hope.

He stared at the old leather book on his lap. It was beginning. Whoever had Eli now had the Key. The artifact panther head began to glow brighter.

Henry handed a very exhausted Duncan a clean towel when he finally emerged from Eli's chamber.

The young man leaned against the closed door. He sighed and wiped his face. "He's stubborn. So bloody stubborn."

"Takes after Anthony."

"Bugger!" He hit the wall with a growl. "Too much like fucking Raven!"

He leaned his forehead against the wall and sighed.

Henry frowned. "Weren't you able to—"

"Yeah, yeah, but I had to force him…all the way. I had hoped to seduce him, have him return the affection. I had…"

Tears rolled down his tanned cheeks.

Henry hadn't seen him cry in decades. Not since Anthony's death. He really did not want to hurt Eli.

Duncan let out a small laugh and combed his hand through his mussed hair. "Gods, I need a shower." He glanced back at the door. "Don't yell at him. This'll take time…and he's scared right now."

"We don't have time."

Sighing, he headed toward his own chambers. "He's terrified, Henry. Let him be."

Henry was not willing to take advice from someone like Duncan Porter.

Chapter Eleven

A dream gripped Eli.

Duncan Porter sat in his wheelchair at the top of his condominium in London. Michael Sinclair stood next to him, eyeing the street far below. His face was a mixture of awe and remorse as he watched the people and cars passing by.

Porter watched him carefully. He, too, seemed very remorseful, as if his plans had gone awry. "Are you certain you wish to do this? I may not be able to reverse the process after it has begun."

Michael smiled smoothly. "Of course, Mr. Porter. I understand there's no turning back."

Porter licked his lower lip and gestured for Michael to kneel before him. The youth did so without question. Porter placed his fingers along his temples and began chanting softly.

Eli couldn't make out the words, but was able to see the sudden changes in their auras. The holes that were in Michael's were filling in while Porter's was beginning to deteriorate.

After a few moments, Michael pulled back, his hands gently covering Porter's. "How do you feel?" he asked.

Porter was looking around as if caught in a trance. He blinked and looked at Michael. The elderly man smiled. "Different. It's not so noisy."

"Are you sure this is what you want?"

"Yes. Thank you."

Michael stood and smiled. His whole aura was different, as if he was no longer the same person. "Good. We have a second chance of finding the Key."

Porter only nodded and began eyeing the street below. "You'll find him. You have the power to help him."

Michael was no longer looking at him, but at the starry night sky and the waxing moon. "I hope. Chaos's power is far stronger than I thought and he has learned to tap into it."

Porter wheeled his chair closer to the edge. "You can do it. I've already seen the future."

Michael glanced over his shoulder in confusion. His eyes widened as Porter suddenly pushed his chair over the edge.

"No!"

It was too late for even magick to come to his aid. Michael fell to his knees at the edge and watched in horror as Duncan Porter slammed into the concrete below.

However, it wasn't Porter's death that pulled at Eli. He had heard about the warlock's suicide months earlier. It was Michael's aura that drew him as he followed the older boy running down the stairs until he was outside cradling the warlock's broken body. It was no longer Michael Sinclair's it was—

"Eli?"

He turned his face away from the bright sunlight. An alluring soft purr made him smile. The urge to bury his face in his Familiar's soft fur pulled at him. He couldn't wake up yet, he had to figure out why Michael's aura was so odd. It was right there at the tip of his tongue, but he couldn't bring it to reality. What did Duncan do before killing himself?

"Master Eli, wake up," Cleo's familiar deep voice called more urgently.

Small paws tried shaking him. His arms were extremely heavy as he tried to roll over. He practically could not move them. That seemed odd, but he was willing to let it go for a few more hours of sleep.

"Eli!"

He moaned and hid his face under the blanket.

"Elijah Hawke, get up now or so help me—"

"Alright, alright. I'm getting up," he murmured, forcing his eyes open. Cleo burrowed under the covers and was in his direct line of view. His bright teal eyes shone with a fear he had never seen in him before.

Fear gripped him as he read his lifelong friend. The night before had not been part of the dream. Michael, Henry, everything. They were real. The weight he felt were the large heavy cuff and chains imprisoning him to the bed. His heart sank at this knowledge. If Cleo was with him, what of the others? He tried sensing for Alexis and Miao, but found nothing. That meant very little. A spell could be used to shield them from him.

Seeing his fear, Cleo rubbed his head affectionately under his chin. "Are you alright?"

He wrapped his heavy arms around the small animal and drew him close. "I...Cleo. He...I...oh, Gods, I wish I knew." Swallowing the sob that threatened to overpower him, he petted the cat's head.

"You? Are you okay?"

"He cast a binding spell on me. I can't transform."

The chains were long enough to let him sit up comfortably. They were thick and extremely heavy. A spell to increase his power would be the only way to break them, but that would not keep Michael and Henry out. Looking around, he lifted the heaviest pieces of furniture with his mind and piled them against both the bedroom and bathroom doors. That would not keep them out for long, but at least it would slow them down. Hopefully enough for him and Cleo to escape.

That small use of magick almost drained him. He couldn't understand why. Telekinesis was one of his most natural gifts. It never tired him, but for some reason took more concentration than normal. He had to take a moment to gather his strength once more. He tried covering an unexpected yawn. "Why am I tiring so easy?" he asked Cleo. "It's like he just took my power. I feel so weak."

"I don't know," Cleo confessed.

He rubbed against him, offering what strength he could.

Taking a deep breath, Eli cast a power spell. His strength increased, but not to the degree he had wanted. The chain barely budged when he pulled. Frustrated, he yanked harder, throwing his entire weight into it. The metal bit into the butt of his hands. He winced in pain, but continued pulling.

"They've been charmed," Cleo muttered, stating the obvious. His ears perked and he gazed at the barricaded bedroom door. "Damn!"

"What?" Eli grunted, pulling even harder. He braced a pain-filled foot against the headboard, and pulled even harder. Then he felt it. The aura he had felt the last few nights. It was a unique mix of Sinclair magick and something else. He could not help but stare at the door in fear. He could not remember ever feeling so much fear in his life. His body trembled against his will as he revealed this to his familiar. "Cleo?" he whispered ever so softly. "I'm really scared." Cleo nodded. "I am, too."

The door handle jiggled, causing them both to jump despite themselves.

"Eli?" Michael called through the door. "Eli, are you alright? What's going on?"

He sounded so concerned. Eli bit his lip. They had to get out of there, but he wasn't sure exactly where they were. Michael pounded on the door, calling his name, begging him to answer. He ignored Michael as best he could and returned to his chains. They were still as strong as before.

"Summon all your power," Cleo advised.

"I'm trying."

He winced. The cuffs were digging into his flesh, breaking his skin. His burned feet screamed in agony. Please, just one link, break, he begged. He hands stung as he threw his weight back.

The room exploded around him. Had Cleo not cried out, Eli would never have been able to throw up his shield in time. Chunks of oak scattered across the room. Only the door had exploded, leaving the rest of the furniture in perfect shape. They quickly moved back in place as Michael stepped inside. Eli paid him no mind. He continued pulling. He almost cried out for joy as one link began to bend. The pain no longer mattered as long as that link opened enough to free him.

"Eli!" Cleo cried out.

The bed dipped and a hand fell on his shoulder, another wrapping around one wrist. The power drained from him. He could no longer find the strength to continue pulling. His arms felt heavier than before. They fell to his lap.

"Easy, Eli," Michael's gentle voice whispered across his ear. He shimmed closer, pulling Eli into his arms.

Eli was too tired to resist.

"Come on, it's alright."

All the fight left him as Michael's strange aura wrapped around him. He was sure he had felt it before. There was something so familiar about it. He felt lightheaded as he thought about it. Reluctantly, he rested against his captor.

The weight around his wrists disappeared with a click and he found himself more securely in Michael's arms. With effort, he tried pulling away. "Let me go," he pleaded weakly, too drained to put up a fight once more. The light-headedness increased until he could barely look at the other man. "Don't…"

"Let him go!" Cleo hissed, glaring at Michael with rage. "He's just a kid!"

Michael sighed, inspecting Eli's torn wrists, and wrapped up feet. "Eli, why couldn't you wait until I came back? I would have unlocked them." He cradled Eli's half-conscious form against his chest. He picked up the leather watch that had been torn from Eli's left wrist, Raven's magick circle engraved on the face of it.

Eli snatched the gift Nathan and Scott had given him for his eighteenth birthday and held it possessively, rage freeing him from Michael's spell. "Don't touch that. Let me go." He tried pulling free once more only to have Michael tighten his grip. A dizzying wave of magick swept through him. His eyes felt heavy as he stared up at those eerie blue eyes. "What have you done to me? I can barely…keep my eyes open." Soft fingers caressed his cheek as Michael lowered him back on the bed. His head rested on the large, fluffy pillows.

"I'll get the med kit. You messed up your arms pretty bad."

Almost as soon as Michael moved away from him, the heaviness lifted and Eli could move and think again. He took a moment to gather his strength before sitting up. He clung to his favourite watch. Frost had gone out of his way to design it. It cost him and Scott a few hundred to have it specially made.

Michael was back in an instant, but the cloud of heaviness did not return with him. Instead, Eli could look at him and think clearly. The only blurriness came from his missing glasses, which he found on the nightstand.

Cleo sat alertly next to him as Michael sat on the edge of the bed.

"Easy there. You don't want to move too fast. No need for another dizzy spell." He handed Eli a glass of cold water before fishing through a small case.

Hesitantly he took a drink, watching the other young man carefully. Setting down the glass, he glared at his captor. "What did you do to me?" he demanded.

"Nothing."

"I couldn't move the moment you touched me. I nearly passed out."

He shrugged. "I tried calming you. It must have drained you after the use of your own spell."

"Calming me?" he asked in disbelief.

"I'm telepathic," Michael explained. He took out the antiseptic and dabbed it on the folded skin of Eli's right wrist.

Eli hissed as it stung. He hadn't noticed just how bad he had hurt himself. The skin on the butt of his hands had torn pretty badly from yanking on the chains and had bunched up. They weren't bleeding badly, but the skin was raw.

Michael furrowed his brows at Cleo. "Eli, don't you ever tell that cat of yours to shut up and leave you alone?"

"No."

He couldn't help but smile and pet his hissing feline. His warmth and closeness comforted him.

Michael sighed as he took the tweezers and pulled the skin back into place.

Eli yelped in pain. "Sorry."

Eli watched in fascination as Michael raised his wrist to his lips and kissed the wound. He inhaled sharply as a warm current flowed up his arm. The skin began knitting itself back together faster than Eli's healing power could have ever done. Michael lifted his head as he panted. It was perhaps the most intimate thing Eli had ever felt. There were butterflies in his stomach as Michael moved to the other wrist. This time his tongue delved into the wound. Eli hissed. It stung, but the warm current pushed the pain away, and again the skin knitted itself back together.

The warmth was more sensual, like a full body caress from the inside. He closed his eyes as Michael kept kissing his wrist and hand. The magick traveled through his body, making his feet and toes tingle. Somehow, this was familiar. He knew without a doubt, he had felt such power before.

He turned slightly, a strange need for more filling him. "I know you," he whispered to himself. "I know I know you."

He leaned forward slightly, unconsciously knowing where it all was leading.

"Ow! Son of a—Cleo!" Michael bellowed. He dropped Eli's arm and grasped his thigh as Cleo retracted his claws.

Panting, Eli leaned forward and held his chest. The sensual current stopped as fast as it had begun. He couldn't believe what he had been about to do. "How did you do that?" he breathed, trying to understand why he was so aroused.

"I'm a healer." Still gripping his injured thigh, he glared at the small cat. "That's what I do, heal people."

"You mean seduce people," Cleo countered. "I suppose last night didn't go as planned."

The blow meant for Cleo landed harshly against Eli's hip as he scooped up his friend and jumped off the bed. He stumbled, his feet far too tender to hold his weight. He grimaced in pain, but forced himself to stand.

He stepped back as the older man stood. "What do you want, Michael? I won't be your slave. I don't care what the Sinclairs want, I'm not interested. I won't let you or anyone touch me again."

Holding Cleo tighter, he dared a glance at the open door. They had to escape.

Michael tackled him as he made a break for it, dragging him to the hard marble floor mere feet from his escape. Michael knocked Cleo out of his arms and used his powers to cage the small creature. He pinned Eli to the ground, holding his wrists in one hand above his black head of hair. Eli fought and struggled under him.

"Eli, stop it! No one is going to hurt you," he assured, grabbing his chin. He forced eye contact. "I would never hurt you."

"Liar!"

His face cracked in remorse.

"I'm not as naïve as Cleo and Henry think I am."

He was prepared for the young warlock to hurt him, perhaps even cast a spell to subdue him as he had before. He looked away, refusing to show the fear that raced through his body. He was unprepared for Michael to let him go, nor was he prepared to be pulled into a tight embrace a moment later. Michael buried his face in his hair and sighed in resignation.

"I'm sorry, Raven. I'm so sorry," he whispered.

The nickname triggered the memory Eli had so desperately tried to remember. The person who had nicknamed him Raven and it was a name that had lasted two lifetimes. He stared up at Michael and focused on his aura, ignoring the magick that tickled his body. Unlike in his dream, Michael's aura was full and pulsing with energy. It did not feel the same as it had when he had first seen the young man in his dream. It was different, like after the spell Duncan Porter had performed. Then it hit him.

"You're not Michael Sinclair," he whispered. "You're Duncan Porter!"

Chapter Twelve

Duncan Porter had switched bodies! It wasn't possible. That type of magick was forbidden. Eli's struggles renewed as the warlock held him tightly.

"Eli, no. It's okay. Just relax."

Eli was anything but relaxed. He struggled more only to have the magick flowing through him increased. It overwhelmed him quickly and he found himself holding onto his old rival as the sensation of being caressed from the inside out returned. It was as if he was being fed the healing magick.

"Just relax. You can't walk with your feet as they are."

It was hard not to fight. His body felt ablaze, but in an oddly good way. He was aroused and it scared him. Duncan's lean body holding him down didn't help matters.

"Slowly, Eli, slowly."

It was the most erotic thing Eli had ever felt. No intercourse or fondling. Nothing physical other than being held. The magick was tantalizing. He clung to Duncan as it washed over him in waves.

Then it was gone in a flash. With no memory of how, he found himself on his feet. Michael-Duncan was bracing him. He had to cling to the taller boy to keep from falling. His feet no longer hurt, but his body still tingled from the flow of magick. He never felt such a buzz.

"By the Gods," he breathed as Duncan led him toward a large walk-in closet. "How are you be alive?"

Duncan's eyes were remorseful as he gazed at him. "It wasn't supposed to happen this way. Michael was more emotionally disturbed than I thought. This was supposed to be temporary."

Eli shook his head, pushing back the fuzziness the magick had caused. "Temporary? You switched bodies." His eyes widened as the dream played itself over again. "Michael Sinclair died in your body. It wasn't you."

"Eli, let me explain," Duncan tried. "In March, I only wanted to get to you before Chaos's power took control of you. I...I never wanted to hurt you, but I...I..."

Eli looked away. He did not need to hear Porter's lies again. He didn't want to hear the false promises of love and devotion that had almost trapped him in March.

"I'm sorry, Eli. For everything."

He opened the closet door, revealing a vast walk-in closet with an incredible selection of clothing.

His jaw dropped. Porter had spent a fortune on clothing in the exact style he liked, all in his size. He didn't know what to say and could only stand there as Duncan began searching through them.

"Henry told me your size. I knew he wouldn't have time to pack anything without raising suspicion." He cried in triumph when he found an outfit he liked. He eyed it, then Eli. His eyes brightened and he took it off the hanger. "Perfect."

Common sense returned to Eli and he huffed in irritation. "Look, Por—Duncan, I'm flattered, but—" Duncan pulled him toward the bathroom.

"—I'm not interested in—"

"Strip."

"What?" His mouth fell open at the sudden command. Was he serious? "I don't think so."

Whether or not he listened, Eli did not know. He was busying himself with the clothes, making sure there were no tags or stickers. Eli folded his arms stubbornly across his chest when the older man looked up. "I'm not doing it."

Duncan laughed in delight. "Strip, take a shower and get changed. I'll wait for you in your room." Seeing the doubt in Eli's eyes, he smiled reassuringly. "I won't touch you unless you say so."

Eli was completely flabbergasted when the door shut and he was left alone. The door had no lock. Duncan could easily just walk in, and Cleo was alone with him without his powers. The cat only had his claws and teeth to defend him. Eli was afraid to provoke Duncan by using his magick to lock the door. Duncan may take it out on the feline.

Reluctantly, he removed his clothes and marveled at the fact he had completely healed. Chaos had healed the scars created by Dominique and her pack of werewolves months ago. The new ones had healed almost as nicely. His feet didn't hurt at all. Why did Porter heal him? To gain his trust?

New thoughts boggled his mind as he turned on the elegant Gothic style shower. A huge whirlpool stood off to the side invitingly. How could this have happened? Why did Henry betray him and hand him over to Duncan Porter of all people? Was he under a spell? Henry had been so abusive the night before, so unlike his usual smiling self. He had been acting oddly all week. The fights with Frost. The odd demands to open a portal. The fire last night after abandoning him to Porter. Why else would he do such things? Porter had to be controlling him.

The warm water was refreshing, far more than he thought possible. He let it cleanse his weary body. His unbound hair cascaded around his shoulders. Resting his head against the tiled wall, he gave into the urge to sob once more.

Why could no one leave him alone?

Eli held Cleo close as he sat in an elegant old dining room. According to Porter, it was one of the few rooms to not be upgraded. Nothing modern resided here. The castle was hundreds of years old, standing long before Anthony's time, even that of Merlin, the great magician of times long past. It was enchanting with the old suits of armor standing guard along the walls. Oil lanterns, marble pillars and large bushy ferns decorated the great hall. The windows were large with a magnificent view of the Irish sea. Had the situation been different, he would have seated himself before one of those large arched windows and spent the day watching the surf. Perhaps even paint a picture. The scene was breathtaking.

The maid who had attended to him earlier that morning, Claudia, was serving them breakfast. Duncan had insisted Eli could have anything he wished. Chefs from all around the world served him, many of which lived within the castle walls or state houses upon the huge estate. He was more confused than hungry. Duncan had Claudia bring him poached eggs and ham. A basket of fruit sat in the middle of the long mahogany table.

Not caring whether or not it was bad manners, Eli placed Cleo on the table and let his familiar take what food he wanted. The cat settled to Eli's left, his teal green eyes never left Porter, in a constant state of readiness.

Eating was nearly impossible. Eli's stomach churned with each bite. It tasted delicious, finely cooked with all the right spices yet he could not eat it. Finally, he laid his fork down and gave up. Anxiety rolled through him. What did Porter want from him?

"Is the food not to your liking?" Duncan asked, nibbling on his whole-wheat toast.

Eli's head shot up. The older man had been so quiet that he had almost forgotten he was still there. Those ocean blue eyes that did not belong to him watched Eli with emotions he could not quite place. It unnerved him. The retort he wanted to give fell short.

"It's not the food," he finally said with all the defiance he could gather, but it barely came out as more than a choked murmur. Swallowing hard, he tried glaring instead. "It's the company." He inhaled sharply as his rival stood, not helping the fear that bubbled inside him.

Duncan rounded the table, appearing as unthreatening as possible. He brought the basket of fruit closer and took a seat next to him.

Henry watched them from his seat, his gray eyes regarding them suspiciously, but he made no move to interfere. He hungrily ate his meal without a care in the world.

It took strength to keep from flinching as Duncan touched his cheek. He bit his lip as he felt magick swirl around him. It wasn't arousing this time, only calming. The sickness in his stomach eased.

"Better?"

It took a moment to realize Duncan had spoken. Eli looked up at him in confusion. Why was he trying to make sure he was comfortable? It was as if he was trying to be his friend. "Ah…yes. Thank you."

Duncan smiled, patting his knee. "You can be very stubborn, Eli. You make yourself sick with worry."

Cleo snorted in the background, but Duncan's words rung true. At least in regard to the last year or so.

Sitting back, Duncan gestured to the barely touched plate of food. "Go on, eat. I'm sure you're famished."

Eli ignored the suggestion. "What do you want with me?"

"I already told you. Once Chaos's power is under control you can go home."

He stared into his rival's eyes. "I don't believe you. You tried kidnapping me in March. Had Raven's Guardians not—"

"Interfered, there would be no need for this now," Duncan sighed as he took some green grapes from the basket. "I'll admit I have many personal reasons for wanting you here and my methods are a little unorthodox, but they work when you let them. I helped Raven once. I can help you."

"When did you help Raven?"

"In Spain. Nathaniel had sent Henry a telegram saying he was very sick and that Henry should hurry. Henry asked me to join him in hopes that my magick could heal you." He bowed his head. "Do you remember?"

Eli could recall Henry being in Spain. Anthony's best friend had traveled all the way from England to be by his side. They had talked for hours, Henry helping him outside to the Syfferns' garden so they could sit in the beautiful sunlight. There had been another man, a few years younger than Anthony. Anthony didn't like him, something about a baby sister and Nathaniel. One had been severely hurt, the other dying. Nathaniel-Frost was fine so it had to have been the girl who died.

"Try to remember."

Eli couldn't stop himself from closing his eyes as Duncan placed his hands on either side of his face. The calming warmth increased placing him in a small trance. Images from his past life became crystal clear. He was in the past, but not in Anthony's body, even though he could feel everything his past self could. He was a viewer not a participant.

* * *

Anthony was enraged as the young man sat next to Henry Griphan. Anthony didn't get angry often and there were few people in the world he could honestly say he hated, but Duncan Porter was one of them. There were crimes the man had committed against him and his family that he could never forget nor forgive. Henry knew all about them.

Why would his friend even consider bringing the warlock to him, especially at this time?

"Calm down, Anthony," Henry said, placing his hands on his shaking shoulders. He made him sit down. "Porter's the best healer in all of Europe. You know that. We don't have time to search the Americas for another one."

"So, he's a healer, what's your point?"

Henry scowled. "The illness must be making you dense."

Anthony didn't look so good. His usual bright tri-blue eyes were dull and tired. His hair, although in the same usual style and freshly washed, had no shine to it. His pale skin almost surpassed Nathaniel's. He was incredibly worn and tired. "Henry," he muttered, wanting to get the exact reason Porter of all people was at his mother's family's home.

"He can help you. He has already agreed to it."

Anthony raised a questioning brow to the young warlock. The dark-haired man gave a nod, smiling enthusiastically.

"No," Anthony said firmly.

Henry slapped his forehead. "You are dense!" he almost shouted. "Anthony, this is no time to hold a grudge. You're dying or have you forgotten? Duncan's magick can counter it. Just give the man a chance!"

"Raven," Duncan interrupted, catching both their attention. "I know you can never forgive me for my past sins and I can never make it up to you, but if my gifts can help you in any way, please let me try."

If looks could kill, Anthony was sure he would have set Porter ablaze. "Is that so? How do you replace a murdered little girl? Or how about the morale of a boy that was almost burned to death? For that matter, how do I explain your presence to him?"

"We all know you erased Nathaniel's memories of that day. He no more remembers Duncan than the other Guardians." Henry took Anthony's hands, making the smaller man look at him. "Won't it be worse if we did nothing?"

Anthony shook his head. He could not forgive Porter for the death of his sister.

"It was an accident. I only wanted to get your attention, not kill her," Duncan pleaded.

"And Nathaniel?"

"A horrible mistake. Rage blinded me to his youth. Anthony, please, we need you."

Anthony could barely remember the last time he had heard Porter plead with him. It had been nearly twenty years. He had been pleaded for something far different back then. Still, he could not trust him, not after losing Elizabeth. He shook his head. "I'm not into the Sexcraft, Porter. Even for this."

"But—"

A huge smile crossed Henry's face as he spotted Nathaniel entering the garden. "I love that boy's timing." He gave Anthony a sly grin. "Let's ask Nate what he thinks. Nathaniel! Come here, lad!"

"Henry!" Anthony cried in objection as his angel took to the air and flew to them. "There are days I hate you."

The police chief waved the comment away. "I'm not too happy about it either, Tony, but we're running out of options."

"Can you ever let a person die in peace?"

"Nope."

Nathaniel landed next to Anthony and bowed graciously to their company.

His smile grew at the sight of Henry. "Henry!"

"What? No Uncle Henry? I'm disappointed," the redhead gave Nathaniel a bear hug, practically crushing his wings to his back. "How're you doing, my boy? Getting taller by the day, I see."

To say Nathaniel was beaming from the comment was an understatement. Henry was an uncle to him. He was built like an ox, but was as loveable as a puppy. He gave affection to all of Anthony's creations.

He sat Nathaniel down and knelt before him, his big hands covering Nathaniel's much smaller ones. "Nat, I've got a big question for you. I know all about you and Anthony."

Amethyst eyes grew wide with fear. "H-how?"

Henry placed a finger to the youth's lips to hush him. "That doesn't matter."

Anthony covered his face in embarrassment, not of his relationship with the youth, but Henry's line of questioning. Porter's smug face didn't help either. He seemed to be eyeing the faery in ways he'd rather the warlock left alone. "Touch him and I'll kill you," he whispered across the table.

Porter blinked and focused on something else. Considering how seriously he had taken him, Porter must have honestly believed his magick could help Anthony.

Henry paid no attention to them as he spoke to Nathaniel. "You know Anthony's sick, right?"

Nathaniel nodded. It was something he had to deal with for the past few weeks.

"What if I said there may be a way to help him?"

The faery's eyes brightened. "How?"

"Well, my friend here is a healer. He can absorb the illness and direct it elsewhere. He'll need a lot of time alone with Anthony."

Anthony groaned at the very idea. "Tell him why, Henry."

"You sure?"

A small nod answered him.

"Ahm…okay." He held Nathaniel's hands a little tighter. "Nate, uh…it involves the Tantra…uh… Sexcraft. Not very many people use this form of magick anymore, but Duncan is an expert at it and well…he wishes to use it on Anthony to heal him."

The boy's eyes were wide as they stared from Anthony to Duncan and back again. "Anthony?"

Henry took his chin and turned his head back to him. "Anthony won't do it unless you're okay with it. You won't be able to touch him for the first few days. So, the question is, what do you think?"

"I…" He stared at Anthony's pale face and dim eyes. "I'll do anything to help him. If this can heal you, then try it," he said softly.

Anthony sighed, gazing at the young fey. Leaning over, he hugged him. "Are you certain, Nat?" He combed his fingers through the long, silky mane.

"Of course, Master Anthony," Nathaniel said formally in front of their guests. Luckily, his face pressed on the other side of Anthony's, hidden from the others. "I love and trust you," he whispered against Anthony's ear before kissing the exposed skin of his neck.

Anthony only smiled and hugged him tightly.

* * *

Anthony folded his arms across his chest as Duncan laid out the tools of his trade. Scented candles stood on every free space, which was more than usual. It had been years since Anthony had left his home in Spain to live in Canada and the sudden return had left little time for him to bring many of his belongings. Only the necessities, Nathaniel had said. Anthony was too sick to argue and Selena didn't dare argue with her brother that day. His angel wanted him home with his family as soon as possible. Anthony didn't mind. He was proud to see Nathaniel could take charge when needed.

"Are you ready?" Porter asked, lighting the last of the many candles.

Anthony frowned, stepping up to the large windows. "We've been rivals since childhood, Duncan. Why should I not believe this is another attempt to take my power before I die?"

"Just because we're rivals doesn't mean I want to see you dead." He laid his hand flatly on Anthony's back. "We were friends once. Had I not been foolish, we still would be. I meant what I said about Elizabeth and Nathaniel."

A warm current spread from the hand on his back throughout his whole body. It made Anthony lightheaded and he had to hold the window frame to keep from falling. "What do you get from this?"

"You're so tense," Porter replied, moving his hand in circular motions.

"We'll have to work these out before we start."

Anthony could vaguely remember being led to his bed or his clothing removed. Duncan's hands were so soothing that he found it hard not to relax under his touches. Each taut muscle loosened to the point that he felt he would fall asleep.

Duncan untied his long ponytail, pushing his ebony hair over one shoulder and out of the way. "Feeling better, aren't you?"

Anthony could only give a murmured response as he felt Duncan reposition his arms on the pillows and knead the tension out of them. His skilled hands worked each muscle until Anthony's body was so loose he felt as if he were floating on a cloud. Their coupling was as gentle and relaxing as the message. Their magick melded together as Duncan drew the illness from Anthony. The colour returned to Anthony's cheeks and his eyes brightened, slowly bringing back the old Anthony Sinclair.

* * *

Eli found himself in Duncan's arms. His head rested heavily against the other man's chest. They sat on the floor, his chair tipped on the ground. Cleo and Henry stood nearby, watching him with worry. Sitting up was dizzying and he found himself forced to continue leaning against Duncan. The warlock seemed more than content to hold him.

The memory seemed unreal yet he knew it spoke the truth. Duncan had tried to save Anthony. He was in love with him and Anthony had not found out until it was too late. The feelings were never mutual. Anthony resented him for the death of his sister and the near fatal injuries to Nathaniel.

Eli sighed, leaning further into Duncan's arms. He couldn't pull himself away as he slipped in and out of consciousness. The vision was unnatural and drew from his power more than normal. He closed his eyes and relied on Cleo to protect him.

Selena paced the living room. Paced the foyer. Checked every phone over and over again to make sure they were working. There was nothing wrong with the phone lines. Everything worked perfectly yet Henry had not called, and it was nearly noon! She continued her frantic pacing while Frost opened himself to the spiritual world. He was having as much luck as she was. There was no sign of Eli or Cleo's auras and the forest spirits only confirmed Henry had carried Eli to a waiting car. It vanished down the road moments later. With it, all trace of Eli and Cleo.

"Damn!" Selena screamed. She slammed her fist into a wall.

She pulled it out and rested her palm open next to the gaping hole. Tears rolled down her cheeks as the frustration finally got to her.

"Henry would never…"

Biting her lip, she punched a number into the phone. Her hands refused to stop shaking as she held the receiver. Holding it to her ear, she waited for someone to pick up. After a moment, a warm friendly voice answered.

"Pietro, it's Selena," she said, cutting off his greeting. "We have an emergency. Eli has been kidnapped…. Henry, we believe… Yes. Tell the Sinclairs the present Eli's family from Canada and their Guardians are seeking sanctuary."

"What?" Frost whispered, standing next to her.

She covered the receiver. "It's for Alexis's and Miao's safety. Whomever has Eli and the others, may come after them. Sinclair Manor is well protected. They'll be safe. Hmm...yes? Pietro, I need to bring her today. We have only three days to the eclipse. If Raven's prediction was correct, we may have Armageddon on our hands. Remind Richard what happened with the High Council the last time Eli lost control, and tell him to times it by a thousand. Eli has more power now than he ever did before."

There was a long pause. She leaned against the small table and gazed at the others surrounding her and Frost. There was still so much they did not know about Eli, or Anthony for that matter. There were many things Anthony had only told her and Cleo in preparation for Eli. She had always hoped Anthony would be wrong.

"Richard, how nice to hear your voice. We believe Henry Griphan may have kidnapped Eli. Yes, I know Henry would only do what's in his best interest, but we don't know where he is and we can't sense Eli or Cleo's auras. Yes, completely gone." She took a deep breath and let it out slowly. "Thank you. We'll be there in a few hours." She hung up and eyed the teenagers. "Go pack. We're going to visit the Sinclairs."

Amazingly, they didn't ask any questions or object. Alexis and Sif helped Miao up the stairs, his ankle still bugging him slightly. Frost and Scott waited patiently for the kids to get out of earshot.

Selena took a moment to center herself. There was so much Nathaniel had not been told due to Anthony's illness. Secrets Anthony had managed only to tell her. Dark secrets. "Before Anthony died, he used a lot of his remaining power to block all the dimensions he had created."

Frost nodded, obviously remembering that day.

"He then created a key and a lock, hidden within both halves of his soul."

"Eli and Dad," Scott stated.

Selena nodded. "Yes. There was also a puzzle box that foretold when the Key would become active, but is controlled only by the Lock. I had always thought Dan already had it, but it must have been lost at some point. You see, Eli has always been able to open dimensional gates. He's done it many times. Subconsciously of course, and only in the astral realm. Anthony kept him from opening them in the real world and protects him in his dreams.

"There was no problem until Chaos possessed Eli and boosted his power level." She stared off to the patio door in thought. "Anthony said when Eli was in his late teens an unfathomable power would surge within him. Every portal will unleash itself and devour him unless both halves are united as one. The light and dark, and the power bestowed upon the gods are released."

"What does that mean?" Scott asked in utter confusion.

"That unless we can find Dan and get him here in the next two days, there may be nothing left to save."

Chapter Thirteen

The rain was coming down hard. His slippered feet had no grip as he ran down the dark streets. It was hard not to fall in the large puddles. He forced himself back to his feet after each fall. The scrapes on his knees stung, but he didn't care. There wasn't much time left. Tears fell room his weary eyes. The train tracks weren't far now. He could see them through the sheets of rain. Maybe there was still time. If he could make it to the other side…

Four sets of lights appeared down the street on the other side of the tracks. A train whistle screeched not far down the track. He ran faster as his fears grew. He had to stop them. He had to save his Mommy and Daddy.

The three cars chasing the sedan boxed it in as they approached the tracks. The family car was magically forced to a stop in the path of the oncoming train still yards away.

He slipped in another muddy puddle less than twenty feet from his parents' car. The other cars moved away as the train bore down on them. He could not get up fast enough.

Through the front window, he could see his father cradling his mother as she sobbed. His kind face buried in her silky black hair.

A scream tore from the child's throat as the train slammed into the much smaller vehicle. The car was crushed and pushed over a hundred yards down track and all he could do was scream.

"Mum! Da!" he cried over and over again.

Forcing himself to his feet, he ran down the side of the tracks to the crushed sedan. The conductor tried grabbing him as he ran past. His heart pounded as he reached the car. It was compacted to almost half the normal size. The windshield was crushed and what appeared to be a mass of raw meat met his eyes. Only the strands of silky blue-black hair and purple Asian dress identified what was left of his mother, but none of it made sense to his young mind.

Movement caught his attention. It was barely human, but movement meant life. Going to the driver side door, he pulled on the handle. The twisted metal and raw flesh jammed the door, but the six-year-old continued to pull. He had to save his Mommy and Daddy.

Closing his eyes, he sobbed and screamed for help. The funny feeling that he got in his stomach when his gifts appeared, filled his stomach. It ran up and down his arms as he pulled on the door. With a cry of surprise, he ripped the door off its hinges. It felt far too light to be real. Throwing it aside, he peered into the eerie car.

Another scream tore from his throat as a bloody, meaty hand grabbed his wrist. A torn, broken face stared down at him with bloodshot eyes. What remained of his mother seemed to be pushed into his father, making them into one grotesque being. There was no question she was dead. Yet amazingly enough, his father was still alive.

"Eli." His father's usually soft voice choked with obvious pain.

"Papa!" Eli cried, trying to wrap his tiny arms around him, but was pushed away. "Da, wha…"

"Run! Go now before they—"

Large arms wrapped around Eli, pulling him away from his father. The big man lifted him off his feet and carried him away. Kicking and screaming, Eli tried prying his way free. "No! Let me go! Da! Papa! Let me go!"

"Easy, Eli. It's okay. Everything's going to be okay."

He twisted around to see his Grandpa Henry holding him. The old man seemed oddly calm.

"No. Let me go. Da's still alive. My dad's alive!"

Grandpa would not listen. He held Eli tightly as he walked to the waiting car. Eli struggled. He had to save his dad. Something that felt like electricity ran through his body, surpassing the butterflies in his stomach. He tried reaching for his parents' ruined car, wishing with all his heart that he could reach it.

The fender moved the more he concentrated. It ripped off the rest of the car and flew toward them. Surprised, Eli lost focus and it dropped out of the air.

Henry cursed under his breath and handed him to another man. "Take care of him, Duncan. I'll be back in a moment," Grandpa Henry said as he turned back to the accident.

The other man was also in his mid-seventies. He wrapped his arm under Eli's rear and the other around his back. There was something different about him. Eli couldn't understand how, but he could no longer fight. Warm currents flowed through his body like a warm blanket. He felt tired as he lowered his head on the man's shoulder. The warmth of the car barely broke the trance he was in. His body was maneuvered so he half-sat, half-lay in the man's lap. Pale blue eyes watched him with great care.

"You're soaked to the bone," Duncan said, wrapping him in a warm blanket.

He held Eli close, rubbing his hands over Eli's cold, wet body. Warmth radiated through him, warming his body, and drying his clothes. Sleepiness threatened to claim him as the strange man cupped his cheek.

"So beautiful. I can see Raven in you."

The words made no sense and Eli was too tired to ask what he meant. His eyes fluttered close, barely opening when Grandpa Henry climbed into the driver seat.

"It's done. They're both dead."

Eli's eyelids shot open at his grandfather's words. "No!" he cried, twisting in Duncan's arms. "Papa was still alive!"

With force, Duncan turned him back around. "It's okay, Eli. They're in a better place now." A soft glow emanated from his hand as he placed it in front of his small face. "Sleep."

He wanted to fight, to prove his father was still alive. That there was still one family member who still loved him out there, but he couldn't. He felt lightheaded and the butterflies in his belly were doing loop to loops. His eyes rolled back and with a small moan, he slumped into the stranger's warm embrace.

* * *

Eli twisted and turned in his sleep. Treacherous memories of the past assaulted him over and over again as for the first time in years he remembered in vivid detail his parents' murders. So many details he had forgotten. It was as if Duncan Porter who had opened a floodgate to the past.

So many memories.

Duncan had been a more active member of his past than he had imagined. Far more than he ever wanted.

He rolled away from Cleo and curled into the fetal position in hopes to push the visions away. Even asleep, the tears would not stop coming. Sobs racked his body as he buried his face in the numerous pillows.

Cleo pawed his shoulder, but the light touches did nothing to awaken him.

A firm hand fell on his shoulder instead. "Eli?"

The firm shake startled him. Instinct caused Eli to roll out of the touch. His hand grasped the Totem hanging around his neck. It morphed to his long sword with barely a thought. He moved quickly, the blade coming down on the man's throat.

Pain radiated from his wrist as it suddenly twisted back. The sword returned to its totem form. Eli was forced to lie down once more as Duncan straddled his hips and held his wrists firmly on either side of his head. He struggled beneath the larger man until he could fight no more. Lying beneath Duncan Porter, he allowed himself a few shaky sobs as the realization of his captors being his parents' murderers overwhelmed him.

"Murderer!" he sneered through the sobs.

"Eli," Duncan sighed.

Eli felt Duncan's mind scan his. A small frown crossed the other young man's face as well as a deep sadness. He pulled Eli into his arms and hugged him. "I'm so sorry."

Despite the anger and hate, Eli clung to him. "Why?"

He wanted to pull away, to fight, to do something, but allowed Duncan to pull him off the bed instead. The lights came on as they crossed the room.

Duncan's power.

They sat at the small poker table in the dinette where Eli took a few moments to steady his breathing. His mind raced as Duncan fetched drinks out of the fridge.

All these years he always knew they were murdered, no matter how many times Henry and Nan said it was otherwise, but he never figured

Henry had anything to do with it…and Porter? Why? Why kill his parents and not him? He was only six. Completely defenseless. Why was he spared?

Duncan placed an iced tea before him, then took a moment to fuss over Eli's sleep tangled hair, untangling the knots, and straightening the sleep-induced curls. Every morning since coming to the castle, Duncan had gone through this routine. Not even Selena fussed over him so much. Duncan straightened the collar to Eli's silk black pajamas as he sat across from him. As always, he smiled at him with a mix of worry and devotion. Like a lover. It was the same expression he gave him all those years ago, cradling his soaked little body in the warmth of his car.

"You were dreaming of your parents," Duncan stated as he opened his can of iced tea. "I'm sorry you had to see that. We never thought we would have a vision of their death or try to save them. We weren't prepared for you."

"What?"

There was a deep sigh. "You won't be able to sleep tonight, I see."

Taking a drink, he fell into deep thought.

Cleo jumped into Eli's arms and rubbed his cheek affectionately. Did the feline know about his parents' deaths? Did Selena? They had been so intent on keeping him away from Duncan and the High Council, were they hiding something? They had said it had something to do with when he was eight, but he could never remember any bad times at that age. Yet Cleo had not become his guardian until two months after his parents passing. There were so many things he had forgotten over the years, maybe, like his parents' murders, something else had happened when he was eight that he had forced himself to forget.

"Your destiny was at risk. Your mother had convinced your father to move to Spain to be with her family. There were great business opportunities for him there…but you would have been exposed to the Syfferns."

"So? I would have grown up with Miao. What was the problem?"

"Raven came to you when you were seven. You may have been sent to Canada far too early. They would have sent you to find Daniel Dion before you were ready."

"It was Anthony's wish for Daniel to succeed him, not me. I would have followed his wishes either way."

"Yes, but your training would have been more disciplined and Daniel may not have been able to handle the full extent of his power. Had they been able to get their hands on either of you, I fear what they may have twisted your gifts into."

"That's a stupid reason if I ever heard one."

"Think about it, Eli. The Sefferns always worshipped Anthony as some demi-god. Had you been with them when your powers first unleashed themselves, when Raven began talking through you, you would have become their antichrist. Your mother refused to see reason. I could have trained you."

Sighing, Eli took a sip of his own drink. "And when she died, why didn't you just take me?"

"And let the police learn it wasn't an accident? Once we had the conductor under my control, it was easy to make up a story. If you went missing at the same time, they would've known something was up and the Sinclairs would have put two and two together." He smiled sadly. "No, Henry took you back to your grandmother. You used to sleepwalk. He just *found* you wandering and your grandmother never asked, even after the police told her about the *accident*."

Eli felt hot tears behind his eyes. "And Henry? When he left me with you?"

Duncan was silent for a moment, his gaze never leaving Eli as if he were judging his ability to handle the truth. Finally, he said bluntly, "He broke your father's neck."

Shocked, Eli could only stare at Duncan. He looked down at Cleo's surprised face. He wanted to cry, but the hot tears turned into something far more lethal. He smashed his fist through the table, surprising both Duncan and Cleo.

Magick mixed with rage filled him, lashing out at the objects around him. The wide screen TELEVISION flicked on, but filled with snow as Eli stormed past. Small objects trembled on the dresser. None of it fazed him.

"I trusted him!" he raved, his eyes bright and wild. "He was Anthony's best friend! Mae loved him! Why? Why would he kill my parents? He treated them like his own children!"

He was trembling so hard now that he feared he would fall. Henry had practically raised him. How many times had he sat on his knee as a child? Or hugged and kissed him goodnight? All those years spending every holiday at his cabin. All that time he was staying with a murderer? His parents' murderer!

Duncan wrapped his arms securely around him. He didn't say anything, just held Eli and let him rant. Soothing sentiments brushed across his ear when he finally relented to the sobs that filled his chest. He found himself rocked like a small babe, Duncan's cheek resting against the back of his head, when they finally sat on the floor. Duncan continued to hold him until the trembling ceased and Eli slipped into restless slumber.

The next day was heart-wrenching for Duncan. Eli refused to leave his room, refused to eat. He would not even move from his bed. He lay there as if in a trance, staring off into space. He had barely spoken a word since waking. Not even Cleo seemed able to get through to him.

Duncan leaned against the doorframe and watched the youth worriedly. Henry was next to him, an angry frown tugging at his lips. He had no sympathy for the youth.

The knowledge of his parents' murders was taking its toll on Eli. He could not help but pity the young man. He should have known it would affect Eli in such a way. He should have known Eli would react like this. There was no point in seeking revenge though, and Eli knew that. He was overpowered here. They had only scratched the surface of the secrets Henry had been hiding from him. Duncan didn't want to see the outcome should he ever learn the full truth.

"He doesn't remember, does he?" he finally asked Cleo.

He had been so sure that Eli at least remembered their past together, but somehow he must have blocked out all the testing and training he had gone through with the High Council. He had forgotten all the time they spent together when Eli was eight. In the end, that was a good thing. Things had gotten out of control back then.

"No. Selena erased what she could." The cat looked up with a frown. "Be thankful. You would not be able to control him otherwise."

Henry growled in frustration. He folded his arms over his broad chest as he watched Eli. His eyes were hard as he regarded him. "We don't have time for him to mope." He glared at Duncan. "Take him."

He shook his head. "I'm trying to gain his trust. Forcing him into the craft will just push him away. It was never his form of magick anyway."

"Fine," Henry snarled, storming into the room.

Eli didn't even look up as he stood in front of him. For a long moment, Henry just stared down at him. At first, Duncan feared the worst. Feared Henry would beat the young man, but he didn't. Instead, he scooped up Eli's inert form and stormed past Duncan and Cleo, giving a deaf ear to Eli's protests and struggles.

Duncan and Cleo followed closely as Henry took Eli down flights of stairs until they were in the bowels of the castle. There the science labs and training facilities were located.

Eli stood on his own two feet, trying to pull out of Henry's grasp. The old man wasn't fazed in the slightest. He pulled Eli to the first training room and shoved him in, locking the door the moment the young man was inside, alone.

"Set the exercise at maximal danger level. He'll snap out of it the moment he realizes we're not playing games."

"Henry!" Cleo snapped, enraged. "Let me in there!"

Henry only grinned as they entered the observation deck. "You can't swim."

Thankfully, Eli can, Duncan thought as he pressed his hand against the large bulletproof window. These rooms were made to help those with extra-ordinary powers learn to handle them. This wasn't Eli's first time in one. When he was eight, he had gone through testing for several days, spending hours using his powers. It was tiring for the young mage and very dangerous.

The water slipped from the large reserve, filling the room as it had many years earlier. It seemed to take Eli a moment to figure out what was going on. Rather than panicking as he had when he was eight, he seemed not to care, as if drowning would be far better than participating in their test. He sat in the cold water until it was nearly to his chest, his eyes closed and head bowed. He was nothing like the little boy who had been franticly searching for higher ground. The look on his face spoke volumes. He was at peace with the world and ready to join his parents.

It tore at Duncan's heart and he suddenly wanted nothing more than to be with him and ensure him his life was worth living. It was worth fighting for.

Someone else got to Eli first.

Eli's brows bunched together in sudden anguish. A single tear rolled down his cheek before he stood. His eyes had an unearthly glow to them as he rose out of the water. An annoyed expression crossed his face as he levitated above the rising water.

"Raven!" Cleo cried, placing his small paws against the window. He gazed out at his master in relief.

The energy that radiated through and around Eli was different, far from what he had witnessed during his childhood. Duncan wasn't sure how to describe it. It wasn't as if he were looking at Eli Hawke, but at a younger version of Anthony Sinclair. Even with his hair tousled, his glasses still in his room and clothes soaked, Eli had undoubtedly handed himself over to his past life. Or Raven simply took over to prevent the boy from drowning. Whatever the reason, Eli was no longer with them.

Even Henry was impressed. "Hello, Anthony," he called through the loudspeaker.

"Why are you doing this, Henry?" the deceased magician demanded as he floated higher. The water was rising far too quickly, lapping at his bare feet within minutes.

"Make Eli cooperate. He won't be harmed if he does as we say."

"He knows what you did. How you murdered his parents. He'd rather die than work for you."

"That's possible."

Fiddling with the controls, something Henry had helped design some thirty years ago, he unleashed cybernetic arms from the ceiling and walls.

They ensnared the surprised mage. The tentacles dragged him under the water before he could free himself. His struggles lasted a few heart-stopping minutes before he became deathly still.

Duncan's heart froze in fear. Eli could not have drowned. Not Eli. Eli was one of the best swimmers he had ever met. Even as a small child, he could hold his breath for nearly five minutes. Maybe the robotic arms wrapped too tightly around him. He bowed his head in remorse.

Cleo made a small whimper. "Please, no," he said softly.

A soft glow caught his attention. Opening his eyes, he stared in awe as Raven's magick platform appeared below Eli's feet. It glowed bright gold, filling its master with light and life. The teen opened his eyes, his past-self still shining through. The water began bubbling as if being boiled. The ends of the robotic arms holding the mage began melting away. It was almost as if Eli's body was a source of unfathomable heat. Slowly the water began to vaporize. Eli's glow became as bright as the sun.

Duncan shielded his eyes as it exploded outward. Water turned to steam and the robotic arms melted into unrecognizable scraps of metal.

Eli slowly descended to the ground. Once his feet touched the now-warm metal floor, his knees buckled and he fell to his hands and knees panting.

"Thank the gods," Cleo breathed.

Duncan sighed in relief, half-laughing. "He loves scaring us."

Henry was actually smiling proudly. "That he does. Causing me heart attacks has always been his favourite past-time." He hit another button.

"What are you—"

Flames rose from the floor, surrounding Eli. They rose in height and intensity until they threatened to consume the young man. Eli was still glowing as if one with the flames. His arms spread and fingers stretched, and let the flames lick at them. A coy smile crossed his lips as one hand vanished within the flames. They turned from a raging red inferno to a glacier of ice. Soon the room looked like the arctic.

Eli stood in the center. Raven's keen eyes observed the room with distaste. Raising his unscorched hands, he sent fireballs at every piece of equipment that looked remotely threatening. He destroyed all the cameras recording the session. Turning toward the observation booth, he sent his energy toward it.

"Damn!" Duncan cursed, snatching Cleo off the computer console just seconds before it exploded. He stumbled back in awe as electricity ran the length of the board.

Henry stood back in surprise. "Well, I think he's upset."

"You think?" Cleo cried in astonishment. "You're not dealing with Eli any more, Henry. That's Anthony down there and angering him is never a good idea."

Thunder boomed throughout the room. Duncan peered through the window. Eli was standing before the large metal doors. The magick was building around him. Raw power. Not just Anthony's. Fire and ice mixed around him in surreal patterns. A chaos of natural powers so raw Duncan could feel it even through the two feet of titanium that separated them.

Henry pressed his hands against the window. The magick was drawing him as it had many years ago. The strength of it drew him like a magnet. It was far stronger than anything Eli exhibited since giving up half his magick to Daniel Dion. He pushed past Duncan and hurried down the stairs.

Duncan watched as the doors began to melt at Eli's touch, the sound of thunder was still echoing throughout the room. Eli was throwing everything he had, or at least what he thought would scare his abductors the most, at the door. He seemed to be taking his time and actually enjoying himself. Definitely Raven's technique. He was almost through.

Duncan just made it down the stairs when Eli broke through. Henry and two guards were there, waiting for him. The guards had their rifles aimed at the young mage, but it didn't faze Eli in the slightest. The weapons were telekinetically ripped out of their hands and dismantled. The young man levitated past them and glared down at his grandfather. Anger radiated through his whole being.

None of it bothered Henry. He was smiling lovingly at Eli.

Always the good, loving grandfather.

"That's my boy! I knew you could do it!" he declared, throwing his arms open wide for an embrace.

Carefully, Duncan approached the mage. Anthony was still in charge, which meant Eli had gone dormant. Why? They usually mixed together. For Raven to be completely in charge, something had to be seriously wrong with Eli. The truth about Henry and his parents must have shattered him. He really must have wanted to die when the training room was flooded. Had Raven not taken over he may have very well drowned.

"Eli?" he tried, hoping the young man would answer rather than Anthony. "Are you alright?"

Eli, or rather Anthony, paid him no mind. His entire attention was on Henry. He floated closer to his supposed grandfather, keeping just out of reach. "You've disappointed me, Henry. I entrusted Eli's safety to you and you've betrayed him from the time of his birth," Anthony said in a flat voice.

"Perhaps," Henry said, lowering his arms. "But some things were needed for his training. Do you think he could have found Dion had I not taught him to be ruthless? To take advantage of Daniel's weaknesses? Quite frankly, I still think he should have the all the power."

"I choose Daniel. Eli has a separate destiny." His bare feet touched the ground. Standing, he stared up at Henry for a long moment. "Why are you doing this? You were my—" He gasped sharply as Henry closed the distance between them and pulled him into a bear hug. Maybe Anthony forgot Eli was still young and much smaller than the old man. Only a third his size. Physical strength was definitely at a disadvantage.

"I only asked one thing from you, Tony. You refused me." He just gaped at him in utter confusion.

"All I wanted was you to bring Dorothy back to me."

"I can't bring back the dead."

"No, but you could open a gate to her. You could have brought her spirit back." He buried one large hand in Eli's velvety hair, holding him securely. "I've worked eighteen years training Eli. Don't think that just because you surface every now and then that I will let you get in my way."

Duncan watched as Anthony's confusion cleared and understanding filled his eyes.

"That's what this is all about? Henry, it's been fifty years, let her go. She doesn't want you to mourn forever." He winced as Henry's grip tightened and his head yanked back.

"Have you ever tasted immortal blood, Tony? It's intoxicating. Far more than any drug or liqueur ever created. Duncan and I debated for years whether or not magicians tasted the same. It's different, not as sweet as immortals, but far more addictive and potent."

"Nathaniel," Anthony breathed in realization.

Seeing the horror in Eli's eyes Duncan hurried to Henry's side. "Henry, no. Not like this. There's no need to put Eli in further shock."

Henry ignored him. "Yes, Nathaniel." He stroked Eli's cheek. "You angered so many people when you called upon your Guardians. They were so unlike the Fetch. They had life, consciousness, and a will of their own."

"Why? Why Nathaniel?"

"He was beautiful. An angel in either form. He had an innocence that Selena didn't possess. She had street smarts, fought her faery nature, and learned about the world." A smile graced his lips. "They both take after you. Your light and dark. If I can't have you, I might as well take Eli."

"Let go!" Anthony growled, trying to pull free. "You won't have him or any of my Guardians!"

A new guard came around the corner. Seeing Eli struggling against his grandfather, he hurried to Henry's aid.

"No!" Duncan ordered, but it was too late.

The young guard raised the rifle and slammed the butt of it across the back of the young man's head. Eli fell forward into Henry's arms, but the blow wasn't hard enough to knock him out, only daze him. A small trail of blood trailed down the back of his neck and onto Henry's fingers.

While defenseless, Eli-Anthony was yanked firmly against Henry and lifted off his feet. His pajamas shirt was ripped open and the old man's sharp nails tore into the soft flesh beneath. Anthony ground his teeth in pain.

"Henry, stop!" Cleo cried as the man's mouth fell upon the wound.

Duncan held him tight, refusing to let him near his master. Duncan watched in mild horror as Henry drink in Eli's life force. He had only watched this form of vampirism on occasion, but it surprised him that Henry would choose Eli as his victim. It didn't surprise him how fast Eli succumbed to Henry's feeding. He slumped in the large man's arms, his head falling against Henry's shoulder. He was barely conscious. Henry refused to stop feeding. Scared, Duncan rushed to Henry's side and tried to pull Eli out of his arms.

Annoyed, Henry glared down at him. "What is it?" he demanded. He shifted Eli's weight.

"He's barely conscious."

The glaze that covered Henry's eyes cleared. Fear and worry took its place. He shifted Eli in his arms as if he weighed nothing at all, his strength increased by Eli's energy.

Eli was slightly pale, his breathing labored, but he was still awake. His hazy eyes stared up at Henry in horror.

"Oh, Lord," Henry breathed, hugging Eli tightly. "I…I'm sorry. Eli…Eli, say something."

"What are you?" Anthony's voice murmured, but Eli's under toned it. "How…"

Henry only chuckled in relief while Duncan held his chest. *This was too close*, thought Duncan as he brushed back Eli's hair. *Henry could have killed him without even realizing it until it was too late. What if I wasn't here to stop him?*

Good cop, bad cop? Cleo wasn't sure. They both seemed to care and love Eli in their own ways. He knew Henry loved Eli more than anything else, but it seemed as if the old man was trying to push Eli into Duncan's arms, even if it meant scaring the living hell out of him. It was all an act.

Cleo nuzzled Eli's chin as his eyelids fell closed. Whatever Henry had done to him had drained him considerably. Eli could barely keep his eyes open. His chest sported a horrid bruise over deep scratches. Cleo avoided it at all cost as he settled on his young master's stomach. It was impossible to tell who was forefront in Eli's mind, Anthony, or himself. It had surprised him that Anthony had not been able to defend himself against Henry, but Eli's depression could have been taking its toll on him. The young man was torturing himself for trusting the man he thought of as his grandfather for so long. It wasn't his fault, but Eli was just as stubborn as his past self, if not more.

Henry took them to the *games room* on the next floor and laid Eli on the large Queen Anne sofa while he fetched some ice and water.

Duncan sat next to them on the floor, trying desperately to get Eli to open his eyes. He took the ice from Henry and brought it to Eli's lips. It moistened his dry lips and dripped into his mouth. "Eli? Raven? Nod if you can hear me." Eli nodded at Duncan's request.

"Good." He brought the ice cube to Eli's forehead. His brows bunched together, but he didn't protest.

Cleo marveled at how well Duncan looked after Eli. He fussed over the younger man as a parent would. Or lover. He made sure Eli ate, even if it was just a little. Claudia brought fresh clothes for him. There was no telling whether or not it was really Eli or Anthony in charge. He refused to speak. Rage reflected in his eyes whenever he looked at Henry. All Cleo could do was rub against him and offer what comfort his feline nature would allow. Duncan, as scary as it was, even petted him for his efforts.

"Don't pick a fight."

Miao looked up in surprise at Nathan's crisp voice. Selena stormed past him in an outfit that really didn't suit her bubbly, bouncy nature. A black pants suit with small two-inch heel boots that the loose pant legs concealed. The top was also black, slim fitting in the chest, loose in the arms. She had her hair tied back in a tight braid. Dark blue sunglasses adorned her gently tanned features. She jumped into her Porsche and gave a quick glance at Miao and Alexis.

"Fights been picked, Nate. If the Sinclairs are behind this, I want to know before we leave Alexis and Miao with them," she said dryly, revving the engine.

"And how do you expect to find out? They're not just going to tell you."

She smirked. "I'll persuade them. Frost knows the way to the manor." Barely giving Nathan enough time to back away, she roared off in a cloud of dust.

Nathan waved the dust away and frowned. Walking back to the SUV, he shook his head. "Forty-years, yeah right. Frost knows the way through the busy streets of Cambridge. Could've at least given me an address. Wonder how many Sinclairs are in the phone book," he muttered. Leaning against the van, he gazed at Miao and Alexis.

"Any ideas?"

They both shook their heads. Other than going to Cambridge and praying Frost could find his way, they had no other ideas. Selena was supposed to take them, but at the last-minute, she had changed her mind. Richard Sinclair was the head of the family and apparently Eli's third or fourth cousin. He was a little jealous that Daniel and Eli had inherited Raven's power rather than him. He also had many misgivings about Eli's training being so informal. Selena said he was a good man; she just didn't want to take any chances on him having something to do with Eli and Cleo's disappearances.

Despite the lack of directions, Nathan ushered everyone into the van. He climbed in the driver seat next to Scott and pulled away from the cabin. Following Selena's trail of magickal residue was much easier than any of them had expected. Soon, Nathan navigated through the highways as if he had been born and raised in England.

Alexis was shuffling her tarot cards, talking in a hushed voice to the spirits within. So far, none of them had any answers. Windy was off searching again, communicating with the local forest sprites and spirits, but none were of much help.

Frowning, Miao held the framed photo he had given Eli as a belated twelfth-birthday present. It had been made after summer camp, when he had finally confessed his feelings to Alexis and forgiven Eli for all the trials and tests he had put them through. Miao had had a long talk with his mother and she had confirmed everything Eli had told them, right down to him being the reincarnation of Anthony Sinclair.

Miao was not in awe of Eli as he had been of Anthony, instead he thought back to all the time they had spent together that summer and the way Eli always watched over Alexis. Those eyes were that of a father, maybe even a big brother, but not of a possible suitor. Of course, being cousins helped. Although it must have been weird having two cousins on completely different sides of his family dating. His eyes were so sad at times, very lonely. They still were.

With Melissa's help, Miao got a group picture of everyone. Eli, Selena, and Cleo were already back in England so they took one Melissa had snapped before the big move and digitally put it in with the group. Then they added an old photo of Anthony behind Eli and managed to get all the Guardians in their true and false forms. Everyone from the Canadian group signed it and the school yearbook and he sent it to Eli with an apology for his actions while Eli was attending the camp.

After that, they had become best friends and very close cousins. Eli loved the picture and hung it in the most expensive frame he could find. It looked so real, like they were all actually there. Such happy memories, even if they weren't real.

"The wind spirits still can't find them," Alexis whispered. She began reading them as tarot cards, hoping one of the spirits may have an idea. The Four of Cups appeared on top. "Someone from the past." The Judgments and Eight of Swords came next. "To influence his power, using the elements of shadow and illusion to hide himself."

"And Eli," Miao threw in.

"Hidden in both time and space," she murmured, turning another card.

"What does that mean?"

She drew one last card and stared at it in utter confusion.

"Hope."

"Hope? What could that possibly mean?" He frowned and folded his arms across his chest. "Someone from the past, I'm guessing Raven's, hidden in shadow and illusions, somewhere apart from time and space, searching for hope. Hope for what?"

An idea came to him. Now that she was their mistress, Alexis powered the cards, but they still held a strong connection to Raven's present incarnations. "Ask them if he's okay."

She flipped the next card. Ten of Wands. "Lost." She sighed in restraint. "I don't know, Miao. The cards are confused. It's like he's a doppelganger. He exists, but doesn't. Another realm perhaps. Goddess! Why is this happening?"

"I don't know."

She leaned into his arms and sighed. They were driving themselves insane, trying to figure out why Eli had become such a target the last year. Or maybe it had been his whole life. There was still so much they didn't know about Eli let alone Anthony Sinclair.

But why would Eli's own grandfather abduct him? Something just didn't feel right. If the Sinclairs were involved, then Miao's family needed to know. The Elders would know what to do. They were one of the few magick families that could counter the Sinclairs. He prayed this didn't come to another war between the two factions.

The plane touched-down at the London terminal mid-afternoon. The hustle and bustle of busy travelers slowed Daniel's progress to the rental booth. He needed a car and fast. He could feel Alexis and the others on the move. Places he could only conclude had something to do with Anthony Sinclair popped into his mind. Cambridge, Sinclair Manor, Duncan Porter. Cambridge and Sinclair Manor stood out above the rest. That was where they were headed. Duncan Porter seemed to have something to do with Eli. Somehow, the deceased warlock was in fact alive and Eli was with him. Alexis and the others were going the wrong way.

He held himself steady as he rented a car. Eli's emotions were jumbled, but a deep sense of depression overwhelmed him. From his half of Anthony's spirit, he knew a terrible revelation had befallen Eli.

Something that simply tore at the young man's soul.

Mentally, he reached out to him. He could see his young ebony haired twin sitting in a vast garden, huddling within himself. He wrapped his arms around him. The young man started harshly, but relaxed quickly. His whole demeanor changed as their minds met. After a few short moments, the fear drained away from Eli and calmness washed over them both.

Sighing in relief, Daniel pulled out of the airport parking lot. He had to go to Sinclair Manor first, gather the troops. He didn't have the power to go after Eli alone. Only their added magick could counter Porter's.

Chapter Fourteen

"Daniel?" Eli whispered.

He could feel warm, loving arms wrap around him. They weren't physically there, but they felt real. He laced his fingers through the invisible ones and relaxed. Soothing energy swept through him. The embrace reminded him of his own deceased father. A small longing plagued him as he tried to recall exactly what his father looked like. Daniel Dion's face appeared instead. They did sort of look the same, considering they were twins.

You're not alone, Daniel's voice whispered in his mind.

So much like his father. Alexis and Scott were so lucky to have such a kind man as their father. He suddenly realised he barely remembered his own father. It had been twelve years since he had lost his parents, but knew his father had been a kind man...fond of telling him bedtime stories. It seemed funny, now that he thought about it, neither his mother nor father had blue eyes. His father's were hazel and mother's a deep chocolate brown. Ian Hawke had been a successful businessman, while Suzanne Syffern ran a small real estate business out of their modest home. They weren't exactly rich like Nan and the Sinclairs, but they were more than well-off. He never regretted a moment of his life with them. They were his life, and he missed them dearly.

"Are you alright?"

Eli glanced over his shoulder at Duncan. The older man stared down at him with worried eyes. He gave a nod and looked back down at his sleeping guardian. After several days of no sleep, the small familiar had finally passed out. After all those days of watching over him, it was only right for Eli to now watch over him.

"Still won't talk to me?"

He shook his head. Duncan just wouldn't take the hint that he wanted to be alone. His sighed as he felt the warlock move closer.

"A little childish, wouldn't you say?"

Eli rolled his eyes. "I'm eighteen," he snorted in disgust. "It's allowed."

He raised a brow as Duncan yipped in glee and plopped down next to him. It was indeed the most childish thing he had ever heard from someone supposedly in their eighties.

"I've got a sentence out of you! The most since morning!" He combed his fingers through Eli's think hair. His eyes saddened. "I'm sorry. That wasn't how I wanted to show you the training facilities. Last time we started off easy and worked our way up. Henry just wanted to get your attention."

"Last time?"

Duncan frowned for a moment and looked up at the clouds. "You were very young. Eight, if I remember correctly. It had been Halloween and the Council had decided it was time to test you. You spent a few days with Sara and me. Selena…she must have erased all of it. Explains why you didn't recognize me. I wasn't trying to hurt you in March."

"Selena hated you."

"I know."

"Why?" He bowed his head in shame. "I loved you too much to give you up. We fought. You almost died."

Eli had no memory of it, nor did he care to. Whatever had happened back then had probably been erased for his own good. Aaliyah had a tendency to search through his mind when he was very young and discard anything that was too painful to him to remember. It was her way of helping him focus. It was probably the reason he couldn't remember what his parents looked like without a picture.

"Don't worry about it. It was a long time ago and I'm not exactly proud of some of the things I did to you."

Somehow, if he remembered, Eli doubted he would be allowing Duncan so close to him.

"But that's all changed. You'll master Chaos's power. You'll open and control the alternate worlds. You will be the Oracle you were born to be."

"Oracle? No…my visions aren't a gift. They're painful and I can't control them. Someone always gets hurt or dies."

"Fate," Duncan said softly, cupping Eli's cheek. "They are painful because you fight them. Just relax, let them come. I promise, it won't be so bad."

Eli thought about it. Sister Maria used to tell Anthony the same thing, and Aaliyah used to tell him all the time. Alexis seemed able to control her sight. Unfortunately, splitting his power with her father had not freed him of his ability to see into the future. There were days he was simply jealous of his other half. At least Daniel managed to live a normal life.

Duncan moved to sit behind him. His experienced hands moved along Eli's shoulders, working out all the tense muscles. The soothing magick flowed through him and he leaned into those gentle, skilled hands. Between Daniel's essence holding him and Duncan massaging his shoulder, Eli felt as if he were laying in the clouds.

"Can you behave yourself tomorrow long enough for me to attend a meeting?" Duncan's gentle voice made its way to Eli's ears. "Henry shall be in charge until I return. It should only take a few hours. I have made it clear for him to discipline you should it be needed."

His thumbs moved to the base of Eli's neck.

"What is he?"

Duncan's warm breath brushed across his cheek. "A vampire of sorts. He absorbs magickal auras. He didn't mean to take so much or scratch you like he did. Like me, he has waited so long for you to mature enough to touch you. Blood can be considered a delicacy."

Eli couldn't help but laugh. "So, you want my body and he wants my power?" He turned enough to look Duncan directly in the eyes. "Neither of you are going to let me go, are you?"

"When you're ready. The more you cooperate the faster you can leave."

He raised a brow. "Meaning?"

"Participate in the tests. Let Henry feed from you—" Eli's eyes widened to saucer size. "—just a little. I'll help you any way I can." He wrapped his arms around Eli from behind and rested his head next to the smaller man's. "I'll let him feed off me as well. That way he won't take too much from you. All I want is a little affection. I have waited over half my life to be with you once more." Taking Eli's chin, he gently turned him until their lips were mere inches apart. "I love you, Eli. I always have. You're the only reason I'm still alive."

"I…" Duncan silenced him with the softest of kisses. It was like the brush of butterfly wings. It reminded him of goodnight kisses Selena would give Anthony in her childhood, but this was more sensual with a deeper meaning. He found himself returning the kiss with a passion he had not thought possible.

"Let me worship you," Duncan was saying between kisses. "You are like a god."

His lips moved to Eli's chin, then neck.

Eli's eyes fluttered shut and he raised his head, ignoring the fact that Cleo was stirring on his lap. He moved his little friend onto the bench and slid closer to Duncan. A fire raged in his stomach, ignited by the soft kisses. "I'm not a god," he whispered. "Just a magician."

"No, Eli," Duncan corrected, raising his head to kiss Eli's cheek. "You are much, much more." Taking his hand, he pulled Eli to his feet. "Come, let me show you what you truly are."

Maybe it was his curiosity or the passion in Duncan's voice and eyes, he wasn't lying about his feelings, but Eli allowed his rival to lead him back to the castle. Cleo's protests fell on deaf ears.

Sinclair Manor was one of the largest and oldest in mansions England. Built way back in the Middle Ages, it had over eighty bedrooms, although not even half were in use. It was a sanctuary for any Sinclair or their descendants. Until eight years ago, Jonathan Sinclair had ruled the manor. Anthony's father had lived to be in his early hundreds.

Now his grandson, Richard, had taken over. He had taken after Jonathan in every way. He ruled over the Sinclair clan with an iron fist, sifting through those with strong magickal potential and those who posed a danger. Such as Elijah Hawke. There were many reasons for that. His strange quietness, powerful aura, and defiant nature. Training his was impossible. He followed his own path, much as Anthony had before him. It didn't mean he wasn't welcomed. Far from it. Richard encouraged it as much as possible. Anthony's old bedroom was reserved for the young sorcerer. Indeed, Eli's future was the talk of the house.

It was something Selena had grown to resent and was happy Nan had taken custody of Eli rather than any other member of the Sinclair family. Mae had decided it was safer for Eli to be with her, someone who loved him for being himself and not simply the reincarnation of her late brother. She never pushed him past his limits. It had been the biggest fight amongst all the Sinclairs, Richard had reason to fear Eli. So much power was hard for one person to control and he was fearful that one day it may come to control him rather than the other way around. Mae had been a good teacher and had Aaliyah and Henry to help her, but Selena could not help but worry now. So much had happened. What if Eli finally lost control? What if he became the threat Richard feared? No one knew the full extent of Raven's power, even split in half, and no one knew what Chaos's power was. Mixed together, they could spell devastation. She knew, without knowing, that if such power was unleashed there would be no stopping Eli. Short of killing him, and that was one thing she refused to let happen.

Standing in the great hall, she wondered, had Nan done the right thing? Would Eli's power have been more stable if he had been trained by the Sinclairs? Would any of the bullshit with the High Council have happened if they had been there to interfere?

"Perhaps. Perhaps not." A deep, thick British voice answered her thoughts. A tall, muscular man with dark brown hair and eyes and an expensive Armani suit, stepped into the great chamber. "Nothing is coincidental. Destiny would have found him either way."

"Destiny?" she mocked, leaning against the large round table. "It's his destiny to suffer? To be tormented?"

"Perhaps. Even the greatest of sorcerers must suffer to gain wisdom." The older sorcerer sighed and sat on the edge of the table as well, foregoing the seats as Selena preferred. Formalities were saved for group meetings. "A shadow has befallen the young man. His future is cloudy, destiny uncertain."

"What do you mean?"

He shook his head. "Many things. He could become the Oracle he was born to be or…or the string of destiny has come to its end. It could be worse, however. Chaos may very well descend the Earth at his hands. He still holds much of its power, but nothing is certain at this point."

The Sight, much like Eli's, allowed Richard to pierce the veil of time and space, see what few mortals, even those with magick, could see. To learn he could not determine Eli's future was disconcerting. Her fears grew. What had Henry got Eli into? Why was his future so undeterminable? "Someone with Sinclair magick entered his room the other night," she said absently.

He raised his head. "What?"

"I'm not sure. There's a strange mix of magick. Sinclair and something...darker, tainted but familiar."

The middle-aged man raised a brow. "Before his disappearance?" She gave a small nod.

"Odd. No one of our clan would do such a thing."

Her eyes closed. "He was frightened, confused. Said he didn't remember a thing. I'm sure whomever it was is also holding him."

"If it is a Sinclair, we can track him, but... No. It couldn't be..." He fell into deep thought as she fingered one of the beautifully craved chairs. "Eli is eighteen, correct? And Dion is in his mid-forties. Hmm...perhaps...perhaps this is destined." He held out his hand. "Come. There is something I should have shown you years ago."

Confused, she followed him through the winding corridors to the old library. What could he possibly mean by all this being destined?

Cleo frowned in worry. More-so than ever before. Eli was laying sound asleep, spooned against Duncan, their fingers intertwined. The most recent *test* had taken a lot out of Eli, but he seemed oddly content, happy even wrapped in Duncan's warm embrace. It was a complete change from earlier that morning.

If only Eli could see this was all a ploy set into motion by Henry and Duncan. He didn't seem to understand that this was exactly how things were supposed to be. He was forced to take refuge in Duncan. Yet Cleo didn't have the heart to separate them, not at the moment anyway. He could not remember the last time Eli looked so peaceful in his sleep. No nightmares, visions, or flashbacks.

Duncan was propped on one elbow, lovingly playing with Eli's long ebony, locks that made him look so feminine yet strong, and all the little things about Anthony that now reflected in Eli. Cleo was sure that was the only reason Duncan was so interested in Eli. The look in his eyes was anything but malevolent. They were tender as he pulled the sheet to Eli's shoulder and kissed his cheek.

The warlock climbed out of bed and put his shirt back on, but instead of leaving, sat back down and watched the sleeping mage a little longer. It was almost like the days when Anthony was dying and Duncan was caring for him. It was a little disconcerting. He had the same look he had the day he realized his magick could not save Anthony.

"You're so sad, Raven," he whispered to Eli. "Far more than when you were Anthony. Why?"

"Is he alright?" Cleo finally asked in worry, his curiosity getting the best of him.

Duncan gave a small nod. "Just fine. Exhausted."

"No doubt."

"If I could only channel his power. Figure a way to destroy or transfer whatever Chaos gave him. Then maybe…" he sighed and reached over to touch Eli's bare shoulder. He pushed back a stray lock of hair. "Why won't he let me train him? Why does he have to be so stubborn? He finally lets me touch him, love him and he still rebels."

"That surprises you?"

Duncan almost laughed. "No. Raven's spirit is strong." He shook his head. "He doesn't understand the danger he poses. He doesn't remember what a threat the eclipse poses when mixed with the power of Chaos. Perhaps there's another way, something I missed." He turned to face Cleo. "What would Anthony want most in the entire world? What does his heart still yearn for?" A smile spread quickly across his lips as the answer donned on him. "Cleo, take care of him. I'll be back soon."

Confused, Cleo watched as the young man rushed out the door.

What Anthony wanted most? What did he mean by that? All Anthony ever wanted was peace and to be left alone. He shook his head. Porter was insane, that was all there was to it. Jumping onto the large bed, he sat next to Eli. His young master smiled happily in his sleep as Cleo curled up next to him.

Eli was not sure what scared him more—standing in the training room once more or awakening to find his eyes as black as obsidian. They were slowly returning to normal, but the change was unexplainable. All he could figure was the exchange of magickal energies he had with Duncan. The spell Duncan had used to relax him had more of an effect than either of them had expected. Eli couldn't remember the last time he had felt such passion toward anyone. Thankfully, Duncan had kept him from doing anything he would have regretted. He really didn't have time to ponder any of it right now.

The room filled with holographic projections, simulating real-life terrain. Everything looked so real, the rolling hills, the bright summer sun. The moon was unusually bright as well and incredibly close to the sun. An eclipse? He shielded his eyes as the silvery orb moved over the sun.

Something inside him burned in reaction. A pulsing in his chest, not his heart, propelled him to levitate. Floating high above the false earthy ground, he drew in every bit of magick that resided in the castle. Focusing it into a small ball, he thrust it before him. Its glow grew brighter than a thousand suns, nearly blinding him as he attempted to open a gate. Its brilliance was surreal.

Inside the orb, he could see into other realms. People, places, and creatures, he had never seen before danced before him. He stared at it in awe. So many worlds. He raised his hand to the glowing sphere.

If only he could open a door to one of them.

Eli, no! Anthony warned, but Eli refused to listen.

Just one portal. Give Henry what he wants and he would be set free. As his hand neared the orb, it began to pulsate, growing brighter until it exploded, unleashing its force upon Eli. He was thrown back by the sudden force. Landing heavily on the ground, he whacked his head, dazing himself. Shaking his head, he gazed up. A small dazzling tear cut through the fabric of space. He stared at it letting his magick see into the other side. His eyes widened.

"Mum? Da?"

He reached out to the two-inch portal. It couldn't be. It wasn't possible. Yet he saw them as clear as day. His heart raced as the tiny portal grew smaller.

"No! Wait! Don't go!"

His bruised limbs refused to move. Summoning all his power, he tried to keep the portal from closing. If what he saw was truly his parents, he had to see them. He had to make sure they were okay...but his magick failed him. It vanished in a blink.

"No!"

Henry's large arms were suddenly around him, preventing him from going after the small portal.

"No. No, you've done what you could. You need your rest before we try again," the old man commanded gently.

Eli fought, more desperately than ever before. "I saw them! I saw them!"

"Who?"

Even as the question was asked, Eli could feel Henry lower his head to his shoulder. The sleeve of his tank top pulled aside and his foster grandfather's lips met bare flesh. Eli felt a soft pull, the same as the day before as his magick slipped from him. He wanted to fight, wanted to make Henry stop, but his promise to Duncan prevented him from doing so. He reluctantly did as Duncan requested. Tilting his head to the side, he let Henry feed. It wasn't painful, not like last time. In fact, other than becoming sleepy, he felt nothing.

"Hmm...that's enough for now," Henry whispered, letting Eli recuperate in his arms. "Who did you see?"

"My parents," he said softly, resting his head against Henry's broad chest like he use to as a child.

"Anyone else?"

It took a moment to recall. His mind felt fuzzy. "I don't remember."

"A woman? Blonde? Think, Eli. Did you see her?"

"I...I can't remember."

Henry growled, but reframed from striking him. Stroking Eli's long hair, he grinned. "It doesn't matter. The first stage has begun. Soon you'll be strong enough to open the portals. Both halves will finally be reunited."

Chapter Fifteen

They were on their way to Cambridge. He could sense them as they headed to Sinclair Manor. Tracking them was easy. Their added magick was like a flashing beacon. Skipping through space and time, it was easy to catch up with the SUV between East Retford and Newark. His sudden presence and magickal aura must have caught the driver off guard. The vehicle skidded to the side of the highway and came to a stop. It was exactly as Duncan and Henry had planned.

After leaving Eli asleep, he had gone to Henry's chambers filled with excitement. He was positive he knew what was wrong with Eli. He wasn't just being stubborn. Even if he was one of the most powerful magicians in the world, his power came from his past life, from Raven, and he only possessed half Raven's spirit, which meant he was not nearly as strong as he once was. Forfeiting half his magick to Dion only weakened him more. Then there were the magickal tools, books, and Guardians. They were a part of Raven's daily life. With only Serenity and Cleotro, Eli must have felt lost and lonely. Well, that was going to change. First to reclaim the tools and then Dion, the books, and the Guardians would surely follow.

The problem was how to convince Dion's daughter to surrender them. From the months of observation, he knew Alexis Dion had become very close to *her* Guardians. Eli was very fond of her and her friends. Hurting any of them would only push him into further depression. Duncan had to work carefully. If the woman was as naive as she appeared this would be easy.

Soon Eli would be whole once more.

The passenger side door opened and a tall, dark-haired man stepped out. He motioned for the driver, whom Duncan guessed was Nathaniel in his human form, and the others to stay calm. Duncan knew from the magick he and Eli had exchanged that this was Scott, Nathaniel's fiancé, and Alexis's big brother. His magick wasn't as strong as the others, but he was a seer. His sight gave him an advantage over the others.

The young man approached the limo cautiously.

Duncan could feel his senses stretching, searching him. Time for introductions, he decided. Not waiting for his chauffeur to open the door, he got out and walked to the front of the long, black car. He smiled politely and bowed his head. "Mr. Scott Dion, my name is Michael. I'm a friend of Eli's."

The young man, approximately three years older than Duncan's present form, froze and stared at Duncan. "Where is he?"

"Safe…sort of."

"What do you mean?"

Duncan gestured to the van. "May I speak to your sister? She has something that belongs to him."

Scott's eyes wondered to the driver side of the van. They could both sense Nathan's anxiousness. "I don't see how that's your business. If Eli wants it, bring him to us."

The guy was smart, no doubt about that. Probably would not let Duncan near the woman without the proper incentive. "He's rather occupied."

Raising his hand, Duncan produced a crystal orb. Inside, an image of Eli-Raven struggling against the robotic arms as the water rose in the training room. "You see, Eli's magick is failing him. Only Lady Alexandria has what is needed to save him."

Maybe Nathaniel saw everything through the rearview mirror, or maybe his connection and love for Dion allowed him to see through the taller man's eyes, but he was out the car door instantly. He transformed to his faery form in mid-stride and Scott literally had to grab him to prevent the faery from attacking Duncan.

"Let him go!" bellowed the enraged fey. Silver ice crystals formed in his hand even as Scott forced that hand down.

"Nathaniel, hmm…I heard the happy news. Congratulations."

His eyes glowed in rage. "What do you want?"

So easy. Nathaniel, or Frost as he seemed to prefer being called in this form, would do anything for Anthony. "Raven's tools, we both know Eli should have them. That's why his magick does not obey him. Yet everyone still wants him. Time is running short."

Indeed, it was. The robotic arms pulled Eli underwater.

Frost's eyes almost bulged at the sight. He trembled in rage and fear.

"Call Alexis, Frost. Tell her to give me the tools."

"No…" The fey's voice trembled.

Duncan tried another angle, knowing he had only a short time before Eli would free himself. "How long can he hold his breath? Three to four minutes. Maybe more if his magick works. Perhaps even a minute or two? He is such a strong swimmer, but he is still only human."

Frost's eyes closed, fearful. "No," he suddenly said, his voice cold. "I can't sense him. How do we know that's not just a projection?"

The fey was smart. Always had been. So maybe this wasn't going to be so easy. It was time for plan B. He had been prepared just in case. After spending days with Eli, he had become capable of creating any number of illusions of the young man. The vision of Eli under water stayed, but instead of freeing himself, he struggled until he could no longer hold his breath. Bubbles escaped his mouth and seconds later, the young man passed out.

Frost's eyes were fearful at the sight. Perfect!

Pulling out his cell phone Duncan, pretended to call the castle. "William, get him out of there quick. What? Damn it, man! Have you not been keeping an eye on him? Take him to the infirmary now!"

They watched in horror as the water drained until Eli was lay motionless on the ground. The image closed in on Eli to show he was breathing. Barely.

Duncan made himself look distressed. "Damn! He'll be fine, I assure you. We have the best doctors in England, but…he really does need his tools, Frost. His magick isn't what it used to be."

Now Alexis and the future Syffern Clan head were getting out of the SUV. The girl was running and her boyfriend tried to hold her back. Seeing Eli in the crystal ball made them terrified. Easy prey.

"Will he be alright?" she pleaded in a trembling voice.

"I don't know." Opening his senses, he slipped into her mind. She was an open book to him. Her metaphysical shields were not as strong as Eli's and, as he discovered to his surprise, she had never had the need to hide her thoughts. They were pure, like her body. Love and concern for her family and friends filled her. She was just as Eli described her.

You have the power to help him, he whispered into her mind. *Raven's mystical tools can heal him. The crystals have healing magick.*

She seemed to take the bait, her hand going to the pouch on her hip. "Can the crystals really help him?" she asked, staring at the orb as one of his servants picked up Eli's unconscious form.

"I hope so. Raven had a strong bond with them. It may still exist." Or at least he hoped.

"Alexis, no," Miao said harshly. "He's lying."

Scott nodded in agreement. "You can't surrender them. Not even for Eli."

Nevertheless, the woman was unsure, concerned with her friend's safety. She stared up at Duncan with pleading eyes, begging for the truth. Her telepathy was not nearly as strong as Eli's, but they seemed so much alike. Almost like two sides of the same coin.

Eli's light.

Duncan had the urge to touch her, share his magick as he had with Eli. Learn all her secrets. There had to be a reason Raven had chosen her as his heir rather than Eli.

She stared up at her brother for a moment as she chewed her bottom lip. Her hand fell to her pouch. "Celeste," she called to the spirits within the crystals. "What do the spirits think?"

The spirit in question appeared before them. Her long cotton-candy pink hair swirled around her as her butterfly wings framed her. "We fear for Raven's reincarnation's safety, but it is our Mistress' decision. We will follow your wishes."

"I…" She swallowed hard. "Protect Eli. Take care of him and return to me safely." Tears slid from her closed eyes.

Why was she not fighting him? Surely she was not this trusting? Her emerald eyes were mirrors of Eli's sapphire ones. No, she did not trust him. He could feel the binding spell she was placing on her tools. No one but she or Eli would be able to call upon them. That was alright. Duncan had no interest in using them.

Miao grabbed Alexis's hand before she could hand over the pouch.

"No!" he growled, pulling her back toward the SUV. "Eli would not want this!"

"But he's hurt! Maybe dying!"

"We don't know that."

"I do! I can feel him."

That seemed impossible. Not even Frost could sense him. There was something different about her. A sense he had not felt in almost sixty years. There was more to her, a reason her connection to Eli was so strong. Her eyes, hair…she looked like a Sinclair. An older version of…Elizabeth Sinclair, Anthony's baby sister. No, she couldn't be. Yet it explained so much—their desperation to protect each other. The way Eli would often buy her stuff without a thought of price of reward. Duncan doubted either of them even knew of their connection. It gave him another angle to work with. "He's like a brother, isn't he, Alexis?" he asked carefully, not wanting to alert her too much. "If it were Scott or Frost you would surrender the crystals. Why not him?"

"She'll fight first," Scott growled.

The elder Dion took him by surprise when he roundhouse kicked him. The wind knocked out of him in a whoosh as he hit the ground. Scott was fast. He grabbed the collar of Duncan's shirt and raised a fist to his face, threatening to break his jaw.

"Do yourself a favor, kid, take us to Eli and you might walk out of this."

Duncan just stared at him wide-eyed. He had definitely underestimated the young man. Scott was not only fast, but also strong and agile. He needed a new plan. Staring up at Scott with wide, frightened eyes, he began to tremble slightly.

"They'll kill him!" he suddenly exclaimed. "They said if anyone followed me, he's dead! You don't understand. His powers, those that demon gave him, are out of control. They had a priest try to cleanse him, rid him of the evil, but they couldn't. That's why they're testing him. If they weaken him enough they could cast the demonic powers out."

"And the crystals?"

"To help him recover."

"Who?"

"The—the High Council."

"Where?"

"I can't tell you."

He pushed everything he had into Dion's mind, eliminating all doubt of his truthfulness. He made Scott believe him.

Scott glanced at Frost, who had his mystic bow aimed at Duncan's head. "Well?"

"He was the one in Eli's room the other night. Same magickal aura." His violet eyes narrowed. "I don't trust him."

But what if Eli dies? Duncan mentally whispered.

The psychic message made Frost reconsider. "But can we take the chance?"

Sighing, Scott let Duncan go. "No, but we can't just hand over the crystals. How can you guarantee he and those spirits will be safe?"

"Give me three days. I swear they'll be safe. I'll protect Eli with my life."

He wasn't lying. He would give his life for the young mage.

Reluctantly, Miao let Alexis go. Hurrying to them, she shoved the pouch in Duncan's hands.

"If anything happens to them or Eli, I swear I'll hunt you down and show you just what power they have," she swore with a growl.

Flabbergasted by her threat, he could simply nod. Maybe she wasn't the cream puff he had thought.

"I understand," he said with a gracious bow. Backing away, he kept his gaze on the magick users. They were nothing like he had expected. Far tougher. Yet somehow his plan had still worked with little more than a few bruises. Slipping into the limo, he ordered the driver to take him home. He still had a meeting with the High Council.

Hopefully, they could keep Alexis and her friends busy until after the eclipse.

Alexis's eyes glowed softly as she silently called out to her spirits. "Shadow and Mist, create a trail for us to follow. Keep it attached to me and Eli at all times. Stay hidden from all outsiders," she whispered.

A thin shadowy line, not an inch thick, slipped from her feet and attached itself to the rear of the limo. A small layer of mist concealed it. Turning on her heel, she marched back to the SUV. She eyed each of them. "Let's find Selena. We can track Eli in a few hours," she commanded, taking charge of their small group.

***

Run!

The command rung through his ear like a gunshot, but he did not question it. He ran down the smoky corridors as fast as his little feet would carry him. His small body stung, his legs still felt numb, but he refused to stop. He had to escape. If he didn't, the strange man would hurt him again. Touch him in ways he knew were wrong. The man was close, his shadow demons lapping at his bare feet.

Stay ahead of them. Don't let them touch you, the voice warned.

They moved in ways that were beyond human logic. Every time he fell under the hall light, creating his own shadow, they leapt at him. He was almost at the door when one wrapped around his ankle and pulled him to the marble floor. He squealed in fear as the shadow began to consume him. It was cold, numbing. The feeling to his feet was lost, soon followed by his lower legs, then knees. He screamed as it neared his hips.

"Help! Cleo! Selena! Help me!" It was at his waist, nearing his chest. Not again! Please not again, he pleaded to the voice in his head. He felt sick, lightheaded.

"Somebody, please help me," he whispered, reluctantly succumbing to the creature. His eyes closed and he lay back as it moved closer to his shoulders. He was so cold. The eight-year-old was barely conscious of the blue flame that suddenly consumed the creature. Warmth filled his body, but the grogginess refused to leave. A warm muzzle rubbed his cheek. "Hmm..." he moaned, trying to force his eyes open.

"Master Eli."

One eye finally opened to find his glasses askew on his nose. He fixed them and stared up into the black, furry face. "Cleo?"

It seemed like a dream. Rolling over, he wrapped his arms around the panther's neck and hugged him. He had never wanted to hug his Familiar so much in his life. Cleo nudged him onto his back.

"Hold on, little one. We're going home." Spreading his large black wings, they took to the air.

Eli held onto his guardian, trying desperately to come fully awake. The cold November wind tore through the thin material of his pajamas, chilling his flesh as they flew through the open bay window. They circled the castle in search of Selena.

A battle raged off the north perimeter. The scent of smoke and magick filled the air. The castle was on fire, something Eli had caused in his escape. Many magick users were trying to bring it under control while others fought off Selena's attacks. Lord Porter was not among them. Maybe the old man was dead.

Perhaps the fire had taken his life. It didn't seem possible.

"Selena!" Cleo bellowed, alerting her to Eli's safe rescue.

Happy to see them, she waved and left the battle to join them. Eli smiled. Good, they were together again. Now they could go home and forget the strange man.

Come to me.

That voice! Not Mr. Anthony's, but— He barely had a chance to ponder it before his eyes glazed over and he fell off Cleo's back. Three hundred feet in the air, he plummeted. Selena screamed his name as she and Cleo flew after him, crying out for him to use his magick.

He felt weightless, as if someone was carefully carrying him back to the burning castle. Old, seemingly frail arms caught him on the roof. A magickal shield wrapped around them, protecting them from the heat of the raging inferno and keeping the two Guardians at bay. Eli knew instantly, even through the haze of his mind, that Porter now held him. The man's aura snaked around his small form.

"Easy, Eli. That's enough," Porter said gently. "You know this is futile."

Eli could not struggle, could not even move under the spell Lord Porter had placed on him. Gently lowered to the roof, he found himself forced to stand as the old man knelt before him. Those hands that had abused him in so many unthinkable ways, cupped his cheeks. He wanted to pull away, cry out for help, but his voice was stolen from him as he stood like so many of the castle's many statues. He could not cry, no matter how much the tears threatened to come. Porter's thumbs brushed the edges of his eyes, under the large wire-rim glasses.

"Shh…shh…no need for that. I know you're scared and I'm sorry, but this is your home now. I will guard and protect you. In time, your Guardians can join us. I only wish to help you and love you as my own personal God." His head came close to Eli's. Dry lips brushed his forehead and moved slowly down his nose. "You are a God, Eli."

Those lips claimed him. Outwardly, he did nothing more than close his eyes, but inwardly Eli was screaming. He cringed inwardly. Why was this happening to him? Why wouldn't he leave him alone?

A white fire began burning in the pit of his stomach. It filled his eyes and reflected against the back of his eyelids. The fear left him as he felt it grow. It was the same force that had come to him earlier, that had helped him escape and set the castle on ablaze. He pulled at it, begging for its help. Just as Porter pulled him closer against his body, the force sprang forth, shoving the gray-haired man back.

The spell was broken. Eli had full control of his body once more. He ran out of the shield toward his frightened Guardians. The air was hot, smoking from the raging fire, trying to fill his lungs and block his route. Behind him, Porter was screaming for him not to run away. Eli knew the warlock was on his heels, trying to catch him once more. He fought his way through the thick smoke, more scared of Porter than the fire.

The fire was eating away at the roof. Nearing the peak, it gave out under him.

Eli didn't have a chance to scream…only react. Instincts from a lifelong past kicked in. He grabbed a barely singed railing and dangled over the raging fire.

"Eli!" he heard Selena scream. He knew they feared the worst.

"Selena! Cleo!" he called, trying to pull himself up.

Selena's beautiful face peered through the hole down at him. Relief covered her features. "Hold on tight," she instructed. "I'll be right down."

The hole was too small for the faery to fit through. She disappeared in search for another route to him.

His arms stung as he held the railing. It was getting hot, burning the palms of his hands. It hurt too much to fight the flood of tears.

"Eli?"

He gazed up to see Porter kneeling on the rail. He seemed at ease balancing on the thin rail metal.

"Hold still, Eli. I've got you."

"No!" he cried. He tried to move. His hands screamed in agony as he moved them along the rail away from his captor. The flesh tore, fused to the hot metal.

He cried even more.

"It's okay, Eli," Porter cooed, kneeling down further.

He wrapped his arms under Eli's and lifted him up. His magick once more wrapped around Eli, making him wrap his arms around the man's neck as they moved toward safety. Eli clung to him, not only because of the spell, but too scared and hurt to fight any more. His hands burned with such a heat that he feared he would never be able to use them again. Porter instructed him to wrap his legs around his waist for better support. He did so without question. They were nearing one of the huge windows when Cleo and Selena came crashing through two others.

The fire roared to life with the new source of oxygen.

Porter paused in confusion as he stared at the two Guardians. He placed a hand against a wooden beam for balance. Steam came from the contact of ice and fire.

"Let him go!" the great cat bellowed, firing his blue fireball at him.

Too surprised to block the attack, Porter was only able to turn enough to spare Eli from more injury. The second shot shook his grip on him. He let go against his will. His footing slipped and they both plunged to their deaths.

Eli cried out in fear, but the flames never engulfed him. Opening his eyes, he found Selena cradling him. He threw his tiny arms around her and cried on her shoulder as she and Cleo flew him to safety. She held him close, ensuring everything would be alright.

The other magick users did not stop them as they flew to the waiting vehicle. His teacher and Watcher, Aaliyah McNeil, ran to the passenger side and opened the door. Cleo changed to his borrowed form in mid-flight and went inside. Selena changed shortly after touching down. The soft fabric of her red and cream gown changed into a wool burgundy sweater and jeans. She grunted as her strength returned to that of a fourteen-year-old girl's and was forced to move Eli's weight to one side in order to slip into the vehicle. Once inside, Aaliyah gunned the engine and they tore off into the black night.

It seemed an eternity before anyone spoke. Eli clung to Selena as if she were the only thing real near him. The rest was a dream. It had to be. Klaxons filled his ears as fire trucks raced to the burning castle. Cleo sat in the backseat, making sure they weren't followed while Selena chanted softly, her soft fingers carefully moving over his burned hands, slowly healing them.

After almost twenty minutes, thirty kilometers from the stronghold that had held him captive, Aaliyah slowed the car down and pulled to the side of the road.

She set it in park and undid her seatbelt.

"Eli…" she began, turning to face him.

He buried his face deeper into Selena's hair, not wanting anyone other than his Guardians touching him. He didn't want the Priestess to yell at him for what he did. A sharp cry of protest escaped his lips as she pulled him out of his faery's arms. She placed him on her lap and hugged his trembling form.

"I'm so sorry. I had no idea they would want to keep you. Are you alright? Did they hurt you?"

He nodded before he could stop himself. He wiped at his tears, but they refused to cease falling.

"Where?"

He froze and looked away, ashamed to even voice where Porter had touched him. Aaliyah knew just by his actions. Biting her lip, she gestured to his groin.

"Down there?"

Once again, he nodded against his will.

"By the Goddess!" she cried, hugging him tight.

His head rested against her breast as she shook in fury. He had never seen her so angry.

"We're going to the hospital," she suddenly declared, handing him back to Selena.

"N-no!" he pleaded, trying to come up with a good excuse. "I…I look just like Raven. He wanted to touch me…feel me. I couldn't stop him. I tried. Honest…but he…he took control of me. Made me. I was too weak. I should've been able to stop him. It's my fault!" A new batch of tears took hold of him as he pleaded for forgiveness.

Selena's arms tightened around him. "No…honey, it's okay," the faery cooed.

"It's my fault," he continued to cry. "I let him."

Aaliyah shook her head, cupping his wet cheek. "No, Eli. You're just a child. Lord Porter is a grown man. He should know better, but he's a very sick man. None of this is your fault. It's his. Remember that."

"Aaliyah…"

Eli slowly opened his eyes, squinting at the harsh sunlight. What was that? He could not recall anything like that ever happening to him. He could still feel the childhood fear he had. How he had fought not to go to the hospital. How he hated the doctors touching and probing him. Even awake, he could see his child self sit in the kids' playroom while Aaliyah talked to his grandmother and the doctors. Selena was sitting next to him, trying desperately to cheer him. His face buried in her shirt as he pleaded for her to make him forget even as Anthony's voice warned it was the wrong course of action, that it would only make matters worse in the future. He had not cared at the moment. It was the only way to keep his sanity. Selena, bless her heart, had done as he requested.

She had switched forms and placed her power-hand on his forehead. She *erased* all the pain and suffering he had gone through that week and replaced the missing memories with a happy post Halloween week where they tormented Cleo with sweets, played games, and went to school as they normally would. He could barely remember Aaliyah and Nan reprimanding Selena for such a foolish act.

Duncan must be pulling these memories back. Not all of them. He was thankful for that. Whatever happened in the past to scare him so could not have been good by any means. It was obvious he was molested, perhaps even… He shook his head. No, Duncan would never do such a thing to an eight-year-old. He had his problems, yes, but he would never, couldn't possibly harm a small defenseless child. Could he? If he did, why would he want him to remember now? Wouldn't that only turn him against the warlock? Unless it was Anthony trying to show him the truth.

Of course, just when he was beginning to like the guy, Anthony had to show him some revelation. It did explain Selena and Cleo's reaction to Porter-Duncan when he appeared in Ravenwood. If he had been hurt in any way, they would have defended him and kept him hidden in any way possible. It was only natural; they were his Guardians.

He brushed his fingers over Cleo's tiny form. No wonder the mighty familiar worried so. He had not been able to protect him when he was little so felt it necessary to do all in his power now to protect him. Silly little familiar. It wasn't his fault. None of them knew what was going to happen. There was little any of them could have done to avoid it. Live and learn, that's what Anthony would say. At least they had escaped. He wasn't going to brood about it.

No, he was going to find out the truth. If Duncan had indeed hurt him as a child, there was hell to pay. The castle being engulfed in flames all those years ago would look like a camp barbecue compared to what he would do this time. A firm, large hand squeezed his shoulder as he moved to sit up. Gray suit pants met his vision as he noticed his head lay on Henry's lap.

"Slowly, Eli. Not so quick or you'll get dizzy again," the former General advised, adjusting himself to up Eli up. He kept one arm around Eli. "You passed out after the training session."

"After you fed on me," Eli corrected, repulsed by the fact he was sitting so close to the man who had murdered his parents.

"Yes, well considering the amount of magick you expelled, it was to be expected. Extensive use of magick always had a tendency to tire you. Sleep and sunlight were always the quickest way to restore your power."

"I didn't use that much magick."

"You'd be surprised. You were off the charts."

"Humph!"

Henry frowned and let him go. "So much rage for one so young."

"Live my life and ask me *why*." Eli stood, picking up Cleo as he did so. He stepped out of the shade and looked out over Duncan's vast property, then to the old castle. Everything was as it were in his dream. Except the castle looked almost new. Obviously, it had been repaired after the fire.

He turned back to Henry. "You murdered my parents. Destroyed my life. Why? So, Duncan could make me his lover? So, you can have an everlasting supply of food? How many times did you feed from me before bringing me here?"

He gestured at Henry's more youthful build. Indeed, the power he took was decreasing his age. He now looked as if he were in his mid-fifties. His gray hair had almost completely returned to strawberry blonde. He even seemed more muscular if that were possible.

"A few times," Henry admitted, lighting his pipe. "Usually when you were asleep. I tried to resist, but after watching you and Duncan make love, I finally gave in." He looked off into the distance before looking up into Eli's troubled eyes. "Ever wonder why, when you hardly ever get sick, you managed to catch the flu so hard when you were twelve? Or why for a week you had pneumonia and no one could figure out how or why? Every time you generate a large dose of magick, it took a few days to recover. You would not have noticed, Eli," he explained, noting the hurt in Eli's face. "I would sit next to you, maybe read you a bedtime story or just check up on you, and hold your hand, kiss your forehead and drink in just a little. Enough to quench the thirst. I tried to never take enough to hurt you."

"And when Duncan posed as Frost that night?"

"I drank from your lips. You were in such a trance that you never cared."

Disgusted, Eli turned on his heel. "Don't expect that to happen again, Henry. Once I'm free, you'll never see me again, except, perhaps, in your nightmares. Believe me…that can be *very* possible."

Henry only laughed as Eli stormed off. "Not until you're nineteen, my little Raven. Until then you're mine to do with as I please. Be happy it's your magick I want. You would not survive some of the things I can do to your body."

Eli forced himself not to run as the man taunted him. Evil, far worse than Chaos, he thought. He sighed. No, the demon had been just as bad. Why had Anthony not known about Henry? Had he been fed on as well? Maybe it was buried deep into his subconscious.

He didn't know. Didn't want to either. This was all too much. He had to figure out what Duncan had done to him when he was eight first, then he would deal with Henry. Yes. All he needed now was a plan and a way to learn the truth. Then, hopefully, find a way to escape.

Placing Cleo on his shoulder, he walked back to the castle. The answers he sought were hidden somewhere in there. He remembered Duncan showing him a massive library in the west wing. It was three stories high and took up over an acre of the castle. Duncan said he was welcome to any book, even spell books. Maybe he could find something to counter the spell placed on him as well as find a way out. It would take forever, even with his magick, to sort through all those books, but it was worth a try.

After changing into some clean clothes, the others full of sweat from the training session, he stood in the center of the library. Using his magick, he called out to the spell he needed, summoning the correct book with his heart. It took an eternity for his mind to scan through the thousands, maybe even millions of books. So far nothing. After an hour, he had not even reached a tenth of the books and his head was beginning to hurt.

"Eli, you're going to wear yourself out," Cleo warned as the young man removed his glasses and rubbed his weary eyes. "Sit down."

"Hmm...no. I've got to—" he blinked when he found Cleo pushing him onto a step, "—find a spell."

"It won't help if you pass out. What if Duncan finds you sprawled on the floor?" His small brows came together at the thought. "Then again he may leave you alone for a few days. Too worn out."

Eli leaned on the seat. No, Duncan would go nuts if that ever happened. Probably make him go to bed and nurse him until he was well. Duncan would not leave his side, making it impossible to find an avenue of escape or the whole truth. Staring at the mosaic ceiling, he sighed. "We've got to get out of here," he murmured. "I haven't seen a phone or computer anywhere and that blasted shield is too strong for my magick. I can't even reach Selena telepathically."

Cleo curled up on his lap. "Maybe he has an office somewhere. There should be a phone there. Probably tapped, but it'll be better than nothing."

"We don't even know where we are." It seemed hopeless. Absolutely hopeless. All he knew was they were beside the Irish Sea, in a castle hidden in time and space. Even if Selena remembered the location of it, she would never be able to break through the shield. Her magick was only as strong as his, and that was very limited at the moment. Maybe, just maybe, her power mixed with Frost's,

Alexis's and Sif's could break it.

The castle was huge. How would he ever find the office before Duncan returned? Cleo sat next to him as he stood. Time was running out, they had better start the search.

Oddly enough, it had not taken half as long as Eli had figured. His senses picked up a very guarded section on the second floor. It seemed a little odd that an office would be guarded, and by two Lycanthropes no less. Did Duncan suspect he would attempt a break-in? With Cleo at his side, he hid around the corner and watched as the guards talked. Neither had any serious magick. Nothing he couldn't handle at least.

The younger of the two seemed the easiest. His mind was untrained, no metaphysical shields to protect him. Eli planted a desperate need to use the bathroom in his mind. A small ache in the groin helped hurry the man along. Giving his partner a pleading apology, he took off down the hall.

The older guard was not at all pleased. He wanted a break, needed a coffee and donut. Apparently, he wasn't being paid enough to stand in front of some doors all day. He was a former American police officer spending his retirement in England, apparently the wife's idea.

He hated the rain.

His mind was a pit of loathing that was quickly giving Eli a headache. The guy obviously hated working for some *British brat*, but he was planning on screwing Duncan out of millions. Tell the tabloids about his little secrets, or take his frustrations out on him in other ways if he didn't get his money. *Nasty bastard*, Eli concluded. Maybe there was a way to work on the man's greed.

"Now what?" Cleo asked, peering around the corner.

"Hmm…"

Eli pulled out the Totem from his shirt, more than thankful Duncan had not taken it from him. He chanted softly, calling forth the powers of the elements to transform it. The golden totem morphed into his staff. He held it high. "Spirits divine, create a mirrored image of myself and Cleo."

A magickal mist swirled before them, reflecting their images perfectly. The mist solidified into perfect reflections of them. Eli smiled happily at his creations. "Two are always better than one."

"I doubt Selena would agree," Cleo teased.

Eli only laughed. "She loves us."

He peered around the corner again. The Lycanthrope had yet to smell their scent. Turning back to his twin, he raised a finger to his lips, singling it not to talk. "Listen," he said softly. "I want you two to lead him away long enough for us to get inside. I'll call you when we're ready to leave. I'll need you to distract him again. Understood?"

"Yeah," the other Eli said.

He, too, peered around the corner.

"Be careful. I don't know when Porter's coming back," he warned. His eyes widened in surprise when his twin suddenly hugged him.

"You, too," the spirit said before he and the second Cleo took off down the hall.

They got the guard's attention instantly. He started yelling about restricted areas before chasing after them. Eli waited almost a full minute before slipping into the office with Cleo. It was large and surprisingly high-tech. A huge screen covered one wall. Shelves of books, CD ROMs, video tapes and DVDs lined the wall behind the desk. A PC and laptop sat upon the desk next to an old-fashioned phone. Pictures old and new hung from the walls, sat on the desk, and took up what free space there was on the shelves.

Eli felt as if he had just entered the Twilight Zone or the Hall of Raven. The pictures on the walls were portraits of Anthony Sinclair, ranging from his childhood to the time of his death. The small pictures scattered throughout the room, which almost tripled in number, were of him. He stared at them in a mixture of horror and awe. He found baby photos and rare ones of him with his parents. There were even a few with Selena and Cleo where he wore his battle costume. It was disturbing. He could not figure when most of them were taken. It looked as if Duncan had someone spying on him all his life. It was not what he had expected. He thought he would find pictures of Duncan's family, his children, wife, and grandchildren. Not this.

"I think he surpassed obsession," Cleo whispered. He flew around the room. He landed on the shelf and began searching for the spell book while Eli moved around the desk. "Let's just hurry and get out of here. This is starting to creep me out."

"Yeah," Eli muttered as he picked up a picture of him and his parents. It had been Christmas, Henry dressed as Santa Claus while his mother helped him unwrap his present. His father was smiling proudly down at him. He had to have only been two in it. He smiled sadly at it as he traced his fingers over his mother's form. She had been so beautiful.

Blinking back tears, he picked up the phone and dialed the cabin's number. After ten rings, he hung up. Okay, no one there. Probably still searching for him…or gone home. He shook his head. No, they wouldn't leave him.

He began punching in Selena's cell phone number when something caught his attention. Placing the receiver back on its cradle, he stared at the black photo album. It had a strange feeling to it. Duncan's aura was recent on it. More photos. Not of him hopefully. The knot in his stomach grew tighter as he opened it. Sure enough, a large picture of him covered the first page. There was a note underneath.

Elijah Derek Hawke, age 8. October 31
First Samhain with the High Council and Porter Family.
After hours of debate with the Sinclairs, it has been agreed Eli would spend a week with me and Sara. I'm surprised Richard allowed it, but due to the child's unusually strong magick, it is time to test his abilities and control.
Both Sara and I are surprised by just how much he has grown to look like Raven. He says his former self talks to him. He has drawn many pictures of Raven's Guardians. His skill is just as excellent as Anthony's. I hope it is in every other category as well.

There were many pictures showing the testing he went through. The whole event was documented. There were notes about videotaped tests, but other than the tests being a little harsh, there were no explanations to why he had been so scared of Duncan. Closing the book, he looked at the shelf. There *had* to be another album. This one was just for looks. A video tape drew him and next to it was the hidden album, half the size of the other and easily concealed. He pulled them both out. They felt cold, unnatural. They were Duncan's most prized possessions. His chest knotted in fear. He did not want to look at them, but could not stop himself. Shoving the video in the VCR, he hit play.

"Hey, I found it!" Cleo announced, holding up a large book between his two front paws.

"Hmm…oh, good," Eli said, looking up from the VCR. "Hide it outside, somewhere safe. I'll meet you upstairs in twenty minutes."

"You sure? You can watch those in your room."

He shook his head. "No, I still got to get a hold of Selena and I don't want Duncan finding out I was watching these. I won't be long. Promise."

He waved as his little friend shrugged and opened the window. A moment later, he was out of sight.

Sitting back down, he quickly flipped through the photo album. Disgust filled him with every picture. Slamming the book shut, he glared at the video stream. The photos had strengthened his sudden hatred for Duncan. If the video was what he feared, he had more than enough to justify his outrage and need for retribution. He could already feel the power building within him.

The wall-mounted television came to life, revealing a child's bedroom. A little boy no more than seven or eight sat in the middle of the huge bed playing with what looked like a Transformer. The toy was floating in front of the child, its parts transforming from robot to tank and back. The boy's, obviously Eli, brows came together in concentration as he made the toy change forms. It had three or four of them. In tank mode, it's turret rotated until it faced the door. The door opened and a small missile shot at the elderly man stepping inside. A tiny smile came to the raven-haired boy's lips as the missile hit the man's shoulder.

Eli snickered at his younger self. Obviously, little Eli wasn't too fond of Porter back then either.

"Eli, that's not very nice. Is that any way to treat your grandfather?"

The little boy gave him a puzzled look. "You're not my grandfather."

Porter sat next to him, holding a large children's Fairytale book.

"'Course I am. I bought you all these cool toys and clothes, didn't I?"

"Yeah."

"And this is your room, right?"

Little Eli shrugged, playing with his Transformer. "I suppose."

"And you want me and Raven to be happy, don't you?"

The boy made his toy change again with his telekinesis. "Mr. Anthony is happy," he said innocently.

"He'll be happier if you're with me."

Porter gently raised his chin, making Eli look up at him.

"No."

"Why not?"

He shrugged, returning to his toy.

With a sigh and shake of his head, Porter pulled him onto his lap and opened the storybook. He held the child in ways not appropriate. Eli's anger grew as he watched his younger self's confusion. The child honestly didn't understand what was going on.

The limousine pulled in front of the old castle. Duncan smiled as he looked over the leather book, pouch of crystals, and magick tools. Everything was going as planned. It had taken years find Raven's book on dimensional gates. Although the language was one he could not read, he was sure it would be of some assistance to Eli. The young man's mind would quickly translate it. After all, he had written it in his past life. Even if Raven somehow warned him against it, curiosity was Eli's biggest weakness. He would study the book and learn. Then he would open the gates and Duncan would finally find peace. Soon…soon it will all be over.

He was tempted to slow time even more. As much as he wanted to end all this and let Eli get back to a normal life, he had grown very attached to Eli. He gave him a new reason to live. He wanted to show him so much. Not just in the sense of magick, but the world. Maybe after last night they would finally be able to be together. Truly together. To have their magick meld together as it had was amazing. Every sense, every touch, had been wide open, filled with light and brilliance. It was truly magickal.

Duncan was in love with Eli, so much more now that he was grown. There were things they could do now that they could not so many years ago. Eli looked identical to Anthony. He never realized just how much he had missed his former rival until recently. Hearing his voice through Eli's lips now and then was a rare treat. He was in love with Eli far more than he had been with Anthony. There was something that seemed missing in Eli that needed to be filled. Something he was sure he could fill.

After the confrontation with the young sorceress, he had placed a few rumors of her possibly attacking the High Council. Now all he could think of was wrapping his arms around Eli's warm body and watching the tide roll in under the sunset. Too bad it was not a full moon. The reflection would have been breathtaking. One day he would have to take the young mage sailing. According to Henry, Eli had never been out to sea. It was definitely an experience he would love to share with him.

He hummed to himself as he entered the castle's huge double doors, giving his butler a brief nod in greeting. Climbing the stairs, he gazed at the pouch of crystals. Their magick was vibrating as if they, too, felt the attraction of the reincarnation of their former master. He smiled.

The transformation would be easy. They would succumb to Eli's will as they were meant to. Soon everything would be as it should.

"Where is he?"

Duncan's head snapped up as Henry's voice boomed throughout the hall. Clenching the pouch and book tightly, he rushed into Eli's room, ignoring the guard nursing a broken nose. Henry, looking much younger and healthier, was shaking Eli by his upper arms. The youth's eyes were wide with fear, more than he had ever displayed before, even that first night. Yet there was something else odd about him...and Cleo. He could sense Raven's magick, but not Raven. The teenager was one of Anthony's spirits.

"Tell me!" Henry boomed.

"I...I don't know."

Rage flared in Henry's eyes and to Duncan's utter surprise and horror, he brought his hand across the fake Eli's face, sending him sprawling on the bed.

"I highly doubt he would want me to hurt one of his precious imps. You're only doing as he asks." Grabbing a fist full of hair, Henry yanked the spirit's head back. "Tell me where he is or I'll punish you just as I will Eli. Worse perhaps."

He brought his lips close to the spirit's ear.

"Do imps bleed?"

"That's enough!" Duncan finally growled, slamming the book and pouch on the dresser. "Let him go, Henry. He's terrified. You should have asked Claudia to scan his mind. It would have been faster."

Motioning Henry away from the scared spirit, he climbed onto the bed and sat next to him. The false Eli was trembling like a leaf. Stroking his tousled hair back, he placed his hands on either side of his face. If the aura weren't so different, he would have sworn it was Eli in his arms. However, this one was not as defiant as the real one. Opening his senses, Duncan swam through the youth's mind. Beneath the fear, an image emerged of the second floor. Eli, the real Eli, gestured for the fake one to distract the guard protecting his office. Something about contacting Selena Hawke.

He let the spirit go and sat back. "Damn, I should have known better." He gazed at the still hopping mad Henry. "He's downstairs, in my office. We may have trouble if he managed to contact Selena. How long has he been missing?"

"Almost an hour. They last saw him in the library."

Duncan frowned. That didn't give them much time.

Eli clenched his stomach as his younger self screamed in agony. He felt sick. How could anyone be so cruel and sick? The whole time the child cried, Porter spoke words of love, while stroking and caressing him. The child was a trembling pile of nerves being held tightly against the old man. When Porter was finished with him, he laid the child down.

Tears dotted Eli's eyes. *A pedophile*, he thought grimly. Duncan Porter was a pedophile. He had molested him when he was only eight. No wonder he had begged Selena to erase his memory. How could anyone live a normal life with something like that haunting them? He wished to the Gods he had never found the video or photo albums.

"Eli!"

He jumped at Duncan's voice. Blinking, he stared at the young man standing in the doorway. It was hard to believe he was the same man that had violated him so many years ago. He wanted so much to believe it was some mistake, that it never happened. That the Duncan Porter in the video was a different man, but he knew it was true. Everything Duncan had ever told him was a lie.

"Eight? I was eight when you first..." His voice cracked as the video continued to display his younger self-struggling against the man. "Why?"

The other man seemed genuinely confused. He gazed at the big television screen. His eyes widened. "Eli...Oh, God! How...no, you don't understand."

As Duncan rushed toward him, Eli lost his cool. All the rage he had been trying not to let loose suddenly unleashed itself. His powers pulsed, filling and strengthening his aura. The energy in the room became a crushing weight as his magick filled it. A hurricane of psychic power lifted the antique desk off the ground, scattering everything onto the ground and threw it through the large television screen. The numerous pictures shattered. Anything not bolted down rose and swung around the room, destroying everything it struck.

Duncan raised his shields, protecting himself and Henry from the flying objects. "Eli, stop! That's enough!" he ordered, inching his way closer.

Raven's magick circle appeared beneath Eli's feet. The windows exploded outward as the winds swept around him. He directed all his rage at Duncan, taking great pleasure at each attack that made it through the shield.

"Ugh!" Duncan cried, clenching his shoulder. "Henry, subdue him."

Eli's foster grandfather moved out of the shield, ignoring the objects flying at him. Eli's focus was entirely on his rival and he failed to notice Henry move behind him until it was too late. Henry hit the back of his head with one of the statues, causing Eli to crumple at his feet. His magick dispelled and everything fell to the ground.

The world spun as Eli raised his head. It hurt when he tried to focus. With a pitiful groan, he pushed himself to his knees. Too stunned by the blow, he could not avoid the large hands from grabbing his upper arms and pulling him into a bear hug with his back pressed firmly against Henry's chest. In such a position, Henry was able to easily absorb his magick and there was little he could do to stop him.

Duncan took his chin, forcing eye contact. Anger, fear, and worry, all were mixed in those eerie blue eyes. "What the hell were you doing? Selena won't find you. Not here."

"How could you? I was eight!" Eli demanded once more.

"Eli…" Sighing, Duncan pressed his lips against the mage's. "How could I not?"

Disgusted, Eli spat in his face. "I hate you," he sneered. It sounded childish, but it was true. "I will always hate you."

"One day you will learn to love me."

"I will die first."

Duncan's eyes saddened for a moment as he brushed long wispy strands of hair from Eli's eyes. "What am I to do with you? What can I do to make you love me? To make you understand this is for the best."

"Never."

Was he insane? Did he honestly think that after everything he had just seen that he would fall in love with him? Eli struggled against Henry's crushing embrace. There was no way he was ever letting Duncan touch him again.

Duncan rubbed his forehead. "We'll have to discipline you," he muttered. "Take him to his room. We'll deal with him and the other one there."

Why Henry decided to squeeze him tighter was beyond Eli. His ribs screamed in protest as his breath caught in his throat. Drawing air into his lungs only increased the pain. His vision soon became blurry from lack of oxygen. He fought the urge to close his eyes. He would not pass out. There was no way he would let what happened as a child happen again.

He lost track of time as Henry carried to his chamber. He found himself dumped on the floor, gasping for air. The twin of himself rushed to his aid. The spirit's arms wrapped around him protectively.

"Are you okay?" his twin asked, his voice wavering in fear.

Eli sucked in a deep breath. "No," he said flatly. He glared at Duncan as he stood over them. "Anthony always thought you were screwed up, but I don't think he ever considered just how sick you were."

"He knew I would love you from the moment you were born. Told me to stay away from you," Duncan explained. Yet his eyes still had sadness to them, as if he no more liked what happened than Eli did. "Even cast a spell to keep you and Daniel hidden. Worked on Daniel perfectly, but you...you were just too powerful." Folding his arms across his chest, he glanced at Henry and nodded. His eyes closed as the big man moved toward the twins. "I would have found you either way. Hmm...so who do we start with first?" A smile totally void of mirth crossed his lips as Henry snatched up the fake Eli.

"No!" Eli protested as his double cried out. "Illusion, re—"

Duncan moved as fast as lightning. He slapped a hand over Eli's mouth and poured his power into him. It overwhelmed the younger man, making it impossible for him to call the spirit back to its true form. Kneeling behind him, he forced Eli to watch as Henry dragged the spirit to a bare section of a wall.

No! Don't hurt him! Eli cried telepathically. He struggled and fought to be free, but Duncan's powers weakened him. He gasped inwardly as he felt a sense of regret wash over him. He tried turning his head just enough to see Duncan's face, but the magick refused to let him.

I'm sorry, was all he heard.

"Five straps for the imp. Then five for Eli," Duncan instructed Henry in his most commanding voice. "Maybe this will teach you to listen to us." Still the sense of regret filled each word.

Eli had no time to ponder it. Henry removed his belt and wrapped the buckle in one hand. The spirit was shoved face first against the wall. His screams mixed with the crack of the belt shattered Eli's heart. He would have screamed, too, in defiance of his poor spirit as he was whipped over and over again, but Duncan held him tight. All he could do was watch and pray.

Cleo frowned as he jumped through the open window. Stupid gardener had to spend nearly fifteen minutes chasing him with the hose. It had taken forever to hide the spell book. Then he heard Eli's screams. With the gardener trying to catch him, it was almost impossible to get back to the castle. Humans were such odd creatures.

The bedroom was oddly quiet. He had expected Duncan Porter to be with Eli. Something told him it would not have been one of his more pleasant visits. Whatever Eli had found before they had parted just didn't feel right. He knew he should have stayed with his young master.

The room was empty except for Eli asleep on the oversized bed. His back was to him, but he seemed okay. A little early for him to be sleeping though, he thought. The sheets lay over his body, not tangled in the slightest as they would be if Porter had been there. Surprised and curious, he jumped on the bed and padded up to his master.

"Eli?" he called softly, fearing the young man was sound asleep. He placed a paw on his back.

Eli hissed, wincing at his friend's touch. "Ahh... Cleo, please...don't."

Confused, Cleo pulled the sheets down his back and growled in rage. Nasty slashes marked the mage's back, running through his tattoo. They were raw, sticky with dried blood. He knew when he had felt Porter's aura that Eli would be punished if he were found in the office...but this? It didn't match the tenderness the warlock had shown that morning. At least Duncan had taken the time to clean most of the wounds.

"They beat you."

"Yeah," Eli grunted. Taking Cleo's small paw, he pulled him in front of him and gave a weak smile. "It's okay. It hurts a little, but I'm fine. Don't worry."

The cat's teal eyes watched him carefully as Eli drifted in and out of slumber. He was in obvious pain, but refused to admit it. Sighing, he smoothed out his master's furrowed brows and snuggled closer to him.

"It's my job to worry about you, Eli," he said softly. "Especially when there's a maniac after you."

Chapter Sixteen

The front door to Sinclair Manor blew open with such force the old hinges rattled and threatened to break. The butlers and guards stood back as the small group of magick users stormed in. Their united energies were more than enough to make anyone flinch.

Frost stood protectively in front of his mistress as they followed Selena's aura through the foyer. He paused when they emerged in a large sitting room. Sinclair magick flooded the old family mansion, blinding him to the exact number of Sinclairs around them. Were he not so close to Alexis and Scott, he may very well lose them amongst their distant relatives. Yet of all the Sinclair auras surrounding them, one pulsed with a very familiar light. It had warmth the others seemed to lack. It called to him with a force only Raven's descendants had ever produced.

They followed it to the adjoining drawing room where Selena and a man, who Frost guessed was Richard Sinclair, awaited them. Another man, in his early forties, sat at a window seat overlooking the huge property.

Selena jumped on him the moment they were all in the room.

"Frost! You made it! What took so long?"

"Michael Sinclair," Frost growled, glaring at Richard. "Stole the crystals."

"What?" Selena gasped, staring at Alexis.

The woman had been oddly quiet since her tools were taken. It was as if she still silently communicated with them, learning everything she could about her cousin's disappearance. So far, all she knew was Eli was hurt.

"Is everyone alright?" the tall man by the window asked. He held the wall as he stood and turned to them. His soft brown hair and hazel eyes surprised everyone.

"Dad!" Alexis cried, for the first time coming completely out of her trance. She ran to her father and braced an arm around him to help him stand. "What are you doing here? Are you alright? Why didn't you call us?"

Daniel Dion was wincing in pain. He carefully maneuvered Alexis's hand to his arm. "There was no time, Alexis, honey." His voice changed slightly, a little deeper with more of an accent. Frost couldn't help but gape at him, although he should've known better by know. "Things are happening far faster than I anticipated."

"Raven?" Alexis breathed, staring up in surprise. The surprise turned to worry at the sight of her father's pain-filled eyes. "What happened to Eli?" she suddenly demanded as she made him sit on the velvet sofa.

Richard Sinclair leaned against the grand piano and folded his arms across his chest. "He arrived an hour ago, saying he was the reincarnation of Anthony Sinclair. The other half at least," he reported with a sense of doubt in his voice.

"He is," Frost replied, ice filling his voice. He knelt before the elder reincarnation and helped Anthony unbutton his shirt.

"I wasn't doubting him. I could sense Raven. I had first thought it was Eli walking into the house. Thought I'd ground him for giving us all such a scare," Richard countered, mimicking Frost's coldness. "Fifteen minutes ago, he took an attack, as if some physical force were after him." He gestured to Daniel's back as his daughter peeled back his shirt. "Then those appeared, bleeding heavily."

"They stopped shortly after," Selena finished.

Scott inspected the wounds with a doctor's eye. "But no one touched you…Alexis said Eli was hurt. You don't think…"

"Anthony's spirit connects them spiritually and psychically," Frost murmured.

Scott shook his head. "The twin syndrome? I don't know."

"Twins? There's almost thirty years between them," Richard said doubtfully.

Frost frowned. Obviously, the new leader of the Sinclair family knew very little of Anthony and his style of magick. He was amazed that the man had not freaked over his appearance. Then again, his glamour was fully in place. Even in his faery form, he could not show his full self. He had a glow about him that reflected the moon perfectly. He had to tone that down around mortals. Those born under the moon were strongly attracted to his aura. Richard was obviously born under the sun. He was not as powerful a magician as he boasted. How he had become the head of the Sinclairs was a question Frost was too polite to ask. "They are twins. Two halves of the same soul. Age is not a factor in this spell," Frost said sharply. He smiled reassuringly at Daniel. "Are you alright?"

"I'm fine, Nate," Anthony's voice answered. Daniel's eyes closed. "Eli blocked me from taking over. He would not let me spare him the pain. He believes if he suffers the torment alone, it will strengthen him so he can take his revenge later. It's a way of defying them. To prove he is not weak."

"Why?"

That question alone seemed to eat at Anthony. "Henry and Duncan Porter..." Daniel looked Frost squarely in the eyes. "He's alive, Nate, and he wants Eli. He loves Eli, but..."

"Eli learned the truth," Selena whispered in sudden understanding.

She, too, knelt before Daniel as if waiting for their creator's reincarnation to tell them a story.

"Yes, but Duncan has changed. The man you met today, Michael Sinclair, is really Porter. They somehow switched bodies."

"Oh, Goddess!" Selena covered her mouth.

Stealing another's body was illegal in the magick world. Punishable by death, unless proven an accident or necessity, which was even harder to prove. It was no doubt to be a willing trade. It also met Porter now had a lifetime in which he could harm Eli.

Daniel's eyes closed as he grimaced in pain. Sweat broke out on his forehead.

Frost turned to Richard. "Can someone bring him a glass of cold water?"

"I'm alright, Nate," Daniel insisted.

He nodded. "I'm sure, but you're not used to being psychically attached to anyone. Your body may not be able to handle the stress."

Daniel's head bobbed up and down understandingly. He looked exhausted, understandable, considering the long trip from India.

Knowing Anthony, Daniel had most likely not slept during it. Probably monitoring Eli even before he was kidnapped. How long had it been since he slept? When alive, Anthony could last a week or so with only his magick to sustain him, but Daniel was still new to the magick world. He needed sleep and food.

The water came faster than Frost had expected. Richard, using his magick perhaps to alter the molecules in the air to create the ice water, handed him the glass. Frost held it out to Daniel like a small offering. Hesitantly, Daniel took the glass, his soft brown eyes staring up at his relative. They did look an awful lot alike. Definite cousins.

"Thank you," Daniel, not Anthony, said with a nervous smile to them both.

"You're welcome, Daniel." Richard rolled the name as if trying it for the first time.

His gaze flicked back to the two Guardians before him. Anthony's voice resumed. "Eli's confused. Porter's age now and how he's been treating Eli with such kindness while Henry, the person he trusted most, abuses him. He knows the truth about everything now. Everything he suppressed from his childhood is coming out. It's overwhelming him."

"Will he unleash his power if it continues?" Richard suddenly asked, an odd fear formed in his eyes. "Will it start controlling him?"

"I don't know. His emotions are running rampant."

"But you can get through to him, right?"

"Hopefully."

Alexis helped Scott as he ripped their father's shirt and dressed the wounds. "Dad—Anthony, you're exhausted. You need rest. There's not much we can do for Eli right this moment. If you can return to him, tell him that we're looking for him. I don't know, comfort him perhaps. It might give him strength."

Daniel smiled and Frost could instantly see Anthony in those remarkably British features. Such a contrast to Eli's Spanish features, yet they still looked so much alike. It had to be their smile and the way their eyes twinkled when they laughed. They could easily be father and son.

"Perhaps you're right," Anthony said. When Daniel looked back at them, it was his, not Anthony's, tired and confused eyes staring at them. "Eli was raped when he was eight?"

Selena nodded. She helped him to his feet while Miao, who had stayed completely out of the way, wrapped his arms around Alexis. This wasn't really a discussion they should have in front of them. Daniel gave his daughter a kiss on the forehead before following Selena and Frost.

"He can have Raven's room," Richard suddenly said, stepping forward to lead the way.

"We know where it is," Selena assured him, smiling. "Please make sure our Mistress and her companions are comfortable."

"Of course, Lady Hawke."

"Lady Hawke? Our Mistress?" Frost whispered once they were in the long corridor leading to the spiral staircase. "What are you not telling me?"

"Because of how young Eli was when I became his guardian and the fact that his parents were deceased, and Mae and Henry were in their late seventies, I was named Eli's spokesperson. After what happened with Porter, we refused to take a chance with Eli so I talked to the High Council for him." Her gaze fell upon Daniel. "I was given the title for Eli's benefit. The Council would otherwise demand Eli's presence, despite his age or what was done to him. They do not listen to servants."

Daniel frowned, but nodded.

"How did you get here?" Selena asked bluntly. "Did you sense Eli was in danger?"

Daniel blinked and glanced thoughtfully at the ceiling. "I had a vision, then a strong urge to be near Eli. To hold him and protect him. I found an orb. Four sections, each representing one of the Guardians. There was a book...Gaelic... Anthony's...hmm..." He held his head for a moment, his knees suddenly weak. "I'm so tired."

Frost caught him as he slipped on the last step. Putting one bare arm over his shoulders Frost supported him as they made their way to the bedroom. He was actually surprised when they entered the room. Unlike at the cabin there had been no change to Anthony's room. There was no evidence to show that anyone else had ever occupied it in the last forty years. Jonathan Sinclair must have arranged things that way for Eli's benefit. It was still decorated as it had been so many years ago.

He sat Daniel on the large bed and helped Selena pull down the covers. Although still awake Daniel allowed them to tend to his needs. Frost actually liked the thought of taking care of him. He was just a few years older than Anthony had been the last time he had been with him.

Frost shook his head. No, Daniel was the fatherly side of Anthony, and Scott's father. It was different than with Eli. Eli was still a young man but still in need of protection and comforting. The young man looked so much more like Anthony than Daniel as well.

Was that why all these weird things were happening to him? Because he was more like Anthony than Daniel? Was that why his own feeling toward Eli were so strong? One day, would his feelings change? Would his desire for Anthony overcome him as it had Duncan Porter? He hoped not. He loved Scott and cared very deeply for Eli, but he was not in love with the young mage.

Anthony had said Porter was in love with Eli, changed himself for the young man even. Was it because of Anthony or Eli?

"Dan, you said Porter loved Eli. Why? Is it his power or because he's Anthony reincarnated?" he asked, needing to know.

Daniel shook his head. "No. It's more than that. I think…I think Duncan actually loves him. Just him. Now at least."

"What?" Selena's eyes hardened. "He would not have known about Eli had he not felt Anthony's power within him. He would never have—never done the things he did. He was trying to get back at Anthony by hurting Eli because it was the only way he would ever feel it!"

Daniel pulled her into his arms and cradled her as he would one of his own children. She cried openly even as he began dozing in and out. She cried for Eli's lost childhood, something she had tried and failed to save. Caring for Eli was so much harder than Alexis. His past life was a hindrance.

Frost patted Selena's back, gently pulling her off Daniel as the professor passed out. She sobbed until there were no tears left and then finally exhausted herself to slumber. He laid her next to Daniel. He doubted Dan would mind. There was nothing sexual between the two. They were all family. He left them to rest and returned to the drawing room. Scott was sitting where his father had been, staring out the window. Alexis and Miao were missing.

"They were assigned rooms," Scott explained, not even looking up. "Sif's staying with Alexis. Miao's going to contact his mother. Eli's under their protection, they may be able to help."

"No. The eclipse is soon. There's no way the Syffern Clan can help. We're on our own." He sat on the other end of the window seat. His long hair pooled on the floor next to him.

Scott pulled Frost's bare foot up and held it close to his chest. His fingers massaged under his toes, causing Frost's eyes to flutter shut. The fey groaned, leaning back and letting his love rid him of the stress gripping him. Unconsciously, he began caressing the inside of Scott's thigh. Scott hummed appreciatively.

"Those marks...whips?" Scott murmured, thinking out loud.

Frost had actually been trying not to ponder the cause of the wounds, nor the vision of Eli being tortured. Now that Scott had voiced his fears, the visions swarmed him. He gave a small nod. "Whip, belt, cable...could be anything. Eli's very willful. This was their way of trying to control him."

"You're cynical today."

"I've seen it happen before."

"Anthony?"

Frost stared out the window, over the meadow and rolling hills. Sunset was approaching and the city lights were flickering on in the distance. Sheep-raising country, he reminded himself, his mind on his childhood and chasing fireflies with his siblings and Anthony. It was a place he could easily see a young Eli running through and getting lost in the garden's maze.

He silently prayed to every god and goddess he could think of for the young man to be okay, but knew deep down Eli wasn't. He felt helpless just sitting there, unable to help him. Even worse for letting Scott comfort him, but if he didn't, he would drive himself insane as he was sure Selena had.

"That kid is such a brat no one will be able to control him."

Frost's head snapped up at the comment, not sure if that was really how Scott felt about Eli. He hoped not. He wanted them to be friends. Scott winked and smiled, banishing all his fears.

"Another day and they'll be begging us to take him back. Besides, it gives me one night where I'm not competing for your attention."

"Scott!" Frost objected.

He knew the taller man was not actually happy about what had happened, that he was trying to cheer him up, and not let him lose hope, but the comment was totally uncalled for. Had it been anyone else, he may have struck them.

Scott gave a lopsided smile and, grabbing his knee, pulled him closer. The giggles came before Frost could stop them. "Scott, stop. Scott!" he cried as his beloved tickled his sensitive areas. He only hoped the Sinclairs did not misinterpret their playfulness for lack of caring for the missing friends.

* * *

Eli laughed as Aaliyah wrapped her arms around him and rocked him as he tried packing his suitcase. The mansion had been a buzz of business since he had announced the opening of the Book of Illumination, just two weeks after his tenth birthday. In a way, it was an odd birthday present. Not that he was complaining. This was what he had been training for. In two days, he would be traveling halfway across the world to a land he had only dreamed of. Aaliyah was so excited to show him her mother's homeland, making it impossible for him to pack properly. He hugged her arms and rocked with her.

"You'll love Ravenwood," she was gushing as she had for the last few days. She kissed his cheek. "What is she like?"

"Pretty," he said softly, thinking of the girl he believed to be the other half of his soul. "Athletic, stronger than she believes."

"Much like you."

A blush raced up his neck and cheeks. In a way, they did have a lot in common. He couldn't wait to meet her. Nor could his Guardians. Selena was still deciding what to pack. She dropped a fifth skirt onto Cleo's head, declaring it wasn't cute enough and that she needed a new wardrobe. It meant another shopping trip in which she would not only shop for herself, but pick out a pile of clothes for him that he did not need. He didn't mind, one last shopping trip would be fun. He had a craving for jellybeans.

A sudden cold chill made him shiver. His eyes slid closed and he leaned against Aaliyah. Tiredness gripped him as familiar magick seeped into the house. He couldn't place it yet he knew it was dark. Fear gripped him as a voice, not Anthony's, whispered in his mind.

"Yes, I'm here," he whispered before he could stop himself.

Aaliyah felt the magick, too. Her grip tightened around him as she poured her magick into him, pulling him out of the trance he was slipping into. Her amber eyes turned cold as she looked at Selena.

"Check it out," she commanded.

Her hand took Eli's firmly and pulled him toward the study where most of the weapons were stored. A confused Cleo followed close behind.

Mae Sinclair met them in the hall. Her pale blue eyes stared down at Eli with worry. "Hide your aura, honey. Don't let anyone sense you," she instructed.

"Aaliyah, keep him hidden."

"Yes, ma'am."

The Priestess surprised Eli by picking him up and half-ran into the large room. She carefully dumped him on the old leather chair that was dubbed Eli's due to Anthony, and knelt before him.

"Listen to me, Eli. Some bad people are at the door. I want you to stay right here." Her eyes darkened slightly. "Anthony, make him stay put," she said sharply, addressing his past self.

It was as if he were bound to the chair. His hands clenched the armrests, back straight, legs dangling. His eyes became more watchful as Aaliyah knelt before the weapons chest and unlocked it. She pulled out the sacred sword, a magickal weapon Eli had given her, through Anthony's instruction. She used it to seal the room from the rest of the world. Once she was satisfied it was secure, she placed on kiss on his forehead and hurried out the door.

There were several moments before the spirit of his past self released him. Muted arguments shook his senses as he fought to climb out of the huge chair. When he first touched the locked door, a warm current ran up his arms. He silently cursed Aaliyah and his grandmother for their over-protectiveness, wondering why they were so concerned about the visiting magick user. Why they were so insistent he hide. He hated to hide.

Curiosity got the better of him. Aaliyah used Anthony's magick to seal the room. He was, in essence, Anthony. He could manipulate that power to get out. A tiny smile crossed his lips.

The heat of his power rose from the pit of his stomach like the breath of a singer, and moved to his hands. It passed through his fingertips to the invisible shield. He felt it vibrate and pulse under the power.

Come to me, the strange voice whispered once more.

He paused, feeling Anthony pull back the magick he had been born with. Maybe this wasn't a good idea, he rethought, but someone was calling to him.

He had to fight for control. Why Anthony wanted him to stay in the room like everyone else was unusual. Normally the deceased mage was just as curious as he was. A hole finally opened in the seal and Eli was able to open one of the double doors and slip out before the seal could repair itself. Cleo followed, urging him to return to the study rather than follow the strange power to its source.

"Eli, go back to the study. It's safer for you there," the panther insisted. He grabbed the child's sleeve with his teeth and pulled the other way.

Eli resisted and peered around the corner at the bottom of the stairwell. Nan was at the door, talking with a man in an expensive gray suit. He was a little younger than his grandmother, but leaned heavily on a wooden cane, varnished so dark it looked black. His wrinkled old face held a pleasant smile as he spoke.

He seemed to know Nan, yet the elderly woman obviously did not like him. Selena and Aaliyah flanked her as if ready to attack him.

Eli concentrated on his face. Somehow, he knew this man. He was sure of it.

His heart began to race as the man's gaze slipped past Nan to him.

"Eli, go to the study now," Cleo growled.

Something in Eli snapped. Fear froze him in his tracks. He knew the man, but could not place him. Nor could he comprehend the uncontrollable fear that had such a firm grip on him. He suddenly became very aware of the shadows around him. "Not again," he whispered. The shadows seemed to move unnaturally around him.

The man's eyes sparkled at the sight of him. "Hello, Eli," he called. Nan's arm shot out as he tried to pass her. Their eyes met and he frowned. "It's his birthday. I have a gift."

"I'm sure. Leave my home, Duncan."

"In a moment."

Eli gasped as the man teleported. Cleo nudged him back up the stairs to the study.

"Run, now!"

He didn't need to ask, he knew, this man was dangerous. The first thing he feared was this man was after his magick books and weapons. Perhaps he came looking for information on the exact whereabouts of his other half. Somehow, this man knew about his past life, or at least that he was connected to the Raven.

He raised his metaphysical shields as the other magick surrounded him. It was not enough. He came to a standstill mere feet from the study's doors.

The strange man stood just in front of the doors. He knelt before Eli, smiling gently. He held out a small, decorated box and spoke as if he were Eli's grandfather. "Hello, Eli."

"Hello," Eli whispered in a small voice as he tried to take a step back. His feet refused to move.

Scared, he raised his shields as high as he could, for all the good they were doing him. The man raised one hand, caressing the cobalt energy surrounding Eli. His smile grew.

"You've grown so much stronger since I last saw you. Your power is impressive." His hand slipped through the protective shield.

Eli's eyes widened. He could feel his shield fluctuate under the man's power. He was powerful. More than Eli thought he could handle. Anthony surged within him for a moment, then fell oddly silent. Eli's eyes slid shut and he pitched forward. Before the man could catch him, Sinclair magick enveloped him. Opening his eyes, he found his grandmother's arms wrapped tightly around him.

Her magick surrounded them both, pushing the elderly man away. It was the first time he ever recalled Nan using so much power and it was flaring, overriding his own.

"I want you to sleep, baby," she whispered, her magick swirling around them.

Once again, he had to fight to keep his eyes open. They were so heavy, yet Anthony was on his sister's side. He made Eli close his eyes, but he refused to sleep. Eli listened carefully to the two grownups as the magick filled the house.

"Duncan, get out. You can't have him," Nan growled. She was so angry her power burned with rage.

In his mind's eye, Eli could hear her chanting a warding spell on him, something that no one would be able to break until her death.

Maybe even beyond. "I'm only here to wish him Happy Birthday and good luck on his mission. I'm not here to harm him or any of you." The man sighed. "I simply believe he should collect the books for himself. They are, in a sense, his anyway. Let him be what he was born to be."

"He will do Anthony's will, and correct his mistake."

"Are you sure it was a mistake and not destiny?" Somehow, the man managed to push through Nan's power. He pushed the decorated box into Eli's hands and brushed his lips over his aura, above his forehead. "Happy Birthday, Raven," he whispered.

Eli felt him disappear a second later and Nan sighed in relief. Her magick dispelled and her old knees gave out. Eli managed to pull himself awake in time to catch her. He wrapped his arms around her waist, but he didn't have enough physical strength to keep her standing. She dragged him to the polished wooden floor as she passed out. "Nan? Nan!" he cried, shaking her. "Are you alright? Please wake up. Nan?"

Aaliyah was holding him a moment later. "It's okay, honey. She's just exhausted. It's the most magick she's used in ages. It tired her out."

She gestured for Selena to help her carry the elderly woman to her room.

* * *

Eli was dreaming of the past again, Duncan could sense it, even peek into the youth's mind. It had been the reason for the break in of his office. Eli was starting to remember. It was good in one way, but made Eli hate and fear him even more, and just as they were beginning to become friends. Proving he meant no harm would take precious time they did not have. For now, Duncan had to concentrate on the wounds lining Eli's back.

Although they no longer bled, they would leave nasty scars unless he healed them.

Shrugging off his silk pajama shirt, he slipped under the covers and wrapped his arms around the smaller form. Total skin contact would heal the wounds much faster than anything else. He focused on each lash separately, taking on one injury at a time.

Ignoring the hateful daggers Cleo was throwing as he peered over Eli's shoulder, Duncan brushed Eli's long hair aside and kissed his bare shoulder. He rested his head next to the young mage's and drew in all the pain and cuts covering his body.

"Hmm…" Eli murmured. Instead of pulling away, he leaned back into Duncan's arms. "Aaliyah…"

* * *

Nan's aura was flickering. He could feel it even in his room. It had been doing so for about twenty minutes, but with Aaliyah's arms wrapped protectively around him, her body spooned against his, and Cleo, in his panther form lying across their legs, he could not get up to check on her. He wiggled, trying to loosen Aaliyah's grip. She hugged him tighter, her breasts pushing against his back, but did not wake up. "Aaliyah, I've got to go to the bathroom," he pleaded softly.

She murmured something incoherent and let him go. It took great effort to escape the crushing weight of Cleo's big body on his legs. When he was finally free, he slipped off the bed and padded in his bare feet to his grandmother's room. The door was slightly ajar due to the number of times Selena had been checking on her.

Sliding it open, he peeked inside. Selena sat in an armchair next to the window, sound asleep. Nan lay on her bed, eyes closed, her breathing shallow. Her long gray hair spread over the pillows like the halo of an angel. She looked like an angel. Crawling onto the four-poster bed, he laid next to her, his head resting on her chest.

Her aura was fading as surely as he listened to the erratic beating of her heart slow. Her thoughts were still crystal clear. He listened carefully as she spoke to him without moving her mouth.

The wrapped box the strange man had given him sat on her nightstand. He picked it up and carefully unwrapped it. Inside was a baby dragon hatching from its egg. The statue was made out of pure silver, carefully handcrafted. It was beautiful and rather unique. He instantly loved it. He had been born in the year of the dragon. It was his symbol. Carefully. he placed it in Nan's hands and moved her fingers over it. He smiled when she remarked how beautiful it was.

Lying back, he rested against her. She began talking about his mission, heatedly explaining how he must hide himself, even from

Nathaniel and Sif. How he had to be strong and patient with his other half, and promise to always be good.

"I promise, Nan," he whispered, hugging her tighter.

Her aura faded into non-existence shortly after that. Staring at the statue still in her hands, Eli began to cry. She had given up all her remaining power to protect him and enforce the warding spell around their mansion. Had he listened to Aaliyah and Cleo, Nan would still be alive. Nan may have held no ill will toward him, but for it, he still felt guilty. Even as she passed from this realm to the next, she had forgiven him, explaining he always had a curious nature, a love for mischief. He had done what was in his nature to do.

It only made him feel worse. He clung to her until Selena awoke and held him, also trying to explain that her death had not been his fault. She was old and her time would have come either way. All he could do was cry.

* * *

Wiping back the tears, Eli found himself in the dreamscape. The bridge of shining lights twinkled all around him. He had returned to his eighteen-year-old body, hair long and flowing over his shoulders. It had been a long time since he had thought of his grandmother's death. She had had a beautiful funeral, surrounded by family and friends.

It had been the first time he had given himself fully to his past self, letting Anthony take control because he could no longer handle everything that was happening…that was going to happen. He had needed a break away from reality. It was also when he fell in love with Aaliyah McNeil. No, Anthony had fallen in love with her because she was the reincarnation of his lost wife. Eli had only echoed those feelings until he, too, could not bear to be without her. Funny how that had yet to fade, even after being separated for so many months.

"Love can do that."

He looked up to find Anthony standing on the bridge with him. The elder mage was smiling warmly, holding his arms out to embrace him. Eli almost ran into his arms. The large cloak wrapped around him as he buried his face in Anthony's robes. He smelled of lavender and musk. Eli smiled. In the dream world, Anthony felt as real as anyone in the real world.

"Are you alright, Eli?" Anthony asked, wrapping his arms around his smaller frame.

"I am now."

Anthony only smiled. "Why did you shut me out?"

"You took the blow from Henry. I couldn't let you go through it again."

Anthony combed his fingers through Eli's hair. "That's very noble of you, but I could have protected you."

"Not after what I saw."

"Eli…"

"It wasn't your fault. I was eight, not strong enough to protect myself and I was not yet willing to let you take charge. I was scared."

"I know. Somehow, you must escape. Your friends are still looking for you. They want you to be strong."

"We're outside of time and space. How can they possibly find me?"

Anthony leaned his head against Eli's and sighed. "Energy comes in many forms. Utilize and dispel that which is hidden."

* * *

"Hidden?" Eli murmured in his sleep.

Duncan winced in pain and buried his face in the back of Eli's neck. All the injuries healed quickly, but they marked Duncan's back. He felt the pain Eli had. It was all he could do not to cry. Instead, he held Eli tightly and whimpered as he tried to heal himself. That wasn't as easy. He had to separate the pain, focus on each wound separately. It was much easier to heal others.

Cleo, amazingly enough, had climbed over the blankets to stare at his back. He was oddly quiet when he returned to Eli's side. His teal eyes were confused and he forcibly made Duncan pull away from Eli long enough to peer at his master's bare back. There was not a single mark on him, only a slight redness.

He looked up at Duncan. "You healed him and brought it upon yourself. Why?"

Duncan caressed Eli's arm and snuggled closer. "I caused it," he whispered. "I did this to him."

He didn't just mean the lashes, although he did regret them. He meant Eli's whole childhood. The abuse, the lies, the fear, even the revenge he had sought for his daughter back in March and how he had desired Chaos and Raven's power.

He was willing to give that all up now for Eli to love him. To feel his heart's true desire touch and kiss him of his own accord. After everything that had happened earlier, his hopes were crushed.

He only hoped returning Raven's magickal tools would make the young man happy. It would be a serious boost in his power if they changed back to his own tools. Soon Eli would be the true embodiment of power and beauty.

Henry growled under his breath as Duncan snuggled even closer to Eli. They were spooned together in a protective embrace. Duncan's back was toward the window, protecting Eli from any form of attack. Even if someone were to strike from the doorway, they would have to go through the older man first. It was cunning and even though Henry meant Eli no harm that night, he could not help but disapprove of Duncan's tactics. He should have waited until morning to heal Eli. He should have made the child beg, swear an oath to do as they say. This only complicated matters. Eli had Anthony's strength, his relentlessness. There was no doubt in his mind that things would only get worse. He knew Eli. He was not easy to control and kindness could only go so far.

Closing the door, he walked back to his room. He felt so much stronger after consuming Eli's magick. He left his cane in his room. He no longer needed it. Even with one fake leg, he had more than enough strength to walk straight. It seemed the only way to subdue Eli without hurting him was to take his magick. To do so before he used it meant the child could not open a portal. Waiting left him flowing with magick. Much more to feed on, but he recovers too fast. Somehow, they had to keep him from causing trouble, but Duncan would object to chaining Eli again.

Slipping into bed, he smiled at the fact that none of his joints hurt for the first time in years. A little more magick from Eli and he would be just as youthful as Duncan, although he planned to stop once he was in his mid-twenties, when he was in his prime. No need to go any younger. It was too bad his leg could not be replaced by a new healthy one, but that was not within Eli's power. Only a true Lycanthrope could re-grow lost limbs. Even then, he would have to have been a shapeshifter before the accident. He had learned to live without it for nearly sixty years and had grown accustomed to being crippled. It was something he did not worry about.

Tomorrow he would make Eli open a bigger portal than the speck of light he had that day. He would show Eli he was just as strong as Anthony, and that Chaos's powers were not needed. Hopefully, even destroy it before it consumed the young man. It was his worst fear. Eli's friends and even Duncan assured that the demon was gone, but he was not willing to take the chance. He prepared himself for the worst.

Patting the vial of Holy Water he received from the Priest of St. Peter's, he closed his eyes. The blessed Father appeared to agree with his fear for Eli. A demonic possession to such a degree could destroy the world of both magick and norm. As a soldier, it was his duty to protect England even at the cost of his grandson's life. It was also a chance to reunite with his long-lost wife. Only time would tell whether or not his fears were justified. He truly hoped he was overreacting.

The two young men were picture-perfect. Had he brought a camera with him, he would have snapped a picture. It wasn't often he got to see the two like this. Smiling, Daniel placed the blanket over his son and Frost. As he tucked the blanket around Frost, he noticed the white gold engagement ring on a chain around the silver-haired man's hand. His smile grew. So, Scott had asked him. Good. Frost looked so happy, his legs intertwined with Scott's, and his son gently held one foot as if to massage it. Frost twisted when Daniel brushed his hair back over his shoulder. He opened his eyes and gazed up at him.

"Mr. Dion." He brushed his bangs aside. "Is something wrong? Are you alright?"

Moving to get up, he was surprised when Daniel placed a hand on his shoulder and made him continue sitting. "I'm fine, Frost. My back has healed, amazingly enough. Please, Frost, after all these years, you should know to call me Dan."

He gave a nod. "Of course, Dan."

"So formal. You should be more like Nathan. Lighten up. Not just with Scott either." When Frost smiled, Daniel almost yelped with glee. He touched the ring Frost held. "I see you said yes."

Surprised, Frost blinked and stared down at the white gold ring. "Yes. You knew?"

"Scott asked for my approval. He was worried because you were another man and you could not provide me grandchildren." He winked. "I told him to adopt."

Frost burst out laughing. "I wish Eli took it as well." He moved his leg so it sat next to Scott. The taller man murmured in his sleep and wrapped his arms around Frost's legs, trying to pull him close.

"He's young and has a crush on you. The downside to being Anthony's reincarnation."

"And you?"

Daniel chuckled. He knelt next to the window seat. "No, Frost. You are like a son to me. I have felt that way since I first met Nathan."

"The fatherly side of Anthony." Frost turned to the window. It was pitch black, not even a star in the sky.

Daniel watched the worry grow in Frost's violet eyes. There was no moon and the stars were hidden from them. There should have been a silver sliver of moon by now.

"Is Eli alright?"

Daniel was silent for a moment. He followed Frost's gaze. The city twinkled like a jewel. "I don't know. For once, his mind is set on his own life, his own past. Duncan is unwittingly making him remember everything he had worked so hard to forget." He sighed. "His emotions are running rampant. Anthony is trying to keep him calm, but...every time he loses his temper—gives into his emotions, his powers become unstable. They have unleashed themselves on several occasions already." His gaze fell to the ground. "Richard may be right about Eli."

He hated admitting that, but he could feel Anthony's fear. The young man's anger was getting the best of him. It clouded his judgment and made him make rash decisions. It hurt just knowing the pain he had gone through. Daniel, himself, had grown up not knowing his parents. They had either died or abandoned him when he was very young. He had grown up in an orphanage with only his name and an old picture to tell who he was.

He had made his way through life on countless jobs until he graduated University, became an archaeologist, and met Christina. He married the woman of his dreams, built their home, and had children. He rarely gave his childhood a second thought after that. He only concentrated on his family and work. When Christina took severely ill after the car accident and passed away, he had thought it was the end of his world. He never told Scott, Debra, or Alexis she had been with child.

It took a long time to come to out of that depression, upon which time he had done numerous stupid stunts. Christina had been his life, his entire world, but in time, he learned his world still consisted of his three children and that they were his life. He consoled Alexis through her nightmares and helped Scott deal with the ghosts he actually was seeing, but there had been little he could do to help Debra, and when she ran away, he thought he had failed as a father. There had been no time in his life for magick or mystical creatures until he met Eli. Sure, he had known about Frost for years before that, but he never let it get to him. Nathan and Frost were simply part of his family and that was that.

He wondered about a great number of things since meeting Eli Hawke and learning of his past life as Anthony Sinclair and their joined soul. He never wanted to believe any of it. From the moment he met Eli, he knew there was something different about him. Maybe it was the odd quietness that had befallen him the first time they met.

The knot in his stomach grew tighter and he could feel Anthony within him. Wherever Eli was, time seemed to pass at an erratic rate. His thoughts flashed through Daniel's mind like rapid fire, causing a slight headache. Subconsciously, he withdrew from Anthony and Eli's thoughts. The miraculous healing of his back had been caused by Duncan's magick. Oddly enough, he had been momentarily able to sense the warlock. He did seem to truly care for Eli.

"I don't know. Maybe. So much has happened to him. If he loses control..." Frost closed his eyes. "Without the crystals, we won't be able to stop him. It would be as if Chaos really did take control."

Unconsciously playing with the long tail of Frost's braid, Daniel shook his head. "Duncan won't let that happen."

Frost raised a brow. "I thought maybe Henry..."

He shook his head. "Henry's pushing Eli, making him use his magick. If Eli loses control, Henry won't be able to stop him.

Duncan is the one who keeps him grounded."

"But Porter—"

Daniel felt Anthony stir in uneasiness. Eli must be on the verge of waking. Wherever he was, it was morning. He stated the conclusion they had come to earlier that day. "—loves him. He really loves him."

Frost wrinkled his nose in distaste. "I haven't heard anyone call Porter by his given name in decades."

Even to Daniel, the name sounded foreign on his lips, but it was the name Eli was using and, for some reason, so must he. Maybe Eli's feelings were more than mere hate. "The tides are turning, Frost. There is more happening than meets the eye."

He stared down at the silvery hair in his hands. There was a soft radiant glow to it as there was to Frost's alabaster white skin. Yes, something was indeed going on with Duncan Porter. There was another reason to Eli's abduction. The eclipse wasn't the only reason. It just didn't feel right. Somehow, he had to translate Anthony's book. It held the answers. He was sure of it.

Chapter Seventeen

"Morning, Eli," Duncan chirped.

Eli shielded his eyes from the sun pouring through the open windows. He frowned at the sight of Duncan putting his shirt on. It didn't endear his sense of safety, only increased the possibilities of what may have happened after he had passed out. The mere fact that Duncan had slept with him was enough to prove that he had been up to something.

Rolling out of bed, he walked past the warlock without a word. He slammed the bathroom door shut and sat on the toilet in deep thought. They had to get out of there. He could not stand another night in either Duncan or Henry's company. He could not bear to have either of them touching him again. He was too angry to cry. All he could think of was escape.

The bathroom door opened a crack.

Narrowing his eyes, Eli drew a little magick into his power-hand and aimed it at the opening.

"Eli?"

He withdrew the magick instantly as Cleo slipped into the spacious bathroom. Relaxing only a little, he sat back. "Stupid bathroom doesn't have a lock." At his friend's hurt expression, he shook his head. "Not to keep you out, just Duncan. Who knows what might happen if he walked in while I'm showering. Either way...I should wash the blood off my back." Which oddly enough was no longer hurting.

"Eli, that's what I wanted to talk to you about," Cleo said, nervously glancing at the door. "Duncan, ah...he healed you last night."

"Yeah? And..."

"That's all. He just healed you. Held you all night."

That was surprising. "Watch the door. I'm going to have a quick shower."

Duncan was not in his room when he emerged from the shower. Surprised and relieved, Eli forewent the fancy clothes his captor usually tried to dress him in. If he wasn't a captive, he would have gladly worn them. They were his style, but he put on a pair of jeans and t-shirt instead.

While in the large closet, he spotted a small duffle bag. Not even bothering to wonder why Duncan had given him one, he began packing a spare pair of pants, sweater, t-shirt, underwear, and socks. Going to the bar fridge, he began pulling out several cans of soda. Today was the day of their escape. That alone calmed him considerably.

Cleo watched him in silence as he finished packing the small bag. Eli had knowingly left more than enough room for the cat to hide once they were past the border of magick. His ears twitched as he followed Eli out of the large closet. Eli watched his familiar in confusion as he jumped on the dresser and poked at a black pouch.

The black leather shone with the care its owner took of it. Eli's hand hovered over it in hesitation. Fear etched itself over his brows. "No, it can't be." He whispered. The strong sense of Alexis's magick filled the aura around the pouch.

Picking it up, he opened it and pulled out the crystals and small tools, weapons, and tarot cards. He spread them over the table to make sure they were all there. All the spirits were there, greeting him as he looked them over. At least they were all safe, but how did Duncan get them from Alexis?

Running down the stairs, he stormed into the dining room, clenching the belt of the pouch so as to not hurt Raven's creations in his rage. Duncan was sitting at the head of the table, waiting for him while Henry stood by one of the large windows.

"If you hurt her…" Eli began, holding up the pouch and shaking with such fury he was ready to lash out at either one of them. "I swear I'll make you wish you never saw me."

"Alexandria willingly gave them to me for you," Duncan explained, gesturing to one of the seats around the table. "You need them, Eli."

"For what exactly? Alexis is Daniel's heir, not me. She was granted Raven's tools and crystals. The spirits belong with her."

"A mistake. They should have been yours." Duncan smiled, using his magick to pull out the chair nearest to him. "Come, sit down. Let us talk about this. With a little spell casting, they can be yours and—"

"No! They are Alexis's now. She is their Mistress and I will not take them away from her." He turned to storm out of the room when Henry stepped in front of him. The big man stared down at him. "I won't do it. Neither of you can make me." He stepped back as Henry went to touch him. "You can beat me all you want. I won't do it."

"Eli!" Henry called as he ducked under him and raced out of the room.

Eli didn't care what they did to him now. He didn't believe them. Alexis would never give up the crystals. Not even for him. If she was hurt, he would make them suffer. Now more than ever, he had to escape. He had to find Alexis. Reaching his room, he was tempted to grab the duffle bag and make a run for it, but still had no idea how to break through Duncan's shield.

Placing the pouch on the table, he sat down. It was depressing, sitting there, not being able to sense the outside world. If he could, he would be able to sense whether or not Alexis was alright. Maybe even enter the astral realm to talk to her…but Duncan's spell prevented him from doing so.

"Master?" Cleo asked, sitting on the table before him.

Picking up the pouch, Eli opened it and fished out the colourful crystals once more. Their essence swam around them as the spirits within awoke at his touch. Odd. They were no longer his to command, why would they react to him? He needed answers quick. He had to talk to one of the spirits who were able to speak. His fingers fell on the Moonstone. He hesitated. The spirit that had helped him yesterday, although not necessarily the same as the one he now held, had been severely hurt. He could not endanger another, even if it was just to talk. He was about to move to the next crystal when his door flew open.

Henry stepped inside and slammed the door shut. He towered over Eli and glared down at the pouch. For the first time, Eli noticed he was no longer using his cane. He sighed inwardly. His magick was making Henry so much younger and stronger if he could walk on his fake leg without the need of his cane. He gasped as Henry snatched the Moonstone from his hand and studied it with angry eyes.

"The same spell twice, Eli? How very unlike you. Are you trying for ten lashes? I'm sure the spirits wouldn't appreciate it."

Taking the stone back, Eli placed it with the rest. "I was going to ask her if Alexis was safe."

"You don't trust Duncan?"

He laughed bitterly. "You saw the video, Henry. You know what happened when I was eight. How can I?"

"I saw the television blow up. Nothing else. When you were eight...I didn't know Duncan would do that when I made the arrangements."

"You?"

Henry leaned against the dresser and sighed. "I've known Duncan since I was eighteen. He never touched a child before and I never thought he would. He has loved Anthony from the moment they met. Shyest kid I ever met. He didn't know how to tell Anthony until he found out about the arranged marriage with Xyan Syffern." His gray eyes took on a faraway look as a faint smile spread across his lips. "He loved Tony right to the day he died and swore to protect you as best he could, even when Tony begged for him not to. Anthony was delusional near the end and Duncan was very protective of him."

"He said Anthony tried to hide me from him."

"A last-minute spell that Mae advised him to do. She was afraid for you and Daniel. Anthony had a vision of what had happened— would happen—when you were eight. I thought it was just the illness speaking or I never would have allowed you to spend time with Duncan and Sara. I never thought he would ever touch you, Eli. Honest. Anthony's magick must have been too much for him to ignore. I'm sorry."

"But you helped hide me after that. Why are you allowing this to happen now, after so long?"

"Because of Chaos. Because of the eclipse. Duncan has the power and knowledge to help you. When he came to me and told me what was happening and reading all Selena's letters and her fear of what the Chaos demon may have done, I had little choice."

"Duncan went to you about this?"

"He was concerned. Eli, you have no idea how serious this can be. The eclipse caused chaos in the past. It feeds the demon. It may no longer be in you, but you still hold a lot of its magick. You are the Key to numerous portals. The familiar can use you as a channel and move through these portals without care. It will destroy our world. Not even the fey have the power to stop it. Only you."

Eli stared at the crystals in his hands. Once again, he called the Key. Dominique had said the same as had Duncan. Maybe he should learn more control. If what Henry said was true, the entire magick world may be relying on him. How could he ever trust Duncan and Henry? No, he had to escape and find out from the Sinclairs if it were true. They would know and know how to deal with it. They were still the most powerful magick family in all of England. "Is there a *Lock*?"

"Yes, Daniel Dion, I believe. That's why I have been writing to him. I was trying to get him to visit with you and your friends. At least, then we would have been able to shut down the portals faster. Without him, you're on your own." He took a step around the table. "We didn't have time to track him down. Duncan says he's made arrangements to bring him here."

Eli closed his eyes, holding back his emotions. It wasn't possible. The whole world could not be depending on the magick that flowed through him and Daniel. There were so many magick users in the world, yet it seemed as if they didn't matter. They never did. He swallowed the lump in his throat. "He's with the Sinclairs," he whispered, terrified that Henry would go after his soul's twin next.

A ragged gasp escaped Eli as Henry pulled him into an embrace. It was warm and tender, reminding him of all the times Henry had held him through his life. He didn't bother pulling away, rather wrapped his own arms around the large man's waist. The sudden need for human contact overwhelmed him. Even if Henry absorbed some of his magick, he didn't care as long as he was held.

Henry didn't absorb his power. He stroked Eli's hair, talking gently and promising to take care of him as he always had. Eventually, he managed to convince Eli to go back downstairs for breakfast. Cleo stayed behind to look after the crystals, not trusting anyone but Eli near them.

Eli ate very little, his stomach churning from the news Henry had given him. The day became the same as any other. Henry had him back in the training room, facing off against many sequences, all designed to push his powers to the limits. Eli held himself in check the whole time, not letting his magick get out of control and destroying the room as he really wanted to.

Somehow, Duncan had charmed the room to contain any extensive power he wished to use. Instead, Eli focused on the portals for which Henry and Duncan continued to demand. In fact, Eli actually wanted to open at least one. The one he had seen his parents in, but it wasn't working. He could not remember how he had done it the last time.

Worry for his friends ate at him as well. How did Duncan get Alexis to give up the crystals? Was Henry going to go after Daniel? For what exactly was the Key and Lock created? That question made him question his entire existence. If Anthony had created a Key and Lock in the form of two humans, were Eli and Daniel even really human?

The constant line of questions made him lose focus. He leaned against the debris from one of Henry's robots that he had been fighting and sighed. This was ridiculous! He could not focus with all these unanswered questions. If he could just hear Alexis's voice and know she and her family were safe, everything would be fine.

He did want to open a portal. He really did. He wanted to see his parents again. It was as if they were still alive…on the other side. He had never truly believed in Heaven and Hell, but he knew everyone went some place after they died. There had to be.

He touched his chest in deep thought. Anthony had to have existed in another realm after he died, before either he or Daniel was born. A part of him had to still be there. Why else would the first portal to reveal itself be to the Land of the Dead? Perhaps Anthony was trying to show him something, a chance to say goodbye to his parents.

He closed his eyes. If only he knew for sure that Alexis and Daniel were safe. He needed to talk to the spirits. They had to be okay. If something had happened to either of them, he would know, wouldn't he?

The doors to the training room opened, finally letting him out. He didn't hesitate, glad to be allowed out. One of Duncan's servants stood in the hallway, holding out a bottle of water and towel for him. It surprised Eli. He had expected Henry or Duncan to be waiting for him, but was happy, nonetheless. He wasn't sure of his revolution yet.

The Land of the Dead may not have been the portal they wanted, but it was the first one they were going to get.

Claudia met him on his way to his room. Her eternal pleasant smile lit up her pretty face as he neared her.

"Lord Porter and your grandfather won't be able to join you for lunch, Lord Hawke. They ask for your forgiveness but they are trying to repair Lord Porter's office," she said with a small formal bow.

"Oh…" He smiled inwardly. This was perfect.

"May I ask what you would like for lunch?"

He smiled brightly. "Actually, I was hoping to wander the grounds today. Can you make a picnic for two?"

"Deux?"

"Yes, me and Cleo."

"Your cat?"

His smile grew. She obviously didn't know about Cleo being his familiar, or the fact he could talk. Not a very good telepath, unless Duncan had put up some blocks so his staff would not freak out over a talking cat. "He likes tuna," he said innocently.

The confusion left her and she nodded. "Of course…and you?"

"I'm not picky. A few sandwiches, fruits, and drinks. I'm very hungry after that workout."

She smiled. "Yes, sir." She hurried off to the kitchen.

Eli continued to his room. He had to shower again. So much use of magick had worked up quite a sweat. By the time he was done and changed, Claudia had brought a large basket of food to him. It sat on the table next to the pouch. Cleo poked his head into the basket, to check out what goodies they had been given.

"Don't eat anything, Cleo," he instructed as he pulled the duffle bag out of the closet. Although the bedroom and bathroom had security cameras, even though Eli doubted they were really for security purposes, the closet did not. Even if anyone kept a constant eye on his movements, no one would have known what he was up to.

Duncan had given him a number of sketchbooks, boards, and paints, obviously knowing his love of art. He slipped a sketchbook and paint board on top of the clothes, effectively hiding them. He slung a paint stand over one shoulder and picked up the basket. To any onlooker, it would appear he and his *pet* were going on a picnic and doing some painting. No one would have guessed he was about to attempt an escape. It also gave him an excuse in case it didn't work or he was caught too far from the castle.

Cleo hid the pouch in the basket, then flew inside himself. His little head poked out the lid and gave him a lopsided smile. Eli prayed he wouldn't get into the sweets. Last thing he needed now was a hyper cat.

He made his way outside with little trouble. Many curious servants and groundkeepers asked what he would paint. Most were very kind, begging him to show them his work once he was finished. They surprised him. It seemed few knew he was a prisoner. All seemed to think he was Duncan's or rather Michael's younger cousin.

Apparently, they had orders to treat Eli like family. It was easy to read their thoughts. Not very many of them had any magick and those that did, only had small amounts, healers, and seers, but no true defensive or offensive powers. Duncan obviously liked to be above his servants in power. Easier to control those under him.

He paused under one of the many terraces to the huge garden. Plants of very variety grew around him. Fountains with some of the most elegant statues he had ever seen since childhood spread about the property. It made him homesick. He missed his mansions in Ipswich and Ravenwood, and resented having to give them up over something as silly as repairs he could not perform himself.

His land had not been half as large as Duncan's, but it had been just as elegant. He had taken good care of it. The vast garden maze, tall apple trees and climbing rose vines had been his pride and joy. He loved feeding the swans first thing in the morning. Things he could not do now that both mansions were gone.

As much as he loved his new home in Ravenwood, it would never be like Anthony's and he still did not know how to react to that. In a way, he was no longer living in Anthony's shadow, yet that in itself felt strange.

Passing a large shady pond, he made his way toward the far end of the estate. Through the lining of brushes and trees, he caught glimpses of the deep blue Irish Sea. He paused in his hike to admire it.

Years earlier, he could remember dreaming of it. He had wanted so bad to explore its depths or sail across it to the far land of Ireland. It had been a fantasy for as long as he could remember. Folklore and tales of the faery people had always captivated him. The land had magick different from England and Asia.

He always wondered what it would feel like to stand on those shores, barefoot and feel the Earth spirit talk to him. Was Gaea different there? Would the land's magick welcome him as North America's did? He could not help but wonder. England and Ireland were so close yet worlds apart. One day he would go, he promised himself.

Cleo jumped out of the basket and led him to two boulders under an apple tree. He waited as his little companion pulled out the large old book from between the boulders. Taking it from him, Eli opened it to the page Cleo indicated.

"Basically, the mix of his telepathy and the Sinclair blood you now share nullifies many of your powers. You can cast a spell on anyone but him. It's far stronger than any spell he cast on Anthony."

They sat down under the tree and looked over the journal entry together. It was a complicated spell, one that had been in the works for over sixty years and only now working. "What do you mean?"

"Henry was telling the truth about Porter. He did love Anthony. Very much," the black cat explained. "but when Anthony would not fall in love with him, he tried to control him."

"But that didn't work."

"No. Anthony's willpower out-matched most, but Porter did find a way to enter his mind and calm him enough to make mental suggestions."

Eli froze, staring at his friend. "Like back in Ravenwood when he touched me? It was as if someone caressed me from the inside out. I would have done anything he said."

"Yes, but it only works when he's close to you or Anthony. He normally had to be touching you or use one of his shadow creatures when you were sleeping. It's why your mind gets all fuzzy when he touches you. Even the small caress or kiss can put you in a trance, and whatever he does, you will enjoy."

He blinked, his stomach, knotting. "But the first night here, he touched me and I fought back. His magick didn't work."

Cleo smiled sadly. "You were scared, chained to a bed in a room you had been tortured in as a child. So much fear can override any calming spell." He eyed his young master carefully. "Any such spell can be a form of assault, Eli. He mentally seduces you and then takes you."

"That's how he did it when I was a child, isn't it? If that didn't work, he would threaten to spank me." He shook his head. Those were memories he did not want to lay around. "But once we break through the shield, our powers should return to normal, right?"

"It appears so, but you must focus all your magick into opening a tear. The shield is almost as powerful as Anthony's strongest ones. He's had sixty years to perfect it."

Looking up, Eli stretched his senses. They were close to the border. A dull-red energy field, invisible to the average person, sparkled a hundred yards into the lush forest. Standing, he pulled his totem from his shirt and changed it into his staff. Cleo stepped next to him as they approached the shield.

Kneeling, Eli studied it. It would take considerable magick to pierce it. Laying down the basket, duffle bag and art supplies, he quickly reorganized the bag. Carrying so much stuff would only slow him down. Using a spell to make his clothes smaller, he packed all the food he could in the bag. Adjusting the pouch, he strapped it around his waist and right thigh.

Melissa thought of everything when she designed Alexis's battle attire, he thought, moving his leg. The pouch was firmly against his leg and had a buckle over the flap to keep the cards from spilling out when Alexis had to move quickly. The sorceress was well known for her jumps, twists, and flips. The gymnast needed equipment that moved with her. The pouch was something that Anthony could have used.

He dumped the paint stand and basket in the bushes where he hoped no one would find them, but kept the paper and board. Cleo could only fly him so far in his true form before his wings would give out. He was designed for speed, not distance. They would need to find transport if they wanted to get back to the cabin before the eclipse. Lord only knew how much time they had left when they stepped back into real time and space.

Taking a deep breath, he raised his staff to the shield. Electricity ran up and down its length as he brought the head against the shield. He tightened his grip, focusing all his magick on the task at hand. He silently prayed to the spirits for help. He felt the crystals vibrate against his leg. Their combined power raced to his staff in a show of help. His staff glowed brightly with their added magick. The blades of the dragon crowning the top of his golden staff sliced through the shield as if it were paper. An opening just wide enough for him and Cleo to slip through appeared within moments.

It felt like walking into another realm. Nausea gripped Eli the moment he passed through the shield. Time seemed to slow down, causing colourful lights to dance before his eyes. He stumbled, grasping a tree trunk to steady himself. It took a moment to get grounded, to remember Duncan had sped up time on his property, turning one day into many. It was early in the morning in the real world and time. Pitch black compared to the beautiful sunshine on the other side of the shield. It was better than being forever trapped in the castle.

His strength returned within minutes. The numbness he has been feeling the last few days subsided and his power returned to full strength. His senses heightened completely and he felt whole once again. It brought a smile to his lips. The first step to freedom was done.

Staring up into the night sky, he frowned. No moon. That was odd and discomforting. There was no light to lead them. It was easy enough to solve, he thought as he and Cleo proceeded into the woods. Thousands of tiny glowing lights danced from the pouch and surrounded them as the tiny glowing spirits took the lead.

Duncan threw the broken pieces of glass in the pail and sighed. Eli certainly had a temper. He took after Raven in every way. He had never expected the young man to break into his office or use a spirit to distract the guards. He should have. Anthony would have done the same…had, in fact. However, that was a lifetime ago, another place and time. He was still surprised that Eli had forgotten everything that had happened ten years ago. He had assumed as much in Ravenwood and had been thankful. It gave him a clean slate.

There were things for which even he could not forgive himself. A tear rolled down his cheek, completely taking him by surprise. He brushed it away and stared at the damp finger. Why, after so many years, was he feeling so guilty? Eli's words rung in his mind, *I hate you! I will always hate you!* He had been so hurt, so full of rage when he declared his hate. Duncan wanted so bad to explain why. To tell him just how much he loved him. Or maybe let him forget once more.

Block out everything that had happened so long ago, but that would be like living a lie. How could Eli ever truly love him without knowing the truth?

He was getting soft. In the real realm, he had little more than two days until the eclipse. He could make that into months, even years inside his property, but that would cause Eli to grow up far faster than natural and he still had a long life to live. No, another week or two at most. Just enough time to train him and hopefully prove his good intentions.

Having Henry with them was proving to be the cause of some of their difficulty. It was as if Henry was subconsciously feeding Eli the memories of his past. Every time he fed on Eli's magick, it broke one of the young man's carefully placed shields. It was as if he wanted Eli to fight Duncan.

If that were so, how was he to heal Eli? He could never discover or control what power Chaos may have given Eli. Duncan was beginning to suspect the demon had left him nothing but a heightened healing factor and slightly more sensitive telekinesis. There was nothing demonic within him, only Raven's spirit.

It would appear that Chaos had truly returned to the Void without cursing its host. That was a relief, although he had no idea how Eli would respond to the eclipse. Raven's book had said the Key would be the cause of the portals opening and Eli seemed to have no knowledge of how to do that. He had to learn. If luck was with them, things weren't going to be as bad as Raven had predicted. If only Eli would calm down and let him help him. Too bloody stubborn for his own good.

Something on the edge of his consciousness flickered. It wasn't big, just a small drain in his power that lasted a mere moment. He almost ignored it, believing that one of his servants had passed through the shield protecting his estate. Maybe Claudia was off to the market again. She had said she had to go to town.

His mind traveled out over his vast land to see the time of day. He didn't know why he had the urge to check, but he did. It was very early in the morning. The new moon was high in the early morning sky, obscured by heavy clouds. The scent of rain filled his subconscious. Just small approaching showers. It was far too early for any of his servants to be traveling outside the shield.

A knot formed in his stomach as possibilities ran through his mind. He had not felt Eli since Henry's training session. He thought that the young man was probably asleep, resting after the long and exhausting use of magick plus Henry's now normal feedings. Henry had never mentioned anything other than Eli had not yet opened a gate that morning. The knot grew as he tried to feel Eli's subconscious mind with no luck.

Dropping the chunk of broken computer parts in the garbage, he rushed up the flight of stairs to Eli's chambers. He had to take deep breaths once he reached the oak doors. He was overreacting. He had to be. Eli was in his bed, sound asleep with Cleo curled up next to him. Lord and Lady, please let him be here, he pleaded turning the doorknob.

He knew, even as he opened the door and walked in, Eli was not there. Nor were the crystals or Cleo. He didn't need to check the closet or bar fridge. He knew. Eli had run away.

Chapter Eighteen

Had the sprites not been shining around them, Eli doubted they would have been able to see anything. Even as his eyes adjusted to the blackness, he found he was tripping on the undergrowth far too often.

Cleo had returned to his full size to help balance Eli, but after the fourth time of Eli nearly twisting his ankle, Cleo declared they were flying. Eli didn't have a chance to argue before he found himself on the panther's back.

The mighty beast spread his huge wings and took to the air. Eli held on tight, protectively wrapping himself around his guardian as they rose above the branches and leaves that tried to reach and hold them down, some snagging on his jacket. They rose into the cloudy, starless sky. A light drizzle washed over them, but Cleo was determined not to let it hamper them. The shining spirits instantly followed. The playful sprites split themselves in two groups, the first staying with them while the other kept just above the tree line to make a path for them to follow. They found the highway and kept to it, passing the first small city in hopes of finding another.

Eli suspected Duncan would search Holyhead first, expecting him to look for help there, but he wasn't that foolish. He wanted to get as far from the castle as possible during the night and go to whatever town they were near by dawn. Yet after a few hours of flying and walking, Eli began to tire. Even Cleo was growing restless. Distance flight was never the panther's strong suit and Eli was much heavier than he was as a child. Tension was building between the great cat's shoulder blades as he tried to stay in the air. No matter how much Eli rubbed it, the tension continued to build and Cleo was slowly beginning to descend. "Cleo, land. Your wings—"

Cleo growled, shaking involuntarily. "Not until we're past the strait. The water will dampen their magick for a while. Give…us…time." He huffed as he pumped his wings harder.

Eli frowned at his stubbornness. "You're tired."

"Humph! I failed you once, not again."

"Cleo…" A smile graced his lips. The cat was just as bad as him. Scratching behind Cleo's ear, he laughed. "At least they kept us together, Cleo. I don't know what I would do without you." He hugged the cat's neck in traditional Selena fashion and giggled, doing his best impression of his cousin.

Cleo grunted under the tender assault. He never liked being *hugged* and it only made Eli laugh more. The face Cleo made was almost as funny as seeing him on a sugar high. Smiling, he buried his face in the soft blue-black fur. Cleo purred affectionately, his tail wrapping around his Master's ankle.

They flew for another hour, passing many farms and small towns. The blackness of night hid them from anyone who may have been looking skyward. A very worn Cleo landed in a field, completely exhausted and hungry. A river ran into a nearby forest. They followed it into the woods, walking nearly another kilometer before Cleo began dozing as he walked. Concerned, Eli found a small clearing for them to camp.

The spirits grew brighter as he began rummaging through his duffle bag. He was actually starving, but had not wanted to bother Cleo. It had taken all his strength and concentration just to keep them in the air. He estimated they were at least thirty to forty kilometers from the castle, in the hills of Colwyn.

His tired mind laughed. It had always been an odd name. Pushing that aside, he pulled out two tuna sandwiches and unwrapped them for Cleo. He pulled out a highly-stacked roast beef and cheese sandwich for himself and a cola. He smiled. Claudia had packed a lot of food for them. Maybe she had thought either Henry or Duncan would join them.

It was a good thing though, there was enough to last them a day or two if they were careful with it. Cleo did not really need food to sustain him, the sun gave him his power, but the great cat had become accustomed to eating and Eli was not about to deprive him of anything but sweets. Well, until they got home…then Cleo could go nuts on all the sugar he wanted.

Soft snores made him look up from his sandwich. The winged panther was sound asleep with half a tuna sandwich next to his muzzle. His large wings twitched in the gentle breeze. Under the soft illumination of the firefly like spirits, he looked picture-perfect.

Wrapping the leftover sandwich, Eli put it back in the bag, making a mental note that it was Cleo's. He finished off his own food and drink, then stretched out next to his friend. There were only a few short hours until sunrise and they needed what rest they could get.

Thanking the sprites and dismissing them, he slipped into slumber, unconsciously wrapping his arms around Cleo. The rumble of the cat's purr lulled him to sleep.

Selena awoke with a start. Magick swam around her. Eli and Cleo's essences were strong, almost as if they were right next to her. She expected to see the youth and cat curled next to her when she rolled over. An image of the two played before her, then vanished into nothingness. Blinking, she stared at the rumbled sheets next to her. Where were Eli and Cleo? Whom had she been sleeping with if not them? Anthony's magick was all around her.

Her memory slowly kicked in. Daniel Dion had come to England. He had had a vision of Eli. She could sense Eli again. What did that mean? Had he escaped his captors? She smiled. If she could sense them, that meant they could communicate and she could track them down.

Jumping out of bed, she virtually flew down the stairs. Alexis and Miao met her at the doorway to the sitting room. Alexis's eyes were bright, knowledge spilling from their emerald depths. Giddiness bubbled within Selena at the sight of the young woman. Alexis knew. She could feel Eli, too. By the look of Miao, he had a vague sense of Eli, but could not feel him as strongly as they could. It did not matter as long as they could feel him.

Throwing her arms around Alexis, she squealed in delight. Alexis bounced up and down with her practically at tears with joy.

Several groggy members of the Sinclair family approached them. No doubt, they, too, had sensed Anthony's magick. The whole household was most likely up now. That was more comforting than words could say.

She threw on her brightest smile and half-danced into the room. "Frost, Scott!" she called, singsong like. She bounced in, latching herself around Daniel's neck. She planted a kiss on the professor's cheek. "Do you feel him? I almost held him in my arms. I can smell him. I can smell Eli as if I was actually holding him!" she giggled.

Daniel only smiled, patting her hand. "Are you sure that's not me you're smelling?"

She sniffed his hair and neck. "Nope. You smell like musk, just like Anthony. Eli smells more like—"

"The ocean," Sif said, standing next to Alexis. He went to Daniel and Selena. His tiny brows came together. "They're by the sea. I can smell Cleo. He had a tuna sandwich!"

Scott raised a brow. "What?"

"He's been teasing me," the husky cried.

Miao shook his head and laughed. "Astral realm."

"Sif, do you think of anything other than your stomach?" Frost questioned from his perch on one of the elegant sofas. Shaking his head, he stood. "Daniel has tracked Eli to the Irish Sea. This side of Holyhead."

Selena smirked, still holding Daniel tightly. Amazingly, he didn't seem to mind. In fact, he seemed more than content letting her hang off him. The only other person to ever do that was Anthony. Scott and Frost usually yelled at her after thirty seconds. "Good thing. If they were on the other side, they'd be in the sea." She gave Daniel another peck on the cheek. "Andy, I love you…you, too, Dan, love."

He chuckled and squeezed her hand, much as Anthony used to.

"I love you, too, Selena, darling."

Her embrace tightened. The endearment had been purely Daniel's. It made her feel as if they were just one big family.

"Selena, I can't breathe."

She giggled, letting him go. "Oops, sorry." She rubbed the back of her head. "So, we go get them, right?"

Daniel nodded. "You, me and Frost will head toward—"

"Not you," Frost said sternly. He folded his arms across his chest. His icy gaze did not falter as Anthony slipped into Daniel. "You have little understanding of your powers and will be more of a hindrance than help."

"I—"

"No, Anthony, Daniel. You will stay here with the children and Sif. The Sinclairs will protect you." He raised a hand as the older man began to object. "Whoever kidnapped Eli, may very well come after you. The Sinclairs are a family of powerful magicians. No one will get near you and Alexis here."

"Dad, Scott is better in the field than you, especially when it come to combat," Alexis said in Frost's defense. Seeing her father's eyes narrow, she bit her lip. "I'm sure you can take care of yourself, but magick battles can be tricky and you're just not trained for it. You're not like Eli. You're not ready yet. Anthony, please don't do this."

Anthony's anger reflected in his eldest reincarnation's eyes. He frowned deeply for a moment before sighing in restraint. "Of course. You are both correct. Daniel has yet to develop his metaphysical shields or any defensive magick. Eli has been subconsciously calling to him. Daniel only feels the need to be next to him. To protect him like only a father would their child."

"We understand, but for both of your protection, it is best if you stay with us," Richard said with a tired yawn. He looked over his guests, many of which were still tired.

Selena grinned when she caught his eye. A silent message passed between them and Selena's grin grew.

Groaning, Richard nodded. "Pietro will find you an appropriate mode of transportation."

"The SUV—" Scott began, but stopped when Selena raised a hand with a devious smile. He glanced at Frost in confusion.

"Yes, the SUV would be a good idea." She gave the two men a wink before following the young blond-haired man out of the room. Normally it wasn't this easy to get Richard to bend to her wishes.

Pietro was small, built much like Frost, only a little shorter, which for Frost must have been a new experience. Nathan had been the second shortest male in High School and college. Frost never mentioned anything about the young Sinclair's height as they followed him down the long dimly lit corridors and Selena was happy for that.

Pietro was a little sensitive about it. His mother's family came from a small region in France and had little magick, but where he lacked in physical strength, he gained in his father's magick. He certainly wasn't the most powerful Sinclair, but he was impressive. As children, he and Selena use to play together all the time, she and Eli visited the Sinclairs or Pietro visiting Mae Sinclair's home in Ipswich.

Eli had loved when they spent time with Pietro because he never cared about the fact Eli was the reincarnation of Anthony Sinclair. Sometimes, if Eli said anything about being Anthony, Pietro would tackle the young man to the ground and tickle him until he declared he was Eli Hawke. If Eli didn't or couldn't stop laughing long enough to, Pietro would start searching Eli's pockets, calling out for Eli, and threatening not to buy any sweets for his *lil' buddy* until he found him.

On two occasions when Eli was only six or seven, he had actually laughed so hard be peed his pants. He had almost cried, believing Pietro would be mad but the older man had only laughed and declared he had found a very wet Eli rather than getting upset. He had even taken Eli in to get changed, saying that it was nothing about which to get upset. Accidents happened. It had caused Eli to adore Pietro even more.

Whenever they spent the night together, Pietro would spend half the night telling them scary stories in hopes of scaring them. While Selena, as much as she hated to admit it, ended up squeezing one of her teddies, Eli would bounce up and down, adding onto the story to scare her even more. They both had wild imaginations.

In many ways, Eli was Pietro's *pet.* Eli always followed the older boy around the mansion. It was hard to keep them separated, let alone get some private time with Pietro when he and Selena were in their mid-teens. Pietro had been Selena's first steady boyfriend and was still her best friend. He was in for a surprise by Eli's growth.

They stepped into the large garage. Scott whistled at the sight of well over a dozen vehicles. Pietro was also the Sinclair resident mechanic. Over half the cars, vans and motorcycles were equipped with magick users in mind. Most had an intake designed to absorb excess magick that may overheat the engine and cause the vehicle to die or worse.

It was a complicated design that came from Pietro's computerlike mind. All windows were reinforced, not so much for bulletproofing, but because you were never sure what a rival magick user may send your way. The rest of the body and frame were also reinforced for such reasons.

Truth be told, it only gave a few extra seconds, maybe minutes to escape, but if someone really wanted you dead, not even that could protect you. Each vehicle was also warded to keep people from trying to steal them. Any thief who tried to take one would instantly think better of it and move on. It was the same type of warding spell Eli had placed on their car back home.

Pietro led them to a black SUV with matching black tinted windows. It was one of the heaviest equipped vehicles the Sinclairs owned. Its twin sat next to it. Both were used by the Paranormal Investigators, a small group within the Sinclairs and surrounding magick groups who went out to deal with aggressive demons or spirits that were either causing harm or becoming severe annoyances to the community.

It usually turned out to be a grumpy faery not happy with the modern world or a playful goblin just trying to scare the public. The Elves were usually quiet and kept to themselves. There had been times when a demonic presence had called upon the team. Such things as demons attempting to break into this realm, a demonic possession, the odd fallen angel, vampires, or a rouge Lycanthrope were not uncommon.

The amount of monsters in the world was uncountable. Others…well there was a good reason for the magick community to monitor them. The public would be in shock if they really knew what surrounded human-kind.

The vans were loaded with weapons to deal with such creatures, both magickal and man-made. If none of them worked, which was very rare, they were screwed. There was nothing like an enraged monster ripping your heart out. Selena had seen it happen to one of the Investigators when they had upset one of the faery Sidhe Queens. The creature the fey had as a pet tore into the man like raw meat. She and Eli had barely escaped with their lives.

Pietro smiled as he handed her the keys. "Tell Little Bit I have a whole bag of jelly beans with his name on it as long as he comes home safely."

"He's not that little anymore." She raised her hand just over her head. "He's getting big."

"Three inches taller than you? Mon Dieu! I can't call him my little buddy anymore!" He feigned horror. "How will I pick on him if he's bigger than me?"

Scott laughed. "That's not hard," he teased, looking over the vehicle. "I pick on him almost on a daily basis."

"And you were going to dump me for him?"

Selena giggled as Frost rolled his eyes. "Pete, as much as I love flirting with you, we must be off."

He took her hand and brushed his lips over her knuckles as he always did after long periods between visits. "Of course, my lady," he said in his best nobleman impression.

Flashing a coy smile to the other two men, he left to open the main garage doors. It was obvious he didn't like either Scott or Frost. Well, at least Scott. It was true that when she was seventeen, she was going to dump Pietro for the soccer star, but he was already taken. As for Frost, Pietro seemed at awe, but it was very un-Sinclair-like to gush over a faery. All that meant in Pietro's case was he would wait until Eli was safe before he began his endless line of questioning of what it's like to be an *angel*. Although Selena was pretty sure Frost was anything but an angel.

Selena climbed behind the steering wheel. Frost, now in Nathan's form, sat next to her while Scott took the back. He took a moment to marvel over the technology filling the back. Two laptops were built into the back of the front seats, both with satellite link up. It helped track down paranormal occurrences and link up with someone who may be better in a certain field. The weapons were stored under the seat in a strong box.

"Ready, boys?" She gunned the engines, making Scott jump and forget the computers. "Let's go find Eli." Waving to Pietro, she drove out of the garage and pulled down the long driveway to the street. Finding the trail Alexis's spirits had created, she kicked it up to one hundred and twenty kilometers per hour, shifting into her false form as she drove.

"Can you sense him?" Henry asked for the umpteenth time since they left the castle.

It was beginning to annoy Duncan. He had instructed the driver to go slow. It was easier for him to search the surrounding woods for Eli.

There was no fear of traffic, it was still far too early for many people to be on the highway. It was a slow process, but if Eli had his metaphysical shields in place, they would practically have to be on top of him for Duncan to truly sense his aura. Henry was anything but patient. He was pissed off, but Duncan ignored him. It took great focus to find Eli.

After discovering Eli was missing, he had sent some of his people down river to see if he had gone that way. They had strict orders not to touch him. Duncan, himself, was going to retrieve him. They would, if all went well, make him run toward them. Catching Eli and Cleo was not going to be hard. At least he hoped not. They had been on the run for four hours and would be incredibly tired by now. A few magickal obstacles would further advance the cause. As soon as he located Eli, he would increase the destructive nature of the approaching storm. Eli would have to use his magick, enabling Duncan to pinpoint his location.

They were nearing Colwyn Bay as dawn broke. The sky was a deep gray with a streak of blue-green, a storm sky...a sky full of promise.

Not five minutes out of Colwyn Bay, Duncan's senses prickled. He smiled, looking out of the tinted window to the south. Not ten kilometers in sheep country, Eli and Cleo were hiding, sound asleep near the river. Prefect. As long as they stayed where they were, he could catch up with them in ten minutes.

Picking up his cell phone, he dialed the number for his men on the boat. "Outside Colwyn Bay. Look along the river bank." Hanging up, he instructed the limo driver to turn right at the next intersection.

"You found him?"

He gave Henry a satisfied smile. "Yes. Sleeping like a baby."

"Let's keep him sleeping, shall we?"

Closing his eyes, Duncan fully relaxed. His mind slipped into the astral realm easily as the sound of rolling tires lulled him into a trance. His astral body left the limo, flying ahead of them over trees and farmland. Deep under the foliage of the forest, mere feet from the river, Eli laid curled next to his panther guardian. Descending slowly, he hovered over his prize for a moment, watching Eli's slow, even breathes. He looked peaceful. Ignoring the pang in his stomach, he forced his way into Eli's body.

Eli gasped, his eyes fluttering open for a moment before closing.

Cleo opened one eye and studied his young master. With one large paw, he pulled the slim figure closer and went back to sleep.

* * *

The bridge of stars stretched out before him. Curious, he began walking along the dream bridge.

"Anthony? Anthony?" he called, looking in every direction. The spirit of his past self was nowhere to be found. Frowning, Eli moved on. Maybe Anthony was asleep. Do ghosts even sleep? He laughed at himself for such an absurd thought. Anthony slept when his mind slept so that wasn't often, if ever. So where was Anthony and why was he in the dream realm?

"I'm sorry, Eli."

Spinning around, Eli found Duncan standing behind him. The older man's head bowed. When he looked up, grief filled his eyes.

"I'm sorry for the abuse, the lies. Sorry for taking your family from you and then kidnapping you and for allowing Henry to feed from you." He swallowed hard, his eyes teary. "I'm sorrier than you will ever understand, but I can't let you go."

"Try and stop me," Eli snarled, summoning his staff. He was ready to fight, die even to escape. The bridge began to change. It grew, climbing up his legs and making it impossible to move. It was like one of Duncan's shadows creatures, only made of light. It climbed up Eli until it reached his upper chest, then stopped. A cocoon of pure light ensnared him, but did not hurt his eyes. He struggled as Duncan slowly approached him.

"You see, if Henry finds you awake and you fight us, you're likely to be beaten, far worse than last night. If you're asleep or come peacefully, he may be gentle."

"Let me go!" Eli growled, trying to summon his power to break free, but the staff was also encased in the light. Anthony, Anthony, please, help me! he pleaded. As Duncan came closer, hope began to fade. He was trapped, and unless he could wake up, Duncan and Henry were going to find him. He shook his head. This couldn't happen. "No," he whispered.

Duncan touched his cheek. "Don't fight me, Eli. I won't hurt you. I swear. I never meant for you to be hurt."

The words brought no comfort. He continued to struggle, fighting, and mentally calling for his magick to obey him. Nevertheless, nothing worked. Not even Anthony answered his pleas.

Eli?

He fought, ignoring the whispered voice.

Eli, wake up.

Finally, the power within him began to build. The power to escape was hot and raw.

"Don't do this, Eli. You don't know what Henry is capable of," Duncan pleaded as he, too, sensed the growing magick. "Please, Eli, you're only making matters worse."

The power became a burning sensation.

Focus, Eli. You must wake up.

The cocoon of light crumbled around Eli like many shards of glass. Staring at the warlock, he sneered angrily. "You can't stop me, Porter. I will not be some slave for you or Henry."

With an inaudible growl, he forced himself to wake up.

* * *

"Shh!" Cleo growled softly as Eli awoke with a start. He placed his muzzle against Eli and a paw on his side, preventing him from moving.

A thin ray of light danced through the darkness of the trees coming off the river. It wasn't from the sun. A spotlight, Eli realized with horror. They were coming by the river.

The spotlight moved above their heads, but the darkness of the woods kept the two hidden until the light swept past. Once they were out of the light's path, Cleo nudged Eli over the edge of the rock platform into the brush. Keeping to the shadows, Eli grabbed the duffle bag and his glasses. Keeping low, they ran deep into the forest, back toward the highway.

"What happened? You went into a trance," Cleo asked as he ducked branches and avoided up growing roots. His wings vanished to keep from being snagged.

Eli panted as he forced himself to keep pace with the mighty cat. Cleo had a nasty habit of forgetting he was human and unable to keep up with him at times. "P-Porter invaded my dreams. W-was trying to keep us here."

The sky grew dark. Large drops of rain splashed on the heads. The wind began to howl, blowing harshly and ripping at the light green leaves of the trees. Rival magick beat at them as they avoided falling debris.

Sparing a glance skyward, Eli took note of the oddly coloured sky. Green-gray clouds with a hint of red. Hurricane skies. It wasn't normal in England. Duncan must have been causing it. Just to catch him? That was insane! What if there were innocent bystanders?

Yelling behind them alerted Eli to the boatmen chasing after them. He could not sense Duncan among them. One small blessing at least. However, the men were armed with what looked like rifles. Duncan would never have someone use a gun on them. Henry…Henry must have made them come armed. Why? Did Henry suddenly want him dead? Unless they were loaded with tranquillizer darts. Eli almost wished they were real bullets. Better to die than be forced back into Duncan's arms.

Flipping open Alexis's pouch, he blindly pulled out a crystal. "Wood!" he cried, not even looking to see if he had pulled the right card. "Block their path." He silently prayed the spirit would do as he asked. He threw his own nature magick into assist the spirit.

The ground shook before them as vines and roots intertwined and began growing upward. They leapt over them as the undergrowth grew faster, higher, until it was above their heads, but it was not yet dense enough.

Eli spotted the highway up a head. He boosted his speed as much as possible without falling. A small explosion echoed behind them, signaling a gunshot.

Pain rocketed through the back of Eli's neck. With a gasp, he grasped his neck. It stung, but he could not allow himself to focus on it. He kept running, ignoring his drooping eyelids.

Why Aaliyah McNeil had woken so early in the morning and why she had decided to drive halfway across the country while visiting a good friend for the week had her confused. The urge had been so sudden and the need to visit Holyhead after so long seemed to have no apparent reason. In fact, Holyhead was not a town she really wanted to visit ever again. However, before hitting Colwyn Bay, she had another strong urge to turn around. It didn't make sense. It felt like she was driving in circles.

She had sensed Eli, or rather Raven, in two different sections of England, Wales and Cambridge. She knew Eli was visiting his grandfather and she had been planning to visit him before he left. Well, if she could muster the courage. After the last time they talked, she feared he would not want to see her. His heart was broken and needed time to heal. She was terrified of hurting him again.

However, a second aura? Why would Daniel Dion be in England? For that matter, why would one of them be here in the middle of nowhere?

Cambridge, she thought, checking her phone. Maybe the Sinclairs would know what was going on.

Halfway through dialing, she passed a long black limo. The auras within it were dark, but familiar. Curious, she gazed at the black windows. One was a Sinclair yet not. It was as if the Sinclair aura was hiding or protecting another's. An older one. She focused harder, penetrating through the well-developed facade.

"By the Goddess!" she gasped, putting her foot on the gas. It couldn't be, but she knew it had to be. Duncan Porter was indeed alive. What was he doing out here? Why had she not noticed his aura when she passed him on her way toward town? The aura in the woods must be what he was after. It was close, running fast.

She had to beat Porter.

She cried out as two dark shadows burst through the thick forest and onto the highway, directly in her path.

She hit the brakes. There was no time to think. She couldn't even come up with a spell as her tires squealed in protest. Vines shot up from the earth, meters from the front of the car. They formed a barrier, cushioning the impact. When she hit, it was with force of a punch to the gut. Eli clung to the hood, winded, but not seriously hurt. Aaliyah watched in amazement as the young mage pushed himself to his elbows. Ocean-blue eyes peered through the pouring rain, glazed over in pain and shock.

Shifting to park, she threw open the door and ran to him.

"Eli!" she cried, wrapping her arms around him.

He didn't fight or struggle as she led him to the left side of the car. Opening the passenger door, she gestured for Cleo to jump in back. She sat Eli in next and quickly shut the door. The limo was approaching quickly. Porter must have sensed her. Behind the wheel of the Mercedes, she shifted into gear and tore down the road. "Hold on, Eli."

The youth gripped the dashboard not saying a word. He looked ready to pass out and was clenching the back of his neck as if in pain.

"Cleo, take out their tires," she instructed as Eli's head began to bob. "Stay awake, Eli. Do up your seatbelt."

It took a moment for the young mage to do so. He looked at her in confusion. "Aaliyah?" he whispered as if trapped in a dream.

Cleo roared behind them, his blue flame exploded from his mouth as he leaned out the window. He sent ball after ball of fire until the front of the limo erupted into flames. Aaliyah watched in satisfaction as it swerved to the side of the road and came to a halt.

Aaliyah flashed Eli a grin, only to discover he had lost consciousness. Concerned, she reached over and touched the back of his neck. It was sticky with blood and a small dart was piercing his soft skin. Very gently, she removed the tranquillizer dart and studied it while keeping an eye on the road. It was still half-full, meaning he didn't get the full effect of the drug. He should only sleep a few short hours, not even. Thank the Lord and Lady for small miracles.

"So, what happened, Cleo? Porter's supposed to be dead, but I sensed him just a moment ago." She glanced at him through the rearview mirror. "There was a Sinclair aura hiding him."

The cat nodded. "It's a long story, Mistress, but I'm sure you can guess what he was after," he said formally, bowing slightly to his master's former love.

She shook her head, squeezing Eli's hand. "Even in death he never gives up." A gasp tore from her throat as her hand brushed against the leather pouch against his leg. "The crystals?"

"Porter forced Alexis to give them to him. He wants Eli to turn them back to his own."

"Why?"

"I wish I knew."

Eli looked uncomfortable, sitting with his chin against his chest. His neck was going to be stiff.

"Cleo, by the door there's a button to lower Eli's seat. Push it until he's halfway back. Thanks."

The panther did as asked without question. The seat lowered until Eli was half-laying in it. His head rolled to the side and his breathing became soft and shallow.

"Good. Now there should be an Afghan back there somewhere. Can you pass it to me?"

Instead, Cleo changed to his false form and dragged it to her. He placed it on Eli's lap, then began covering him entirely. Within mere moments, Eli began looking better. Cleo curled himself on the youth's lap.

Aaliyah petted him affectionately. It had been so long since she had run her fingers through his soft fur. It surprised her how much she actually missed the two. "Are you guys okay? How long were you in the woods?"

"All night. We broke out of Porter's fortress early this morning."

She nodded. Eli was exhausted for more reasons than one. He needed protection and for once, she was ill equipped to take care of him. Her hand fell to her swollen belly. There was someone a little more important for her to worry about. It didn't mean she wasn't willing to help her young friend, but the Sinclairs were better equipped to protect him. Moreover, if Dion and his children were in Cambridge, all the better. He could return the crystals with no trouble to Alexis. Maybe she could help him.

The sky was suddenly black as night. The rain grew heavier, the wind harder, hammering into the sides of the car. The ground shook with the force of an earthquake causing the small car to bounce along the road. She looked out the window only to find she could no longer see the road. "Damn!" she cursed, slowing down slightly.

"Black out. This is hurricane weather."

"What?"

"Porter, he must have—" She gazed at Eli's unconscious form. "He wants us to stop. He thinks we won't risk Eli or my baby's life to go through." She bit her lip. Her baby's life was in danger. Porter was trying to give her an ultimatum, Eli, or her unborn child. She couldn't abandon Eli. Not to Porter...but her baby...

Cleo shook his little head. "He won't hurt Eli. He... he seems to genuinely care for him. Maybe even love him."

She closed her eyes for a second. She had to choose, now, before the car was ripped in half, Eli, or the baby…Eli or the baby. Her brows came together as she opened her eyes. A determined scowl crossed her face. She threw an arm across Eli's chest to brace him as she gunned the engine. "I'm counting on that." She floored the gas paddle.

"What are you doing?"

She refused to answer. The rain and wind pounded on the car, threatening to tear it in half. Bracing herself for the impending force of the hurricane, she prayed to her Gods that was doing the right thing. The only way to protect Eli and her child was to get as far from Duncan Porter as possible, even if it meant driving into the eye of the storm.

Her imagination began working overtime as she thought of how long Porter may have had Eli. What had the warlock done to him in that time? The images from seven years ago played in her mind—the hospital, the frightened doctors. She had no doubt that everything from back then was repeating now. If she slowed down, Goddess only knew what Porter would do to them. Either way, her child was now in danger.

Taking a deep breath, she willed the storm to break. She pleaded with the divine to let them through unharmed. Blood pounded in her ears. Fear squeezed at her chest as she unconsciously squeezed her eyes shut. The pressure against the car was suffocating. Her fingers tightened around Eli's shoulder. Lord, Lady, please help us, she pleaded.

"By the Gods!" Cleo cried.

Her eyes flew open. The blackness enveloped them in a thickness impossible to cut through. It was total with no escape. They were going to be torn in two.

Then, as quickly as it started, the blackness dispelled. Soft gray rain clouds covered the sky with no hint of the horror they had just faced. The rain became a soft pitter-patter and the wind a gentle breeze.

Aaliyah was almost giddy with laughter. She let go of Eli and patted Cleo. "Thank the Goddess!" she cried. Porter did care for Eli, enough to make sure he wouldn't get hurt. There was a plus side to his obsession. She smiled at Cleo. "Are you hungry?"

The cat stared at her as if she had sprouted another head.

"Eli looks as if he could use a pick-me-upper," she chuckled, nodding. The baby was kicking. It was more than likely upset by their near-death experience. She was so famished after the excitement that she could not believe it had only been an hour since she last ate.

Duncan rested his head in his hands. *Too close*, he berated himself. Too damned close! He never suspected McNeil of such bravery, especially in her condition. They would have been crushed had he waited another second, and he would have truly lost Eli.

He heaved a large sigh and lifted his face to the rain. It was refreshing after the strain of controlling the storm. He still could not believe he had lost Eli, and to that Priestess of all people. What was she doing so far from London? No matter the reason, he was still in trouble. If the Sinclairs learned he was still alive, they would be in an uproar over Michael's death. They would never believe the truth. Everything was falling apart. A large hand grasped his shoulder, shaking him out of his thoughts.

"Now what?" Henry demanded, angrily.

Henry was so much stronger now that he was feeding off Eli's magick, but it was only temporary. In a few days, maybe even weeks, he would once again return to his true age. He had a month, perhaps two at most, before he was crippled once more, unless he was able to feed. It meant without Eli, Henry would begin feeding on Duncan, and he was not going to be gentle either. Not now that Duncan had let them escape. Why Henry refused to take on one of the Guardians, Duncan would never understand. Their blood was immortal and would permanently slow his aging after only a few short feedings. It had worked with Nathaniel. Frowning, he pulled away from the big man. "Fix the limo and try to track."

"What do you mean *try*?"

"Try. As in, if McNeil puts a warding spell on him that I can't break, we're screwed."

"You better find him, Duncan. You assured me this would not happen."

"And you said you could control him!" Duncan gasped as Henry shoved him against the black vehicle. Henry pinned him there and glared into his face.

"Remember all those stories about me during the war?"

He nodded numbly. Fear was beginning to build in his stomach. There had been many horror stories back then, none of which he had ever believed, until now.

"A good share of them was true." Henry gave a sly smirk and whispered very softly. "Find Eli before I prove it."

"Yeah, yeah, sure, I'll find him."

Henry flashed a friendly smile and slapped his back. "Good man."

Henry was losing it, Duncan decided, moving cautiously away from him. He moved to the front of the limo and quickly helped the driver fix the engine while his mind tracked Eli throughout the countryside. He suddenly wanted Eli to escape. It was for his safety. Henry was insane if the rumors were true. He feared to see what would happen if Henry got his hands on Eli now. It didn't take a genius to know he would kill Aaliyah and her unborn child to get to him.

The music was too loud, Selena knew, but its steady pounding kept her from drifting completely into her thoughts. She needed to focus on the road, not Henry's betrayal, not the many horrible things that may have happened to Eli and Cleo. She didn't want to think about the marks that had appeared on Daniel's back or how they had disappeared short hours later.

At least she could sense them still. After hours of driving, she had feared Porter and Henry might catch the two before they found them. However, Eli was sneaky and she had no doubt that with Cleo's help, he could elude his captors for a few more hours.

Please be safe, Eli, she prayed silently. Just a little longer. Nathan and Scott sat, stony faced, lost in their own thoughts. She was certain they were both thinking the same thing. How to find Eli quicker? Reaching over, she squeezed her brother's hand and offered a smile. "We'll make it," she declared, despite his doubtful look. "We'll make it."

Nathan nodded, but the doubt in his eyes only increased. He was also worried about the others, she realized. Frost did not trust the Sinclairs at the moment. After everything that had happened in the last few days, she couldn't blame him, but it would have been more dangerous to bring Alexis with them without her magickal tools to help protect her. She had not completely mastered her powers yet to work without them. At least the Sinclairs, Sif and Miao were there to protect her and her father. Besides, despite her conflict with Richard, he would guard them with his life. He was a loyal friend.

Scott's hand reached past them and turned down the volume of the pounding music. The loud voice made no sense at first and Selena had to concentrate to understand.

"…eak hurricane made landfall ten kilometers west of Colwyn Bay. Other than toppled trees along the highway, no serious destruction was reported. Crews are already out repairing downed hydro lines. Electricity is expected to resume late this evening. This is the first hurricane in nearly sixty years to hit this area. In other news…"

Nathan blinked. "Eli?"

Scott nodded. "It has to be. He's in that region, Dad said."

That didn't make sense. Eli would not cause a hurricane. Not unless Duncan and Henry were after him and Cleo. Only if they got too close.

Glancing at the speedometer, she frowned. They were already doing over a hundred. Pressing down on the gas, she brought them to a hundred and twenty. Both stared at her. There was no other choice. They had to find Eli before Porter. They were on a highway with no police or cars in sight. They could afford to go past the speed limit.

His head hurt. It felt as if the blood was pounding against his eyelids, making it impossible to open them. Rolling his head to the side, he winced. That little movement almost made him sick. His neck stung like a son of a bitch. Reaching up, he rubbed it and yawned. He had never felt so worn-out in his life. The blanket slipped from his chest to pile on his lap. A muffled cry made Eli open his eyes a crack. "Cleo?"

The cat poked his head out from under the blanket. "Master?"

His teal eyes lit up. "How do you feel?"

Closing his eyes, he sighed. "Tired. Where are we?"

"Flint."

"How? Who…"

He remembered being hit by a car. Not hard, but enough to knock the wind out of him. Then there was wet, silky red hair brushing across his face as someone helped him into the car. Golden amber eyes had met his. It all seemed like a dream. There was no way their savior was who he thought.

The driver side door opened, making him catch his breath. *Please, oh please let it be her,* he pleaded. His heart fell when he saw the large belly.

Reminding himself to breathe, he undid his seatbelt and helped the pregnant woman. After all, she had saved them. It would be rude not to offer a helping hand. "I've got it," he said, plastering on his best smile. He took the two large bags from the woman and moved them to the backseat so she could get in.

"You're awake!" She smiled and bent slightly to look at him.

Eli's jaw dropped. "Aaliyah?"

Her smile grew. "Hi, sweetie. Here."

She handed him a tray of coffee and slipped into her seat. Setting a large paper bag on her lap, she pulled out a breakfast sub. Taking the coffees, she handed him the huge sandwich. She placed the coffees in the holders, then gave Cleo a bagel from the bag.

"How… What are you doing so far from London?" He shook his head. "I mean…thanks. I…it's hard to explain."

"It's okay, honey. I've already put two and two together." She gestured for him to put his seatbelt on as she started the engine.

He did so quickly, then stared at his egg, ham, and cheese sandwich. It had everything he liked, tomato, ham, lettuce, and mayo. Aaliyah knew what he liked. It seemed funny sitting next to her. He had never dreamed of them ever being together like this again. His eyes wandered to her belly. She was huge! How many months was she?

"Porter's alive, isn't he?"

He nodded, biting into his sandwich.

"Did he…hurt you?"

"Nothing I couldn't handle." Looking out the window, he swallowed. "Something has happened to Henry."

They slowed to a stop at the intersection. Aaliyah's worried eyes turned to him. "He's not…"

"He's alive, but he's changed, Aaliyah, he's not the same." He stared at the road thoughtfully. "It's like he's a completely different person. Maybe Porter put a spell on him or something. It's just that he…"

"It's okay, Eli."

He turned to her with serious eyes. "No, it's not okay. He's become a psychic vampire! He's getting younger each time he feeds from me…and stronger." His eyes were wide and fearful. He didn't want to admit it, but he was no longer sure who he feared more, Duncan or Henry. Duncan may have hurt him in the past, but Henry had totally betrayed him. It was still hard to believe it had actually happened, and by Henry of all people. A single tear rolled down his cheek as he closed his eyes. Henry. He loved Henry so much it was painful. How could he have ever betrayed him?

"Oh, Eli."

He felt her cup his cheek and wipe away the tear. At some point, she had pulled to a side street so she could hold him. He buried his face in her bosom and sobbed. She cradled him, rocking gently as he trembled.

"It's okay, baby. Let it out."

Sniffling, he stared up into her amber eyes. "How did you find me?"

Smiling, she kissed his forehead. "The same way I did when we first met. I just felt you."

It took a few minutes for him to relax enough to sit back. Not that he wanted to. He would have held onto her forever if he could, but then she would not be able to drive. Wiping away the remaining tears, he began nibbling on his sandwich.

They left the small town behind as they hit the open road.

The clouds had broken up to reveal a beautiful blue sky. It was going to be a beautiful sunny day. He smiled suddenly as realization hit him. They were on their way home finally. He laughed softly to himself. Alexis and Miao would be so happy to see him. He could practically feel Alexis bouncing into his arms, squealing in laughter. In fact, he could already hear Scott and Miao taunting him. Scott seemed to enjoy tormenting him. He was exactly what Eli pictured a big brother to be. Alexis had no idea how lucky she was. He could not wait to see them and Daniel.

"So, you went shopping?" he asked around the rim of his coffee cup. He could not help but smirk. He never thought Aaliyah the type to go shopping while on the run.

"Well, I was checking out your duffle bag. It must have been ripped while you were running, so I pick up a new backpack and a few lunch supplies. Plus…" She reached behind her and stretched her fingertips. A blue baseball cap flew to her. "I thought if we could tie your hair up in a way we could hide it in the cap and take off your glasses, we can trick Porter's goons. Mind you, Porter's another story. My warding spells are nothing compared to your grandmother's."

He nodded.

"Hers protected me until I split Anthony's power."

"Don't blame yourself. It had to be done."

"I know. Only Anthony's warding spells could completely counter Duncan's."

"Duncan? Since when did you get on a first name basis?"

He stared at his last bite of sandwich with guilt. How do you tell the woman you love that you have developed feelings for your rival? A man no less?

"Eli?"

"We sort of became friends—for a short, very short time. Then I found out the truth and everything went downhill."

Her eyes were wide as she stared at him. The car began to swerve to the right.

"Aaliyah, the road!"

She snapped to attention and corrected their path. "What do you remember?"

"My parents, the time with the Porters, Nan's death. Only bits and pieces, but it was enough. I learned the rest when I broke into his office."

"I'm sorry. I wanted to tell you everything but...I also wanted to protect you."

"I know. I was bound to find out." His blue eyes gave her a weary look. "I just want to go home."

She nodded and gave a small reassuring smile as she placed the hat on his head, making sure the visor fell over his eyes.

He chuckled and fixed it. It felt almost like old times. Taking off his glasses, he folded them and placed them in his jacket pocket. Braiding his hair back, he used a few of Aaliyah's pins to keep it up in the hat. He fished a cosmetic mirror out of her purse and held it close to his face. He frowned slightly. Without his glasses, he looked twelve. As long as it fooled Porter's men, then he had no complaints.

Chapter Twenty

Sinclair Manor was almost twice the size of Syffern Mansion. Unlike Miao's home, the manor was a maze of halls on six floors.

Some parts were very old with no electricity, while others were so modern you would never have thought it had been built in the sixteen hundreds. It still had that "old" feeling. It was so dark with the wood panel walls and burgundy carpet. Antique style lanterns lined the walls. The spirits of old filled the place. It was almost overwhelming. Miao could not recall ever walking through such a place.

Holding Alexis's hand, they wandered the place of Raven's birth in wonder. To Miao, the dark halls were depressing, not at all a place he could imagine children playing. It was nothing like the mansion Anthony had owned in Canada or the one in Ipswich. They were much brighter and friendlier. Too bad Eli no longer had either.

He sighed as they came to another dead end. Where was Anthony's room? They had been working, using only their senses, but Anthony and Eli must have played in every hall. It was a good place for hide and seek, he had to admit. It was one of Eli's favourite games.

"This place is huge," Alexis muttered.

"Our one chance to learn all Anthony's childhood secrets and we're lost!" groaned Miao. He leaned against the wall and frowned.

"Eli's not even here to stop us or make up a dozen stories."

"We should have asked Sif."

"He would never let us in Anthony's room."

She seemed thoughtful as she leaned on the wall across from him. "Well, let's try my Dad's aura. He hasn't been all over the house yet and he was in the room last night."

"Perhaps." Stretching his senses, he followed his girlfriend's father's magickal trail. He could "feel" that Mr. Dion was in the garden with Sif and Mr. Sinclair. A smile stretched across his lips as he found the room he desired. "We should have thought of this earlier."

She grinned playfully. "What would you do without me?"

Grasping her hands, he kissed her passionately. "Sit in Spain with my cousins and siblings tormenting me."

She giggled at that. Once again, the chase was on. They ran down a few corridors, down a flight of stairs until they came upon a corridor they had previously missed. A door, like all the others, glowed a pale blue. Had it not been for their gifts, they would have completely missed it.

Alexis slowly opened the door. "Dad?" she asked, even if they both knew he was outside.

The room was spacious, as large as Miao's back in Spain. Wallpaper with the moon, sun and stars adorned the walls in blue. The canopy had a similar embroidered design along with the quilt and pale blue sheets of the four-poster bed. An oak dresser with a long oval mirror sat across from it. There were several shelves with ornaments, books, and pictures along the far wall next to a big reading chair, lamp, and desk.

Jackpot, Miao thought as he went to the desk. His mother may have had Anthony's journal from the last twenty years of his life, but he was sure the mage had left many things behind before moving to Canada or Spain. His mother would kill him if she ever found out he was snooping through her grandfather's room. He grinned childishly as he opened the top drawer. A small leather book with a worn spine met his eyes. "Yes!" Sitting in the big chair, he began flipping through it.

"Wow!" Alexis exclaimed, holding a large, framed photo. She sat on Miao's lap and showed it to him. "She's beautiful."

"That's Xyan Sinclair, my great grandmother."

"She looks like your mom." Her fingers traced over the photo. "Anthony looks so young."

"He was seventeen when they married. Mom says it was arranged shortly after Xyan's birth to keep the bond between our two magick families strong. She was only nineteen or twenty when she gave birth to Naomi Sinclair. After she died and Anthony ran away, the families began blaming each other for his heartache."

"He really loved her."

Miao gave a nod. "Anthony had several lovers after that, but never married again, or so I've been told. Some say they buried his heart along with her body."

"He just needed time to heal." Her fingers brushed over Anthony's childlike features. "I can't believe how much Eli looks like him."

"Yeah, you'd think he was Anthony's great-grandson rather than me."

"We now know where your mother gets her looks," she teased, getting off his lap. She put it away and looked at the others as he began flipping through the old pages of the book.

Small sketches filled the first few pages. A few scribbled notes filled the spaces. He deciphered what he could, but the words were barely legible. He was disappointed. Somehow, he had thought Anthony always wrote clearly. His handwriting was worse than Eli's was! Miao frowned, returning the book to its draw. "Can you still sense Eli?"

"Yeah. The spirits have been very active. Protecting him, I suppose. They're getting closer, but I don't think he's strong enough to teleport himself and Cleo yet." She picked up a wooden horse from the shelf and smiled. "Wow, Anthony's father must have made this for him."

Going to the window, Miao gazed down at the vast garden. Sif was sitting next to an elegant stone fountain, watching as Mr. Dion strolled along the path, inspecting the assortment of plant life. Mr. Sinclair was with him. There was so much they still didn't know about Anthony and his family.

"Funny," Alexis whispered, puzzlement in her eyes. "Selena said Eli stays in this room whenever they visit the Sinclairs, but..." She waved at the objects in the room. "There's nothing of his here. Nothing remotely modern."

"So?"

"So, doesn't it seem odd?"

"I suppose."

"Hmm, it's as if they expected him to be just like Anthony."

He turned to her suspiciously. "What are you getting at?"

"It's as if Anthony's father wanted Eli to be Anthony. He wanted Eli to relive his life. I suppose after Jonathan died, Richard kept it the same, but you'd think they would've had something separate for Eli."

"Maybe Eli didn't want anything. He can be a little odd at times…and Anthony does take over now and then."

She shrugged, unconvinced. "They have electricity in here. Why not a radio or television or even modern-day toys or games?"

"Britain is very different from Canada, Alexis. Eli was raised in a wealthy family whose way of thinking is a little odd." He took her hand. "Come on. There's nothing here." This was a lie. The room vibrated youthful happiness. At least Anthony had a pleasant childhood. Something told him that was more than Eli had.

Nevertheless, Alexis was right. It was almost as if everyone was trying to make Eli into Anthony. Why? It did seem weird. It may explain why Eli was the way he was. It explained, too, why Anthony's spirit surfaced more often than it should.

Why did this feel so much like home? The gardens, the house, even roaming around the servants' quarters, it all felt familiar. It even smelled right. Daniel took a deep breath and closed his eyes as he breathed in the sweet smell of the hanging roses.

"Here, Mama, over here!"

"Right there, Andy?"

A smile caressed his lips as he watched the five-year-old show his mother where to plant her roses and lilies. The young Spanish woman was beautiful in her flowing robes and long black hair. He could smell her sweet perfume and once again, the fact that this was home played before him.

"You will take care of them for me, won't you, Andy?"

"Yes, Mama. Will Papa let us plant a cherry tree?

She laughed. "Anything you want, little one."

Daniel sighed, placing his hand on the very tree Anthony had asked for. It stood tall and proud, full-grown compared to the little sapling Anthony had so carefully planted those many years ago. He remembered the child's bright eyes as he cared for it. Helena Sinclair had loved her garden so much, as had Anthony. "Oh, Mom, I'm sorry it took so long for me to come home," he whispered to the phantom image before him. "I'm sorry I could not protect Eli."

"Dad?"

He turned, blinking away the memory of Anthony's mother. Alexis and Miao stood down the trail a bit. Smiling, he opened his arms to his daughter who instantly ran up to embrace him. "Hi, honey. You two keeping busy?"

She blushed, obviously guilty of something. "Yeah. You?"

"Remembering."

At her confused expression, he ruffled her hair. Did Eli feel like this the first time he moved to Ravenwood and entered Anthony's old mansion? Did phantom images of memories not his own haunt him? Daniel was sure of it.

Eli changed into the new clothes Aaliyah had bought him. Both the clothes he had been wearing and those he had packed were soaked. He would have used a spell to dry them, but that would only alert Duncan to his whereabouts and he wanted to keep a low profile. Therefore, while Aaliyah bought gas, he used the station's bathroom to change into khakis and a t-shirt displaying a hideous looking happy face with a bullet in its forehead. Definitely not something he would normally wear. Both the pants and shirt were too baggy for his taste, but that was the style, or so Aaliyah said.

Once they were back on the road, they drove in silence, listening only to the soft music coming from the radio. It was smooth and relaxing and was able to give Eli a chance to forget about Duncan and Henry. So far, Aaliyah's warding spell was working like a charm. Neither Duncan nor any of his magickal friends had spotted them. Not so much as a fetch peeked through the windows. It was a pleasant surprise, and for once, Eli liked the surprise.

"You sure you don't want me to take you all the way to Cambridge?" Aaliyah asked for the umpteenth time.

She knew the answer long before he even awoke that morning or she would never have bought all the supplies, but she didn't like the idea of leaving him. He couldn't endanger her or her baby. He refused to allow any harm to befall them, no matter how strong Aaliyah's magick was.

"Yes, I'm sure." He offered an encouraging smile. "Even if Porter had the foresight to know where I'm going, his men will never recognize me. If I have to use magick, I will. The crystals seem to be listening to me. Alexis must have asked them to. They'll protect me, so will Cleo."

He doubted it would be necessary. He could not feel Duncan anywhere in a hundred kilometers radius. Probably still trying to fix the limousine. Waiting at the bus station, they would never be discovered. Not only would the crowd of people cover his aura, but also he didn't even look like himself any more. He changed his whole appearance using a relatively simple and energy efficient spell.

His skin was now tanned, and his hair tinted brownish-red instead of its natural blue-black hue. The eyes had been the hardest part. They were such an intense shade of three blues that it was hard to picture them any other colour, so he pictured Alexis's beautiful emerald ones. They never got that green, but he did manage a nice smoky green shade. When he looked in the mirror, he didn't even recognize his own reflection. His eyes were wide and he looked like a cross between Nathan and Scott. If it weren't for his magick, not even Selena would recognize him.

"Honest, Eli, it's no trouble. I'm going to Sinclair Manor anyway.

Look, I'll drive you."

"Aaliyah."

A small tear glistened under her right eye. She sniffled, wiping it away. "Money! You don't have any money on you."

"I can conjure some from my account."

"No, no, I insist." She zipped open her purse while trying to steer and pulled out a wad of bills. "Here. There should be enough pounds to get you on the bus and buy some snacks. Don't get Cleo high on sugar. You'll probably have to transfer buses so call me every stop. I'll meet you at the Manor and—"

He brushed his lips across hers. "Thank you. For everything."

She stared at him for a long moment. "You're welcome."

They were just pulling into the Crewe bus terminal when she took his hand and placed it on her swollen belly. There was a small kick and Eli could not help but gasp. The baby was really moving.

"When you get to Cambridge we have to talk about my lil' kick boxer," she said, parking the car.

Confused, he could only nod. It was her turn to kiss him. It was gentle and full of promises neither could ever keep. Eli bit his lower lip. He missed those tender kisses even if they were wrong. He missed being held in her loving arms.

"Thank you, Aaliyah," he whispered as she handed him the new backpack full of supplies. He opened the door and climbed out, Cleo sitting on his shoulder as usual. He paused before closing the door. "I do still love you."

Her gentle amber eyes saddened slightly. "I love you, too, Eli." But it wasn't the same. It would never be the same.

"Take good care of him, Cleo," she instructed before waving goodbye and pulling away.

Eli waved, but his heart sank. She had rejected his love once more. Why did he even bother trying? Stuffing his hands in his pockets, he went inside the terminal. It was busy, crowded even. Standing in line, he waited nearly twenty minutes to reach the ticket booth.

An elderly woman smiled at him. "How may I help you, dear?"

"One way to Cambridge, please."

She nodded and punched the request into her computer. "Okay. Name?"

"Hmm…" He had not had time to think of an alias.

"Name?"

"Oh." He chewed his lip for a moment. "Mc… MacLauchlan. Elijah MacLauchlan."

He wanted to say McNeil because of Aaliyah, but it no longer felt right.

"You okay, sweetie?"

He nodded, handing her the money for the ticket. "Yeah, just have a headache."

She nodded understandingly. "There's a little gift shop near the rear of the building. They may have aspirin."

"Thanks. Can you tell me when the bus leaves?"

"You just missed it." She checked her schedule. "There should be another in an hour or so."

"Oh." He thanked her again and moved off. "Now what?" he murmured to Cleo. There were so many people it was easy to hide among them. Unfortunately, Eli had to keep his metaphysical shields high. There were too many thoughts for him to deal with without it. It was almost suffocating.

"Let's get something cold to drink, then call Selena. I'm sure she's worried."

"Yeah," he agreed.

The moment they stepped into the small store, Eli had to turn around. There was no way he would ever make it to the counter. There were too many people. He would have to wait until the line was smaller. He found a coke machine near a line of old-fashioned phone booths. Once he bought a Sprite, he found an empty one and stepped inside.

The booth was unusually large compared to the newer ones on the other side of the terminal. They were very old, made of wood with a small bench and table. The phone sat kitty-corner wise. He took a moment to compose himself before inserting coins into the phone slot.

"Who the hell?" Selena growled, turning down the stereo once more. She glanced at Nathan who was getting grumpy over the fact that he had yet to eat. They were all starving. She was tempted to stop at the next drive-through and get them all something.

The cell phone connected to the dashboard was set on speaker, making her hands free so she could focus on the road. She punched the receive button and brought it to life. "This better be good," she demanded gruffly.

"I always thought my voice was good to hear."

"Eli!" she gasped. She giggled, turning to Nathan with a broad smile.

"Where are you?" Nathan asked.

"Crewe's bus station. You?"

Nathan took the map from Scott. "Ah… Nottingham. Well, in five or six minutes. We should hit Crewe in two hours."

"Great! Hey, if you see Robin Hood, say hi for me."

Nathan burst into laughter. "Are you okay?"

"Just fine. Listen, my bus will be leaving before you guys arrive. Why not meet me halfway?"

"Not a problem," Scott said quickly, leaning between the two seats. "You better be on that bus, you little creep."

The young man was silent on the other end as if he feared Scott was actually upset with him. If Scott noticed it, he showed no remorse. In fact, he played on it.

"Do you have any idea what you put us through?"

"Scott, not now," Selena growled softly.

"Scott," Nathan threw in warningly.

"Miao sprained his ankle searching those damn woods. Did Raven honestly have to own so much land? Alexis's been crying and Dad's having visions."

Eli's voice trembled, "Sorry, I—"

"Do you know what I'm going to do to you?" He paused for effect. "I'm going to flip you over my shoulder, spin you until you're too dizzy to even think of a spell and then tickle the daylights out of you, and Frost is going to help."

There was a soft sigh followed by giggles. It sounded childish but joyous. "After what I've been through, you can tickle me to your heart's content. Is Alexis and Miao okay? The spirits—"

"Yeah, do you have them?"

"Yes. They're okay." There were a few murmurs as Eli talked to Cleo. "Sure. Cleo's going to watch for the bus. He's getting a little antsy."

Selena grinned. "You tell my baby brother he better be good or I have a whole bag of sugar with his name on it!"

"You're so cruel!"

She only laughed in merriment.

The bus was already there, but was in the middle of being cleaned. It gave Cleo time to find a good seat for Eli. Keeping to the shadows, he sneaked onto the big bus and began looking about. The back would be best. If he were alone, no one would bother them. Eli needed time to think and Cleo doubted Eli would be able to keep up a fake interest in anyone who may sit next to him.

He found the perfect seat just two rows down from the lavatory. It had a god-awful view of the television. No one in their right mind would want to strain their neck to watch whatever movie the driver may put on. Eli rarely watched movies so would not be bothered by it. Most likely, the other passengers would prefer seats with a good view.

To his despair, the driver came in. Hiding quickly, Cleo waited until the driver finished his clean up before coming back out. As he headed for the door, the driver shut it and engaged the lock. Cursing, Cleo jumped on the front seat and watched as the man strolled away. "Great! Just bloody great!" he growled.

Scott was still going on about the many ways he was going to torment him. Eli could not stop laughing. Half of Scott's threats were absurd at best. Hanging him upside down in front of Alexis's bedroom window, or worse, nude in front of Melissa's. He felt as if his cheeks would explode if he didn't stop laughing soon. Of course, Scott made sure to include Nathan and/or Frost in each scenario, which, of course, had Nathan in an uproar of chuckles.

It felt so good to be joking around with them once again. Selena was fuelling Scott's rants by giving up all his secrets, including the ones she had swore never to tell. Eli didn't mind. Well, not until she threw out some of Anthony's secrets. Yet he still could not contain the laughter. So, what if Scott knew Anthony talked in his sleep or even sung now and then? As long as Frost didn't start making comparisons with Scott.

Selena began going on about a new movie she and Melissa would make. She planned to save money by getting him and Alexis to do the special effects.

"You're crazy, Selena," Eli laughed, leaning against one wooden wall.

"That's why you love me," she snickered.

"That's why? I thought it was because of how sweet you are."

"Such a kiss-up. I'm going to make you cook dinner tonight."

"Fine! I don't love you." More laughter filled Eli's ears. "I'll just have to take Frost as my guardian. I'm sure Alexis would understand."

Instantly, Scott renewed the threats.

He had to hold the phone at arm's length as Nathan, laughing just as hard as Selena, assured Scott that Frost would never leave him. Unless, of course, Eli made things very interesting for him. Apparently, Eli had a lot of learning though if he wanted to be as good in bed as Scott was, but if Frost had to, he was willing to teach him. It only got Eli into more trouble as Scott threatened to castrate him. Eli laughed. It might be worth it. He was just bringing the receiver back to his ear to retort to Scott's latest threat when it was snatched out of his hand. He turned in shock only to be rammed against the small table.

"Eli's been a very naughty boy, Selena."

Chapter Twenty-one

Eli gasped. His chest pressed against the cool wood as the receiver dropped next to him. Dazed, he didn't have a chance to fight as Henry yanked his arms back and bound them behind his back with a thick leather belt.

Somewhere outside the booth, he could hear Duncan's soft chanting as his magick once again failed to protect him. A binding spell was wrapping around Eli and he could not call upon the spirits to help him. He struggled nonetheless, hoping beyond hope to free his hands. He refused to allow them to take him again.

Henry growled behind him. He lifted Eli up and slammed him into the hard surface.

Eli yelped as his head smacked the wall. His head was swimming as he tried to lift it.

"Little brat," the man sneered. H smashed his fist into the small of Eli's back.

He cried out as Henry beat him for the first time in his entire life. Blow after blow landed against his sides and back yet no one outside heard his cries for help. His knees buckled as the pain became too much to withstand. Henry grabbed him by the throat as he began to slip to the floor and hauled him back up.

"Stop crying, boy," Henry sneered. He squeezed his throat between his large hands. "Take it like a man."

Eli barely registered Selena's screams on the other end of the phone, nor Nathan's curses. The crushing weight against his throat grew in intensity until he blacked out.

Duncan continued chanting, ignoring Eli's cries that no one else could hear. He isolated the phone booth, soundproofing it so no one heard the fight inside. Eli's screams were starting to concern him. He knew Henry would punish the young man the moment they found him, but this was too public. He waited a few more minutes. They needed Eli to come peacefully. There was no need for the locals calling the police.

When ten minutes went by, he became worried. What was taking so long? It shouldn't take this long to subdue Raven's reincarnation, especially if he had no magick to call upon.

Storming up to the booth, he threw open the door. Henry looked up in annoyance from his seat. Eli sat on the floor, half-hidden under the table and phone, but within arm's reach of the large man. His hands were tied back and he looked in massive pain. Faint swelling covered his half-hidden face. He was also paler than usual. Some serious bruises were going to appear on him. It was to be expected. Henry had been really pissed at having to chase after Eli. "What's going on?" Duncan demanded, glaring at Henry.

The other man held up the phone receiver with an innocent grin. "Talking. Eli was just telling Selena he wasn't going home. He actually likes being with us."

Duncan shook his head. "We don't have time for this." Kneeling down, he tried to help Eli to his feet. The young man skirted away from him, trapping himself in a corner. His eyes were wide and fearful as Duncan moved closer, like a dear in the headlights of a Mac truck.

Duncan raised his hands to show he had no hostile intentions. "It's okay, Eli. I'm not going to hurt you." He crawled slowly to him, opening a slight space between himself and the door. As Eli tried to bolt through the opening, Duncan caught him. A pitiful moan escaped Eli's lips as he tried to struggle. After a moment, he became still and closed his eyes, sobbing ever so softly as his glamour faded.

Duncan held him gently, resting his cheek against Eli's sweat dampened hair. "Shh...it's okay. Everything is going to be okay." He gazed up at Henry as he hung up the phone. "What did you do?"

Henry cold gray eyes regarded him with loathing. "Subdued him. Now he is yours. You can take him without fear of him ever running or objecting again."

Frowning, Duncan held Eli a moment longer before helping to his feet. Eli's clothes would have to be changed, he noted with distaste. He needed something more dignified. It took a few moments to fix

Eli's hair and materialize appropriate clothing. He untied Eli's hands, watching as he stared at the ground, never meeting his eyes. Duncan sighed inwardly. In a way, Henry had finally done the impossible, he had broken Eli's spirit.

"Come on, Eli," he said softly. He tilted the young man's chin up. Fresh tears glistened underneath long lashes. "Let's go."

He wrapped an arm around Eli's shoulders and led him to the waiting limo. Eli was oddly quiet as he sat in the backseat, curled up in the corner. He said nothing as Duncan and Henry climbed in. The driver shut the door and started the engine. As the large car pulled away from the curb, Duncan moved closer to him, his hand falling on his knee.

Instantly, Eli pulled his knees to his chest and looked away.

"Eli, I told you what would happen. I warned you."

Still Eli didn't answer. Only a soft murmur escaped his lips, but it was barely audible. Ragged breaths clouded the tinted window.

Duncan glanced at Henry as he rifled through the packsack Eli had been carrying. "Where's Cleo?"

Henry shrugged. "Don't know."

"Eli?"

He shook his head.

Sighing, Duncan brushed a lock of inky black hair from Eli's face. "I'm sorry, Eli. Really, I am."

Nevertheless, he knew that no words would ever heal the hole Eli now felt in his heart.

They sped down the highway, the van accelerating to over two hundred kilometers per hour. Selena shook with rage, determined to catch up with Eli before they lost him once more. His screams still echoed throughout the van, silencing all three of them.

Henry had sounded so different, not at all the man she had grown up with. The sounds of him hitting Eli shook her. Henry had never raised a hand to Eli in his life. Frost's story was running through her mind. Would Henry hurt Eli as he had Frost? Had he in the short time Eli was gone? Fear ate at her stomach as the questions with no answers piled up.

Twenty minutes into Crewe, they sped past the bus heading to Cambridge. A teal aura pulled at her senses, forcing her to slow down. Taking a sharp U-turn, she went after the bus.

"What the hell?" Scott bellowed, gripping the back of her seat. She growled, honking at the bus. "Bugger!" The bus refused to slow down.

Frustrated, she swerved in front of it, ignoring Scott and Nathan's protests. The bus finally slowed to a stop as she parked the car. She was out her door before either could say a word. The bus driver opened the door as she ran to it.

"What's the meaning of this?" he demanded.

"Sorry," she said. She pushed past him and ran into the bus. The passengers stared at her in disbelief as she searched each seat and carry rack. At the very back, hidden deep in the shadows, she found Cleo. Large teal eyes stared at her in fear.

"Selena, they found him," he whispered. Frustrated tears slipped down his black furry cheeks.

She picked him up and held him gently. Taking one more look around, hoping Eli was hiding somewhere, she left the bus. Nathan was trying to explain the situation to the driver to no avail. She took his hand, once again apologizing to the driver, and hurried back to the SUV. "We don't have much time left."

"They found him," Aaliyah whispered to herself.

She turned the Mercedes around at the next intersection and headed back to Crewe. Guilt rang through her as she berated herself for leaving Eli.

There was nowhere for Eli to go. Henry sat across from him, emptying his bag, going on about the clothes he had been wearing at the bus station and the *foolish disguise* he had created with the glamour spell. He held up the bus tickets for him to see and ripped them into many little pieces.

Eli looked away, his heart broken. The tickets, although no longer any good, had given him a sense of hope. Now they, like Cleo, were gone. His throat burned as he sighed. It was torn from all his screaming and Henry choking him. Talking was impossible. It hurt too much. Henry only smirked at his turmoil.

Duncan sat next to Eli, completely oblivious to his situation. He continued to stroke Eli's hair, trying to coax him to talk. Oddly enough, he seemed reluctant to use his powers to learn what was wrong, even though he understood Eli was not happy at being captured once more. There was a small current of magick in his hands, only enough to sooth Eli's pain.

Closing his eyes, Eli leaned his head against the tinted window. Now what? Henry was even more brutal than before. Every time he absorbed his magick and became younger, the man seemed to lose a certain amount of his sanity. In the phone booth, however, he had simply beaten him in such a way Eli had no choice than to surrender or suffer worse. However, no magick or energy was taken from him.

Duncan, who had been angry with him, was now worried like a mother hen. The more Eli only answered with a shrug or shake of the head, the more he would try to pry Henry for answers.

"He's just stubborn. Use a spell or something."

Eli's eyes widened as Duncan stared down at him in consideration.

He shook his head and offered Eli a kind smile. "No. If you don't wish to speak to me, I understand. You're upset and worried about your friend." He gave Henry a hard look. "I know Henry hurt you, but you were warned."

He opened his mouth to talk but no words came out.

"Just tell me you're alright."

He tried, but it hurt far too much. All he could muster was a small squeak. His head swam with a pounding migraine. Telepathy was out of the question for the moment. He touched his throat instead, hoping Duncan would get the idea.

"Oh, Raven," Henry suddenly crooned. He gave Eli a lopsided smile that made him look drunk. "Raven, please come out and play. Eli doesn't want to talk to us anymore."

They both stared at him in confusion. Had Henry completely lost his mind?

To Eli's surprise, Henry got on the floor and knelt before him. He would have scooted further away had he not pinned himself in the corner. Henry placed his hands on either side of Eli's hips and stared into his eyes.

"Tell him what happened in the booth, Eli." His smile grew devilish when Eli could not answer. His voice became singsong. "Oh, little

Raven, won't you speak to me? Won't you let me drink from those lips that offer so much power?"

His lips came close to Eli's. Eli ducked out of his way and stared at Henry in horror. What was he trying to do?

"Henry, let him be," Duncan said sharply, grabbing his arm.

The older man glared at him and Duncan instantly backed down.

It was the first time Eli had ever seen Duncan cower. His fear of Henry intensified. What had happened to make Duncan fear him? He had more than enough power in his pinkie to handle Henry. Didn't he? It appeared Henry held something over him now.

"I haven't fed in hours," he whispered, taking hold of Eli's black clad arms.

Other than his hands and face, Eli was completely covered. They were the only two places Henry could feed from. He tried to make himself small as Henry moved closer. His eyes squeezed shut as large fingers moved along his jaw.

"Say something to us, Eli. Make Anthony come out and visit." His breath moved across Eli's ear, his tongue licking the lobe.

Eli inhaled sharply as Henry latched onto the skin just below his right ear. The large man's weight crushed against him and he was pushed into the back of the soft seat. He felt like a vampire. Henry wasn't just absorbing his auric energy, but was literally suckling his neck. Eli wedged his hands free and tried desperately to push him away. Henry countered by wrapping an arm around the small of his back and wrenching their bodies firmly together. Eli's hands fell to his sides. There was no way to free himself. He was trapped.

"Atta boy," Henry whispered against his ear. "Just relax. It feels good after a while. Ask Duncan."

A haze filled Eli's mind as Henry continued his crazed feeding. Henry expertly moved his head to the other side to continue feeding. Duncan's frightened face met Eli's gaze. It was true. Henry had been feeding from Duncan as well. They were both victims to Henry's vampirism.

Something on the edge of his senses alerted Eli to Anthony's Guardians approaching them quickly. He gazed up into Duncan's matching eyes. The warlock could feel them, too. It gave Eli renewed energy. He forced his way free, dislodging Henry from his feeding.

First rage, then confusion flashed in Henry's eyes as Eli rolled onto his knees and peered out the back window. He looked at Duncan. "What…"

"The Guardians," Duncan explained simply, watching Eli as he smiled.

Eli would have laughed if he could. Selena and Cleo were so close now. He could feel them and Frost. Even Scott. Smiling brightly, he waited for the SUV to come into sight. Knowing Selena's style of driving, he didn't have to wait long.

"What do we do?" Henry asked, his hand falling on Eli's back as he gazed out the window as well.

"Let him see them."

Eli's smile grew. Was he serious? Was he really going to let him see his friends? His smile faded. It had to be a trick. They had to be up to something. What had Henry said to Anthony about Nathaniel? He fed off him, too, once, a long, long time ago. It had been the reason why he had not appeared as old as he really was. What if they planned to use all the Guardians as such a source of power? No, he would not let that happen.

As soon as the car slowed at the side of the road, Eli threw open the door and jumped out. The pouch was still strapped to his leg. He summoned his shield, mentally begging it to throw up a shield behind him to keep Duncan and Henry at bay. It didn't work, his magick still bound by Duncan's spell.

His stomach churned as he kept running. Selena would be rounding the bend any moment. He had to keep as far ahead of the other two as possible. It was the only way to warn her in time.

As if on cue, the Sinclair black sports utility van came tearing down the road. Selena was a reckless driver to say the least…but she knew how to move fast and how to stop just as quickly. As the van got closer, Eli began waving. Only a few more seconds and she would be close enough for him to teleport inside, then they could hightail it home.

A clear energy wall formed in front of him. His mind barely registered its appearance before he collided into it. He kept himself upright and placed his hands on the shield. No, he cried in dismay. Trying to keep himself from crying, he focused on the approaching vehicle. If he could not escape, he could at least save his friends.

Selena, stop, he ordered, focusing hard on his cousin. *Turn back. It's a trap!*

Don't worry. We're here to get you, she answered.

No. Selena, listen to me. It is a trap! Henry wants you as a power source. I'm sure of it. Please, turn back now.

She did the opposite. Parking the van, she and Nathan changed to their faery forms and jumped out, followed by Scott, and what looked like a nasty crossbow.

Please, Frost, stop her.

The silver-haired man listened about as well as the other fey. Frost's mystical bow appeared instantly, aimed at the limo.

"There's a shield," Frost growled to the rest. He kept his aim steady.

Cleo stood in his winged panther form between his siblings. His teal eyes stared anxiously at Eli. "Are you alright?" Eli nodded.

Frost's violet eyes were watching him carefully. "Eli?"

He stared at him for a moment before closing his eyes. He opened his mouth to speak, but frowned when no words would come out. *I lost my voice. Please, Frost, I know what Henry did to you. He will do it again. Take the others and go before they catch you.*

"Not without you." Frost's eyes widened in terror. "Eli!"

Henry's large arms wrapped around him, pinning his arms at his sides. One hand folded around his already damaged throat, crushing it further. The Guardians watched in horror as he was lifted off his feet. Eli's throat burned as it was again squeezed. There was a small popping as the blood rushed to his ears. His eyes widened as he felt the strain on his windpipe. He could not breathe. Henry was going to kill him.

"Come, little Raven, let them hear you scream," Henry taunted as the world became fuzzy around the edges.

I can't breathe, Eli thought, prying at Henry's fingers. Henry had planned this. He had let him run out of the limo. It was all a trap. The Guardians would surrender to save him. Struggling was out of the question with Henry's superior strength.

"Henry, no! Let him go!" Duncan demanded, rushing up to them. He pulled at the hand crushing Eli's neck. "He can't breathe!"

Henry let go long enough to backhand Duncan. The warlock fell to the ground in surprise while Eli burst into a coughing fit. Eli sucked in large gulps of air and tried to regain focus. Selena was screaming. Frost and Cleo were trying to bring down the shield. Henry was talking about Raven again as he lifted Eli right off his feet. It was all fuzzy, a mixture of visual and audio stimuli that made little sense. It felt like he was watching a really bad movie in slow motion.

"Do you want them to watch as I drain the very life from you?"

Henry breathed against his ear. "I want to play with Anthony."

If he wants Anthony so bad, fine, Eli thought as his mind cleared. He began pulling at the power building within him. The power Anthony had given him from past life to past life bubbled over. He raised his head to the heavens, his eyes glowing brightly. Raven will come to Henry indirectly, Eli declared to himself.

Dark clouds filled the sky directly above them. Lightning danced across them.

Bigger, he needed them bigger, stronger. His magick platform came to life beneath his and Henry's feet, increased his strength. A maelstrom of wind howled around them. The elemental power was unfathomable as it tore up the highway and rose to the darkening sky above.

Henry's grip was like tempered steel. He held Eli tightly as his aura flared. One large hand snaked under Eli's top to grasp bare skin.

Immediately, he began absorbing the new flow of energy.

Eli gasped and increased the power of his magick.

"You're not trying hard enough," Henry taunted, his lips falling to his neck.

"By the Goddess!" Selena gasped.

Eli's powers were accelerating far too fast towards a destructive nature. The circle of power was glowing white-hot. Porter's shields were all that were protecting any of them, but as the power continued to increase, they began to fluctuate. It wouldn't be long before it simply buckled under the strain.

She gazed at up the sky in horror as thunder clapped so loud it shook the ground. Lightning flashed, striking toward the Earth. "Down! Get down!" she ordered, jumping on Cleo, and forcing him to lie on the ground.

Following her lead, Frost dragged Scott down. His large snowy wings wrapped around them both, protecting them from the oncoming explosion.

Henry's hand moved further up Eli's heated skin. It was too intimate for Eli's liking. As fast as he could call his magick, Henry would drink it in. The thunder clapped above. *Now,* Anthony whispered in the back of his mind. Watching the lightning dance, Eli called it forth, demanding a bolt to strike between him and aim at Henry. A part of him wanted to pull back that power and spare his grandfather, but the man that held him was no longer his grandfather. He was a stranger trying to hurt him and his friends.

The ground exploded around them seconds before the lightning hit. Debris bounced off the shield and settle around them. The lightning struck milliseconds later.

Henry cried out in agony as electricity ran through both of them. He dropped Eli and fell back, writhing in pain.

Eli rolled as he hit the ground, using his years of training to avoid getting hurt. Getting as far from Henry as possible, he took a moment to catch his breath. He looked over to Selena and Frost as they protected the other. A small laugh filled him. They were all okay. Good. With Henry down, they were safe.

The world swam around him. Leaning heavily on one arm, he tried to bring everything into focus. Where were his glasses? He had no idea, but he felt dizzy and worn. How much had Henry taken from him?

Laughter forced him to look where Henry lay. The old man was sitting up and was anything but old now. He was staring at his hands as if seeing them for the first time.

Eli's lower lip trembled. He looked exactly as he had the day Anthony died. He was now in his early forties. Gracefully, Henry stood and stared down at him. He was still growing younger right before Eli's very eyes. It wasn't possible!

Terrified, Eli began inching backward. No, this cannot be happening. The lightning should have rendered him unconscious, if not killed him! There was no way any human could absorb that much energy.

"We should do that again," Henry slurred, stumbling forward, obviously drunk on the power. "Such a high."

Eli sent energy bolt after energy bolt at him, trying with all his might to stop Henry's advances. Henry merely absorbed them as they hit him, pulling at Eli's power even from a distance.

No, Eli mouthed, shaking his head as Henry got closer. Please, no. He couldn't take any more. His head hurt as the dizziness finally overwhelmed him. He slumped against the pavement, already knowing his fate.

"Stop!" Frost cried out.

Eli looked up as Frost pressed his hands against the shield. It sparkled at his touch. Henry turned toward him as well.

"Henry, stop. Let him be. He'll die if you continue this." Frost waited until he had Henry's full attention. "You buried Anthony. Do you really want to bury Eli, too? I don't."

Henry paused to consider it. For a moment, he looked like his old self, caring and loving. Then it passed. "You would take his place?"

"Yes."

No!

Frost flinched at Eli's panic-stricken cry. He stared at Eli for a long moment.

Duncan knelt next to Eli as he fought to get up. He had to stop Frost. He wouldn't let his friend sacrifice himself. Not for him. His strength left him as Duncan wrapped an arm around him. He collapsed against the older man.

Don't let Henry take them, he pleaded.

"It's okay. You're going to be alright," Duncan whispered, ignoring his pleas. He helped Eli stand and began guiding him back to the limo. "Don't worry about your friends. They'll be okay. I promise."

Eli was too exhausted to fight or object as Duncan made him lay down. Duncan's hand fell to his forehead and a soft chant filled Eli's ears. The urge to fight to stay conscious left him. He leaned into the warmth of Duncan's arms. For the first time in ages, he wanted someone to care for him and make him feel safe. Oddly enough, Duncan now exhibited that sense of security he needed. Eli didn't know why, but he allowed himself to relax.

"Let me see him," Selena demanded as she watched Eli disappear into the black limousine. "Henry, for Christ's sake, I'm his guardian. You raised us. How can you do this to him?"

"You would never understand, Selena," Henry never looked at her, but kept his stare firmly on Frost. She had never seen a hungry look in him before.

"His magick has reversed your aging," Frost said coldly. "Like mine slowed it. Only he's human, you have to feed more often."

"What?" Scott cried, aghast by the notion.

Cleo nodded. "Every time Eli uses his powers."

Selena's head was swimming. Henry, her grandpa, was a psychic vampire? No, there had to be some other explanation. She had to see Eli. "Henry, please, let me see him," she begged. "Grandpa?"

Henry stared at her for a moment. He melted after a moment. As far as Selena knew, she was the only one who could make him do that.

"You can see him, darling." He raised his hand to the shield.

"Take my hand, love."

She hesitated. Was it a trap? Would he feed from her next? Tentatively, she placed her hand against his. The shield opened and he took her hand, pulling her through. Once she was on the other side, he let her go.

"Go ahead. He's most likely asleep though."

Eli was indeed sleeping when she got to the limo. He curled up in Porter's arms with tear-stained cheeks. His throat was red and swollen, starting to bruise. Yet he seemed oddly calm and relaxed in the warlock's arms.

Ignoring Porter's surprise, she placed a hand on Eli's cheek. "Eli? Baby?"

Henry raised his hand once more. "Your turn, Nathaniel."

With a restrained sigh of defeat, Frost raised his hand to Henry's. If this was the only way to save Raven's reincarnation so be it, he thought, silently praying Alexis would understand his decision. She may be his Mistress and friend, but a part of him would always remain loyal to Anthony.

Frost's fingers were millimeters from Henry's when Scott suddenly grabbed his wrist and yanked his arm down. The taller man pulled him away from the shield and stepped before him. His grip was so tight, Frost actually thought his love would leave bruises.

"What will happen to Eli if you continue feeding from him?" Scott glanced at Frost with concern. "The Guardians will be forced to return to faery or fade away without their magick. What about Eli?"

Frost stared at him in shock. Scott would never give up on Eli just to save him, would he?

Trust me, Scott whispered in his mind.

But Eli?

When Henry simply glared at them, it dawned on him. Eli was human, despite his magick. He may lose his magick, but he would not simply fade from existence. He would die slowly from exhaustion more than anything else would. He would need a source of power to re-establish his own, making him into a vampire of sorts as well. While that was happening, Henry would need a secondary source of food.

"Nathaniel, come here."

Scott's grip tightened. "What happens if he dies? You'll start aging so rapidly your heart will fail from the stress, won't it?" The vein on Henry forehead looked ready to pop.

Scott persisted. "You're addicted to his power, aren't you? Immortal blood slowed your aging and now Eli is unwittingly making you younger. Your very own fountain of youth. Bet his is better than any drug on the market."

"More than you can imagine."

"Oh, I've got a strong imagination. I can see Eli dying in the near future. You'll drain him…just as you did Anthony. Then what? He'll never open your precious gates if you keep taking his magick. All that training for nothing. Yeah, I know exactly what you're doing with him."

Frost stared at Scott in disbelief. Was that why Anthony died? Henry had absorbed his power until he had nothing left to give? Yet, Scott wasn't giving up on Eli, he was trying to get through to Henry. He was trying to get the man to see reason and logic. Surprisingly, Henry seemed to be listening.

"You're right about the gates. Whether or not he masters them, they'll open on the eclipse. Would it not be better if he had the strength to close them? Frost and his siblings will be needed to protect this realm from whatever may come through. After that, Eli should have no trouble finding the portal you want, but not if he's too weak to even stand on his own." He smiled warmly. "Let me train him."

They both stared at him in confusion.

"And what can you do that I can't?" Henry growled, losing his patience.

You're losing him, Frost warned, ready to step forward.

"I can see into the spiritual world. I can guide him."

Henry frowned. "Duncan can do the same."

"And how successful has he been?"

Henry's icy glared turned back to Frost. "Come here now, Nathaniel." When Frost refused to move, his eyes darkened with rage. "Fine." He turned on his heel and stormed toward the limo.

"Damn," Scott muttered, letting go of Frost. "I thought for sure..."

Frost watched Henry in fear for a moment. "Selena..." he murmured, glancing at his beloved. "Damn! Selena!"

Her magick poured through her power-hand into Eli. He was so weak it was painful. Porter kept on hand around Eli's waist and poured his own magick into Eli's swollen neck with his free hand. Even though Selena could feel his magick mingling with hers, Eli's throat was not healing. For some reason Eli was fighting them.

Porter's willingness to help caught her off-guard. She expected him to fight her, but instead he held Eli protectively and allowed her to do as she wished. Anthony's message from Daniel played over and over in her mind. Porter was in love with Eli. It was obviously true just by the way he was caring for Eli. Eli seemed content in his rival's arms. It felt like some soothing spell was keeping him calm.

"Eli," she whispered. She stroked his sweat-dampened hair. She increased her flow of magick so he would awaken. Her smile grew when those beautiful eyes she adored so much fluttered open. "Hi, baby."

He mouthed her name, then winced, touching his throat. No words would come out. "You lost your voice?" He nodded.

She glanced at Porter. "Did Porter do it?"

He shook his head.

"Henry?"

He nodded.

"He choked you."

Another nod.

It explained why Eli had stopped screaming abruptly on the phone. "Did he beat you?"

Eli closed his eyes, but nodded. A small yawn escaped his lips as he looked back up at her.

"You're tired, aren't you, honey?"

He shook his head, but it was obvious he was.

She gave Porter a cold stare. "You know Chaos is no longer in him so why do this?"

Porter looked away, his blue eyes revealing his true age. "We still don't know how the eclipse will affect him. Henry says he reacted to the simulated eclipse the first day, but not since. Raven's predictions—"

"Are always correct."

He shook his head. "Eli is, despite how much he fights it, ruled by emotion. The first time, he was coming down from a magickal high."

Porter fumbled for the right words as her red eyes flared scarlet in rage. "We mixed our powers. There were a lot of emotions running wild through him. I believe that's what caused the opening. If his emotions run rampant when the real thing happens, he should at least know how to control it."

"There is less than forty-eight hours left. How do you plan to have him trained in time?"

"I've slo—"

Eli made a sudden noise, his eyes wide with fear. *Selena!*

She didn't realize what was happening until it was too late. Henry grabbed her from behind and pulled her tightly against his hard body. She could not help but scream when he bit into the flesh of her neck. The skin tore and her silvery blood twinkled down her throat. He lapped at it, humming at its sweetness. Selena could do little more than sit in his lap and let him as he pulled her hair to one side.

"Selena!" Frost gasped when Henry finally emerged from the limousine with Selena's unconscious form.

The faery was much paler than he had ever seen her before. Her mahogany hair fell over Henry's big arms in disarray. A shimmer of silver stained her neck and lips. Her clothes were slightly torn and dishevelled.

Henry smirked at them as he laid her on the road several feet from the shield. He bent over the young faery and gave her a passionate kiss that made her whimper in discomfort. With a grin, he stood and climbed into the limo. The black vehicle sped off.

Disgusted, horrified and concerned for his sister, Frost went through the shield the moment it began to fade. He fell to his knees next to Selena and pulled her close, noting with distaste she had to hold one strap of her gown up to cover herself completely.

She looked up to him in a daze. "H-he's not the same. That's not Henry!" she cried, burying her face in his chest. "It can't be. Henry has always been the most loving man I know."

Tears dampened his tunic as he rocked her. This was bad, very bad. Henry had ravished Selena, right in front of Eli, and taken some of her power. It didn't make sense that Henry would do this now after caring for the two for so many years. There had to have been any number of times he could have taken what he wanted from either one of them while under his care. Why now? Something had to have triggered the sudden change. Something big like when Anthony had died and Henry had done the same to him.

Cleo sat on his haunches next to them, rubbing his head affectionately against Selena's side. "I know, Selena," he whispered.

"He's getting out of control," Frost muttered into her hair. He carefully helped her to her feet, mindful of her ruined clothes. "We've got to get to Eli before they vanish again."

Scott helped him lead Selena to the van. They got her in the backseat with Cleo and let her rest. Frost climbed into the driver's seat with Scott next to him. Shifting gears, he returned to Nathan's form then stomped on the gas. There wasn't that many miles between them. As long as he could still sense Eli, they had a chance.

Henry sat back with a pleased grin. He held the cell phone up to his ear, his smile growing. "Yes. A black SUV. R0195. I want the faeries captured and brought to me. You can do what you wish with the others."

He hung up and dropped the phone next to him. His gray eyes roamed over the two across from him. Eli still lay in Duncan's arms, slipping in and out of consciousness while Duncan poured his magick into him.

Henry rubbed his thumb over his lower lip in thought. "I never thought Selena would taste so good. Like wild berries after a summer rain. Better than Nathaniel for sure."

Eli's eyes narrowed. Anthony would never have allowed Henry to abuse Selena as he just had. He hadn't simply fed from Selena, he sexually assaulted her. Anthony would have killed Henry long before allowing him to hurt any of his children had he known what the man was capable of, but Eli was helpless to stop him.

"Nathaniel tasted like strawberries. Did you know that? Strawberries and moonbeams. Maybe, if you're good, I'll let you taste them."

Frowning, Eli turned in Duncan's arms until he faced the back of the leather seat. Duncan continued to stroke his hair. He prayed that Selena and Frost were strong enough to fight Henry's men. He could not bear the thought of Henry hurting either of them more than he already had. Maybe it was best if they just forgot about him. They should turn back to Sinclair Manor where they would at least be safe from Henry's insanity.

Of all the years they've known each other, Scott had never seen Nathan this angry. He was driving just as fast and reckless as Selena had been. He was thankful for his seatbelt and made sure Selena was wearing hers. Cleo stayed in his true form, using what magick he could to empower his sister. They needed them both strong when they confronted Porter and Henry again. They should have caught up to them by now.

Nathan's eyes were glowing violet. Frost's rage was like a wall around him, reflecting the power building around them. It made the willowy man look extremely dangerous.

They were approaching the bridge when a red Jeep Cherokee and gray Hummer came tearing down the road at either end. The passenger leaned out the window of the jeep and fired at them.

Nathan swerved, his eyes wide and fearful. "What the hell?"

"Looks like Porter doesn't want us catching up," Scott muttered, turning to watch the jeep speed past. It turned and continued to fire at them. This was not exactly what he had been expecting when they began their chase. Magick, yes, but this?

"Henry sent them," Selena corrected. She cupped her hands together, willing what magick she had left into them.

"What do you mean *Henry sent them*?" Nathan demanded, swerving another array of bullets.

"The van's bulletproof. Don't swerve." She opened the window and threw the sparkling sphere toward the jeep. It rolled along the road, under the jeep and exploded, making the two attackers retreat. "He's been feeding from Porter, too. Daniel's right, Porter does care for Eli. He's trying to protect him."

Nathan glanced in the review mirror. "You're kidding."

"No."

"We might have a friend on the inside," Scott mused with a small smile. Perhaps this Porter could be of use. If he truly cared about Eli, he might see reason to set him free. It was a chance they would have to take.

Nathan grunted in irritation.

Obviously, he didn't trust Porter and wasn't about to. Not that Scott blamed him. He still remembered Nathan and Frost's reaction when Eli had lost faith in them due to Porter's mind tricks. It had taken forever to calm them. Even after everything was sorted out, things had changed. Nothing was the same after that. Frost was even more protective now than before, especially with Eli.

He was constantly checking up on each of them. Eli was more inclined to spend time alone with Frost or Nathan. Even to do something as mundane as playing cards, working in the lavish gardens they both owned, or the odd movie. As much as Scott hated to admit it, he was a little jealous. He liked the kid, but not when he kept his love overly busy.

The van jerked forward as the Hummer slammed into the rear. Nathan held the steering wheel tightly, trying desperately to keep control as they were rammed again. They were getting close to the bridge. He stomped his foot on the accelerator. The Hummer kept pace, still ramming into them.

"Selena, get them off us!" Nathan ordered as a corner of the van lifted off the road.

She created another orb but before she could drop it out the window, the van rocked so hard, she was thrown against the back of Scott's seat.

The orb blinked out of existence. Selena murmured a curse as she rubbed her forehead.

Scott reached around to check her as the Hummer pulled back. "Gun it!" he ordered. The command fell short as the Hummer rammed them again, this time coming from the passenger side. The metal of Scott's door crunched as it pushed inward. Scott pulled his legs out of the way and held Selena as she clung to his seat.

They wanted to push them over the bridge!

Both tires lifted off the ground. Tools and weapons slid across the floor of the van, hitting the far wall with small scraping noises. The van tipped dangerously to one side, Nathan's side getting closer to the speeding ground. Nathan gasped, not sure how to maneuver in such a situation. His hands were glued to the steering wheel. He suddenly jerked the wheel to the left as they were hit again. Selena screamed as the van overturned and the wind was knocked out of all of them. Sparks flew as they skidded along the road. There was a sickening crunch of metal against metal as the van crashed into the guard railing of the bridge.

Scott could barely make out the shapes around him. His neck stung as it snapped to the side. Nausea burned his throat as the blood rushed to his brain. Red, the colour of blood, filled his vision until his world went black.

Chapter Twenty-two

An upside-down Selena filled his vision as Scott slowly opened his eyes. He winced at the glare of the bright sun behind her and forced them closed again. His head ached and he had the urge to throw up. He couldn't remember feeling so sick since that frat party Nathan had talked him into going to a few months back. That had been a wild night. This one felt just as bad. Where were they? Why did his chest and stomach feel as if they were going to be ripped in two? He moaned as Selena snapped her fingers in front of his face.

"Come on, Scott, wake up. They're coming," she urged, pulling at his arm.

It took a moment to remember what was going on. He blinked open his eyes and carefully looked around. The van was on its side, windows crushed and metal shards piercing the interior. He looked to his side, fighting back the nausea threatening to make him throw up. Nathan lay unconscious in the driver's seat, covered in blood from his waist down. His forehead also was splashed in blood and his glasses cracked. He must have hit his head against the steering wheel.

I hope he didn't get glass in his eyes, Scott thought absently as he reached for the smaller man. He covered his mouth as phlegm bubbled up in his throat. He had to get out first and then help Nathan. He was no use to his love like this.

Ignoring the glass biting into his hands, Scott grabbed the broken doorframe for support before undoing his seatbelt. Managing to keep himself from falling on top of Nathan, he pulled himself out the window.

The sun hurt his eyes. He squinted and watched as the Hummer turned around at the end of the bridge. They must be coming back to finish us off, he thought in despair. He had to get Nathan out of the van. There wasn't much time left. He moved to climb back inside, but a wave of dizziness almost made him fall. He glanced back toward the Hummer. It was speeding toward them once more. "Nathan! Nathan!"

The ash blond man groaned, holding his head. He looked lost and confused. His pale hands bent to his legs. If it were possible, he paled more.

"Scott?" he whispered. His blurry eyes searched for Scott's face. "Scott, my legs…they're pinned."

Think quick, Scott ordered himself. The Hummer was coming back and they were already too close to the bridge. Frost! Frost could save Nathan!

"Change to Frost!"

Nathan was becoming panicky. He pushed against the dashboard, trying to dislodge his legs to no avail. Tears of pain and desperation fell down his checks. He had no idea what to do.

"Frost!" Scott cried, but it wasn't working.

Nathan was too frightened to allow his other self to take over. Scott looked pleading to Selena for advice.

"Teleport."

"Teleport?"

She nodded, her gaze never leaving the speeding vehicle coming toward them.

Looking around quickly, Scott found a small patch of land at the side of the road just passed the bridge. He peered back down at his beloved. "Nathan, listen to me. Look at the end of the bridge. I know you can't see it clear, but there's a patch of land. Do you see it? Focus on it."

Nathan squinted and did as he was told. "Okay?" he grunted in pain.

"Can you feel Frost? M-Ahh!"

The Hummer rammed them once more. Scott held on for dear life as they were pushed ever closer to the edge of the bridge. Cleo jumped off the van and disappeared behind the larger vehicle. Scott didn't ask. He had bigger problems to deal with. He looked down at Nathan who was trying desperately not to cry out in pain. "Listen. If you can't change to Frost, then pull upon his power. It's yours, too. Use it to teleport to that patch of land."

"I don't think I can."

"Focus, Nathan. You can do it."

More shrapnel dug into Nathan's legs as they were hit again. He cried out, no longer able to hold it in. The top of the van hung over the edge and if Nathan wished to, he could look down at the rushing waters below. The roar of the rapids mixed with the engine of the Hummer was almost deafening.

"Damn it, Nathan! Focus! I'm not leaving you!"

Nathan just stared up at him. His voice was oddly calm as their eyes met. "Scott, no. Go. Get out of here!"

"Not without you."

They stared at each other for a moment. Then something in Nathan's eyes changed, they began to glow softly. It was not the strong violet that usually accompanied Frost, but something just as powerful. An aura of silvery blue wrapped around him. Scott watched in awe as the light consumed him and vanished. Scott turned quickly to the patch of land and laughed gleefully as his best friend reappeared. He did it! He actually pulled it off! He couldn't remember the last time he was so proud of Nathan.

"Your turn, darling," Selena said sternly.

The van was tilting dangerously now. There was no place to jump but on the Hummer. If he landed the wrong way on the bridge, he would surely fall into the rapids, if not ran over first. Where was Cleo? He could fly on the panther's back if he were there. Selena was still recovering and as strong as she was, he doubted she could carry him even the few feet to safety at that moment. He braced himself for the coming crash. He had to time it right if he were to jump.

Cleo entered the Hummer through one of the open back windows. Inside was littered with fast food wrappers, pop and beer cans and empty cigarette packages. It stunk. Henry's hired thugs were absolute slobs. No one would miss them, he decided, returning to his true form.

Letting out an earth-shattering roar, he drew both men's attention. Before either could draw their pistols, he jumped the passenger, digging his fangs into the surprised man's jugular. His blood tasted sour, like too much alcohol and tobacco. It was a taste that would take Cleo forever to get a rid of.

The man died quickly with a mere gurgle of protest.

His partner jumped out the driver door before Cleo had a chance to attack him. Blood dripping down his chin, Cleo watched him in distaste. That one should have died, too, but at least he would not have to taste anything else as disgusting as the first. He had managed to stop the vehicle. Or so he thought until, to his horror, the SUV tipped over the edge of the bridge. His eyes widened as he watched Selena and Scott fall with it.

"Scott!" Nathan screamed as the SUV, Selena and Scott fell over the edge of the bridge.

Selena's wings practically exploded from her back as she tried to catch Scott's hand. He was falling too fast. A part of Nathan that felt like Frost but more himself, flared to life. He raised his hand toward his beloved. Pulling all his being into the task, he visualized Scott's descent suddenly stopping and him floating in midair.

Power rushed through his body. Silvery hair fell around his lithe body. Powerful wings formed on his back, but he paid neither any attention. They were normal. They had always been there. He kept his focus on Scott.

It was no surprise when Scott suddenly ceased his rapid descent. He floated in midair for a few moments before Nathan slowly lowered him to the rock shore below.

Once Scott was, safe Nathan took a breath to collect himself. He felt different, lighter somehow, but his legs were killing him. Looking down the length of his body, he found his legs were clad in soft white leggings rather than the blue jeans he had been wearing. He blinked. The pants were torn just as his jeans had been, but instead of his usual red blood, he discovered silver. It made no sense. Even his skin seemed different. It had an alabaster shine to it. It practically glowed! He was Frost.

That wasn't possible! Frost's persona took over when they changed and he fell behind the Moon Creature's powerful shields. Yet it felt right, right down to his bare feet. He could no longer feel Frost as a separate entity, rather it was as if he were Frost. All the fey's memories flowed through him, no longer waiting until he was dreaming. Was this the merging Selena spoke of? Was this what Eli predicted would happen? It wasn't half as scary as he had feared. In fact, he had never felt so at peace with himself. He felt whole for once.

Leaning heavily on his elbow, he felt his wounded legs. Putting pressure on them was out of the question. He would have to fly. For a moment, he wasn't sure how, but the part that was still Frost slapped that idea down. They—he had been flying since he was four.

Stretching his wings to their fullest, he gave them a flap. They felt real. A sharp gasp tore from his throat as something pierced the side of his neck. Surprised, his wings folded within him, vanishing from sight. Nathan gingerly pulled the dart out of his neck and stared at it. A tranquillizer?

"Nice lil' angel," a man cooed. He locked another dart into his rifle. "Don't do anything stupid. Just stay where you are."

"Stop," Nathan commanded, raising his hand. His telepathy reached out and ensnared the man.

The gunman paused, fearful of what the angelic being may do. The drug was powerful. Keeping the man ensnared was quickly tiring Nathan. He tried holding on, hoping Selena or Scott would come to his aid, but his eyes refused to stay open. His arm fell to his side, but he forced himself to stay conscious. Just a little longer.

A second dart lodged itself in his calf. Dizziness gripped him as he tried to keep from passing out.

Where is everyone, he wondered. His arm gave out. He laid in the grass, listening as the man loaded another tranquillizer dart into his rifle. He would not be able to fight a third shot, Nathan cursed. Even supernatural beings could only take so much.

The sickening crunch of bones and flesh made him look up. Selena stood over the man's limp body. His head twisted in an irregular angle, neck obviously broken. Nathan smiled in relief despite his dislike of killing.

Cleo landed next to her while Scott climbed up from the ravine.

They were all fine. Good. The drugs were moving through his system too fast. He finally gave up his battle and lay motionless on the ground. Darkness took him a moment later.

"Frost!" Selena cried, running to her limp brother's form.

Scott looked up as he pulled himself over the edge. What was wrong? he wondered. His breath caught in his throat when he saw Frost lay in his sister's arms. He wasn't moving.

"Please, God, no," he breathed, running to them at full speed. He fell to his knees and pulled the angel out of her arms. "Frost? Frost…"

He fell silent as he rolled Frost over. He didn't look the same. The sharp angles of his face had softened. His eyes seemed a little larger, more innocent. Even the turmoil that Scott usually sensed within him was gone. It was as if for the first time he was looking at the true Frost…Nathaniel. He looked so much like Nathan. So peaceful.

"They merged," he whispered.

Selena nodded in awe.

It was incredible. They had waited years for this and it had finally happened. The timing could not have been better. Why was he unconscious? Did this usually happen during the merging? He brushed back the long strands of silver hair, for the first time noticing the puncture wound on his neck. He caressed it. "Why won't he wake up?"

Selena held out a small dart with a tiny vial attached. "Knock out drug. Twice. He'll be out for a while."

She touched her brother's cheek.

"The Sinclairs should have something to counter it."

He gave a nod and pulled his angel into his arms. Frost— Nathaniel had always been smaller than him, but now he looked simply fragile. There was a new sense of protectiveness. He had to take care of his love. He had to.

"Put him down and step back," a gruff voice ordered.

The gunman from the jeep aimed a Glock at them. Scott glared at him and held Nathaniel tighter. He would not let him go. He was not about to give the person he loved to some maniac. That was why they were attacked. He could hear the man's thoughts. Henry wanted Nathaniel and Selena. He wanted them as food, although he was certain they would be used to satisfy him in other ways, too. They would have to kill him before he ever allowed that to happen.

Selena and Cleo stepped in front of him, forming a living shield. Only Cleo had enough magick left to hold up a real one. His magick bubbled around them. The man had no magick of his own. He never sensed the barrier he would have to try to shoot through.

"If you know what's good for you, lady, you will get out of my way. Griphan wants you and the angel alive."

Selena didn't budge. "He's not an angel."

He clicked the hammer back. "Don't push me."

The sound of a woman's whispery voice singing drew all their attention, but no one else was within sight.

Edgy, the man looked around. He quickly looked back at Selena.

"Come here," he ordered, losing his cool.

Selena stood her ground. "Come and get me."

The song came again. This time as the man looked for its source, Selena threw herself over Scott and Nathaniel. Scott yelped in surprise as the song turned to a piercing sonic scream that tore up the ground, headed directly for them. He held on to all three mythical beings, prepared to be torn to shreds as the ground exploded. Not even Cleo's shields could hold back such a force, he was sure. Whatever was attacking them now was presently stronger than them.

A hideous scream came from their captor as the sonic blast slammed into him with such a force that the man was virtually torn to pieces.

Scott squeezed his eyes shut as the ground continued to explode several feet closer to them. Then it stopped. The force dispelled, leaving little more than a few chunks of flesh that had once been a living, breathing man. Scott raised his head in surprise. Why did it stop? Surely, Cleo's shields were not what protected us.

When the dust and dirt settled, a very pregnant Aaliyah McNeil stood with her arms out stretched, pulling back her power. She studied each of them carefully. Her frown deepened. "They still have Eli," she stated. Her amber eyes closed in remorse.

"You know?" Scott asked in shock. She was the last person he had expected to see or to assist Eli. Although he supposed he shouldn't have been so surprised. The two shared a bond that was unbreakable even in death. Aaliyah had the ability to see into the future. She knew what was happening, but there was a strange sense of guilt written all over her.

"Yes," she whispered, kneeling across from him.

"I can't feel him anymore," Cleo reported. He sat back on his haunches. He looked just as bad as Aaliyah.

Scott sighed. He hated giving up, but without a good sense of where Eli was, they could do nothing. Even if they followed Cleo to Porter's stronghold there was nothing any of them could do to help him. He picked up Nathaniel and held him close to his chest. "There's nothing else we can do. Let's regroup with the Sinclairs and figure out what to do next."

They reluctantly agreed.

Chapter Twenty-three

Eli returned to a state of depression. The moment they pulled up to the castle, he practically run to his room. Frost was in a coma. He could feel his magick fluctuating and there was nothing Eli could do to help him. Even after Frost stabilized, Eli was not sure of his condition…for once they passed the shield around the castle, he lost all sense of his friends once more. It made him feel weak and useless. Worse, he no longer had Cleo beside him for support.

He sat on his bed trying his hardest not to sob. Henry's words still rung in his ears and he could not shake the images of Selena helpless under the large man as he had his way with her. She and Frost were most likely already captured and Henry would be waiting to feed off their magick and worse. Eli knew that Selena would receive the brunt of his attentions.

Eli hung his head, letting a few rogue tears slide down his cheeks. It didn't seem real. Henry was not the same man he had grown up with. This had to be a nightmare. There was no way the man who had beaten him could be the same man who used play with and care for him as a child. He touched his swollen throat. It wasn't possible. There had to be an explanation.

He stared down at the heavy cuffs Henry had insisted he wear again. He was not taking any more chances with Eli. There was no way they would give him another chance to escape. Not that Eli thought he had the strength to now. Even the magick pouch and his totem were taken away just to be certain. It didn't make him completely helpless. The totem was merely a tool to channel his powers. However, without the spirits within the crystals at his side, he felt utterly lonely. He missed Cleo and Selena more than he dare say. He would not allow Henry and Porter to use his emotions against him.

"Henry, this is ludicrous! Of course, he's scared! Seeing those films, beating him, taking him from his friends…it's all too much. We both knew this might happen. Beating him again won't help matters any. Just let him rest and cool down. By morning he should be calm enough to deal with." He heard Duncan sigh behind the closed door. "He needs time."

Henry snorted in disgust. "Time my foot! That boy will learn to do as he is told or I will make sure he cannot walk to a week. Blasted Canadians teaching him he no longer needs to listen to his elders because he was once a great Sorcerer. I'll show him! I'll fu—"

"Henry, please, listen to yourself. He's your grandson. Let me deal with him. I—"

"We've tried it your way. I'm sick of playing kid games with him. It's time he learns that just because he's Anthony's reincarnation he's not bulletproof."

Eli gazed at the door with worn, teary eyes. They had been arguing since they had dragged him back to the castle. Although he still had his magick, Duncan had nullified a good share of it. All offensive spells were of no use. The fact that the warlock had accomplished such a feat had taken Eli aback, his fear rising tenfold. He *could not* escape. He couldn't even defend himself against either of them. They could literally do what they wanted to him now. He did not dare think of the possibilities.

He gingerly rubbed his throat. It still hurt. Why he had fought so desperately to stop Duncan and Selena from healing it, he was not sure. He couldn't talk with it in the condition it was, yet he couldn't scream either. Henry would not have the satisfaction next time he beat him and would tire of him quickly.

The door finally opened, causing him to jump in fear. His two abductors were still fighting over what to do with him. Eli shied back, trying to make himself small and unnoticeable. Duncan gazed at him in distress, his eyes wide with fear and worry. Henry, on the other hand, glared at Eli with evil intent.

This was it! Eli knew it, pressing himself against the headboard as the two approached from either side. They were going to team up on him. He pulled his knees to his chest and watched them fearfully as he tried to avoid their hands. However, being chained to the bed left very little to protect him.

"Eli," Duncan said softly, placing a hand on his knee.

Eli swallowed and stared up at him.

"I'm so sorry. This has to be done. You can't keep defying us and getting away with it."

Horror filled Eli as Duncan went to remove his shirt. He shook off his gentle hands and scooted away only to have Henry grasp his tender throat. Eli knew better than to fight then. Henry could snap him in two with little trouble and no magick. His now youthful form was almost three times stronger than his original.

Please no, Eli silently begged as Duncan removed his shirt, his soft hands sliding over Eli's heated skin. I don't want this to happen. Not again. Please not again. He closed his eyes and look away, willing himself not to be aroused, but Duncan stopped before it could go any further.

"I won't hurt him this way," Duncan growled at Henry.

He pulled away from Eli.

"Beat him all you want, but I will not participate."

He caressed Eli cheek with sad eyes. Leaning close, he brushed his lips against Eli's.

"I can't do it," he whispered, closing his eyes.

"Set up the blasted chains then," Henry snarled.

Duncan gave a nod and climbed off the bed. He walked to the end and lowered a nasty looking set of cuffs from the bed's canopy. Eli's eyes widened in terror when Henry freed him only to drag him to the new set. With little help from Duncan, Henry managed to bind Eli's wrists and ankles. The chains around Eli's wrists were then pulled high above his head, to force him to his tippy-toes. His shoulders stung as his weight was forced upon them.

Eli bit back the whimper as he tried to find a more comfortable way to stand without losing what footing he had and pulling his arms out of joint. It was nearly impossible in such a position.

Eli was sure he was not getting out of this one. He was not going to go down without a fight. He may not be able to use offensive spells, but he did have a few defensive spells left. If only they would work against Henry.

"You look so much like Anthony. You even have his defiant nature. Something I'm about to snap right out of you." He leaned close to Eli. "There are many forms of pain. I can beat you senseless. Whip you until you're nothing more than raw meat. I can absorb your magick until you're bone dry." He ran a finger along Eli's ear.

Disgusted by his words, Eli turned to face him. His eyes were filled with rage and fear. Yes, he feared what Henry could do to him. The man knew everything that had happened to him throughout his life. Narrowing his eyes in hatred, Eli spat in Henry's face, taking satisfaction in hitting the man in the eye.

A large muscular hand went across Eli face in response.

A muffled cry escaped his lips as his head snapped back. He collapsed against his bonds. Maybe that wasn't the best thing to do, he told himself.

"Don't let Anthony take charge," Henry ordered Duncan.

Eli cracked open an eye as Duncan began chanting. Anthony? No, he wasn't going to let Anthony take charge. He could handle this on his own. If Henry was going to do what he feared, he was not going to let someone else suffer for him. He forced himself to straighten as best he could and stood defiantly awaiting his punishment.

A whip cracked just to his left. With effort, he steadied his breathing. He wasn't going to scream. He was not going to give Henry the satisfaction no matter what he did. "You're a coward," he choked out despite his raw and torn throat.

"What?" Henry asked in shock.

Eli glanced over his shoulder and made his voice louder. "You, Henry Griphan, are a coward," he grunted, pushing back the pain.

"You have to chain me and bind my magick just to get your jollies. You disgust me."

He was ready to have his neck broken, the life snuffed out of him. Instead, Henry grabbed a fist full of hair and yanked his head back. "I could care less about your powers. They never saved Nathaniel. I can absorb them just as fast as you can cast a spell."

The whip went across Eli's bare back as Henry stepped away. He managed to keep himself from screaming by biting his lip until it bled. He whimpered softly with each hit, trying to keep as quiet as possible as Henry raved about the tattoo on his back. He was creative with his hits, bringing the whip to Eli's abdomen, chest, and sides as well as his back.

Eli could not hold back the cries of pain as Henry crisscrossed them over the ones before them. Before Henry was even halfway through the *ten* lashes, Eli was screaming in agony. His back was bleeding uncontrollably. His whole body shook with pain. However, for every scream, Henry would add another lash, never allowing Eli to pass out until he was finished and Eli swore loyalty.

Duncan sat on the bed, paralyzed in horror as Eli took the beating.

Daniel's eyes grew wide. Searing pain raced up his back and chest. He doubled over in pain and blindly grasped for something to hold him up. His knees buckled before he could right himself and he fell to the lush grass in agony. His mind was on fire as an overload of psychic pain flooded him. Somewhere, Eli was being tortured. He tried to reach out for him only to be shoved aside.

"Eli…" he murmured, his eyes falling shut.

"Dad!" Alexis cried, falling before him. She grasped his shoulders and gently shook him. "Dad? What's wrong?"

"Mr. Dion?" Miao knelt next to them.

Daniel winced, trying to pull all his strength together. Frost and Selena had failed. Porter and Griphan had captured Eli and were now punishing him for escaping. Henry Griphan was at least. That was where Eli's fear was directed. He was terrified and in massive pain, and his defiance was beginning to falter. Henry was breaking his spirit.

No! Eli, you must be strong. You'll make it through this, he urged, penetrating the shield Duncan must have placed around Eli. He mentally wrapped himself around the young man and held him close. *This is all a bad dream. Close your eyes. Everything will be okay. Go to sleep, Eli.*

There was a moment of tension before he felt Eli slip away into unconsciousness. Daniel relaxed, resting his head on his arm as he tried to catch his breath. Just by the feel of his back, he knew Eli was in horrible shape. His back stung so much he feared he would not be able to get to his feet. At least the pain would not be so bad for Eli while he's asleep. Hopefully, it would give him a chance to regain his strength. He gazed up as Alexis cupped his cheeks.

"Dad?"

He hissed as Miao touched his back. The young man's eyes grew wide as he pulled his hand back to find it covered in blood. He stared at

Daniel in fear. "Eli…"

Daniel nodded. "They caught him."

"But how? Eli's magick...the Guardians?"

Daniel hung his head. "Were not enough."

Tears wielded in Alexis's eyes. "No."

Despite his wounds, she threw herself in his arms.

He bit his tongue as the pain increased, and held her. She had a right to be scared. Eli was one of her closest friends. A brother in many ways. Not knowing what was happening to him yet seeing the torture her father was suffering through frightened her. With every right. It also frightened Daniel.

Pushing back the pain, he forced himself to stand. It was hard. His legs were wobbly and he feared he would fall if he tried to walk. Miao offered him a shoulder to lean on and Alexis instantly went to help him from the other side. In an hour, the wounds would heal. Duncan would see to it. Somehow, he knew the warlock would not willingly allow Eli to suffer for long. He trusted the warlock to care for Eli. He didn't know why, but something told him Duncan was truly trying to help Eli.

Looking up and down the vast corridor, Duncan made sure Henry was nowhere in sight. The former general had gone to his chambers over an hour ago with one of the chambermaids and grumbled about the failure of his men. He was thankful Eli's friends had escaped. It would have torn Eli in two had they been captured. He would likely have done something foolish to free them. After seeing what Henry had done to Selena in the limo, he had no doubt what the chambermaid was going through. The woman had limited magick, nothing like Eli. Henry was likely to get bored of her soon and move on to someone else within the hour. He had to move fast if he were to get to Eli before the young man went into shock.

Satisfied Henry was not wandering the halls in search of his next victim, Duncan slipped into Eli's chambers. The lights were off, but Duncan could see Eli was still the way Henry had left him, hanging from the chains covered in his own blood. Had Dominique still been alive, she would have been on Eli instantly, licking up the blood and offering it to her demons. Duncan sighed. Sometimes it was a good thing Sara had died when she did. As Dominique, she was a horror just as bad as Henry.

Not bothering with the lights, Duncan went to Eli's limp form. He gently raised the young man's bowed head. He was out cold. There was no point in waking him. He could heal the gashes without him being conscious, in fact, it was easier, although he did prefer Eli awake for it.

He moved back behind Eli and stared in disgust at the ruined tattoo in between the young man's shoulder blades. It was no longer recognizable, its unique beauty and vibrant colours hidden under the mass of blood. Henry wanted it destroyed, fuming at how Eli could have allowed such blasphemy to mark him.

Henry believed now more than ever that Chaos still possessed Eli. There was no way to make him believe the truth. He said it was Chaos that made Eli so defiant, that only Chaos would make Eli fight him each time he fed. He refused to believe that Eli was scared of him, that the feedings actually hurt. Of everyone, Duncan knew.

Duncan knelt and carefully undid the chains around Eli's ankles. He slowly moved upward, skillfully checking for any wounds not apparent to the naked eye.

Then, wrapping one arm gently around Eli's waist, he removed the cuffs holding up his wrists. Eli fell instantly into his arms like some rag doll. Placing an arm under his knees Duncan carried Eli onto the bed and laid him down on his belly, careful of the wounds to his chest. Eli made a pitiful whimper, but didn't wake.

Relieved, Duncan went to the bathroom and fetched a bowl of warm water and cloth. He sat on the bed and slowly, gently, washed each of Eli's wounds, softly humming each time Eli whimpered in pain. Henry had made an awful mess. It would take a great deal of magick to heal him.

Henry had done this not only to punish Eli, but also to punish Duncan. He knew how much magick it would take to heal him and he knew how much Duncan suffered each time he had to perform such magick.

Chapter Twenty-four

Henry stared at his journal. The pen shook in his hand as he tried to write. What was wrong with him? He had been writing in the old book since the day Eli was born, yet today, he could not focus on anything but Eli's torn back. He could not understand what possessed him to hurt the boy so. Nor why he bathed in his blood afterwards. He simply craved it with no logical reason. Was he truly becoming a vampire? He shuddered at the thought. There had to be a better explanation.

His eyes felt fuzzy and head ached as if he were drunk. He glanced at the unconscious woman on his bed. Maybe he had taken too much magick. That had to be it. The only reason he had taken one of Duncan's servants to bed was to vent out his frustration on someone other than Eli. He needed some flesh to pound into, a woman to cry out his name in passion. That woman was supposed to be Selena. He wanted to see her alabaster skin glow beneath him, her blood-red hair spread like a halo over his pillows. He wanted to see those amazing wings quiver as she panted for him as she had decades ago.

When did these fantasies of Selena start? He cared for her in both Anthony's time and the last twenty years, as if she were his own child…that was a lie. He did know when it all began…years ago, after Nathaniel was kidnapped. She had wept silently in her room, hiding from the other two Guardians so they would not see her tears. He had consoled her, holding her in his arms and assuring her that everything would be fine, even though only hours earlier he had had been the one to torture her missing sibling.

It was the first time he had seen the woman behind the faery, and even though he was married, he felt a need for her he had never felt before. It took time to seduce her. She wasn't quite as carefree as she led many to believe. It took skill to break through her carefully formed shields and get her to drop her guard. Once he did, he was able to manipulate her in ways that guaranteed she was in his bed whenever he requested it. He'd take her, make her cry out his name over and over again until he absorbed enough of her power that she had passed out. He didn't do it often, Anthony and his Guardians seemed to always be around. When he was able to get her alone, he made such passionate love to her that he wept each time he had to let her go. The reason she had trouble remembering those times was the amount of magick he stole from her. While their relationship changed when she once more reverted to a child form upon Eli's birth, he continued to feed from her. Their relationship was no longer sexual and after so many years, Henry had all but forgotten it. After all, he spent the last thirty years with Mae Sinclair, up until five years ago at least.

Yet seeing her bent over Eli with her hair tossed over one shoulder, had stirred those old memories and feelings. He wanted Selena, needed her even more than Eli's magick.

He glanced up in surprise. Eli's aura was moving about. He could feel the familiar pull of magick that made him hunger for his magick. It seemed too soon for him to be out of bed. The beating he had taken should have rendered him immobile for at least a day or two. Leaving the panties on the desk, he went to investigate.

Eli was indeed up. He walked along the corridor as if in a fearful trance, his gaze darting to every corner, giving each shadow a good long stare before moving around it, as if fearful it would jump at him. His head jerked up when he heard Henry step into the corridor and froze in his tracks before taking a cautious step back.

"No, no! Eli, wait," Henry called as the young man tried to dart away. He caught him before he could get too far.

"I want to talk to you."

Duncan must not have been able to heal his throat yet. Eli made some pitiful noises in protest until he finally realized he could not escape. Henry rested his cheek on Eli's head, gently rubbing a hand up and down his arm. It took a few minutes before Eli relaxed enough to move him without fear of him bolting away. Eli gave a soft whimper as his hand brushed against his back. The wounds were now healed, but still tender. Would be for several days, Henry realized, careful not to touch him there again.

"Shh…Are you alright? Your back still hurts, doesn't it?" he asked gently.

Eli gave a nervous nod.

"I'm sorry I had to hurt you. I—"

He fell silent, guilt filling him as he felt Eli tremble. He held the young man closer, minding his back as he wrapped his big arms around his much smaller frame. "I had to do it, Eli. You know that. How can you learn anything if you are not punished for your wrongdoings?"

"Se—Selena?" Eli choked out, gazing up at him in confusion and fear.

"Hmm…" He buried his face in Eli's hair. "I know. I…want her, Eli. I want to taste her. I want her body. God, help me. I need to be between her legs so bad. I want to f—"

He closed his eyes and stopped himself. *I'm a man of God. A soldier in his army. I can't feel this way for someone I cared for, for so long.*

The urge to feed gripped him as he stared down into Eli's pale face. The young man was just as scared for his faery guardian as he was. They both knew what would happen if she was there. Henry shook his head. He would not feed from Eli or any one today. He had too much yesterday to dare feed again. That Scott bugger was right. He was addicted to Eli's magick.

He gently pushed Eli away. "No…no. Go, relax. Don't wander too far outside. A very dangerous storm is approaching—and stay away from the shield, please. I don't want a repeat of last night."

Eli looked frightened when he nodded. He hurried away without a backward glance, still avoiding the numerous shadows as if they were the plague.

It made Henry sick to see Eli frightened of him, but what was done was done. He had to protect England from Chaos. He only wished there was another way. Yet his numbing mind could not find any. He wanted to feed, needed it like a drug. Maybe just a little taste to subdue him? Just a small lick. He climbed back into to bed, covering the nude woman with his large body.

Eli's heart raced as he ran out of the castle, ignoring Claudia and Henry's warnings of the rain. The pouring rain and pounding thunder echoed in his heart. The rhythm was at once even as his feet slipped in the wet grass. He had hoped to get outside without being seen. Duncan was still sound asleep in his room, recovering from healing the wounds that had been on Eli's back. He had not awakened at all that morning and it was already past noon. Yet the sky was black as night. It matched how Eli felt inside.

There was no escape, but he ran as fast and hard as he could. His chest pounded and the tears rolled down his cheek mixing with the raindrops. He had feared Henry would take his energy before he could get outside. He needed the fresh air. He needed time to think. He needed to be alone.

Falling to his knees, he screamed in rage, letting everything he had been holding in out…not caring what damage it added to his already torn throat. He screamed until nothing more than weak sobs poured from his lips. He covered his face and gave into them. What was he going to do? Even if his wounds were healed, he could no longer handle any of the torment Henry and Duncan were putting him through. He had no idea whom he should trust or whom not to trust.

Henry was his grandfather yet he had turned into a monster. Duncan was his rival yet… yet he seemed to love him.

Why else would he keep risking his life to save his?

Why would he allow Henry to feed from him to spare Eli?

Unless it was all a trick.

What if they were doing this to make him trust Duncan again? What if Duncan forced himself on him again? He may not have last night, but it could easily be a trick. It was too much. It had to end. Somehow, he had to end this before he lost his mind.

The crashing of waves caught his attention. It had the alluring effect of a lullaby. Standing, he slowly walked toward the cliffs. The Irish Sea sang to him like a Siren's call. It was the answer to his trouble. The escape he had been searching for. He would finally become one with the waters he had wished so long to travel.

The waters that were as blue as his eyes on a sunny day were now black and wild. The waves crashed against sharp, jagged rocks below, spraying Eli. It felt refreshing and oddly welcoming. An odd calmness filled him as he stepped near the edge. It was the perfect solution. Step over the edge and it was over. If he did it right, he could snap his neck and feel next to no pain.

Head first.

It was so simple.

No portals.

No Henry. No Duncan.

What was left of his family would miss him as would his friends and he would miss them, but in time, they would understand. It was the only way. He stepped closer to the edge and took a deep breath. So easy and no one was there to stop him. A small giggle bubbled in him. One more step.

No! Anthony's voice cried out.

Eli staggered back in shock. No, he wasn't going to let Anthony stop him. Daniel and the others needed him. As long as Anthony's spirit lived in Daniel, everything would be okay. His life no longer mattered. Nevertheless, Anthony's spirit continued to fight him, pushing him further and further away from the cliff's edge. Eli fought, slowly making his way to the ledge. He had to do this now while he still had the courage to do so, as there may never be another chance.

Daniel's voice mixed with Anthony's, their joined voices telling him it was cowardly to take his own life and forcing him back.

Eli cried out against them. Why couldn't they understand? Why couldn't they understand he just couldn't handle it anymore? He needed release. He needed his freedom. This curse of a life had to end, even if it meant taking his own. They had never been through half the hell he had. How could they ever truly understand his pain?

He sobbed softly as they pulled at him.

Please, just let me go!

Anthony's voice mentally called out for help from a source Eli was unsure of. Whoever they were, it was going to be too late. Eli was determined to jump over that cliff. There wasn't much time left. He pulled and twisted against the invisible hands holding him.

This isn't the way! Anthony insisted, Daniel's voice overlapping it. They held him tightly as Eli listened to the waves call to him. *Eli, please think of what you are doing. We need you.*

"No!" Eli choked out, making one last break for the cliff.

His foot hit the edge and he dove. Arms wrapped around him and pulled him back with such force he and his savior were sprawled on the wet grass. Eli lay panting, dazed, and confused. The arms that held him now were real. They trembled as they held him close. Warm breath caressed his neck as soft sobs filled his ears. He didn't need to turn around to know it was Duncan. Anthony had awakened Duncan to stop him.

"Why?" Duncan whispered, kneeling above Eli. His teary eyes were wide with confusion. "Why?"

Eli closed his eyes. Why couldn't they just let him die? He looked away and just laid there as Duncan hugged him. Now Anthony had betrayed him as well.

"Duncan! Eli!" Henry called over the pounding rain. He ran toward them, his gray trench coat flapping in the wind. He slipped on the grass, nearly falling. "What's going on? Are you both alright? What is Eli doing out here?"

Duncan shook his head, pulling Eli up against him. They rocked back and forth as Duncan began mumbling. Eli couldn't help but stare at him. Duncan was shocked by what he had tried to do. He was genuinely upset, crying even. Eli let him help him stand. Duncan was shaking far worse than he was.

"Why? I don't understand," Duncan whispered. He held Eli's shoulders and stared deep into his eyes. "I never meant for this to happen."

"Duncan, what's going on? What did Eli do?" Henry demanded, laying a hand on Eli's shoulder.

Duncan's eyes flared in rage. He glared at Henry with such hatred Eli shrugged back in fear.

"Don't touch him! Get your fucking hands off him!"

Henry's hand flew off Eli's shoulder as if burned. Duncan wrapped an arm around Eli's shoulders and quickly led him back to the castle, leaving a flabbergasted Henry in the rain. Eli said nothing as they entered the castle. Claudia was at the door with two large bath sheets.

Duncan instantly threw one over Eli's shoulders before taking one for himself. They silently went to Eli's room. Eli half-expected Duncan to pull out dry clothes for him and insist he change right away, instead he had Eli sit in the large wing back chair and knelt before him. His hands shook as he clasped Eli's. There was more fear in those sapphire eyes than Eli had ever seen in him. It made him feel guilty for causing such pain.

"I'm so sorry," Duncan said in a small shaky voice. He held Eli's hands to his eyes. Warm tears spilled over Eli's cool fingers. "What have I done? I should never have brought you here. I should never have involved Henry. I'm so sorry. None of this was supposed to happen."

He wrapped his arms around Eli's waist and sobbed uncontrollably, his entire body shaking. Eli didn't know what to say. He had never seen Duncan so emotional. He placed a hand on the other man's shoulder. Duncan truly would have mourned his death. He was in love with him. Eli instantly hardened himself. That didn't matter. No matter how much Duncan loved him, Eli could not allow him to open those gates to other worlds.

"I never wanted you to be hurt. I just wanted you to love me. I'm such a fool!" Duncan cried into Eli's chest. His arms tighten around his waist. "Please forgive me. I'm begging you. Please... Please forgive me. Say you forgive me."

Eli sighed and combed his fingers through Duncan's wet hair. He shook his head when Duncan peered through his wet induced curls. Eli watched as his heart broke. Tears welled up in Duncan's eyes. Eli wiped some away, blinking back his own tears that threatened to spill from his weary eyes. Duncan burrowed his face against his stomach as Eli brushed his fingers through his hair. No, he could never forgive Duncan for his crimes. No matter how much he wanted to, he could never forgive, nor forget, what Duncan had done to him as a child.

He patted Duncan's head, as Anthony would have one of his children until eventually Duncan cried himself to sleep and Eli moved him to the bed so they could both sleep comfortably.

There was still one escape left open to him, one riskier than taking his own life. Whether or not he had the courage to go through with it, he was not sure. It was a risk he had to take.

Eli gasped when he awoke. His body was stiff as the nightmare pulled away. Warm arms wrapped possessively around his waist and Duncan's face was buried in the nape of his neck. His face was still tear-stained, but he looked sound asleep. Eli carefully moved his arms off him and climbed out of bed. He knew what he had to do. The dream had reminded him how he had dealt with one of his biggest problems ever.

Slipping into the bathroom, he silently shut the door. Taking a few deep encouraging breaths, he stood before the mirror as he had so many years ago and lit one of Duncan's many soft blue candles.

"Or—"

He winced in pain. His throat was still too sensitive to talk again. He frowned at his image and tried chanting the spell in his mind instead.

Oracle of Lunar light, send me now the second sight.

His reflection changed, making him look almost twenty-five years older. Anthony Sinclair blinked and stared back at him. Trying to hold back the tears, he wrote runes above and on either side of Anthony's head. Anthony's eyes widened in surprise and confusion.

When Eli was done, he stood back and wiped his tears away. This had to be done. He had to escape. With a sniffle, he mouthed *sorry*, then blew out the candle. It was done. Nothing could stop the spell now.

He would be free.

Chapter Twenty-five

"Hmm…"

He opened his eyes slowly. Vibrant blurred colours filled his vision. Groaning, he buried his face in the pillow. It was too bright. Waving his hand, he shut the curtains and cast the room into darkness. Better. Sighing, he rolled onto his back. He felt…funny. Something was not right. Things felt strange, out of place somehow. Sitting up, he fumbled for his spectacles that his father had given him many years ago. He was surprised when his finger brushed over a pair of wire-rimmed glasses on the nightstand. He had not worn such a pair since childhood. Odd…

A knot formed in his stomach as he held them. This wasn't the astral realm. Everything felt far too real. He slipped on the glasses and stood before the dresser mirror. His eyes widened in shock. It wasn't possible. It couldn't be!

Anthony gasped at the sight of Eli's reflection. It was not like seeing Eli through the spiritual window they sometimes used a mirror to do. No, this was his reflection, it moved when he did. He groaned inwardly and touched the smooth, cool surface of the mirror. Not again.

Eli, this won't help matters, he whispered to the young man hidden somewhere deep in his subconscious. This wasn't the first time Eli had used such a spell to bring him forefront. It had happened when he was ten as well, after his grandmother had passed on. Normally Anthony's spirit was dormant, watching over his young reincarnation as if he was his own child. In many ways, Eli was just that.

Touching the reflection, he sighed. No, he would not force Eli back. With everything going on, he needed the break. If that meant suffering through Henry and Duncan's torments, so be it. He was not afraid.

Besides, it gave him a chance to figure a way of escape that Eli may not have been able to find.

"Uhm...Eli?"

Anthony glanced over his shoulder to see Duncan pat the bed in search of him. Momentary panic gripped the warlock when he could not find him anywhere on the bed. He finally opened his eyes and looked around the room. Relief filled his tanned face when he finally spotted him.

"Morning. How do you feel?"

Anthony hesitated. He had to pretend to be Eli or things would be worse for Eli when he did return. He opened his mouth to respond, but nothing came but a croak. Grasping his throat, he gazed at the mirror. A nasty bruise still marked it. It felt scratchy and extremely sore. He tried again. "F-fine."

Duncan wasn't convinced. He climbed off the bed and walked rather stiffly to him.

He grimaced, bracing himself against the dresser.

"Your throat, huh? I don't know why, but it won't heal." He went to touch it.

Anthony stepped back.

"I'm not going to hurt you, Eli. I swear. I'm just—" Anthony caught his hand as he tried to touch him again.

"Eli?" Duncan stared him in the eye.

He studied him with keen intelligence.

Anthony dropped his hand as it became apparent his imitation of Eli might not be correct. Eli was supposed to be scared, subdued even. Duncan would not be expecting him to be so willful so soon. However, Anthony knew Duncan. He was not easy to convince.

"Eli?" Duncan did touch his throat this time.

A small flow of magick began to spread between them.

Anthony inhaled sharply, closing his eyes as he tried to imitate Eli's reaction as best he could. It had been a long time since he was a teenager and allowed Duncan so close. He magick was soothing, like it had been so long ago, alluring in a way.

"Eli..." Duncan whispered again, moving closer.

An arm moved around Anthony's waist as Duncan lowered his lips.

Duncan's eyes suddenly snapped open in shock. "Anthony?"

Instantly, Anthony pulled back. Usually, he was better at hiding himself than this. However, Duncan was a strong telepath. Stronger than most. Even years ago, when they were both young, he had a way of bewitching him.

"What? How? Where's Eli? Is he alright?"

Duncan winced, actually grabbing Anthony for support.

Anthony stared at him in awe and worry. Awe for his instant concern for Eli and worry for the sudden pain he seemed to be in. He held Duncan's elbows and helped him to one of the seats around the little table. He gasped when he saw the back of Duncan's white shirt, stained with blood from the wounds he had transferred from Eli's back to his own. They were not healing as fast as the first ones.

He sat across from Duncan and stared up at him. It was the first time he had ever had to look up at his rival. It made him feel small compared to the older teenage body. However, since the *jig was up* as Scott would say, there was no point in not using telepathy.

He buried himself in the depths of his subconscious. I was forced forward, he mentally explained.

Duncan's brows crumpled in despair. "It's my fault. I should never have included Henry. I thought he would help keep Eli calm, make him understand I never wanted to hurt him. I never thought Henry would become so addicted. He was never this way with yo—"

He bit his lip.

"Henry always loved Eli. He spoiled him. Bought him anything and everything he ever wanted, trained him to be the best fighter and magician." He looked at Anthony pleadingly. "You must understand, I—I love Eli just as I once did you. I want to protect him and teach him. Not just about the portals, but about himself, too. Chaos gave him new powers, but they seemed to have gone dormant or vanished."

Anthony nodded, taking note that Henry had once fed on him when he had been alive. Why didn't he sensed it back then? Or did he? Maybe he had ignored it.

"I can't sense Chaos any more. What if it was just a momentary power burst? Maybe nothing will happen at the eclipse, but what if something does? Your own books say so. Isn't it better to be safe than sorry? To know he can control the portals if need be?"

What he said made sense. If the eclipse did affect Eli has he had seen in many of his visions, it would be better if he knew how to handle it, but there had to be a catch. Duncan had to want something out of it as Henry did. *What do you get out of this?*

Duncan looked guilty now. "My daughter, Sara. I just wanted to see her one last time." He looked ready to break down. "I never blamed Eli for Sara's death. I lost her a long time ago. Dominique stole her from me when she was just a child. She put a spell on her when she was just a babe before she attacked you. It was her backup plan should she die."

Anthony raised a brow in surprise, which grew as Duncan continued.

"The day she died, I lost my wife, child, and favourite rival. All in one day."

You were married to Dominique?

Duncan wiped at his tears and laughed. "Yes, I foolishly married her and we had Sara."

Anthony was at a loss. *Of all the people to become a couple,* he thought. They were such opposites except in their magick style, yet it explained why they had worked together to capture him several years before his death. It had been one of the scariest and the weirdest days of his life. Then Duncan had gone out of his way to save him.

"I know, I'm a bad judge of character, but she was so exotic and beautiful. She seemed so sweet and loving." All the traps Anthony had fallen for.

"She was a little wild, but after Sara was born…Raven, believe me, I didn't know she was still after you. I thought she would give up on Chaos. If I had known…when she went after Eli, my heart cried out for him. I left for America as fast as I could to stop her, but his friends got to him before me. When I felt Chaos within him I…"

His brows came together.

"You're laughing at me!"

Anthony shook with laughter. *Do you know the hell you put him through? You and Dom deserved each other!*

Duncan frowned. "You're still a brat."

This coming from you. He shook his head. *Perhaps, but Sara never deserved to be possessed. No one does.*

"That she did." Duncan fell silent, his eyes inspecting his old rival. "I believe Sara's spirit is still out there. Somewhere. Eli may be able to open a portal to her."

Perhaps, but I don't recommend it. The spirit world is forever changing. Anthony glanced at his reflection once more. Under his eyes were dark circles from all the crying Eli had done in the past few days. *He is ruled by emotion at this age. There is no guarantee he can control it.*

"I know." Duncan rotated his shoulders. "Hmm…that's going to take time."

Why did you heal him?

"Because I love him and can't stand to see him suffer." He became silent as Anthony stood and circled the table.

You desire him?

"Yes."

Anthony smiled at his honesty. It was true he loved Eli, but it was also an obsession. The only reason Duncan was being so open was because Eli hid himself so deep in his subconscious. Anthony hoped Eli heard everything Duncan said as well. It was the only way Anthony could think of getting Eli to calm down. If he knew exactly how Duncan felt, maybe, just maybe, they could work together on escaping Henry or curing him.

Duncan gasped as his finger trailed over his back. His shirt was stuck to his back with small patches of blood here and there. Eli must have gone through some real damage for Duncan to suffer so much after trying to heal him. It also meant Duncan had not perfected his healing techniques. It was not uncommon amongst the healers. They often took on one's pain and suffering without transferring it elsewhere.

Anthony didn't need to touch flesh to heal. All he needed was the patient's aura and a strong imagination. Placing his hand on the dresser, he pictured it touching the brick wall connecting to the rest of the castle and far below them to the ground. He kept the other inches away from Duncan's back so he would not hurt him and channelled all of Duncan's pain and injuries to the earth spirit. It hungrily devoured them, leaving Duncan's skin smooth and vibrant.

Duncan inhaled sharply, surprised by the sudden lack of pain and the new energy flowing through him. He flexed his shoulders and smiled gratefully. "Thank you."

The least I can do for helping Eli.

"I wish I knew how to gain his trust."

Time and patience. Give him the time he needs without pushing. Show him you don't mean harm and perhaps, just perhaps, he will come to like you.

"Leave it to you to set me straight," Duncan sighed. "I've missed you."

And I you. Oddly enough, it was true. They fell silent. It had been many years since they had been able to sit comfortably together. Not since after Xyan's death and Anthony had cried his soul out to Henry and Duncan. So many years. It felt odd for them to do so now.

Duncan fished a fudgesicle out of the small icebox and presented it to Anthony. "Here. Your throat must be killing you. I'll bring you some ice cream later. It might be better if you stay in here today. Use illusion or glamour to look like you are still hurt if you like. Henry probably won't bother you much today. Eli scared all of us yesterday, but he might check on you. We can't let him learn you're not Eli. He'll go ballistic."

That was an understatement. He nodded and took the cold treat. He looked around the room quizzically. There were so many high-tech things that only Eli could understand. There were also many books that could occupy his attention for many hours.

"You don't know how to operate any of these, do you?" Duncan asked noticing his dumbfounded stare.

He shook his head.

Duncan laughed wholeheartedly and gave him a quick rundown. It nearly too half an hour before Anthony had the hang of it. The remote made things a little easier, but the numerous buttons were confusing. Duncan set up five CDs in the player and turned it on for him while he chose a book to read. There were many to choose from. Anthony chose one of the horror novels with large doses of magick and settled into the armchair. Duncan left shortly after, promising to bring him breakfast and ice cream.

This was the oddest thing to happen to Anthony, but in a way, he was happy Eli gave him a chance to talk to Duncan in private. It had been so long and for the first time, Anthony realized that he had honestly missed his rival and former friend. If circumstances were a little different, they may have been able to become friends again.

Chapter Twenty-six

The huge double doors blew open with barely a touch as Selena rushed into the mansion. Her torn gown billowed behind her as she ran to the drawing room. He saw it all before she even reached him yet his mind barely registered any of it.

"Dan! Richard! Nathaniel needs help! Where's Alexis?"

Daniel looked up from his coffee. His tired eyes gazed at the faery, his mind taking forever to comprehend her words. A part of his mind was far away, holding a quivering Eli in the dark depths of the young mage's mind. Somehow, Eli had managed to lock himself away from the outside world and a part of Daniel had followed him. He needed comfort and time to heal from his psychological wounds and Daniel wasn't willing to let him face it alone. Even in the fantasy world Eli had created for himself.

Selena grabbed his hand. "Come! Scott can't carry him much longer."

He followed her to the parlor where a very exhausted Scott held the unconscious faery. Frost's wings had vanished and his long hair wrapped around his waist and legs.

"Dad," Scott breathed, shifting Frost's weight. "He won't wake up. I've tried everything," he panted. He appeared ready to pass out as well. "Selena says the Sinclairs have a cure."

"We do," Richard confirmed. "But first we'll take him to his room. Much easier to work if he's lying down."

Scott nodded and followed without question.

"Where is his room?" Daniel suddenly asked, a small knot growing in his stomach.

"Servants quarters of course."

"Since when?"

Richard stared at him in confusion.

Daniel silently cursed Anthony's father once more for degrading his Guardians. "Take him to Anthony's chambers," he instructed coldly. He glared angrily at Richard. "Anthony would never allow his children to be treated as mere servants."

"Children?"

He stormed past the head of the Sinclair family in slight disgust. It wasn't his fault he didn't understand. It was before his time. Still, it was annoying to think someone was willing to think so lowly of a member of his family.

"Yes, children. Mine. He's just as much my son as Scott. It goes for Selena, Cleo, and Sif...and Miao. Either you treat them all with respect or we leave."

The other man's jaw dropped, but he didn't object.

A red-haired woman caught up to Daniel as he followed his son up the elegant staircase. She was as pretty as he remembered, he noted as he gazed at her, and quite pregnant.

"Daniel Dion?" she asked. Her intense amber eyes bored into his.

"Yes?" He blinked as her features changed to that of a Spanish woman with flowing black hair. The fact she was pregnant did not change in either form. "Xyan?"

She smiled. "Aaliyah McNeil."

"Ah...oh, yes, of course. Eli's Watcher."

"Was."

He led her to Anthony's room, his gaze never leaving her. Even though they had not seen each other in years, he could have sworn he knew her in another life. It wasn't just Eli's emotions this time. No, this was completely a past life issue.

Scott was laying Frost on the huge four-poster bed while Selena pulled down the covers. The willowy man lay peacefully, a huge contrast against the dark sheets. Scott was nervously trying to straighten his silvery hair.

"What happened?" Daniel asked as he calmly pulled his son's hands from the ethereal being. "Are you alright?"

"Yes, yes, fine. They took Eli and then attacked us. Nathan was hurt and could not change to Frost. They merged. They merged!" He calmed his excitement. "One of their men shot him twice with this." He handed his father the small vial.

"It's a special tranquillizer designed for those of magick," Selena explained. She sat next to her brother and stroked his hair. "He would be awake by now had he not lost so much blood." She gestured to the large gashes on Frost's legs. "He was nearly crushed when we slammed into the railing."

"Nathaniel?" Daniel brushed Nathaniel's bangs back, noting the subtle changes. Frost and Nathan had indeed merged. He looked as he once had, many years ago in Anthony's time. It gave the fey a softer, younger texture.

His leg was another matter. Silver blood, matching his hair, covered the pristine white trousers. They were torn so bad in places that Daniel would simply have to make him new ones. The idea made him smile. That type of material would be impossible to find. Only the Queen of England or the fey were able to purchase such fabric.

Luckily, the flesh was already healing, leaving only small cuts where the gashes had been so deep. He gently pressed his hand against the wounds. Warmth came to his hands. He visualized the flesh pure and healed, the fabric shimmering white without a tear or snag. He gasped when he pulled his hand back. Nathaniel healed just as he had imagined.

"Direct it somewhere else before it drains you," Aaliyah instructed in a teacher's voice.

It seemed only natural to touch the wall and think of the ground below or some faraway tree in need of nourishment. It was instantaneous when Nathaniel's pain spilled from him into that faraway place.

"You have the touch!" Richard gasped.

Aaliyah smiled at him with pride.

"Raven's magick is strong in you, too," she remarked. She took Daniel's hand. Her hands felt warm in his. "What do you see?"

He stared at her for a long moment before allowing his eyes to relax. The same image of the Spanish woman overlapped hers. His own arms and legs turned to elegant garments. Long black hair fell over his shoulders. Everything else became background clutter. "You, but not…your hair is black. Spanish… My hair is also black. I'm wearing silk clothing. We… you are… are… Xyan?"

She smiled.

"We were married. You were my wife."

"What?" Scott gasped, staring at them with wide blue eyes.

"In our past lives, Xyan and Anthony were married," Aaliyah explained, letting go of Daniel's hands. "When Eli was seven, I did the same exercise with him to test his level of insight. It was instant as it is with your father. Perhaps there is hope."

"What do you mean?" Daniel asked. The urge to hug and kiss his past love slowly subsided. No wonder Eli was so in love with her. When she had left him, it was not just losing a crush and maternal figure, but also his former wife. It was an eternal love, like what Daniel shared with his deceased wife, Christina.

"Anthony was the *Catalyst*. He created many dimensions and other worlds. Eli is the *Key*. He can open all these dimensions and many more. Daniel is the *Lock*, the door that will close the portals from all mortals."

"What?" I don't understand. I'm not some door. I barely have any magick. I wouldn't know what to do," Daniel objected. He stared at each of them. "I can't do this."

Scott gazed at his healed love, then back at him. "Yes, you can."

His love for the being was evident on his face as he held the pure alabaster hand. Nathaniel glowed softly in his sleep, his glamour slowly fading to show his faery form. The moon magick made his skin shine like the full moon. So pure, so full of life.

Daniel smiled as he recalled his past self's memories of the winged being. Anthony loved him in ways he did not his other Guardians. They shared a bond that was more than Master and Guardian. However, Daniel did not share it. He viewed Frost as one of his children and would, as he had for many years, protect as such. Aaliyah touched his arm, pulling him from his thoughts. He followed her to the corridor away from all eavesdroppers.

She rubbed her belly and smiled up at him. "He's kicking again," she replied to his confused look.

He nodded in understanding. When Christina had been pregnant with Scott, he had kicked a lot. Alexis had not been nearly as feisty.

"I... it's Eli. I found him this morning. I should have brought him here, but he was terrified we'd be hurt. I left him in Crewe to catch a bus. That's where they caught him. I'm so sorry, Dan. I didn't want to leave him." Tears glistened in her eyes. "He's like a son to me. I just couldn't—"

He smiled and drew her in his arms. She trembled as she mumbled more apologies. "It's alright. Not even you could have seen what would happen. We'll find him. I promise. Eli is going to be okay." He lifted her chin with his index finger. "You'll see. Everything is going to be alright."

Days had passed on the Porter estate. Eli had yet to return and Anthony was becoming more worried by the passing minute. He wasn't sure what to do to help his young reincarnation. It had been so long since he had to deal with an emotional teenager, but even then, it was not to this degree. So, he did the only thing he could.

The evening was calm as he sat near the cliffs overlooking the Irish Sea. He kept far enough back to keep Eli from making any irrational decisions should he decide to return, but close enough that he could feel the spray of the waves hitting the rocks far below. He had always loved watching the sea on a bright sunny day or while the sun set.

Even on clear night, the water was enchanting. The depths held more secrets than any one person could learn in a lifetime, several even. Childhood dreams of crossing those waters danced in his head. So many folklores, legends, and fairy tales his nanny had told him always inspired him. Ireland had been the reason he had created Serenity the way he had. She was, in every aspect, just as the faeries he imagined lived over the waters.

He tilted his head, letting the wind ruffle his loose hair. It was refreshing with the sprays of salty water splashing him as the waves hit the rocks. He was hoping the starry night would lure Eli out. The young man loved the stars and could easily name every constellation. There were many nights where Eli would climb onto the roof just to gaze at their beauty. Out here, away from the city lights, he could see everything so clearly it was breathtaking.

But Eli did not reveal himself.

Anthony was quickly running out of ideas. What if Eli simply refused to return? He shook his head. No, he's just scared. He needs more time. He closed his eyes and sighed as he felt Henry's aura approach from the east. Henry had graciously not touched him the last four days. It was impossible to believe they had once been friends. He was so different now. So cold. Power hungry. A psychic vampire feeding off Eli like his own private buffet. Yet, luckily, he still did not know about Eli's disappearance.

The large man took a seat directly behind him and pulled him close as if Anthony were just a wee child. His large legs were on either side of him, his strong arms around his waist. Anthony fought the urge to pull away and sat still.

"What are you doing so far from the castle, little one? Not trying to do something foolish again, are you?"

Anthony shook his head, gesturing to the sea and the colourful Northern Lights dancing in the heavens above.

"It is beautiful here," Henry agreed. He rested his head against Anthony's. "You still haven't got your voice back, have you? You know I never meant to hurt you. I have a fierce temper that I cannot always control. You are my grandson, I love you so much."

Lies. Anthony closed his eyes and tried to focus on the sound of the crashing waves. It was relaxing and, despite his anger, Henry was a good pillow. He frowned at the slight pull on his magick.

Henry was feeding again. His lips were brushing his hair lightly, barely touching. It wasn't as overwhelming as before, but he did feel sleepy. He opened his eyes and gazed at the stars. There had to be a way to stop him. He had studied Vampires in both forms of the term when he was young. What had his father taught him?

He inhaled sharply as the answer came. It was so simple, so easy that he didn't know why Eli had not thought of it earlier. Shifting his position, he crossed his ankles, then touched all his fingers together, ceasing the circuit of energy. The posture gave no hint as to what he had done.

Henry pulled back in surprise and confusion. He stared down at him, believing he had only moved into a more comfortable position.

"What did you do?"

Anthony only gazed up innocently.

"Eli, what did you do?"

Anthony shook his head and stood. At least now he knew how to stop him. He pushed the information to where he knew Eli was hiding, hoping it gave the youth a new sense of faith and hope. He started to walk back to the castle just as Duncan ran down the hill.

The warlock was smiling as he walked past.

"Hey, what's up?" he asked at Anthony's smile.

Anthony winked. *I'll tell you later.* He assured with a smirk. Oh, this could be fun, he thought, folding his hands behind him. Henry won't be able to feed any more. He's not going to be so happy. Although Anthony hoped Henry didn't decide to take it out on Duncan. He was beginning to enjoy reminiscing over old times with his former rival.

Duncan just stared at him in utter confusion as Henry stood.

"He stopped me," Henry muttered in awe. "How did he stop me?"

"I don't know," Duncan whispered honestly. He looked from one to the other. His brow came together in anger. "You promised not to feed from him until he was better."

Henry frowned. "He is better. He just refuses to talk."

"Whatever. Leave him alone until I say."

Henry growled under his breath threateningly. "Then I'll feed from you."

"Fine. Later." He threw an arm protectively over Anthony's shoulders and walked next to him back to the castle. "Did he hurt you?"

No.

"How did you stop him?" Anthony only smiled.

The night actually turned out silly. After spending most of the day in the library together, Duncan declared they would watch a movie. It took a moment to recall the meaning of his words, as he realized that he had not watched a movie since Eli was ten or eleven. It was while he was sitting at the cliffs that Duncan finally came up with a good one. *Lord of the Rings* was one of Eli's favourite series of books. It gave Anthony another chance to try to pull Eli to the forefront.

Duncan was like a big kid. He turned the DVD player on then bounced on the bed with a huge bowl of popcorn. He sat the bowl aside and opened his arms for Anthony to join him.

Shaking his head and half-laughing, he sat on the bed next to the warlock. They had become friends, sort of. Maybe it was the fact that in the end they were both prisoners. Henry was now feeding from Duncan on a regular basis, as Anthony had learned by accidentally walking in on them. It seemed Henry was taking his frustrations out on Duncan because he refused to let him touch Eli.

The rival magick user wasn't only protective of Anthony, but very much so of Eli. He constantly asked Anthony how his younger self was if he wanted anything. Sometimes he simply used Anthony as a channel to tell Eli things. None of which Eli responded to.

Duncan playfully threw his arms around him and pulled him to the middle of the bed. "It's a three-hour movie. Best get comfortable."

"You're such a brat," Anthony said softly, careful of his sore throat. It was healing, slowly, but he could talk when he wanted to, not that either of them were going to tell Henry.

Duncan chuckled and laid down, not bothering to pull Anthony down, but letting him do as he wished. It had been this way for days. No advances, spells, or anything to persuade him, just very friendly. Anthony lay next to him, making himself as comfortable as possible as the large television came to life.

The bright colours were captivating. As he had many years earlier when he lay next to Aaliyah McNeil, he was completely in a trance. He never noticed Duncan wrap his arms around him or his head lean against his own. He paid more attention to the story than anything else. The writers and actors portrayed the mystical creatures nearly perfectly. Even though the story was good, Anthony found himself dozing somewhere in the middle.

A tugging at the back of his mind woke him up. The room was dark and the television turned off. Duncan was sound asleep, popcorn scattered all over the bed. Anthony silently laughed at the warlock for the mess as he disentangled himself from his caring arms. The left side of his head stung where he had lain against his glasses to watch the movie. He massaged it as he got up. Last time he falls asleep with his glasses on.

The tugging feeling pulled him toward the bathroom. Rubbing the sleep from his eyes, he followed it until he was standing before the large bathroom mirror. He gazed at it as he yawned. "Eli?" he whispered, trying not to wake Duncan.

His reflection spoke by itself. "I want to go home."

"I know. Soon." He left the mirror and turned on the shower. He didn't need the mirror to commune with the youth. They were one, after all…the mirror simply made it easier to cast certain spells, or talk to one from a long distance…not for those simply talking to another part of them self. *Do you wish to come back?* he spoke through his mind instead.

No.

Are you alright?

I will be.

He sighed and stepped under the warm spray. Eli was so stubborn sometimes. So much like him, it was scary. Surely, Daniel was not like this. Then again, the professor was stubborn in his own ways. *I've been worried about you. You haven't talked to me in days. Even Duncan worries about you.*

Eli fell silent. Obviously, he didn't know what to make of Duncan's friendship either. Was it true or false? *How are we going to escape?*

I don't know. He could have sworn he heard Eli cry in despair.

This was really getting to him. He really wanted to go home, not that Anthony blamed him. The creepy old castle had a resident vampire that was feeding off him. That was enough to make any sane person crack after a while. He mentally hugged the young man. *Maybe it would be easier if we did open the gates.*

What?

I can't bear Henry hurting you. We can stop his feedings, but if he strikes you again, he may cripple you. No amount of magick can protect you if he simply drinks it in. He smiled as Eli finally agreed.

If Duncan could not stand to hear Eli cry, it simply tore Anthony in two. He loved Eli as his own and he had vowed many years ago never to let anything happen to him. Nevertheless, he was only a spirit. There was only so much he could do to protect him.

Eli slowly, hesitantly, pulled himself into Anthony's embrace, wrapped his spiritual arms around Anthony's waist and hugged him tightly. Anthony smiled. Holding Eli in his mind had become so familiar that it felt almost as if he was really holding the young man. Eli was a good kid, just confused. He did not blame him for retreating into the back of his mind.

As he held Eli, he let his own mind wander as the warm water washed away the stress Henry had induced in him earlier that evening. His sense of Eli began to fade even if he knew the younger man had not left the protection of his arms. He opened his eyes to find himself levitating high above the ground.

The moon and sun shone brightly in the day sky. The moon was slowly overlapping the burning sun. Anthony shielded his eyes. The city in the distance glittered like some huge jewel in the summer heat. A tingle in his stomach grew as the moon fully eclipsed the sun. It grew into a painful heat that Anthony could not quench. With a cry, he threw his head back as his magick half practically exploded from within him.

Portals to other worlds opened all around him. Lord and Lady, help us, he thought as creatures, both humanoid and otherwise, swarmed around him. Arms, tentacles, and other appendages wrapped around him, pulling him in either direction. It felt as if he was being torn apart. Somewhere amongst all the pain and confusion, he felt Eli clinging to him. As the pain grew, Anthony was only able to make out one sound. Eli's scream filled his ears and his own cry of agony met it. Then the world faded to blackness.

Chapter Twenty-seven

Duncan sat up with a start. A scream so shrill still echoed in his head.

Anthony.

Where was Anthony?

He looked around, not seeing the magician anywhere. God! What if Henry came in the middle of night and took him? The panic grew as he swept his gaze all across the room. Spotting the light under the bathroom door, he quickly got out of bed and ran to it.

Please don't let Henry be in there with him. Please God, don't let Henry hurt him.

He threw open the door and nearly cried out in relief when he saw Anthony alone. Relief turned back to fear when he saw the youth kneeling in the shower stall, holding the wall as if it were the last thing in the world. He looked dazed, confused, and utterly scared.

"Raven?" Duncan asked softly as he knelt to the shower stall, the water still running. "Anthony, are you okay?"

Those ocean deep eyes squinted up, his breathing labored. The way he held the wall hinted to Anthony not completely being there. It appeared as if he were fighting something. A vision perhaps? Whatever it was, it was causing him to shake uncontrollably.

"Oh, Lord."

Forgetting his clothes, he climbed into the shower and grasped the young man's shoulders. He winced as the rapid flow of magick shocked his hands. Touching someone while they performed magick was unwise, but he had to steady Anthony before it got worse. "Don't fight it, Andy. Let it come. Let the visions reveal themselves."

When the shudders finally stopped, he pulled the smaller man into his arms and let him relax. Reaching up, he turned off the water and sat back in the warm water. His head rested against Anthony's as he stroked the soaking wet hair away from his face. It must have been one hell of a vision to render Anthony, of all people, semiconscious. He could never recall Anthony reacting so harshly to one of his own visions.

The smaller man moaned softly and pushed himself up. He held his head as if it still hurt.

"Anthony, are you alright? Must have been a doozy."

Eli blinked and stared at him. His eyes crinkled in despair and fresh tears came to his eyes. He shook his head repeatedly. "No..." he pleaded, his voice small and lost.

Duncan's eyes widened for a moment. The vision had forced Eli back. Anthony had returned to the spirit realm. Ignoring Eli's protests, he wrapped him in a heavy terry cloth towel and held him until he stopped his violent shaking.

"It's alright, Eli. Shh..."

It took time, but he eventually got Eli to calm down enough to take him to his room. Keeping him wrapped up, he laid Eli on his bed and retrieved his glasses.

"Just relax. Take deep breaths," he instructed and sat next to him. He placed a cool wet cloth against his forehead.

Eli stared at him in confusion as Duncan tended to him. "Wha—"

He rubbed his sore throat for a moment.

"What happened?"

"Shot in the dark? The vision snapped you back from the dream world. Are you okay?"

Eli looked away and sighed deeply. "Yes."

"That's my boy."

It earned him a frown from Eli.

"Look, Eli, I'm sorry. Really, I am. For everything." He wiped Eli's brows and kissed his forehead. "I should have been more responsible. I should never have taken you as I did."

Eli merely closed his eyes and let him care for him.

Duncan sighed softly and continued to wipe away the sweat that had collected on Eli's forehead. The jolt back must have drained him. Eli was already beginning to slip into slumber. Whatever Anthony had seen must have really scared them for them to scream. Duncan could not fathom a possible reason.

Making sure Eli was tucked safely under the warm covers, Duncan leaned back and watched him. His visions always foretold the future. They were always right. Something bad was going to happen, most likely due to the eclipse. Duncan was beginning to have misgivings about the eclipse. Perhaps it would be safer to put Eli in a comatose state that day. Even if he did not see his daughter again, he could not endanger the young man's life. They would find another way.

"Claudia said she heard Eli scream," Henry half-bellowed, throwing open the door.

"Would you hush?" Duncan snapped, glaring at the big man. He left Eli asleep on the bed and went to Henry. "He had an episode." He took Henry's arm and pulled him out of the room. "You've got to completely lay off the feedings with him. He can't help us if you have him terrified or if he's too weak."

"How did he stop me?"

"I don't know. Closed the channels perhaps." He shook his head at Henry's dumbfounded stare. "Listen, that vision really scared him. Let him rest. If you keep feeding from him, he'll be too tired to do anything but sleep."

Surprisingly, Henry nodded. "The two of you have become very close the last few days. Have you…"

The question hung between them. There were many times since Anthony had taken over Eli's body that Duncan had wanted to kiss him, make love to him, but he had restrained himself. It was not Anthony that had made him think twice, but the sight of Eli in pain and crying. The image of him as an eight-year-old had planted itself so deep in his mind that he could not shake the agony he had caused the young man. No, any and all advances toward Eli were now prohibited. There was no way he would allow any harm to befall him. "No. Besides, Chaos is not within him. I would not be surprised if nothing happened on the eclipse. I'll still train him just in case."

"You love him."

He stared at his feet as they walked down the corridor. "Yes."

"Hmm…That's why you've been insisting I feed from you or your staff rather than him."

He nodded. "You tend to take too much when you feed from him. He needs his strength."

"And after this is all over you plan to let him go."

He was stating facts. What was he getting at? Duncan stared up at him in wonder. "Yes. There would be no need for him to stay against his will."

He gasped as he was suddenly pinned against the wall as they stepped in Henry's room.

Henry's hand moved along his throat as the other searched under his top for bare skin. "What if I said I don't want him to leave? That I'm beginning to like it here with servants to cater me and two youths I can control and feed upon." He squeezed Duncan's throat. "Make him yours in every way. Make your power one. I don't know how, but I'll tell you this, boy, Chaos is still in him. I can feel it every time I feed from him. You will control it and him, or you'll only wish I killed you all those years ago rather than this." He leaned in close. "Now about that feeding."

Duncan's eyes grew wide as Henry leaned his full weight into him. Closing his eyes, he gave in to the fate he had created.

* * *

Capturing Raven's guardian had been far easier than Duncan had ever imagined. Henry had slipped into the bookstore and simply told the young angel his Master wanted him and Nathaniel had instantly believed him, not once questioning Anthony's closest friend.

In his human form, he stepped out the back door of his favourite store and looked for his beloved Master. He became instantly defensive when he saw Duncan and changed to his true form, ready to protect Anthony. He had never expected Henry to betray him when the police chief had grabbed him from behind and injected a tranquilliser especially designed to take down magickal creatures. He had barely put up a fight.

He was bound, gagged, and blindfolded, hidden in the depths of the Scottish Highlands with so many magickal barriers that not even Raven himself could locate him. It had been so simple it was frightening.

"The secret to immortality is to take what they have been graced with. Even Nathaniel has the potential to live centuries, even millennia, as does any other faery," Duncan explained as they stepped into the narrow cavern. "An immortal's blood can slow a human's aging process. With time, you will learn how to feed off their auras instead. It is safer and far less noticeable. For now, this is easier."

Henry knelt on the other side of Nathaniel's half-nude form. The fey also had earplugs to keep him from hearing their voices and identifying them. He squirmed as Duncan raised him slightly and ran a razor across his pale, lean chest. Duncan's tongue ran over the wound, lapping up the silver blood as it flowed freely down the alabaster flesh.

Nathaniel cried against his gag.

Pulling back, he offered the angelic being to Henry. "Take it slow."

Henry stared at the young man for the longest time. His gray eyes flicked back to Duncan, uncertain. "He's like a nephew to me."

"Be gentle if you wish, but this coven will not. They dislike Raven's use of magick. They believe these creations are abominations and will use their magick to further their power. Better to do this now."

Henry's brows came together as he lifted Nathaniel to his mouth. The fey whimpered as he suckled his chest. For the first few moments, he hesitated, but as the power of the immortal blood took effect, he began to feed hungrily.

"No. Enough," Duncan ordered as Nathaniel's muffled cries grew in pitch. He pulled Henry off the smaller being. "You don't want to hurt them, only take a little of their magick."

The skin around the wound was already bruising. Brushing Nathaniel's wispy hair back, Duncan drew upon his magick to calm him. Soon Nathaniel laid there, barely conscious, and fully healed, but Henry was already staring at him hungrily, wanting far more than the fey could give.

Duncan fell against Henry when he finally pulled back. His head rested on the broad chest as he tried to regain some of his strength. He didn't have the energy to argue.

Henry lifted him up and placed him on his large bed. He knew Henry was far from done with him. He would suffer for the countless days he had refused to allow him to feed on Eli, and the countless more yet to come. In the end, it was better this way.

He would not allow Henry to touch Eli ever again.

He groaned as he watched Henry undress for bed. His head hurt. Even the softness of the pillows bothered it. He felt too weak to move. He only hoped he wasn't too weak to protect Eli. Why he had ever given Henry the gift of immortality was beyond him, yet now, after fifty years, he knew his stupidity was not only endangering himself and Eli, but also all magick users. Henry would continue to feed for centuries unless stopped.

Chapter Twenty-eight

Alexis sat next to Nathaniel's bed and watched over him while Scott took a break. Sif curled up at his brother's feet and Miao sat at the window seat, still going on about all the secrets he had hoped to find on Anthony. So far...nothing. At least nothing that interested him. However, for Alexis it told a different story. With the exception of the antique furniture, the room was a lot like her father's. The layout was even the same. All Anthony needed was a piano, but that had been her mother's and Anthony had one in the music room to enjoy. The room itself filled with the same love and joy her father's had. To her it simply felt right.

Nathaniel murmured in his sleep. She leaned forward and adjusted the cool cloth on his forehead. Scott was fussing over the slight increase in temperature, terrified that it may be something more. He practically made her and Miao sign a contact in blood, stating that they would take exceptionally good care of him. Of course, she would only offer the best for her Guardians, even if one was involved with her brother.

"Can you still sense the spirits?" Sif asked, lifting his head.

She nodded. "They're worried about Eli. Someone took them from him after capturing him again."

"Doesn't it seem odd that all Anthony's enemies seem to be appearing this year?" Miao suddenly asked. "Other than that Porter guy, everything started happening just lately."

Sif shook his head. "According to Selena and Cleo, this has been happening since he was born. It died down when he gave half his magick to Daniel...but," He nuzzled Nathaniel's feet. "when puberty hit last year, his power once again grew too fast and became unstable. That's probably why everyone became interested in him again."

Scott stepped through the door, holding a large paper bag. "Hey, squirt, how is he?"

"Still sleeping like a babe," she said with a smile. "Where were you?"

"Selena's gone to London to talk to the High Council. I had Pietro take me to town. I needed to get out of here before I went stir crazy," he explained, pulling a big white stuffed teddy out of the bag. Large angel wings stood on its back and a silvery blue crescent moon embroidered on its chest.

Miao smirked at the unusual gift.

"You bought him that? It's so cute!" Alexis declared with a grin from ear to ear.

"Yeah, well, shopping for Frost is nearly impossible. Now that they've merged I thought they—he might like this."

"They look a lot alike," Sif agreed, smirking.

Scott threw him a threatening look, silently telling him not to tease his angel. He placed the stuffie on the nightstand. "Any change?"

Alexis shook her head. "Not much. He's begun murmuring. Something about you and Eli. He's worried about him. What is a *Psychic Vampire*? He keeps going on about one feeding off Eli."

"It's someone who feed off another's aura or energy. In Henry's case, he takes Eli's magick," Scott explained, sitting on the large bed.

"Eli's grandfather is doing it?" Alexis gasped in shock. Henry seemed so nice. How could he be so evil?

She continued, "Did Eli know? Did Anthony?"

Scott shook his head. "I don't believe so, but Henry's been taking a lot from Eli. Somehow, it's making him younger." He stared at his sleeping lover. "When Nathaniel wakes up, I think he should tell me everything that happened between him and Henry. Something tells me he knows what's going on."

Alexis offered a comforting smile. "Did you want us to bring you anything? Juice? Soda? Food?"

He shook his head and squeezed her hand. "Thanks, squirt, but no."

She playfully punched his arm. "Don't call me squirt."

"Fine, monster, whatever you say."

"Scott!"

He only smiled innocently.

Taking Miao's hand, one of the things she knew that irritated her brother, she called Sif and headed to the door.

"Hey, Alexis?"

She paused and looked over her shoulder at her brother. "Yeah?"

"We'll get Eli and the spirits back. Promise."

She nodded. In truth, getting the spirits of the crystals back was easier than any of them would have guessed. All she had to do was call them back and the Wind spirits would transport them to her. Nevertheless, she refused to. They were her only link to Eli and she dare not break that.

"So now what?" Miao asked as they went downstairs.

"I'm calling the Wind spirits back tonight. Make sure Eli's okay. We have today and tomorrow to prepare for the eclipse. Something tells me it's going to take all our magick to stop these portals from opening."

"Do you believe McNeil?"

"She hasn't been wrong yet."

"That's what worries me."

She stopped and stared at him. "What do you mean?"

"She never helped Eli when Dominique kidnapped him. Then she appears out of the blue after four months of Chaos being inside him. Why? Because Porter was after him. Now she's back again, claiming that in her past life she was married to Anthony and wants to help your father rescue Eli. Mind you, she hasn't bothered calling him since his birthday. Is it me or doesn't it all sound a little convenient?"

"I got to go with the kid on this one, Alex," Sif said.

She nodded. It did seem weird, but Ms. McNeil had always been that way. Always showing up when they needed her, then vanishing when she was not. However, she had never done that to Eli until recently.

"I'm just saying we should keep an eye on her. Maybe it's nothing, but it's better to be safe than sorry."

"I suppose." They found her father outside. Dusk was approaching and he seemed captivated by the stars. Aaliyah was talking to him about magick, apparently trying to teach him the finer points of the art. She had less then forty hours to teach him everything about the portals, and how to close them.

Eli sat on the oversized window seat and stared at the sea, imagining once more the distant land of Ireland. A novel sat open on his lap, but he had paid it little mind. He had lost interest after reading the same passage four times. He was bored. Duncan had asked him to play sick for another day just to keep Henry off his back. The warlock was trying considerably hard to keep Henry away from him, but there was only so much Eli could do to keep himself busy in his room.

Although he did not truly trust Duncan, he had considered Anthony's advice. The warlock did seem remorseful for all that had happened in the past as well as what was happening now. He apologized all the time and admitted repeatedly there had been no excuse for his crimes.

Other than the odd training session, he left Eli in charge of what they would do. All meetings were rescheduled so he could attend to Eli's every need personally as well as keep Henry at bay. If Henry wished to feed, Duncan offered himself rather than let him take Eli. Henry didn't seem so keen on the new arrangements and would often beat Duncan for being so over-protective, but the warlock always held his ground. It was becoming common for Eli to heal him rather than the other way around.

It was impressive in a scary sort of way. Eli found himself appalled and grateful at the same time. If Duncan was willing to put so much on the line to protect him, then it could not hurt to at least talk civilly to him.

When he did, Duncan had been ecstatic. He explained how he and Anthony had finally overcome their differences and deep down, Anthony confirmed everything Duncan had said. Maybe Anthony's approval made him relax around Duncan. It had taken time, but Eli was almost comfortable in Duncan's presence.

Eli looked up when a "rap" came to his door. He could feel Duncan on the other side politely waiting for him to answer. He smiled. Duncan had also allowed him more privacy, always knocking, and waiting. He would not come in unless Eli said okay, or he couldn't sense his presence, or something major had happened. Eli smiled at that. Duncan was doing everything he could to make him happy.

"Come in," he called, after a long enough period had gone by. Sometimes, making Duncan wait was fun.

Duncan opened the door and peeked in. "You weren't in the shower, were you?"

"No." Eli quickly looked back outside, hiding his smile from Duncan.

Even if he had began to like the other mage, he was not yet willing to admit it.

"Is this a bad time?"

"No."

Duncan let out a sigh of relief that caused Eli to look up.

"Good. I was afraid I might be interrupting you."

He sat on the other side of the window seat. When Eli refused to look at him, he took the book from his lap and looked at it.

"I don't believe I've read this one. Is it any good?"

"Not bad. Anthony must have been reading it. It's about Werewolves and such."

"When you're done, I might have to read it."

Eli nodded. "Sure."

Duncan leaned on his knees and peered down at him. "So, are you busy?"

Eli raised a brow. "No."

"Want to get out of here for a bit?"

"Okay."

He held out one hand between them. Opening his palm, a gold chain fell out, Eli's magickal pendant connected to the end. "I thought you could use this."

"Training?"

Duncan gave a lopsided grin. "Nope, fencing. Henry says you're good and I remember watching some of your gym classes in London. You were—how do they say it—awesome."

"You watched me?" Eli frowned.

He didn't like the thought that Duncan always seemed to have an eye on him throughout his life.

"Who do you think got Aaliyah her job or you enrolled? I was a little worried about you. Dominique didn't help matters either."

"No, she didn't."

Duncan was silent for a moment.

Eli couldn't help but stare at his pendant. What he would do to have it back. He felt almost naked without his totem and staff. Duncan must have picked up the thought because he began to gently swing it back and forth with a childish grin.

"You are getting sleepy, very sleepy. When I snap my fingers you would fall desperately in love with me," he said in an eerie voice that made Eli cover his face to hold in a giggle.

"Would you settle for fencing?"

Duncan's eyes widened in surprise. "Seriously?"

Eli nodded.

His smile grew. "Definitely."

Eli snatched his Totem. "Then I need this." He was surprised when Duncan didn't try to take it back.

Duncan slapped his knee. "Well than, let's get cracking. I'll teach you everything I know."

"Well, this should be short." Wide eyes stared at him.

With a laugh, Duncan shook his head. "You are definitely Raven's son." He playfully slapped Eli's arm. "Race you." Eli raised a brow, then smirked. Maybe it would be fun. "Sure."

They raced down the hall. Duncan easily took the lead due to his knowledge of the castle.

Eli ducked around the chambermaid as she existed one of the rooms with an armful of soiled sheets. She yelled at them for running, but neither paid her much mind. Duncan called back a short apology but only laughed as she scowled him. Everyone seemed to think he was just another young punk. It made Eli smirk. It was fun watching one of the servants try to scowl at him. He always gave such wide-eyed innocence.

Duncan reached the door mere seconds before Eli opened it. Once inside, they both called upon their magick swords. They took their positions and began fencing in one swift movement. Duncan was trying to *teach* him the fine art of swordsmanship even if Eli already excelled in it. He was trying to point out areas Eli could work on, but each time Eli proved he could do it. After so many years of training, it was second nature. He easily sidestepped the other as he lunged for him, and brought his own sword between Duncan's shoulder blades. Duncan yelped in surprise and slight pain as Eli carefully poked him. Smirking, Eli brought the flat side of his sword across his rival's rear.

Rubbing his butt, Duncan just gapped at him. "That's not fair, Raven."

His smirk grew. "I'm not Anthony. You can't call me Raven."

"Really? Then stop acting like him."

Their swords came together again. "What if I said I'm just doing it to bug you?"

Duncan blocked as the sword came near his head. "I'd believe you."

Eli laughed and swung once more. He hesitated at Duncan's smiling face. "What?"

"That's the first time you truly laughed since coming here."

"First time I had a chance."

His smile grew and he waved a hand dismissively. "And I thought I might have to tickle you to hear you laugh. Take away all my fun."

"What makes you think I would let you that close?"

Those blue jewels twinkled.

"Oh, a challenge. Okay, I'm game."

It sounded like something Pietro Sinclair would say before Eli would laugh and run in the other direction. It was his favourite game as a child. He would climb into an impossibly high tree that the young Sinclair could not climb and wait until the other boy brought him a bag full of jellybeans. As he was climbing down to get the bag, Pietro would usually catch him and tickle him until he was on the verge of peeing his pants. The jellybeans always made up for it. He really hoped Duncan didn't have the same plan in mind.

He raised his sword to ward off the next blow. The way Duncan was now striking was as if to try to get his sword from him. Two could play. Twisting his sword in a spiral motion, Eli pulled Duncan's sword from his hand. Catching it in his left hand, he scissored the two swords and pinned Duncan against the wall. He could have easily taken his head if he wanted.

Duncan stared at him in awe. "You do fight like Anthony. That's it! Your name is officially Raven now."

"Is not."

"Yep. My castle, I declare it."

Eli only smirked. "I've got the swords and I say no."

Duncan seemed deep in thought. "You're right. You're a cat person. How about Pussy?"

"No!" Eli's face was red with barely contained laughter.

"Kitty-kitty?"

"Duncan!"

"No, I'm Duncan."

"Oh, God." Eli shook his head. Duncan was insane.

"I always said you were one. Okay, God, what nickname can I give you?"

"How about Eli Hawke?"

He playfully frowned and looked thoughtful. "Eli Hawke...Eli Hawke... Nope. Just doesn't work. I guess, God, Raven it is." Shaking his head, Eli could not help but laugh. "You're such a—" His eyes widened as Duncan ducked under the swords and tackled him. The swords fell to the ground with a loud clang as he fell backward. Duncan landed heavily on him and quickly straddled his hips. His eyes shone with mischief.

"I thought you said I could never get close enough to tickle you."

"Don't you dare!"

He poked Eli's ribs, causing him to jerk. "What? This?" He poked him again before burying his hand under Eli's armpit.

Eli's eyes grew wide as he tried not to laugh, but Duncan found his ticklish spots fast and was foregoing all mercy as he attacked each one. He began rolling in laughter, unable to fend off his rival's hands. Duncan must have learned about them in the dream world, he concluded. "Stop...stop!" he cried, trying to catch Duncan's hands.

Duncan buried his face in Eli's neck to cover his laughter. Instead of being awkward, for once Eli was actually comfortable with the other hugging him. He never felt so giddy. "This isn't good. What would Henry think?"

Duncan smirked and planted a kiss on his forehead. "Do you really care?"

He wasn't sure why, maybe because Duncan did care for him so much, but he didn't care. In fact, he was beginning to enjoy being with Duncan. From the moment he had picked him off the bathroom floor, things had been different. He smiled and looked at every inch of Duncan's face. There were so many things he liked about him—his eyes, his mouth... He shook his head. "No." Duncan smiled broadly.

"Boys, we've got work," Henry called over the intercom.

Eli chuckled, rolling his eyes. "Speak of the devil."

Duncan got up and offered him a hand. "Oh, I don't know. I think the Devil's nicer."

"Duncan, get up here."

"He bellows," Eli cracked, gesturing to the doors. "You better get up there before he has kittens."

"Be careful," Duncan called back as he hurried to the doors. "Oh, Eli."

"Yeah?"

"There's a party tonight. You must come." It wasn't so much an order as a request. His eyes were pleading.

Eli rolled his eyes.

"It's just dancing with some pretty little witches. Interested? Good music. There's plenty of food and drinks. No Henry."

He gazed up at the observation booth. "No Henry?"

"No Henry."

"Sure," he sighed. "Why not?"

"Great! I'll see you after!"

He slipped out the door with the largest smile Eli had ever seen on his face. A party wouldn't be so bad. It would give him something else to think of. How often was it he got to spend time with so many other magick users?

The moment the door shut, the room changed. The same scene with the eclipse from the first time as well as from his vision appeared. Getting into a defensive position, he awaited the familiar bubble of magick to fill him and began drawing in the magick within those residing in the castle.

"It appears to be working," Henry muttered as Duncan stepped into the observation booth.

Duncan stepped up to the window and watched as Eli levitated. He glowed brightly as his magick took shape. It was much stronger than before. He would do it this time. He would open a portal. "I told you his magick works with his emotions. A little magick to make him relax doesn't hurt." He smiled warmly. "Make him laugh, feel safe and he can do anything. Frighten or anger him and he can destroy worlds."

"You believe that?"

"It's the way magick works." His smile grew as a small portal opened before Eli. It was only a few feet in size, far larger than the first, but not large enough for a human to pass through. He leaned over the intercom. "Hold on to it, Eli. Control it. Don't let anything come out."

"Why?" Henry asked in surprise.

"We don't know what's in there?"

The portal began to flicker. Eli's magick strained as he tried to stable it.

"Hold on, Eli, just a little longer," Duncan encouraged as he watched the youth carefully. He seemed surer of himself now, far more than before. Maybe Anthony had a talked with him. "Is all in readiness for the party?"

"Claudia is finishing the ballroom. She has your servants working over-time. Are you sure this is a good idea?"

"Something has to work. We need him to be completely relaxed. I want him to enjoy his last few days here. Even if it means I must let him go."

Henry silently glared at him.

"Has the sorceress arrived yet?"

"Yes. She's making herself at home as we speak."

He nodded. "This has to work."

The portal flickered once more, then with a torrent of wind, it blinked out of existence. The wind sent Eli flying across the room. He crashed into the far wall and landed heavily on the floor.

Duncan gasped in fear. "Eli!" He ran out and to the practice room as fast as his feet would carry him.

Eli was already on his feet when he reached him. His eyes focused entirely on where the portal had been. He had a frustrated frown. Seeing he was alright, Duncan practically jumped him. "Are you alright?"

Eli nodded without looking at him. "I should have put more power into it, but after seeing those things, I didn't want to take the chance of them coming through." His frown deepened. "It wasn't the portal I wanted."

"What was in it?"

His eyes became thoughtful. He rubbed his chin absently. "Creatures, demons perhaps. With tentacles. Dark magick." He fell silent, deep in thought.

"Like your vision?"

He nodded again. Then he shook his head. "I wish I could remember more."

Duncan gave a reassuring smile. "You will." He wrapped an arm around his shoulders. "Come on, that's enough practice for now. We've got a party to prepare for."

Eli was hesitant and frowned at the space where the portal had been. He was still curious about the creatures he had seen.

"Don't worry. You're getting better. You'll be more than ready by the eclipse."

Eli gave a nod and followed him out of the room.

Henry waited for them just outside the door. He had that look again, the one that spoke of feedings and pain. He was staring at Eli with hungry eyes.

Pursing his lips, Duncan gave him an icy stare. "No."

Nevertheless, Henry didn't bother listening to him. He stepped up to Eli and caressed his cheek. "How do you feel, little Raven?"

Eli stepped back. Fear flickered across his eyes and he looked away. "Fine...Grandpa."

"Atta a boy." He patted Eli on the shoulder. "Enjoy your party."

Eli nodded respectfully. "Yes, sir." He chuckled and left them alone.

Surprised, they both stared at each other. Eli laughed shakily. "I guess I don't taste good anymore."

Duncan bit his lip. Eli's lips were so tempting when he smiled like that. He wanted to kiss them. Instead, he kissed Eli's cheek and kept himself from moving any further. "Hmm...You taste good to me."

Eli's face turned red in a blush, but didn't pull away.

He gently wiped at his cheek and smiled shyly. Indeed, the calming spell was keeping Eli relaxed and making it so much easier for them to be friends. It was exactly how he had imagined their friendship being. He loved seeing Eli smile. His laughter was like music. He would give anything to see that every day of his life until he died. This was exactly how life should be.

Chapter Twenty-nine

Selena growled inwardly, her hands shaking in rage. The Council refused to listen. For some reason, their new leader believed Alexis was a threat to England and not Porter. They even demanded she leave. That was out of the question until Eli was safe at home. They must not have understood her when she said no. Three of their number attempted to capture her with magick. However, those of the new Order forgot she was a creation of Anthony Sinclair, empowered by the blood of the fey. Very few mortals had the magick and skill needed to capture one like her. She used only what magick was needed and resorted to martial arts for the rest. Killing humans was not one of her favourite pastimes.

Throwing her jacket in the passenger seat, she started the Porsche's engine. Scott had been surprised when she decided to wear a pantsuit instead of her normal skirts. She needed to move quickly and tight skirts were never good when pissing off the High Council. The pantsuit was designed for fighting.

Racing out of town, she cranked up the music. It didn't seem right that the High Council would refuse to save Eli. They were never very fond of Anthony, even when his father was their leader. Even now, many of them envied the power passed to Eli. Still, he was young and supposed to be under their protection, even after all the crap they had put him through.

Yet now, they said it was no longer so. If he wished to align his magick with that of other countries, then he had no place in England or most of Europe for that matter. They did not speak for Spain or the southern countries. They would ban his use of magick entirely if they could. Foolish, considering this was the young man's homeland and

Eli had not betrayed anyone. At least their leader did not speak for them all. A few had sworn to help Eli in secret.

Maybe it was the fact that Duncan Porter was still alive that had turned so many against her. They were unwilling to believe that he had taken another body and lived on. It was illegal and immoral and no magick user would ever commit it without facing eternal torment.

Yet Duncan was willing to risk it. She, herself, could not understand how anyone would allow such a fate to befall them. Yes, he had been crippled, stripped of all magick, but was that any reason to let your soul be enslaved by demons for a thousand years? She wasn't sure. After seeing how he held Eli, the love that reflected in his oh so blue eyes, she knew he had good reason. He was in love.

Would Duncan take it further? Had he already? Lord and Lady, I hope not, she thought in fear. A small relationship she could deal with, but anything further, especially after what the warlock had done to Eli as a child, she simply could not allow him to do it again, even if Eli was willing. There was nothing she could do as long as Eli was with him.

She subconsciously fingered the bite mark on her neck. It was fading away, her healing factor already taking care of it. She still could not believe Henry had bit her let alone touched her as he did. She could still feel his hands roaming her body as his lips conquered hers.

Then there were the dreams that gripped her every time she slept or dozed off. It wasn't a matter of reliving what had happened in the limo, but rather it was as if Henry was entering her mind, ravishing her body and soul, and nothing she did seemed to stop him. A part of her didn't want to stop him. It had been so long since anyone touched her in such a way. Her magick usually overpowered any human who tried to make love to her. They called it Elf Struck, and most humans who knew what she was would not dare touch her. However, Henry wasn't exactly human anymore, was he?

It didn't seem possible for him to be a psychic vampire. She had known him all her life and not once had he done anything like this. He even comforted Anthony when Nathaniel had gone missing. Yet, she now questioned even that. During that period, she remembered how Henry had stayed to care for the rest of the Guardians while Anthony searched for Nathaniel. He had comforted each of them and had spent a great amount of time with her.

She hit the brakes as a flash of memory struck her. There wasn't much she remembered about her time with Anthony—usually only glimpses here and there, but now it was almost crystal clear. Henry had spent a lot of time with her. Her heart pounded. Good God! The limo was not the first time Henry had been intimate with her. He had made love to her numerous times when she was Anthony's guardian.

That whole week Nathaniel was missing, Henry had visited her room, consoling her as she worried for her master and brother. He had touched her gently, seducing her until he had her begging to be touched, just as he did every night in her dreams. Even all those years ago, he had craved her flesh, desiring the touch of faery flesh and the powerful magick hidden within.

Nathaniel's story kept running through her mind. It wasn't just her flesh Henry had craved. It was anyone with faery magick, herself, Nathaniel, Mae, Anthony and now Eli. If he had done that to Nathaniel and her, what would he do to Eli?

Pulling into Sinclair Manor, she hit the button to open the large garage doors. She parked the car inside and went into the mansion. It was getting late. All she wanted to do was go to her room and sleep. Daniel had made sure her new room was close to Anthony's. He wanted everyone close together and Richard reluctantly agreed.

She passed Alexis's room and paused at the huge wooden door. Both Miao's and Alexis's auras burned brightly. They were conjuring something. It appeared they were communing with the spirit world.

She stopped at Daniel's room. He had decided to find another room and let Scott and Nathaniel have Anthony's. Nathaniel was still in a deep state of sleep. With a knock on the door, she carefully opened it.

He was sitting on the bed, reading one of the Sinclairs' many magick books. One in fact she had not seen in many years. With the exception of his brown hair and eyes, she could have sworn it was Anthony sitting before her. "Can I get you anything before I go to bed?" she asked, suppressing another yawn.

He smiled, looking more like Anthony by the second. "No, thank you. Have a good night, Selena." As she went to turn to leave, he called her back. "Selena, don't worry too much about Eli tonight. Anthony has it covered."

She raised a brow in surprise. "What?"

He turned back to his book, but it was not Daniel who answered.

"Everything will be alright, Serenity."

Biting her lower lip, she nodded. "Goodnight, Dan."

He smiled again. "Goodnight."

She went to her room next and almost cried out in despair when she opened the door. Cleo was sprawled out in his panther form on her bed. Groaning, she stripped, not even bothering to change into a nightgown.

"Cleo, move over," she murmured. She climbed into bed and him a shove to one side.

"What did they say?" the great cat murmured.

Nuzzling close to her youngest brother, she yawned. "Nothing. Bunch of old crones."

"No respect for the witches."

Closing her eyes, she sighed. "Not when they're willing to give up on a boy just because he moved to Canada."

"That's dumb."

"Tell me about it."

He nuzzled her shoulder and fell asleep, snoring softly. Smiling sleepily, she finally allowed herself to fall asleep, silently praying Anthony was right, and hoping that Henry did not visit her in her dreams again. A hope she feared would die in a few short hours.

Light dazzled his violet eyes. The old lamp's light reflected on a shockingly white stuffed animal. He narrowed his eyes, trying to adjust to the brightness. A stuffed teddy? His lips curled in a smirk. Of all the silly things. He felt giddy as he picked it up. Only Scott would buy such a gift. His heart fluttered as he turned it over. Large cloth wings covered its back. Turning it back around, he traced the crescent moon on its chest. It was the most wonderful gift he had ever received. He loved it.

Hearing a muffled snore beside him, he rolled over. Scott was sound asleep, his head buried in a mound of pillows. With a childish glee, Nathaniel giggled and jumped on him.

"Scott!"

The raven-haired man jumped with a start, blinking uncontrollably. He rolled over and stared at the angelic being.

Nathaniel's long hair covered them like a satin sheet.

"Frost?"

Nathaniel leaned down and captured his lips. "You're amazing," he breathed, feeling Scott smile into the kiss.

Scott pulled back slightly. "So, you like it?"

He held up the teddy. "Love it."

"It's only right now that you're whole. How does it feel?"

Nathaniel became thoughtful. He had not taken the time to consider the change. He no longer felt as if he were two different beings but one. The names Frost and Nathan were now the same, he would answer to either. It only felt right. He could not remember the last time he felt so whole. "Hmm…right."

Scott stroked his high cheekbones. "You look more at ease." Nathaniel lay in the circle of his arms and played with the stuffie. It was something Nathan normally did, yet felt right. There was no difference between him and his human form. His smile grew as Scott wrapped his arms tighter around his waist. "There's no conflict in my mind anymore. No fight for dominance."

"That's good." Scott kissed his silvery head.

"Did we get Eli back?"

Scott stiffened and looked away.

Nathaniel's heart sank at the sadness in his eyes. Laying the stuffie aside, he cuddled his beloved. Scott hugged him tightly.

"I'm sorry, Fr—Nathaniel. I know how much you care for him." He combed his fingers through the long tendrils of silver. "We'll get him back, I promise."

Nathaniel was silent. He really hoped so, but he was losing hope. Entangling his fingers with Scott's much larger ones, he softly hummed a lullaby Anthony used to sing to him as a child, absently caressing his love's long fingers.

The room was glowing. Alexis stood in the center of the room, her magick circle beneath her feet. Miao and Sif sat away from the circle of power and out of the way, yet close enough to help if needed.

She closed her eyes, extending her powers as far west as possible. She knew where Eli was. A magickal force blocked her from sensing him, but told her where he was. Holding out her totem, she changed it to her staff. The gold and silver staff came to life, growing until it was slightly larger than a wand. She twisted it to the west.

"Wind, hear my call. Shed thy confined form and return to thy Mistress!" She did not need to see the Wind spirit to know it had faithfully followed her command.

Eli slumped onto his bed. There was an hour to go until Duncan's party. He wasn't sure what to think of it. Duncan had not said what type of party it was, nor did he prearrange his clothes for the evening as he had the first week of Eli's stay. Eli had no idea what to wear. Was it formal of casual? He never knew when it came to magick gatherings and events. His closet was filled with clothes for every occasion.

Rolling over, he picked up one of the crystals. Duncan had given them back to him, saying he should change them back to Raven's. Eli had to admit he wanted to. They had been a large part of Anthony's life. He loved each and every one of the spirits within. Pulling them out of their case, he smiled at them. "So, what do you think? Formal or casual?"

The crystals glowed brightly.

To his surprise, the Wind spirit emerged. The crystal floated in front of him for a moment before changing to her faery form.

"Wind," he breathed in awe.

The mute sprite smiled down at him. *Hello, young Master.*

Hello, Wind.

The Mistress calls.

His smile grew. So, Alexis could still communicate with the spirits. He gave a nod of dismissal, then paused. "Wind?"

She floated before the window, her misty powder blue form turning to him questioningly.

"Tell Alexis I'm okay and I'll see her in a few days. Give her my love…and Selena." She nodded.

"Oh, and Wind?"

Her transparent form tilted her head.

"Formal or casual?"

Her mental laugh was like the sound of wind chimes. *Formal.*

"Thank you," he chuckled.

The sprite vanished through the air, becoming one with the natural winds of the elements.

Climbing off the bed, he went to his closet. The Wind spirit's advice was to always be taken seriously. She had been one of

Anthony's most trusted advisers. He had lost count of the number of times she had saved Anthony or one of his Guardians. If she said formal, then formal it was.

An expensive black suit hung In a protective cover. He pulled it out and draped it over the armchair. A quick shower and off to the ballroom.

After drying and trying back his hair, he changed into the suit. It was a perfect fit. Shining black loafers matched it to a *T*. He stared at himself in the mirror. Did he ever look like Anthony? Well, a modern-day Anthony at least. He even had the wispy strands of hair that refused to be tied back.

He paused from brushing the strands back. What if this was some trap on Duncan's part? What if the gathered witches and magick users were there to judge him, even take his magick? It wasn't uncommon for those of the magick realm to celebrate before stripping another of their magick. There were always good reasons.

Normally the victim was into the dark arts and they were simply trying to save their nation. Nevertheless, there were cases were innocents were falsely accused and the clans proceeded to take the magick. Yet, Eli felt no hostiles within the castle walls, but that meant nothing. Many of the magick realms could hide their auras. Even with all his powers, it was next to impossible to sense someone when they did not want to be discovered. It took an extremely gifted clairvoyant, like Scott Dion or Aaliyah McNeil, to detect them. He was strong, but not as strong as they were. He simply had to trust Duncan.

Duncan. Eli's feelings for the warlock were so mixed up. A part of him still hated and feared him yet another part trusted him, enjoyed being with him. Anthony said Duncan only had his best interests at heart. He had explained about Sara Porter and why Duncan was so interested in the portals. Duncan wanted to see his daughter as much as Eli wanted to see his parents. In the end, that being the only reason, Eli agreed to help him. He knew what it felt like to lose a loved one.

Adjusting his tie, he went to the ballroom, leaving the magick pouch and crystals hidden in his bottom drawer, one he could actually lock. He hesitated at the grand doors. There was no one in the halls except the odd guard or servant. All the guests must be inside already. He gave one of the two butlers a small nod. They opened the door without a word.

Eli's eyes widened in surprise. Windy was wrong. Loud dance music waft through the doors. There were dozens of youths dancing carelessly inside. All had some form of magick. It was not the party he had expected. He felt overly dressed. Turning on his heel, he started back to his room. He couldn't go in there dressed like this.

"Eli!" Duncan called cheerfully, looping an arm around Eli's, and dragging him inside. "I was beginning to worry." His brows furrowed at the sight of the suit. "I forgot to tell you it was casual, huh? Sorry. I didn't think. That's okay, we'll make do." He quickly removed Eli's jacket and tie and undid the first two buttons of his shirt. "Better. Come, I've got some people I would like to introduce."

They sat at a small rectangular table near the back of the hall. The whole ballroom was converted into a dance club of sorts. Bright lights, loud music and dozens of people filled every corner. Even a refreshment stand was set up in the middle of the room. Considering Duncan's true age, it was hard to believe he was truly enjoying himself in such surroundings. It had to be for Eli's benefit.

At the table were three young women from separate cultures. A North American Native, a Celt, and an Asian. They were all very attractive and powerful. Not as powerful as Duncan or Eli in many areas, but powerful in their own right.

Henry was sitting next to the native woman, a Shaman, he realized. He passed a gaze to Duncan. *What is Henry doing here?* he asked in concern.

Refused to leave without feeding.

Do they know what he is?

Yes. Duncan smiled as the Celtic witch moved next to him. *If they allow him to feed, it's of their own free will.* He smiled at their company. "Ladies, may I introduce young Lord Elijah Hawke of the Sinclair Clan? Eli has honored us with his presence for the last few weeks." Eli smiled thinly. What was Duncan up to?

"A tense week and a half, though," said the Asian woman with a thick Thai accent. She smiled at him with remarkable hazel green eyes, something rarely found amongst her people. "You did not wish to be here, did you, Lord Hawke?"

Eli gaped at her. Her telepathy was extremely good to penetrate his metaphysical shields. Either that or he had not schooled his facial features as well as he had thought. Yet her eyes seemed understanding, soothing. He smiled.

"Of course, he wanted to come. He just didn't know it," Henry slurred. He raised a stein of beer to his lips.

His youthfulness made him cocky, wanting to consume more alcohol than he normally would. Henry had not been one to drink heavy since he and Anthony were teens. Eli prayed Henry would do nothing stupid as he had all those years ago.

The dark-haired woman didn't seem to give a care for Henry's words. Her eyes studied Eli's intently. It was hard not to blink, but Eli could not pull his eyes away from hers. She was searching for something and he felt the need to let her find it. He had underestimated her magick and she was letting him know it.

An uncertain look crossed her face and she gazed at her companions. For a long, unnerving moment, they said nothing. She turned back and smiled softly at his confusion. "You're very willful, aren't you?"

Was that a compliment or an insult? He liked to think of himself as willful. It may get him into trouble, but it often saved his life.

"Yes."

Duncan laughed. "Definitely."

Eli felt his cheeks heat up as Duncan playfully slapped his arm.

"Well, Eli, this is Nala Vye Shen, Maggie MacCorhend, and Coral Anne Dennis. Maggie has been studying Stonehenge during her visit to England."

"Quite fascinating," Maggie said with a broad smile. "Very magickal. Have you ever been there?"

"A few times. My Grandmother liked to visit it. She based many of her researches on its history," Eli answered, mimicking her smile.

"Have you ever watched the sunrise there on the Summer Solstice? It's amazing! The power simply flows through you. It's like being fully recharged from the inside out."

He smiled fully at her excitement. It was nice to see she was enjoying England. Her strawberry blonde hair and bright green eyes reminded him of Alexis. "That it does," he agreed. "So where do you come from?"

"Ireland, on the coast line. You?"

"Ca—"

"Ipswich," Henry said with a growl. He gave Eli a warning look. "Been living up in the Pike Mountains with me since his grandmother passed on."

"Oh dear! I'm so sorry about your grandmother."

Shen seemed unconvinced. She gave Henry a cold stare before turning her attention back to Eli.

Eli also frowned at Henry. Why was he lying?

"Haven't you, Eli?"

Eli shrugged back at the cold rage in Henry's eyes. If he didn't answer the way the man wanted, hell was sure to break loose. "Sort of," he said, bowing his head. If Henry was going to strike, he didn't want to see it. Not this time.

He looked up as a foot rubbed the back of his shin. Shen gave him a rare understanding look. She knew Henry was not being completely truthful. She was offering what comfort she could.

Duncan drew their attention back to him, ignoring Henry's soft curse of Eli's stubbornness. "Maggie, would you like to dance?"

The woman's eyes lit up. "I would love to!"

He took her hand and helped her up. Sparing a glance at Henry and his *date*, he plastered a false smile on. "Henry, do you not have a dream world to raid?"

Henry's face went blank for a moment, then broke into a smile. "Oh yes! Of course."

Taking Carol Anne's hand, he departed.

Confused, Eli stared up at Duncan. "Dream to raid? Who's?" Duncan shrugged. "Just an old friend. Nothing to worry about. Carol is just his guide."

As innocent as it sounded, it made Eli worry. Whose dream was Henry to raid? The list was numerous. Eli only hoped whomever he attacked could defeat him.

Duncan was off before he could question him further.

Odd.

Normally Duncan wanted to spend every moment possible with him.

"You've come to like him," Shen observed.

"Duncan? No! No, no, no. We're rivals. Sort of friends, I suppose. He's better than Henry, but…"

"You worry about your past with him. Can you ever completely trust him? Will he ever do it again?"

He stared at her. "You're reading my mind."

Her smile was gentle. "Your emotions are easy to read when you are truly upset. You are very good at hiding them, but your eyes speak loudly to those willing to listen."

He chewed his bottom lip for a moment, watching as Duncan danced merrily with his date. They looked so happy together. So why did it bother him?

"Would you like to dance?"

He blinked. Shen was now standing before him. She held her hands out to him. Hesitantly, he took them and stood. She wasn't much older than him. Nineteen—twenty at most. She was beautiful. Long black hair as dark as his. Eyes as green as the sea. She was very modern as well. Her ears hosted a rack of earrings. Small braids dangled through her long hair, which nearly reached her rear. A shiny red tube top covered her breasts and she wore tight hip huggers that showed off her ass. She was simply captivating.

Her arms wrapped around his neck. "Just relax. Open your mind. There is so much magick in this room, open yourself to it. It's alright. There is no need to hesitate. No one here means you harm."

She was right. There was no hint of malice in the ballroom. He relaxed and wrapped his arms around her small waist. Almost instantly, he relaxed. He could feel the magick wrap around him, like a comforting old blanket. He allowed his metaphysical shields to fall completely and let the magick take control.

"Don't be afraid, Eli."

"I'm not."

Her lips brushed across his left ear. "Yes, you are." Her hands slipped through his hair to untie his ponytail. His hair cascaded over his shoulders. "Your mind is so tense with worry. Your friends are fine. Trust me. Now try to relax. Let it happen." She let him go long enough to take two Champagne glasses from the waiter. "This may help."

"I…no…"

"Please, Eli. I mean you no harm. Trust me."

She was talking, just talking, and not using magick to persuade him. Had she tried such a trick, he would have said no. Yet, he didn't. Taking the crystal glass, he held it to his lips and sipped some. It was bubbly, tickling his nose. Champagne was something he only drank on special occasions, such as magick celebrations or holidays. He was more used to wine. This particular Champagne, however, had a tangy strawberry taste to it. It was good.

She waited until he was finished before handing both empty glasses to another waiter. They began dancing once again, holding each other as if they had known each other all their lives.

The hours passed by quicker than Eli had thought possible. They danced, laughed, and drank happily, not caring about anyone else in the room. He barely spoke to Duncan and Henry had miraculously not reappeared. Eventually he and Shen made their way to the large hot tub beneath one of the terraces. It was a beautiful night full of promises that Eli was unsure if he were willing to do, yet becoming more interested by the moment.

It seemed like centuries since the last time he had been so relaxed. Shen sat behind him, kneading the tense muscles he had developed since coming to the castle. Her hands were soft, but firm.

Almost as good as Duncan's.

Humming appreciatively, Eli sunk deeper into the warm water, tilting his head back to rest against her shoulder. It seemed funny, but she reminded him of Frost. Strong, silent, and caring. She was full of Moon magick.

Her arms wrapped around his torso. "Better?"

"Much." He squeezed her hands. "Where did you learn that?"

"My mother taught me."

"She must be as beautiful as you."

She brushed her lips against his cheek. "So charming. Duncan should have warned me about you."

Turning his head, he captured her lips. She was startled for a moment before she relaxed and gave into the kiss. Maybe it was the alcohol talking, but he needed the physical touch of a woman, even if it went no further than kissing. Moving forward, he pulled her out from behind him and onto his lap.

She smiled and giggled into his lips. "You're feeling much better."

He pulled back, smiling brightly. "Everyone's so happy," he mused, gazing back at the castle. "They're really enjoying themselves." He leaned on his elbows at the edge of the tub.

"Their auras are strong, vibrant. You can't help but feel their happiness."

"Hmm…"

"Do you wish to join them?"

He thought about that for a moment.

The hot tub was comfy and sitting with Shen was more than pleasant. Nevertheless, the allure of the magick flooding the ballroom was very appealing. It made him feel so much stronger than he had in many days.

He took Shen's hand and nodded as together they climbed out.

It was chilly coming out of the hot water. Steam wafted off their wet bodies, making them look like ghostly spirits. With a basic spell, he quickly dried them both.

Shen gave him a lopsided smile as if saying, *show off*, but she wasn't upset. Slipping back into her clothes, she threw him his. Not bothering to button up the shirt, he zipped up the pants and buttoned it. Together, they went back inside.

The music was loud, the smell of alcohol and smoke thicker than before.

But neither cared.

They began dancing instantly, not traditionally slow, as Eli was accustomed to, but fast, carefree. In some ways, it was more sensual. Shen was really close, her hands caressing his bare chest and neck. He was touching her, too, caressing her curves and burying his hands in her long hair.

It didn't seem like they had just met.

It was as if they had known each other forever.

They resumed kissing, not caring about anyone else. The magick emanating from each guest filled him. He poured his own magick into the mix, letting it take shape as it saw fit.

Another set of arms wrapped around him, but Eli barely noticed, nor did he care. The magick was more concentrated, filling him with more power than he had felt since splitting his powers with Daniel Dion.

For the first time, he felt as powerful as Anthony himself did.

He allowed himself to focus only on his sense of touch, enjoying every touch and kiss Shen graced him with. The hands behind him yanked off his shirt and nibbled at his shoulders as arms snaked around his waist. Mixed with Shen's lips, it was enough to send him wild.

His magick platform flared to life beneath their feet as Eli threw his head back in ecstasy.

Pulling Shen close, he kissed her heatedly even as the person behind him kissed his neck. His magick surged through them, heightening the pleasure they were already sharing.

Leaning back against the person behind him, he shared another kiss while letting his magick take full reign of him.

Chapter Thirty

Raven's magick circle began appearing throughout the castle. It flashed into existence only to disappear seconds later. Many left harmlessly, but several tore into the fabric of space, depositing creatures and spirits from other realms. Eli neither felt nor noticed any of it. In Shen and Duncan's loving arms, his powers expanded, his mind open to new sensations. Petty creatures such as these were now beneath him.

Henry frowned at each new creature. So many dimensions, yet the one he wished still eluded him. He waited patiently, but as the portals ceased appearing, he lost hope. He slammed his fist into the computer console in rage. Why all these and not the Land of the Dead?

Eli did this purposely, he thought bitterly as he led a team to contain the creatures.

Capturing the confused creatures was easy enough. Many were still in shock and did not stand a chance. They were corralled into the old dungeons in the castle's bowels where Henry had them destroyed, allowing only a few choice subjects to live for future plans.

The Wind spirit flew through the night sky as quickly as the currents would allow her. Passing through Porter's shields was easy enough, simply moving with nature. She arrived in her Mistress' room in under an hour. Her Mistress sat on her bed much as Master Eli had. A book sat on her lap and Sif curled around her long legs.

She smiled brightly as the spirit flew in, casting the windows wide open. The spirit swirled around her in greeting. Alexis laughed, opening her arms in welcoming. "Welcome home, Windy!" Alexis declared. "Is all well? Is Eli okay?"

He's in higher spirits, my lady. For days, we feared for his life.

"Days? Eli has only been gone two days...time has slowed where he is, hasn't it?" *Yes.*

"How long?"

He has been there almost two weeks. One week to our day.

The woman paled. "Oh, Lord and Lady!" She began chewing on her lower lip as Sif stirred at her feet. "There is still thirty-six hours left—a week and a half for him. Anything can happen in that amount of time."

Sif climbed further up the bed and rubbed his head against her shoulder.

Windy wrapped herself around Alexis as well, offering comfort. Seeing the youth in pain hurt just as much as watching Eli be tortured. There had to be a way to care for them both.

Wiping back tears, Alexis sniffled. "Give Lord Porter a message, Windy. Tell him if he releases Eli, I will do all I can to open any gate he wishes."

It's not so simple, my lady. Eli is a child of the fey with the powers of darkness. A power that grows no matter how much he tried to stop it. Porter not only wishes Eli to open a gate, but for Eli to be able to control his powers so they do not go rampant.

"What do you mean?"

When Raven's spirit separated, his spirit started a ying-yang effect on Daniel and Eli. A child of the Sun, shrouded in darkness, a child of the Moon, with heart glowing bright. Children of faery.

Her emerald eyes were wide. "Eli has always wrapped himself in a cloak of darkness and mystery."

While your father's heart is open to the world. Even your mother's death failed to destroy that.

Alexis shook her head. "He had to be strong for Scott and me." *Yes.*

"So, what does this have to do with the ying-yang effect?" Sif questioned with a yawn.

Even though Eli is of the Sun, he is the darker of the two. The eclipse will affect them. He is the Key.

"And Dad, the Lock." Alexis pondered this for a moment before nodding. "Fine. Find out where they plan to open the gate. There has to be a place with incredible power nearby. We will be there to stop them. Those portals need to be locked down before someone gets hurt.

Who knows what is hidden in some of them?" She stared at the spirit. "Protect him, Windy. Don't let him stray further into darkness."

Magick still rolled through his body. Even hours after everyone had departed the castle, he still felt their residue. Yet not all had left. Shen lay in his arms, sleeping with her head on his chest. Eli smiled at her peaceful face. Her hair covered his torso like a sheet of satin. She looked like an angel.

Duncan slept on the other side of him. His strong arms around his waist as if telling Shen that Eli was his. How they had ended up in such positions Eli could not remember. They had ended up back in his room and became a triumvirate of power. He was used to such forms of magick. He had spent many nights like this with Selena and Cleo. It was as calming as it was recharging. However, he had never made love to his Guardians during a triumvirate of power. That had been what had tired him out.

Stroking Shen's hair, he snuggled a little closer to Duncan. This had been the best sleep he could remember. He could not recall a more peaceful sleep. Maybe it had been because they had simply tired him out. The magick they shared while in the throes of passion had finally become too much for him to continue. Whatever the reason, he felt better than ever, as if he were on top of the world. Free of all repressing chains.

"Do you like it?" Duncan whispered against his ear with a sleeping yawn. "This sense of power, true power and complete freedom?"

"Hmm…" He smiled. "Thank you."

"You looked like you needed it."

Closing his eyes, he allowed himself to doze off again. "Yes." The magick around them rose. Duncan wrapped a leg possessively around his. His soft snores mixed with Shen's to fill Eli's ears until his own finally joined the chorus as he slipped into the blissfulness of sleep.

He didn't want to wake up when the chambermaid came that morning to remind Duncan and Shen of the meeting with the High Council. He didn't want to lose their warmth or magick, but they had to go. Duncan lazily pulled him out of bed, murmuring an apology while they changed. It was even harder to get Shen up.

Eli's face crumbled as they stood before the meeting hall. Shen smiled warmly while Duncan stroked his hair away from his eyes. This wasn't fair. Duncan had promised they would spend the day together. Shen was supposed to help him direct his focus to open the right gates. Why the sudden change? He felt like a spoiled child, not waiting them to leave his side, but he could not help it. He could not bear a moment without either of them.

"It's just a general meeting. It won't take long. An hour tops. Then Shen and I will spend the rest of the day with you, I promise," Duncan was saying.

Eli only frowned. He didn't want their triumvirate of power to separate. He didn't want to be alone.

Shen stepped in, cupping his cheek. "Eli this is important. An hour, please."

He didn't like it, but nodded, nonetheless. She leaned up and kissed him fully on the lips, but pulled back before he could wrap his arms around her.

"Later," she whispered.

The two slipped into the brightly lit room where several other magick users waited. Duncan gave a small wave before closing the door behind him. Eli leaned against the far wall and stared at the wooden door intently. It was obvious the meeting was about him or why would they not allow him to attend, especially since Henry had been invited?

There was nothing for him to do but wait. He frowned as he went to the courtyard. Maybe he could take a swim. It was a hot day and the sun was shining brightly. A swim would be perfect if he had someone to swim with. He hated swimming alone. He was accustomed to swimming with Miao and Alexis. He liked racing them.

He mentally shook himself. Why am I so needy all of a sudden? I'm not some little boy who needs to be taken care of! Yet even the spirits he worked with could no longer console him. He needed the touch of another human being.

Sitting at the edge of the pool, he let his feet slip in and playfully kicked at the water. What were his feelings toward Duncan and Shen? He had only met Shen the night before, but it felt as if she had always been there, almost like his feelings for Alexis, yet not. Alexis was the sister he had always wanted; Shen was something more. A lover perhaps?

Maybe it was just the magick talking. After all, being trapped in this castle for so long was enough to make him attach himself to any magick user remotely understanding of his situation. She had spoke of some of the tests her own people had put her through and that in fact her coming here was one of them. Although he wasn't sure how.

His feelings for Duncan were still a mystery. He knew he cared for him, enjoyed his company, but was there more?

Sighing, he stared up at the second-floor windows until he found the meeting room. He could easily spot Duncan through one of them. A bored expression filled Duncan's handsome face as he nodded to whoever was talking. He obviously didn't want to be there, either. A small smirk lifted the corners of Eli's lips. Maybe there was something he could do to lighten things up?

Bored. Bored! Bored! Duncan thought miserably. The new head of the High Council simply droned on and on, acting as if he knew and understood the whole situation. He didn't. How could he without doing the proper research? William Larsen had been leader for less than three months and had yet to study all the files on Eli and Raven, or the Dion family.

Those files were huge, practically filing one corner of the massive library in London. Duncan knew the size as he, himself, had done most of the research, at least on Eli and Raven, while other Watchers filled-in the spaces on the Guardians and the Dions. However, trying to tell Larsen the importance of files to the coming eclipse was like talking to a stone wall.

Then again, Larsen only thought of Duncan as a kid, as Michael Sinclair. Just some punk who was keeping Eli from blowing up half of England in an attempt to escape. It was degrading, considering once, not long ago, he had been the leader of the Council for well over twenty-five years.

Shen tried to explain everything to Larsen. She often gave Duncan a warning glance not to blow up at the foolish new leader. It was hard. The man was a complete idiot.

"Last night's experiment proved Eli's powers are ruled by emotion," Shen reported, standing before the gathered group. Talking to several magick covens at once was so much easier with teleconferencing. There was no need for large amounts of power to open enough windows for everyone. "A total of twelve portals were opened, depositing more than twenty different magickal species. When enraged, his powers automatically tried to defend him. While this proves his magick is unstable, it also proves he is one with them. Left to his own devices, he can control it, but place him in an alien situation, one he has no idea how to react to and that same power will take over. It may be of Raven's will, but he easily becomes a walking time-boom."

"And the eclipse?" Larsen asked over the view screen.

She shook her head. "An unknown factor. He may simply fall into a coma until it passes as Mr. Griphan as explained happened when he was a child, or more portals may open. Anthony Sinclair's predictions may yet come to pass yet we are missing that particular book. Eli has always been the Key, but we have never been sure of the date he would come to open all the gates."

"And the dangers?"

"If he cannot close the gates? Great. I suggest a place of great power may assist him. We should have several of our strongest magick users on hand should he lose control. Our added powers should be enough to close each portal."

The head warlock seemed to consider her words.

Duncan sighed inwardly. He doubted Larsen would agree with the video evidence they had given him. To get him to agree to do anything was almost impossible. Even the party the previous night, Duncan had to go over his head to get as many young magick users there as he had. He didn't really expect much help from him.

He gazed out the window and spotted Eli by the pool. He was in his khaki shorts, the ones Eli had proclaimed were his favourites, maybe because Henry wasn't overly fond of them. He was splashing his feet in the pool water, smiling innocently up at him. Duncan wasn't sure how Eli could see him through the tinted windows, but it was obvious he could.

A sly grin passed over the younger man's features. *Bored?*

Bewildered, Duncan gave a slight nod. *A little.*

The mage held up his hand, showing off his Totem. It changed to its staff form. With barely a murmured chant, the courtyard morphed into an elaborate maze. A set of twin Elis began dancing throughout the maze, making a double of everything.

Duncan failed to stifle his laugh as Eli danced with his double. It was identical to how Raven would torment him when they were young, getting him to chase after them only to usually catch the twin and not Anthony. How he missed those days. He leaned on his elbow and watched Eli play, silently wishing to be out there with him.

"Michael Sinclair!"

It took a moment to realized Larsen at snapped at him and a second call before he was able to force his focus away from the window.

"Are we boring you Michael?"

"No, sir."

"Good. Now I will send six members to help you and Shen defend Eli. Try to get Eli to open one more gate tonight and close it himself. I hope that that will be enough. Stonehenge is the strongest site now. I want him there by morning. Normal time, Michael. Any longer and his body may not take well to the time change."

Duncan rolled his eyes in frustration. "He can handle it."

Larsen's eyes narrowed. "Nevertheless, this is his last night. I tire of his Guardians and your family harassing us and threatening war if he is not returned home soon. We do not need another civil war in the magick realm. The Sinclairs are strong and teamed with Raven's heir, they may be unstoppable. I will not remind you of the last Great War."

Before Duncan could shout back that they presently held all Raven's magick, Shen stepped in.

"We understand, Lord Larsen. We will be ready." Her gaze fell questioningly on Duncan. *What's wrong?*

He looked back outside without answering. Eli now had the entire outside looking like space with the maze warping it into another dimension. It was as if he and the castle were floating. Duncan allowed himself a small smile as Eli floated upside down.

The teleconferencing ended and to Duncan's surprise, almost all the magick users gathered at the windows to see what was going on. They had all sensed it, but had somehow managed to not allow it to distract them while Larsen talked. There was a group gasp as they saw what Eli had done.

Biting his lower lip, Duncan got up and took Shen's hand. "Hour's up!" he announced with a childish smile. "Let's have some fun!"

Henry's eyes narrowed as Eli called forth another spell.

The group of magick users watched in amazement and awe as he transformed the landscape again. Simple illusion, but Eli didn't normally display his magick so publicly, even around other magick users.

What was he up to?

Surely, he had not changed his stand on showing off his magick, unless...

He watched as Duncan and the Asian Priestess slipped out of the room.

Eli was doing it to get their attention.

He smiled slightly. Duncan's spell had worked, as had the Priestess's. They had managed to gain some hold on Eli. It meant the youth was finally under some sort of control.

Chapter Thirty-one

Selena continued to stir her coffee in slow, tired strokes. Sleep had practically eluded her. First, her worry for Eli had led to horrible nightmare that had somehow ended with Henry. He had shown her terrifying things that were or had happened to Eli. As much as she didn't want to believe it, she knew the images were true and that Henry had really been in her dreams. She could still feel his big hands roaming over her body as she unwillingly gave herself to him. She could remember without trouble the taste of his lips or the hardness of his body as he touched her. She could still feel his weight on top of her.

She had never been so terrified of him, nor aroused by him. He had been so handsome in his youth. How he kept slipping into her dream world, she could not understand. He had to have had someone with magick helping him. Looking up into those storm-cloud gray eyes as he stood before her in her dream, she could not stop her body from reacting. The way he had tenderly bent down to claim her lips. He had been gentle, loving. He had not hurt her but brought much pleasure. For a moment she thought he was actually in love with her and that, perhaps, she had a hidden crush that only now she was realizing; or maybe she was just beginning to remember what they had shared so many years ago, until he fed upon her, at least.

Everything Frost-Nathaniel had told her about Henry played again in her mind. Did Henry do all this to him, too? Physically? A cold chill ran up her spine at that thought. What about Eli? Some of the images Henry had shown her in her dreams, one of the ways he had managed to get her to do as he wanted—he didn't completely seduce her, she had fought him—were of Eli being punished by him. Did he do more?

Staring at her arms, she almost cried at the large bruises she had allowed Henry to mark her with. Black and blue hand marks covered many parts of her body. She ached all over, but her body would heal fast. She had no worry about that. This was different from other times, as if Henry had really been in her room. That was impossible. Even in the short time Cleo had gone on patrol, there was no way Henry could have gotten into her room without one of the Guardians sensing him. So how had it happened?

"Selena?"

Her head snapped up at Nathaniel's voice. Pushing her sleeves down, she smiled as cheerfully as possible. "Hey, Sleeping Beauty. How are you feeling?"

"Not bad. You?"

"Good."

His eyes narrowed, but not as harshly as he used to. It was more one of Nathan's concerned looks than Frost's impassive one. More proof of the merge. Taking a seat next to her, he took an apple from the fruit basket. "You're an awful liar."

"This coming from you?" she laughed, but his eyes were serious.

"You screamed last night."

"Bad dream."

"Eli?"

"Yeah."

He shimmed closer to her and gave an encouraging embrace.

"We'll find him."

"You don't think Henry would hurt him, do you?"

There was only silence between them. Nathaniel feared the same thing.

Ignoring the pain racing through her body, she wrapped herself in his loving arms.

Cleo, who had been silently sitting next to her, laid his head on her lap. He purred softly as Nathaniel scratched behind his ears.

Selena blinked as a flash bulb went off. "What the—Alexis!" Alexis gave them a cheeky smile as she held up the camera. "Sorry, but Melissa asked for pictures so I thought this was the perfect family shot. Too bad Sif wouldn't get in."

The wolf stuck up his nose. "I'm not into gushy photos." She only snickered.

"Mind you, if Mel was here dressing these two up, he'd pose for pictures," Miao laughed. He sat down at the large dining room table. "So, any idea what to do now? I'm getting tired of waiting. We should go to Holyhead."

"No," Alexis said with a sigh. "They won't be there in a few hours."

Selena stared at her. "What do you mean?"

"The Wind spirit believes they will go to a concentrated source of magick during the eclipse."

"Where?" She practically jumped to her feet. Wherever it was, they had to get there first.

Maybe it was fate or dumb luck, but the phone rang down the hall. A moment later, Pietro stepped into the dining room with a puzzled look on his tanned face. "Selena, phone, love. Sounds important."

She gave a nod and followed him to the old room that was converted into a small office. She picked up the receiver and sat at the desk. "Hawke speaking."

"Lady Hawke, it's Duncan Porter."

Chapter Thirty-two

For half an hour, Duncan had driven himself crazy. Sitting behind his desk, he picked up the phone, then put it down again. He repeated the process several times before finally dialing.

He still wasn't sure it was a good idea. He was certain Eli would not want his friends involved, but Shen was right. Eli could open the gates, but only Daniel Dion could successively close them. If it meant tricking the elder half of Raven to go to Stonehenge, then so be it. However, he had also promised Selena, Eli would return safely to her.

To ensure it, Selena would have to be there to retrieve Eli as soon as the gates closed. He knew Henry would not willingly let him go, not when he was such a strong source of food for him. Henry was also Eli's legal guardian and if he had to, he would bring the courts into it. Then there was the High Council. They would back up Henry's claims as long as it kept Eli's magick among them. Reinforcements were in order.

"Hawke speaking," the faery finally answered after the young Sinclair handed the phone to her.

"Lady Hawke, it's Duncan Porter."

"Porter! What the hell is going on? Henry—" Her voice dropped to a whisper, "—was in my dreams last night."

His eyes closed. He had feared that she was the one Henry was after in the astral realm. "I know. I apologize, but given the choice between you and Eli, I had to choose you."

There was a long sigh on her end. "Is he alright?"

"Perfectly. He can't wait to go home. He misses you." He took a deep breath, toying with one of the photos of Eli that had survived his attack. "Selena, we've tested him over and over again. He can open the gates, control them to an extent, but I fear he cannot properly lock them, let alone find the one we want."

"What did you expect with only half his magick? Besides, we already knew that."

"I thought maybe Chaos…wait, what did you say? You knew?"

There was a soft, mirthless laugh. "Aaliyah McNeil tested Daniel Dion yesterday, and Cleo translated a book he had. You should have read it before kidnapping Eli."

"I don't speak Gaelic."

"Well, you would have enjoyed it."

He sighed. She was trying to bait him, make him feel like a complete idiot. Well, she didn't have to, he already felt like one. "We're going to Stonehenge in the morning. Meet me there?"

"Is this a trap? Are you trying to capture Daniel, too? Only fey magick still exists in Stonehenge. Both you and I know that."

"Yes, but it might be enough to support Eli and Daniel. Do not forget, Raven dealt with the fey in learning to open dimensions as well as call forth you and your brothers. Look, Selena, I know you can never trust me and Nathaniel would rather see me dead than caring for Eli, but please believe me when I say I would give my life for Eli."

"I know."

His eyes grew wide in surprise.

"You love him."

His eyes watered at her understanding tone of voice. It was as if she could see into his heart. "I…"

"When this is over, it's his choice. No magick. Let him decide on his own."

"I will," he promised, and he meant it. He could practically see her nodding in satisfaction.

"Good. What time do we met?"

"Ten a.m. Keep hidden. I'll find you."

"I'll prep the team." There was a pause. "Porter?"

"Yes?"

"Protect him. Remind him we love him. Don't you dare let anything happen to him."

He smiled, giving a small laugh. "I swear, Selena." Again, he saw an invisible nod.

"Good. I'll see you tomorrow."

"Tomorrow."

The line went dead as she hung up.

Placing the receiver on its cradle, he leaned back in his seat. One night left. He had to turn time back to normal in the morning. It didn't give him much time and there was still so much he wanted to do with Eli. So many things he wanted to show him. Luckily, Shen had taken a team to prepare Stonehenge, cleanse it from all negative energies. All he had to do was make sure Eli was there before the eclipse. So why was he afraid to go to Eli now? Because this was their last possible night together, he thought miserably. He held his head in his hands. What am I going to do?

Eli yawned as he adjusted the control to the whirlpool. Spending all day playing in the maze with Duncan and Shen had tired him. All he wanted was a nice hot bath, then to curl up with a good book. Too bad Shen had to leave so soon, he would have enjoyed talking to her some more. She was fascinating and they had so much in common. However, she had insisted they would talk shortly so he didn't bother worrying. She would keep her word.

He was about to remove his robe and climb in the water when the bedroom door opened and shut. Instantly, he sensed Henry rather than Duncan. Frowning, he retied his robe. What could he possibly want other than the obvious?

"Eli?"

"In the bathroom, Grandpa," he called, opening the door. There was no point in hiding. Henry could track with barely a thought. He might as well play friendly though. Maybe he could talk Henry out of a feeding. Fat chance. "Is something wrong?"

Henry backed him into a corner of the bathroom. "Just wondering how you were. We've barely spoken in the last week."

"Oh? I thought you were still angry with me." This wasn't good. Henry, now in his mid to late twenties, had the look of a wild animal. He was hungry and the only reason he was there was to feed. There was no way Eli was going to be able to talk him out of it. Eli let out a little gasp as the back of his legs bumped again the edge of the tub. "We can talk now."

"I don't want to talk."

"Oh. Ah…"

"I'm hungry, Eli." He reached out for Eli, but paused. "Why are you so cold? Why do you fight me?"

He was losing his mind, Eli realized in fright. Every feeding made him even hungrier. How many of Duncan's servants had he fed on? How many witches and healers in the past two weeks compared to the odd feeding he would take from Eli during his childhood? It was all finally taking its toll upon him. "I don't want to fight you, Grandpa. I just want you to slow down. You're taking too much. It's becoming an addiction."

Henry refused to listen. His eyes glazed over as he studied the robe, probably thinking of the many areas he could feed from the pale flesh hidden beneath. "You're so much sweeter than Duncan. Even more than Anthony's Guardians. All I want is a little taste. Satisfy my thirst. You understand, don't you? I don't want to hurt you. You're my grandson, I love you."

"I know." Eli had to find a route of escape before he was either knocked in the tub or pulled into those huge arms. Just as Henry went to touch him, he made his decision and ducked under his arms, only to receive an elbow at the base of his neck. He stumbled to the floor with a yelp. His forehead hit the edge of the shower stall, blissfully missing his glasses. He remained conscious but stunned. He barely had a chance to rub his forehead before Henry was on him.

Struggling with all his might, Eli tried to pry Henry's hands from his shoulders and run to the hall where he could call for help. Magick wouldn't work. Henry would only absorb it before it would do any good. He cried out as Henry harshly rolled him onto his back. His hands were pinned above his head in one large hand while Henry straddled his hips, forcing on his weight down on Eli's legs. Henry was not light by any means. He was incredibly heavier-built than he seemed. He could easily break a leg by simply forcing pressure in the right area.

Henry's free hand snaked inside Eli's robes in search for a piece of flesh from which he had yet to feed upon.

"Don't do this," Eli pleaded for all the good it would do him. "Grandpa, listen to me. This isn't you. You're not like this. It's the magick. It's clouding your mind, making you sick."

For a moment, Henry actually seemed to consider his words. While he was in deep thought, Eli shifted his weight just enough to cross his ankles and have his fingertips meet. No energy flow meant no more feedings.

Henry instantly noticed the change. He began searching every inch of Eli to find the cause only to grow frustrated when he found nothing out of the ordinary.

"Henry…Grandpa, you know I love you, I will always love you. Don't you know that? Can't you understand? You don't need to be young again to feel loved," Eli tried, hoping even a fraction of the old Henry was still there. Tears dotted the corners of his eyes. "Please, let me go."

Henry stared at him. He released Eli's arms, but did not get off him. Grasping Henry's shoulders, Eli shoved as hard as he could, using only a fraction of his magick to get the man off him. It also released the flow of magick and energy he had been trying to stop.

Henry smiled, discovering his secret, and cupped his cheeks, absorbing even that small dose of magick. Eli no longer had a choice. The look in Henry's eyes spoke louder than even his warped mind. Henry wanted him for more than just food tonight.

Increasing the flow of magick, he shoved Henry harder and squirmed as best he could out from under him. Henry's hands flowed over every inch of bare flesh as if in a trance and trying to memorize the feel of him. It was unnerving and Eli wanted desperately to kick his way free, but was far too fearful what would happen if he broke Henry out of his self-induced trance. Unfortunately, Henry came out of it himself when Eli was about to pull his feet free.

He grasped Eli's right ankle in an iron grip and pulled him back. Raising the ankle to his lips, he began to suckle the flesh with a victorious gleam in his eyes. "You can't stop the flow of magick without crossing your ankles, can you, little one?"

He was right. In this position, Eli could not. He tried struggling only to have Henry squeeze his ankle until it felt like it was going to break. His mind became fuzzy as he was forced to allow Henry to feed. He sank back against the marble floor and prayed Henry would finish quickly. His eyes bulged as pain raced up his leg. He screamed.

Henry's mouth was midway up Eli's calf when he bit into the strong muscles hidden under the flesh. It wasn't a love bite by any means. He tore deep into the flesh. His mouth latched onto the hole created by his sharp teeth and was actually drinking the blood rather than lapping at it as he had with Selena.

Eli couldn't think for a moment. What was happening to Henry? Every time he fed, it seemed to get worse. Was he actually changing into a full-fledged vampire?

Not knowing what else to do, Eli threw all his energy and power into the other leg. With a snarl, he slammed the heel of his left foot into Henry's temple, effectively dislodging him from his right leg.

The man fell back in shock and simply stared up at Eli, as he got wobbly to his feet. Too angry to do any more than lean against the vanity, Eli glared back at him. "You just proved me right, Henry. You're obsessed. Far worse than Duncan ever has been." Henry blinked and stood.

Eli hobbled back to his room.

Confusion and rage filled his voice. "I'm obsessed? Yes, perhaps, but only to get that blasted demon out of you, boy!"

"Oh, yes, and that includes absorbing my energy until I can barely move. Or molesting my Guardians?"

"If need be."

Eli rolled his eyes. He couldn't be serious. "Get out," he said tiredly.

"Not until Chaos is gone."

"She's been gone for months!" he finally snapped. "She left because she feared I would destroy her. Follow her example."

"You're going to be exorcised, boy. You've never been this mouthy and it would not surprise me if it was still in you."

"Fine! Whatever! I don't care any more! Now get out!"

Henry stormed past him to the door, mumbling about a good priest he knew. He even threatened to have an archbishop deal with him.

Eli wanted to laugh. If Henry thought the church was going to be afraid of a sorcerer, he had another thing coming. They would flip over a real live vampire long before a magick user any day.

He waited until the door slammed shut, then groaned, and sank to his bed. He held his torn leg and sobbed softly. Thankfully, Henry had not hit an artery, but he still took a good chunk of flesh. It was bleeding badly. Using a little magick, he knitted the flesh back together, silently thanking Duncan for the new spell. His leg stung, but at least it no longer bled.

He flopped back against the pillows. So much for the bath, he thought wearily. His muscles were too tight now and he was not sure if Henry would make another surprise visit. However, he was far too sore and tired to actually sleep.

Adjusting his robe, he rolled out of bed. A little reading should calm him down. He sat in the big armchair next to the open window. The warm summer breeze mixed with the novel was exactly what he needed. Drifting to another world created by the writer was always enjoyable.

A knock on his door drew his attention. He stared at the door in fear for a moment. Henry didn't normally knock. His fears withdrew when he sensed Duncan's rather nervous aura. Oh, no, please tell me Henry didn't go after him because of our fight, Eli prayed as the door opened a crack.

Duncan peeked in.

To Eli's relief, there were no marks on him.

"Eli? Are you up? Can I come in?"

Eli smiled. "Yes, of course." He laid the book down, stood up and nearly fell over. His ankle throbbed. When he looked up, he found Duncan holding him. "Thanks."

"Any time."

Sitting back down, he sighed. "Twisted my ankle," he lied, not wanting Duncan to fuss over him too much.

Duncan gave him a doubtful look. "Was that before or after Henry attacked you?"

Looking away, he frowned. "It wasn't really an attack. He tried to feed, I stopped him. I'll be fine. It barely hurts, already healed…mostly."

Duncan was pushing aside the robe and inspecting his leg.

It was swollen and would bruise, as would numerous areas, Eli suspected, but Duncan was already using his powers to heal the worst of it.

When he looked up, he had the most distraught expression of his face.

"What's wrong?" Eli asked in concern. Surely, Henry had not truly damaged the leg. It didn't feel broken.

"Henry insists we leave tonight rather than in the morning.

It was as he stood that Eli noticed the dark bruise forming under Duncan's neck. Henry had taken his frustration out on the other man.

"He tried to choke you! My God! Duncan, are you alright?"

"I'll be fine."

"No, Duncan, he's losing it! He could have killed you. He bit me. My leg was covered in blood and he was drinking it like wine. He didn't care if I lived or died. Why?"

Duncan rested his forehead against Eli's. "I'm so sorry, Eli. I wish I knew how to stop this, really I do. I promise, by tomorrow night you'll be safe at home with your friends."

"And you?" He felt his throat tighten with worry.

"All that matters now is your safety." His lips brushed against Eli's. "I made Selena a promise I swore never to break, and by God I'm not going to."

Holding Duncan's cheeks, Eli studied him. His words were sincere. "And I won't let him hurt you either. I don't want to lose you." And he didn't. As much as he missed his friends, he didn't want to leave Duncan. Not any more.

With effort, they pulled away from each other.

"We better get ready. Ah…I have an outfit I had planned for tomorrow. I had better pack it. You can wear what you want until then." Duncan rubbed the back of his head. "Eli, I'm really sorry. I never meant for any of this to happen."

"I know."

They moved as one, packing and organizing until Claudia came to tell them the car was waiting. Then, under Henry's dark gaze, they climbed into the limo, both staying as far from the hungry vampire as possible. It was a night neither planned to sleep through.

The moment Selena announced what was going on, the group pulled together. With Scott and Pietro at his side, Nathaniel literally raided the Sinclair armory. Aaliyah was giving Daniel a crash course on magick while they packed the weapons in the SUV.

"Learning how to lock dimensional portals in sixty minutes or your money back," joked Aaliyah as Alexis opened a tiny one.

Although amazed by his daughter's skills, he surprised himself when after only half an hour he closed and effectively locked it. Alexis made large ones, more powerful. As he closed each one, he grew faster and, in essence, more powerful.

It was a feeling Daniel had never felt before. He had only felt totally helpless once in his life and that was the day his wife died; but now? Now he felt powerful, totally in control of himself and his life. He knew that was not true, that it was the rush of magick talking, yet it felt comforting. There was no doubt in his mind they would save Eli. A warm wind ruffled his hair, perking his senses. He looked up as the wind sprite bowed before his daughter. Alexis's face paled. "They're on the move? Already?" The beautiful creature nodded.

"Damn!" She bowed her head. "We have to leave." She gazed at her father. "Do you think you're ready?"

"As ready as ever." However, he wasn't quite sure of that.

Aaliyah stepped up next to them. "Good, because Eli will need your strength."

Chapter Thirty-three

It was nearly ten, real time, when they pulled into Worchester. Twilight reigned over the city, but Eli was too tired to admire it. He had refused to sleep through the drive. There was no way he could trust Henry not to attack either him or Duncan should he allow himself the indulgence. He was going to keep an eye on him no matter how difficult it was. Yet dozing off was unstoppable. He was startled when Duncan woke him as they pulled in front of the Inn. Both groggily went to their shared room while Henry, amazingly enough, shared a room with the driver.

Eli practically fell asleep the moment his head touched the fluffy soft pillows. Duncan slept in the other bed, snoring softly, hugging his pillow as if missing the warmth of a human body.

Sometime in the middle of the night, a firm hand grasped Eli's shoulder and shook him awake. Henry slapped a hand over his mouth as he went to speak. His eyes grew wide as Henry dragged him out of bed. Silently, he was marched out of the room, never waking Duncan.

In the hall, Henry whipped Eli around and dug his fingers into his upper arms. "We're going to the Cathedral to see Father Jacob."

Rubbing the sleep from his eyes, Eli felt for his glasses. "What? My glasses… Hmm… What time is it?" He grimaced as Henry dragged him away from his room. "Grandpa, my glasses?"

"You won't need them."

He was too tired to argue. He simply wanted to sleep, but Henry would have none of it. Holding his wrist tightly, Henry made him use his magick to put on proper attire before flagging down a taxi.

The driver was short and obviously from another country. His English was poor to say the least and Eli had to translate Henry's orders.

Within minutes, due to the driver's unnatural speed or maybe Henry's deathly glares each time they hit a red light, they were at the Cathedral. Eli could not help but stare up at the huge building. Even without his glasses, he could see the magnificence of the ancient church. However, he had little time to marvel over it before Henry pulled him up the steps and inside.

Inside was even more impressive. The high arching ceiling was very Romanesque. He took time to marvel at it all as Henry made him sit in the front row. It seemed like a dream. He never pictured himself in the Worchester Cathedral. He doubted even Anthony had been here.

"Stay put," Henry commanded. As if his words were not enough, Henry's hand cuffed his right wrist to the pew. His gray eyes began suddenly soft, almost like the old Henry. "Don't worry, Eli, I'm going to help you."

His tired mind took a moment to understand. Henry was going to have the bishop exorcise him. He leaned against the back of the pew and sighed. This wasn't a dream. It was a nightmare. Once Henry learned he was wrong and Chaos was indeed gone, it might be the bishop he took it out on. Eli didn't want anyone else to suffer.

Staring up at the decorative cross and altar, he thought back to another place and time. Ely Cathedral, not far from Ipswich, where he had been baptized as an infant, and oddly enough his namesake, was one of England's most beautiful Cathedrals. It had been a place of so many questions and answers, many years before his birth.

"Do you believe in God, Tony?"

"God, Goddess, Kami, Isis, Zeus, Allah… different names for the same essence. Whether it is one God or many, it is still the spirit of the Earth that fills us." Anthony smiled at Henry's flustered face.

"You never give a straight answer."

Anthony caressed the statue of Christ. "Who is to say Jesus was not a magnificent magician whose extraordinary abilities attracted thousands? Was he really the son of God or just a bedtime story?"

"That's blasphemy!" Henry screamed, clenching his fists.

"Who knows for a fact? Were you there? All we have are ancient scripts and no proven facts. Those who translate often change things for their own profit. Does anyone really know what happened in those ancient times?"

"I'm a devout Catholic, Tony. You insult not only me, but also your father's religion."

"I didn't mean any harm, Henry. I only stated my opinion."

He always thought I was evil, Eli thought in dismay. He covered his face with his hands and breathed deeply. Tears trickled down his cheeks. What was he going to do? This could get very ugly very fast.

"My child?"

Sniffling, he gazed up through blurry eyes at a short, budgie, balding man. He wiped the tears away. "Father."

Seeing his wrist cuffed, the bishop knelt before him. Curiosity ruled his pale blue hazel eyes. "Are you alright? Your father is concerned."

"Father?" he whispered before nearly laughing. Henry was pretending to be his father now? A choked sob came from his lips at how ironic that idea was. "I know. Oh, Lord, this is really messed up."

"Do you wish to tell me about it?" The bishop's eyes returned to the cuffs. "For some reason, your father believes you are possessed."

"Do you think so?"

"Why don't you tell me why he thinks so?"

He laughed. "It's a long story and I doubt you would believe it without thinking it is something demonic."

"Why?"

Eli closed his eyes. "Do you believe in magick or reincarnation?"

"Perhaps."

Opening his eyes, he gave a light push of magick. The candles throughout the great hall flickered with small flames, lighting one by one until they all shone brightly.

The bishop gasped in surprise.

"I am a magician, in this life and the last, and perhaps even the one before that. It runs in my family, or what's left of it. Back in November, I fought against the Chaos Demon. She—it possessed me. In March, I finally defeated it by nearly killing myself and then becoming far too powerful for it to control."

"God help us!" The bishop made a cross over himself before taking off his rosary. "Don't be afraid, child."

He pressed the sterling silver cross gently against Eli's forehead. Maybe he expected Eli to scream in agony or whimper in pain, but Eli simply sat there and let him bless him.

"Our Father who art in Heaven, blessed be thy name. Bless our child and protect him from all evil doings." He stared at Eli for the longest moment before removing the cross. "You're clean?"

"Yes. A priest from my local church blessed me the following morning to be certain it was gone." Seeing the fear still in the bishop's eyes, he got upset. "I'm not evil. Magick is not evil. Why do you fear us? You just proved it." He looked away as the tears rushed to his eyes. Clenching his fists, he smothered the candle flames.

"I don't believe you are evil, confused perhaps, but not evil. There are many things in this world that are unexplainable. Many gifted people. You are just one of many." He gently turned Eli's head until they faced each other. "Your father cares very deeply if he is willing to travel so far to get you help. Don't be angry with him."

Eli shook his head. "You don't understand. He got himself into dark magick. It's changing him. He's afraid I may be possessed yet—"

The bishop smiled, patting his knee. "There, there. Your anger is inspiring your imagination. Your father appears to be a noble man who simply worries about you."

"He's not my father! My parents died when I was six. He killed them and then lied to me. Made me think he loved me."

He was completely confused now, but seeing the sincerity in Eli's eyes, understanding quickly came to him. "Oh, Lord. Can you break free? Is your magick strong enough?"

"They're charmed. A warlock made them especially for me."

The bishop tried anyway. Together with Eli, they pulled against the center column of the pew. The old oak creaked, but did not give.

"What are you doing?" Henry demanded. He lunged for the bishop.

The old man stood before Eli like a shield from God. He held of his cross as if it itself could stop the creature Henry had become.

"You shall not have him!"

Henry's eyes were practically blazing. "He is possessed, Father, and very dangerous. He is playing with your mind."

"That's not true!" Eli cried. He felt his insides tear apart. There had to be a way to save the bishop.

The bishop was defiant.

Eli was not sure if he was being brave or stupid.

He stood his ground as Henry towered over him. "He is clean. No demons lay within him. His gifts should be celebrated not feared."

Henry looked past him to Eli. "What have you done, Eli? What magick is this?"

Eli shook his head. "No magick, honest."

Henry grew angrier by the second.

Eli was terrified. It was one thing to go after him, but a man of God? He could not let that happen. Duncan, please don't let these be as strong as the others were, he prayed, pouring every ounce of magick he had into his arms. He gasped in shock when the cuffs gave and he tumbled off the pew. Blinking, he stared at the broken chain in confusion. It should not have been that easy.

Both Henry and the bishop gaped at him in surprise.

Henry was the first to react. He reached behind and pulled a silver revolver from the back of his pants.

Rolling to his feet, Eli grabbed the bishop by the wrist. "Run!" he ordered, pulling him away from Henry.

For a moment, the man didn't seem to understand the seriousness of the situation until a bullet rung throughout the church. Rounding a corner, Eli shoved the elderly man into one of the many offices. "Stay here," he instructed. "It's me he wants." Pressing his palm to the closed door, he charmed it, making sure it stayed locked until Henry was safely off the property.

He ducked as Henry rounded the corner and pulled the trigger once more. His chest pounded as he ran hard. Henry, even with one leg, was fast. His own leg still sore from where Henry had bit him, made Eli slow down. Unfortunately, it also gave Henry a chance at a clearer shot. The third shot grazed Eli's right arm. Fire raced up his arm. Fighting the pain, he burst through the front door of the cathedral and hid in the blackness of the trees lining the river. Kneeling amongst the shrubbery, he watched as Henry began searching for him.

Breathing hard, he called upon his magick to cover him, making it impossible for Henry to see or hear him. Henry came so close at one point that Eli unconsciously began chewing his bottom lip as he clenched his bleeding arm.

"Eli! Eli, come out. I won't hurt you. We'll find another bishop. There's still time," Henry pleaded, stowing his gun. "Eli, please! I'm your grandfather."

Not anymore, Eli swore, creeping deeper into the shadows. I have to get to Duncan. As soon as he was a safe distance from Henry, he teleported himself back to his hotel room.

Duncan awoke with a start as Eli appeared into their room. He gazed tiredly at the younger man. "What's going on? Where were you?"

"It's a long story. Get up. We've got to go." Rushing to the door, Eli charmed it as he had the one at the Cathedral. "Henry will be back any minute. He's gone mad, nearly killed me and a Bishop."

"What?" Duncan blinked away the sleep as he sat up. "What are you talking about?"

"There's no time. Call the limo." He grabbed the backpack Aaliyah had bought him and shrugged it over his shoulders, ignoring his bleeding arm. Before he forgot, he retrieved his glasses from the nightstand and put them on.

Yawning, Duncan called the limo driver in the next room and told him to have the car ready in five minutes, but told Eli to give him ten.

Pacing back and forth, Eli waited as Duncan changed. Henry would not search the church grounds forever. No, he felt Henry close. They could not wait any longer. Taking Duncan's hands, he literally dragged him to the door. They would meet the driver in the garage if need be as long as they left now.

Swinging the door open, he gasped when he found a gun pointed at his forehead. He felt Duncan go rigid behind him and drop his hand to raise his arms as Henry forced them back into their room.

Chapter Thirty-four

"Just where did you boys think you were going?" Henry crooned as he stepped inside. He shut the door with his foot. The gun never wavered from Eli's forehead. "You're fast, Raven, but predictable. Never could leave a friend behind. He would have been a good soldier."

"What's going on, Henry?" Duncan demanded, his voice a little shaky from sleep.

"Get Eli changed and ready for Stonehenge. We leave in twenty minutes."

Turning Eli around, he yanked the backpack off his shoulders and shoved him onto the bed. He threw Duncan another set of cuffs, larger than the last pair and quickly re-aimed the gun at Eli's head. Getting to his elbows, Eli stared at the revolver in fear. Henry's grip was sure and his aim without flaw. There was no way Henry would miss the shot if he dared move.

"Make sure to use a stronger spell this time. He broke the other set."

"Is this really necessary?" Duncan asked. He laid out the satin suit. His eyes were far too wide for his face as he stared at Eli in fear.

Eli gasped as his hair was pulled back, revealing his long column of a neck. He shut his eyes tightly as Henry began to feed. Henry pulled one arm painfully behind Eli's back to keep him from stopping the flow of energy. While Henry fed, Duncan changed all his clothing, all the while objecting to Henry feeding upon him so soon to the eclipse. Eli was only able to make several pitiful groans in objection until finally he was too weak to move let alone fight. It was then Henry finally let him go.

Henry laid him on the bed, gently stroking his hair away from his face after he stowed the revolver in the back of his pants. Eli began hyperventilating. He felt too weak, barely able to roll over. He closed his eyes and concentrated on his breathing. He had to slow it. He had to make it normal before he caused himself a heart attack.

"Easy, Eli. Shh, take it easy," whispered Duncan, leaning over him. His hand cupped Eli's cheek. "There we go. Slowly. Okay. That's it..."

Eli looked up at the two. Duncan was focusing hard on keeping him calm while he finished buttoning the suit jacket. It was an elegant mix of English and Asian design. Expensive, soft, black slacks and turtle-neck completed the outfit. The jacket was a soft royal blue, gold, mid-thigh length and extremely beautiful. Had Eli been able to focus, he would have really liked it, but he became trapped in a haze even after his breathing returned to normal. He was too weak to move, but too wide-awake to slip into unconsciousness. He barely had enough strength to roll on his side.

"Hmm…"

I have to get up. Got to escape, he kept telling himself. He stared up at Henry as the man leered down at him. There was a slight worry in his gray eyes, but it didn't match the rage. Before Eli could object, he was hefted into Henry's large arms.

"He won't be strong enough now," Duncan complained, carrying Eli's bag as they went to the elevators.

Eli watched him silently over Henry's shoulder. Duncan was chewing the inside of his mouth as he stared at him worriedly.

I'm sorry, Eli. I should have listened.

Eli's eyes drooped as they stepped into the cool night air. In the warmth of the limo, he laid down once more with both hands cuffed behind his back and his ankles bound. For the first time in hours, his injured ankle throbbed. He could no longer ignore it. It filled his mind, his consciousness, until he wanted to scream.

Duncan cradled his head in his lap and continued to apologize for not moving faster and allowing Henry to feed. It wasn't as if he could have stopped him. Neither of them could any more. Eli turned his focus away from the weeping man. They were outside Duncan's shields. He could feel his friends and wondered why, only now, did he sense them?

Calming his mind, he reached out in search of them. They weren't far, only several hundred kilometers and moving toward them fast. It felt like a huge source of power. The Sinclairs were with them, he realized in shock. They were coming to help? Why? The Sinclairs weren't exactly fond of him…but he knew he could trust them to protect Daniel and his family.

He focused on his best friend, silently calling out to Alexis. In his mind's eye, he could see her sitting behind Scott in a Sinclair custom-made SUV. She was deep in thought, mentally preparing for the upcoming battle. *Alexis,* he called, reaching out to her.

Alexis's eyes snapped open. "Eli?" she whispered, ignoring Miao's confused look. *Where are you?*

Outside Worchester. We're heading to Stonehenge. We're on our way there.

What? How did you—

Porter called Selena. Are you alright? There was silence for a long period, making Alexis's fears grow worse. Something was obviously wrong, otherwise her father would not have wakened them so early at the hotel. Something must have happened.

I'm fine, Alex. I'm just worried about you.

He was lying. His voice had a small tremble to it that she would never have detected if she didn't know him so well. There was fear pouring through their telepathic bond. She wasn't sure how to help him. Undoing her seatbelt, she reached past Scott and snatched up the CB, clicking on to the channel of the vehicle her father was in.

"Dad, can you sense Eli?"

There was static before he responded. "Yes. What's going on?"

"I'm not sure. Look, can you reach him? I think he needs our strength. Henry might have fed from him."

"I'll find him. Just keep him talking."

The CB clicked off and Alexis sat back. They had to find him fast. He was getting so weak.

"Eli's talking to you?" Miao asked, concern in his voice.

She nodded, closing her eyes. She had to keep him focused or they were going to lose him. "He's growing weak. So tired."

Indeed, Eli was on the verge of passing out, but it was not just due to Henry feeding from him or the lack of sleep. Duncan was softly chanting a renewal spell, offering what power he could, but the cost was to put Eli into a deep sleep.

He struggled against it. As tired as he was, he did not wish to sleep. He could not leave Duncan to defend himself against Henry, even if he *was* bound. However, Duncan was hard to fight.

A gasp escaped from his lips as invisible arms wrapped around him. His fear and anger melted away as an eerie calmness filled him. He forgot everyone in the limo. It was as if they no longer existed. Instead, he could feel a father figure lying behind him. There was no fear in the closeness of his visitor. It reminded him of sleepless nights when he was just a little boy and how he would crawl into bed between his mother and father. His father would hold him while he slept against his mother's chest, whispering that the monsters weren't real, that they would be gone by morning.

However, the monsters were real and they did not vanish simply by the sun rising. It did make him feel safe though, having those same warm arms holding him now. He knew they were not his father's, rather his soul's other half, Daniel. He relaxed into the embrace, feeling warm and safe and silently hoping to feel that safe forever.

It's alright, Eli. We're on our way. Stay calm. Let Duncan help you, Daniel said in a gentle whisper.

"Help me," Eli whispered aloud, forgetting Henry and Duncan were still with him.

I will, but you must remain calm. Duncan is trying to increase your power level so the eclipse does not control you or the magick gets out of hand, he explained.

Let Duncan help, Anthony's voice echoed over Daniel's.

"I am."

"Eli?" Duncan asked in concern.

Eli barely made out his form as the warlock knelt before him.

"Who are you talking to?"

Duncan's face seemed like another part of his vision. "Daniel."

No. Eli, shh...listen, Henry doesn't know we're coming. Duncan does. Don't say anything to alert him.

"My head hurts." Eli closed his eyes. He was so tired now. No!

Stay awake! Yet he could not fight it. The need for sleep was overwhelming.

Sleep renews your strength, Daniel continued.

His astral form held him a little closer. Eli could even feel his breath against the back of his head.

It's alright, son. Go to sleep. I'll stay with you.

Daniel sighed in relief. He gazed at Aaliyah as she drove behind Richard Sinclair's Cadillac. "He's sleeping, finally."

"He can be stubborn," she admitted. "Is he alright?"

"Drained, tired and scared." He frowned. "Something big happened. He's bound and so weak he can barely move, let alone lift his head."

Her amber-green eyes widened. "There's no way he can fight the influences of the eclipse in that condition. Even if he only contained half of his original power, it was enough to destroy half the earth without a single thought."

That was what Daniel had feared. Eli's condition was scary enough and Daniel didn't know how to help him, but throw in the eclipse? It can only end in disaster! "What do we do?"

"Hold onto him. Don't let him go, no matter what happens," Aaliyah instructed with a determined gleam in her eyes.

He rested his head on the headrest and continued to mentally hold Eli. He followed the younger man into the dream realm. It was nothing like he had expected. He found himself in an enchanting forest that felt oddly familiar. He sensed Eli close by. Following the youth's aura, he found a clearing on top of the hill. A small family graveyard sat near a large tree.

Eli was sitting on the brick wall, one leg lazily swinging back and forth, the other perched next to him. He no longer seemed frightened, only curious. His blue eyes were distant, deep in thought as he gazed over the horizon and the deep ocean in the far distance.

"Figured it out," Eli said softly, not looking away from the amazing view as Daniel sat next to him. "Shen was right. Everything is tied to my emotions."

"What do you mean?" Lowering his foot, Eli scooted closer to him. It was almost childlike, but Daniel didn't mind, Eli acted as if it was a big secret he had been waiting to tell the right person.

The youth pointed to a shimmering light a few acres away. "See?"

"What is it?" For a moment, it flashed fully into existence. A portal, small, but showed people and colourful orb-like creatures. His eyes widened as he saw the most beautiful being that had ever walked the earth. His long-lost wife. He would have jumped down to go to her if Eli wasn't holding his arm tightly. The youth shook his head.

"The Land of the Dead. You can't go inside."

"Why?"

His eyes were sad. He must have really wanted to go inside himself. "They're dead. We're not. They will attach themselves to us and we'll never be able to come back."

"You've tried."

Eli closed his eyes and looked away. "This is the one portal I can open, but only in the astral realm. I always thought I was just dreaming until I opened it in the real world a few weeks ago. In the astral realm, I was only seven when it first opened. Aaliyah and Nan were training me. Nan kept saying my power was growing at an incredible pace and had me writing a journal of my dreams that she would read every morning. When she read about the portal, she insisted I never go near it, but one night I saw my parents, so I disobeyed her."

Daniel stared at him in awe. There was still so much he didn't know about his other half. So much he now, more than ever, wanted to learn. He laid an encouraging hand on the man's shoulder as tears glistened in his eyes. It must have been so painful to lose both of his parents at such a young age.

"I just wanted to be with them, even for just a moment. I wanted to tell them I was sorry I could not save them. I went inside, thinking they would instantly find me, but I was wrong. Spirits swarmed me. Selena said I was in a coma for nearly a week. Nan had to come get me."

"Were you scared?"

He had that curious glow to him again. "A little, at first. They came so fast and there were so many. They just wanted to feel an actual life force once more. Mum and Da came and chased them away. They held me the whole time I was there."

He smiled warmly at the memory. "They kept telling me to go home, that I couldn't stay with them, but I refused. I had waited so long to hold them again that I was not willing to let either of them go.

They were my parents. I loved them. Nan had to force me to leave. She came and used superior magick to overwhelm me."

He laughed softly. "Mum and Da helped her. I couldn't believe it. I felt betrayed and lonely for so long. They didn't even let me say goodbye…again."

They sat silently next to each other, watching as the portal flickered and closed only to reappear seconds later. Taking a deep breath, Eli looked up at him.

"Did you get to say goodbye to your wife?"

Daniel nodded. "I was lucky in a way. She died in my arms. It still hurts. It took a long time to learn how to live without her. She was my life, but I had to make my children my life or I would have died right along with her." He smiled. "Now that I can see her spirit and talk to her, it's so much easier."

"I wish I knew her."

Daniel grinned. "She watches out for us quite often. She likes you very much."

"Really?"

He laughed. "Yes. She liked you the moment she saw you. She says you have a good heart and knew you would never let Alexis get hurt."

Eli stared at his hands nervously.

Curious, Daniel took them in his. They were oddly cold. Maybe the circulation in his real body had slowed to his arms because of the way he was bound. "Eli?"

"Can you do me a favor? This will be the most magick I have ever used. I don't think I can handle it. If something happens…if I die, tell Al—"

He looked up in surprise when Daniel crushed him to his chest. "You are not going to die, Eli. I won't let you." He gave the youth a tight squeeze, not sure if he ever wanted to let him go for fear of actually losing him. "You are like a son to me and I never give up on family."

Eli's eyes glistened in joyful tears. He threw his arms around Daniel and smiled. "Thank you."

Resting his cheek against the young man's, Daniel closed his eyes. He would not give up on Eli. He would get to him somehow before the eclipse started. He would find a way to save him or die trying. There was no way he was leaving England without him. Not now. Not anymore. He would protect Eli as would one of his own children.

Chapter Thirty-five

It was just past seven in the morning when they pulled onto the Salisbury Plain. More than half a dozen vehicles were parked in and around the entrance leading to Stonehenge. The land was alive with magick users preparing for the coming eclipse, far more than William Larsen had said were allowed. It wasn't every day one of the world's greatest magicians, or at least the reincarnation, was in their midst.

Everyone knew the legend of Raven. He seemed loved and hated in equal measure, yet worshipped by many as one of the Ancients to take human form.   His unique features mainly caused it, especially tricoloured eyes that were actually three separate shades of blue that made them look like the rolling ocean. All of which echoed in Eli, only he tended to use glamour to hide the strangeness of his eyes. Duncan never could understand why.

The magick users were surprised when they saw they limo pull up. They were not due for another hour of two. Many stared at the windows, hoping for a glimpse of the one that was supposed to save the magick realm. For all Larsen's aloofness, the magick realm still cared and adored Raven. Many would gladly give their lives to defend his reincarnation. It was very likely many would die that day to do so.

Duncan subconsciously stroked Eli's hair as he stared out the window. Many innocent people were going to die that morning. He could feel it. All that was left to save them lay in his lap, so weak that there was no chance of them winning. The gates would open and only heaven knew how many demons would escape before they could close them…if they could close them.

He had poured all the magick he could into Eli, leaving just enough in himself to fight, but it wasn't enough. Far from it. Henry had taken more energy from Eli than ever before. The young man should have been in a comatose state rather than sleep. He needed another magick transfusion before he would be even remotely strong enough to control the portals, let alone close one.

He sighed. It was a good thing Daniel had interceded and made Eli sleep. Had he not, Duncan feared Eli would have had another seizure. He felt so weak. At least he was calm now.

Duncan grabbed Henry's hand as he reached to shake Eli's shoulder. "Let him sleep," he pleaded, smoothing the soft fabric of Eli's jacket. "He needs his strength or it'll overwhelm him."

Amazingly, Henry nodded and opened the car door. He paused to lean down and brush aside a strand of hair from Eli's face. The look in his eyes surprised Duncan for a moment as he looked at him.

"Why couldn't the bishop find the demon?"

Duncan's eyes wandered to the stone temple up the hill. "Maybe there's nothing to find." Thank the Gods for air conditioning, he thought, wiping his brow as a wave of heat seeped into the car. He laid Eli on his side and stepped outside. It was so hot and sunny. Not even the tiniest breeze. Thankfully, Eli was resting in a nice cool car.

Shen approached them with a confused look. "You're early," she declared, glancing at the limo. "What happened?"

"A mishap with a bishop," Henry said offhandedly. He strolled past her to see what everyone was doing.

She stared at Duncan for a long period, making him slightly uncomfortable. How was she able to make him feel like such a child when technically he was old enough to be her great-grandfather? He had to look away from her. "Is Eli alright?"

He shook his head. "I don't know. Henry took a lot last night. There was this huge fight and Henry pulled a gun. Everything just went to hell."

Her gaze darted to the limo. "I thought he might have fed from you. You don't look so healthy."

"I've given every ounce of magick I could to Eli, but it's not nearly enough."

She nodded. "I'll see what I can do."

Surprised, he opened the door for her and handed her a set of keys. "Henry had me bind him. It might be easier if you took off the cuffs."

She took them and sat next to Eli. She quickly did away with the cuffs and felt his head before nodding. She lifted him up in one swift motion and had him lean against her. She tilted his head toward hers, and then with a soft breath caressing his face, she claimed his lips. Eli's reaction was only instinctive. He did not actually awaken as he fed from her lips. The transfer of magick was much as how Henry fed from one's aura, only this was consensual.

Duncan watched it all in fascination. The way Eli's body moved against Shen's as she poured her magick into him. He wanted to join them, join their magick as they had two nights earlier, but he was far too weak for that. He could only watch as Eli gave Shen the attention Duncan so desperately wanted.

"What is this? A magick users' convention?" Scott declared in surprise.

Nathaniel would have laughed, it certainly did look like a small convention gathering, but the power coming from the area worried him. Why were there so many magick users? Were they friend or foe?

Picking up the CB, he clicked it on. "Richard, what should we do?"

"I doubt they're here to hurt Eli. Most likely to drive back whatever comes out of the portals. Find a place to park, then get lost in the crowd. Keep your power level down, kids. We're not here to fight…unless necessary," the Sinclair Clan head said firmly.

This wasn't good. Alexis should not be here, Nathaniel thought in worry. Even with all my magick, I don't know if I can protect her. If they attack…Anthony, give me the power to protect them.

Finding a space to park was easy enough. There was lots of room on the plain, none of it close to Stonehenge, however. It seemed odd how many people were there. There had to be nearly a hundred vehicles.

Taking off his seatbelt, he turned to Alexis and Miao. "Stay close to me and Sif. Don't let them feel your power, Alexis. They may not understand."

She nodded.

"Good. Let's find Eli."

They followed the numerous witches and magicians along the path to the large stone structure. They received many curious glances and friendly smiles. None of them seemed alarmed or concerned about their presences. All seemed welcome.

Not far ahead, Nathaniel felt Eli's presence. Glancing at Scott, he handed Alexis over to him. "I'll be back in a moment."

Scott nodded, wrapping his arms protectively around his sister's shoulders. Miao stayed very close to him and Sif.

Finding Selena and Daniel not far ahead, Nathaniel hurried with them to the head of the line. As they neared the standing stones, he grabbed Selena's wrist and pulled her to a halt. Daniel instinctively followed suit.

Not far ahead of them was Henry, a very young-looking Henry, and he was carrying an unconscious Eli. He looked very tiny in the big man's arms, but healthy. He had a glow to him Nathaniel could not recall ever seeing in him before.

Duncan Porter and an Asian woman flanked them. Both seemed to have a tie with Eli, as if the three had somehow united their magick. Something only Selena and Cleo were supposed to do. Selena noticed it, too. Her whole body stiffened as she glared at them.

They followed silently, hidden amongst the crowd.

Henry laid Eli on the central stone slab and quickly stepped back as the magick users flanked every gateway to Stonehenge. A dozen, in total, on the inside and well over thirty on the outside. The others moved around the structure, but stayed further back, as a last defense. All were ready for battle. If they had to fight them, even with the Sinclairs, it would be four to one.

Duncan Porter knelt before Eli, his right hand on the mage's forehead. After a moment, the ocean blue eyes that captivated everyone opened. He looked upon Duncan with no fear, no hate. The glamour Eli had been using on himself for so many years dropped and for the first time, Nathaniel really saw his eyes. They had a beauty that was not possible for most humans.

Nathaniel's breath caught in his throat at the sight of those eyes. There was a deep sense of longing, a trust and caring that should not have been there. Not for Porter at least. Not for Porter. Even the way Porter stroked Eli's hair was unnerving. They were too friendly to each other, their voices soft so no one else could hear them. Nathaniel suddenly wished he were closer to hear what they were saying.

"He looks alright," Selena whispered, seemingly unconcerned by their behavior. "He's magick level is a little low, but it seems he's using Duncan and that woman as a focus."

Nathaniel gave a grunt. Anthony would never have allowed Porter so close to him. Yet Daniel appeared unconcerned by Eli's behavior as well. He even agreed with Selena.

"With all that has happened, Eli would need a focus." Daniel eyed the two young men with worry. "I just hope Duncan knows what he's doing."

It was too bright, too noisy. At first, Eli had to cover his ears only to find the noise was not physical. It was psychological, or more like magickal. Opening his eyes, surprise filled him at the number of Covens around him. There were Covens from all over Britain. Some of their best were guarding the gateways of Stonehenge. They were oddly silent. The traffic of psychic thoughts was causing all the noise in his head. He raised his metaphysical shields until all he could hear was the beating of his own heart. He still felt Daniel's astral arms around him, but they were much closer now, so much more real. Yet when he looked down to where the arms should be, he only saw a twinkle from the astral realm. Daniel wasn't really there. His heart sank.

"Eli?"

He raised his eyes to see Duncan's worried face. For a moment, he looked up, past Duncan, past the high stone walls, to the sun shining directly above him. The moon, a dark outline now, was slowly moving closer. There were only minutes before the eclipse begun. Fear knotted in the pit of his stomach. What if this didn't work? What if he could not control the portals?

He glanced back at Duncan and the concern in his eyes. He feared the same thing. Even with all the magick users there to protect them, he feared they might die. It wasn't comforting. He closed his eyes. He didn't want to die. Not like this, not so young. Duncan once said he loved his eyes, or rather Anthony's.

When Eli was young, Duncan had always told him he wished he had such beautiful eyes. Michael's were almost like his, not quite, but almost. Eli opened his eyes, pulling back the spell he had created so many years ago after being teased by other kids about them. He let Duncan look upon the three shades, navy, almost black along the edges, sapphire, and the thin ring a gray near the pupil.

It brought a sad smile to Duncan's face.

We're here, Eli. Don't be afraid, Daniel whispered in his mind.

He smiled inwardly. *Dan!*

Shh...

There was no point in looking through the crowd. He could feel his friends. Instead, he kept his focus on Duncan and that sad little smile of his. It would all work out, he thought.

"Hi. You okay, kiddo?"

He couldn't help but smile. Duncan was trying to act so brave when it was obvious his knees were shaking just about as bad as Eli's were. "Yeah."

Duncan got to eye level. "I nearly forgot what beautiful eyes you have."

"Liar," Eli teased. He glanced around the crowd, not really looking for his friends, but curious by the number of magick users. There was so much magick in the area it nearly burned. "What's with all the witches?"

"They're here to protect you, and help close the portals." He gave a smirk. "Even our unexpected guests," he said in a lower voice.

Eli's eyes widened. He knew? He mentally slapped himself. Of course, Duncan knew. He was the best telepath in Europe. His eyes flickered to Henry checking his gun and Shen sharpening her swords.

"Henry doesn't know," Duncan whispered, squeezing his shoulder. They both gazed at the quickly approaching moon as the Head of the Council began his speech. "Soon your friends will be here to help if things get out of hand." His eyes saddened. "No matter what happens, you're going home today." He cupped Eli's cheek, obviously not caring what everyone around them thought. "In case I forget to tell you later, I love you."

Their lips met and Eli could not help but wrap his arms around Duncan and pull him close. A part of him yelled that this was too public, that he should not show such affection for another man like this. Not everyone reacts kindly to such displays, and he doubted his friends would understand why he was kissing Anthony's rival. Especially

Frost. He felt the guardian's anger washing over them. Yet, the fey had Scott. Why should he care if Eli decided to move on with his life? Even if it was Duncan?

"Hmm…" A numb feeling washed over him. The magick users or any other mortal being didn't cause it. Pulling back from Duncan, he looked up. The moon was beginning to overlap the sun.

The familiar pull of magick gripped his chest, stronger than before. His eyes widened for a moment before he shut his eyes tightly. His fists knotted in the front of Duncan's shirt. It felt like he was being burned from the inside out. This was worse than before. Why did it hurt so much? Why could he not push it away like before?

His head sank to Duncan's chest. He was going to burn alive if he didn't figure out what he was supposed to do. "Why…" he whimpered as the pain increased. It was just the start of the eclipse, things were bound to get worse.

Duncan wrapped his arms protectively around him. "Don't fight it, Raven. Let it come naturally. I promise, the pain will go away."

It hurt. Gods, it hurt! The eclipse was only beginning and he could barely stand. Wincing, he forced himself away from Duncan and stood on the ancient altar. It was time. This was what he had been training for. This was what he was born to do. Despite the agonizing pain, he had to focus. He had to control the portals.

"To your positions!" He heard someone order.

The power continued to build, making him whimper as he tried to harness it. The gateways flickered all around him. Where he thought only one gate at a time would open, eleven came to life. The magick from each rushed him at a pace he was unprepared to encounter. A thousand knives pierced him all at once, causing him to feel as if he was being torn apart. Every piece of him that was human shredded away. His flesh burned with the heat of a thousand suns and the howling of many wild animals filled his ears. He screamed.

Chapter Thirty-six

The pain spilled away like a waterfall. It was replaced with the combined magick of all those gathered. They were channeling their magick to him. He could feel each and every one of them. They psychically fed him their strength with words of encouragement. They believed in him. They were willing to protect him and worship as some had once worshipped Raven. It was an odd sensation that Eli had never felt before. He never wanted to be worshipped, not in this life or the last, but their power gave him the strength he needed to control the portals. He was sure he could handle them as long as the magician stood next to him.

A hand squeezed his tightly. Eli looked down to find Duncan holding his hand. His face twisted up in pain. It took a moment for Eli to realize Duncan had been the one to take the pain and clear his mind so the others could freely channel their magick to him. Eli returned the squeeze.

Duncan raised his face to look at him. His face filled with pain, but he managed to keep it out of his voice. "Focus, Eli. They're opening. Don't let them out."

Eli nodded. He suddenly understood his duty. Duncan had not merely been training him to open the gates, but to close them. He was supposed to stop the creatures within from escaping. His magick may trigger the gates, but it could also close them.

He levitated above the altar and opened his arms, drawing in as much of the combined power of all the magick users as his body could hold. Their chants filled his ears, making him focus clearly. He turned that focus on one portal at a time, closing them as fast as possible. It was hard work. A new one would open just as fast as he could close one. He worked fast, but there were more worlds out there than he thought possible. He could not stop the creatures from coming through.

The guards at each portal valiantly fought the mystic creatures back into their worlds. Those that did manage to make their way toward the center were dealt with by Henry, Shen, and Duncan. Swords clashes and gunfire filled Eli's ears. Screams from both the visitors and guards increased to a deafening pitch as the batted raged on.

This wasn't right. The witches died trying to defend their country and him. There had to be a better way. He could not bear to watch them fall. The bloodshed was too much. They were no match for these beings. Forming a large shield, he threw it in front of each portal.

"This isn't working!" he yelled to Duncan. "Clear everyone out. Shield the outside. It'll keep them contained in here."

"What about you?"

"I'll keep trying to close them." Seeing his reluctance, he frowned. "It's the only way."

Duncan's eyes were wide as he stared up at him. He looked away with a sigh. "Everyone out! Code red! Move it, people!" he ordered, taking charge.

Most were hesitant, swords drawn, ready to continue fighting. They stood their ground until Henry and Shen started forcing them out. They took the injured and to a safe distance, joining their fellow magick users. Duncan, Shen, and Henry, however, stayed. They took positions around Eli, with guns and swords ready. Eli took a deep breath as he, too, prepared to fight the ethereal creatures held behind the shield. If he were to die this day, he was going out fighting.

Trying to move past the rushing crowd was nearly impossible. Daniel had to push his way through. His children and the Guardians were close behind him, but the pulling in his chest urged him ahead of them. He had to get to Eli, he had to help him. His chest burned with a fire he had never felt before. All he knew was he had to get to Eli before it was too late.

Making it to the center ring, he spotted Eli levitating high above the altar. His mind was focused entirely on keeping whatever was in those portals from coming out. His shield crackled and sparked, beginning to buckle as the creatures fought it. The strain of the battle was visible on Eli's face as he tried to close the portals.

"Shield!" Alexis yelled from somewhere behind Daniel.

His daughter's magick filled the area, combining with Eli's. Eli relaxed for a moment as the strain was taken from him. He pulled his Totem out of his shirt and began chanting. The totem glowed brightly at its master's touch.

A spark of magick sent everyone in the circle to the ground. It wasn't Eli's spell, but something far worse. Daniel got to his knees and looked around in confusion. The shield covering a portal to Eli's left shattered. "Eli!" he yelled, running full speed to the floating youth.

Eli's eyes were wide as he stared at the tentacles spilling through the portal toward him.

He was in shock, Daniel realized when the mage didn't move. It took precious seconds for the young man to realize what was happening and when he did, it was too late.

The long tentacles wrapped around Eli's lithe form, dragging him toward the portal. Duncan and a woman slashed at the creature with swords as Henry fired into the dark pit. Eli struggled, but did not scream. He was still trying to transform the totem. He suddenly stopped when he made eye contact with Daniel. The fear in Daniel rose as he saw the understanding in Eli's eyes. The young man held his totem possessively for a moment before suddenly throwing it to Daniel. It landed in the sand without a sound.

Without a scream and next to no struggle, Eli was dragged into the portal where he disappeared.

"No!" Duncan cried, fighting desperately to keep a hold on Eli. In the end, he lost.

Daniel echoed his cry as Eli vanished. He didn't know what possessed him then, but he snatched up the magick totem, and while running, finished Eli's chant. It transformed in his hands. The weight of the staff was oddly comforting, as if he had always been meant to wield its power. He ran past Duncan, barely gracing him with a glance before plunging himself into the portal after Eli.

"Dad!" Alexis and Scott cried as they watched their father disappear.

This wasn't good, Selena thought angrily as she rushed to the portal.

Daniel was truly Raven, reincarnated to run inside so foolhardy. She doubted he even had a plan to get out in mind. Frowning, she took the lead.

"Flank them! Alexis, keep that portal open!"

Amazingly, everyone did as she commanded. Scott and Miao guarded the portal. Alexis took Eli's place on the altar, reinforcing the shields' power with her own. Nathaniel and the familiars covered Henry. Selena herself went to Duncan and the sorceress who was trying to help keep any other creatures from coming in. "What happened, Porter? You swore to protect him," she demanded.

The warlock actually looked frightened, but it had nothing to do with her. The Asian woman at his side was holding his arm tightly, preventing him from jumping into the portal after Eli and Daniel.

"He wasn't strong enough," he whispered in disbelief as tears dotted his eyes. "All our magick and he still wasn't strong enough."

Rage took over and he glared at Henry with enough hatred to kill. "I told you not to feed from him! This is your fault!"

Chapter Thirty-seven

Cold, so cold.

Multicoloured lights met Eli's worn eyes.

Am I dead? he asked himself.

He felt weightless, almost as if he were underwater, yet able to breathe. It seemed as if he were like this for a very long time.

Raising his head, he looked around. Long tentacles wrapped around him. He got an upside-down view of the creature that held him. A snake-like creature with such numerous tails moving in and around itself, that Eli could not possibly count them. An oddly human face existed below the snakehead. It drew Eli closer until it nested him amongst the tails. Eli looked away in fear, not sure whether or not he was about to become the monster's lunch.

A part of him could not help but admire the white alabaster of the snake's scales. Had he not been in such a position, he would have loved to take the time to study them further.

This is it, he thought as he was pulled against the body of the snake. I'm going to die. As that thought passed through his mind, a blinding heat passed his shoulder. The creature screamed next to him, its tentacles tightening around him. A cry escaped his lips as his ribs felt ready to crack.

Another blast tore one tail in half, sending silvery blood all over. Eli suddenly found himself floating next to the demon. It gave him a chance to take a better look at his captor. A Lamia? Well, that wasn't good. He had better things to do than be some creature's food.

He gasped as an arm snaked around his waist. For a moment, panic gripped him and he struggled, believing the Lamia had him once more.

"Easy, Eli," a deep voice said as another ball of red energy shot past him to the creature below.

The voice, the strong, yet tender arms around him made Eli blink.

Turning slightly in his rescuer's arms, he looked up to see Daniel Dion holding him. Not just that, but Daniel was commanding the Sun staff as if it were his own. The moon, half-hidden by the sun, glowed brightly as Daniel channeled its power.

Eli was at a loss for words. Daniel had showed very little magickal skill even after receiving half of Anthony's power, yet now he was wielding the staff as if he had been using it all his life. He was successfully chasing away the monster.

"Are you alright?"

Eli nodded. "Yeah. You?"

"Doing good." Daniel smiled down at him. "What do you say we blow this joint?"

Eli smiled happily. "Let's."

Their magick combined as one and transported them out of that dimension to their own world and a scene of havoc.

Levitating high above Alexis and the altar, Eli had to clamp his hands over his ears once more. His senses were on fire. The magick surrounding them was so intense he could not block it out let alone think straight. It wasn't simply the other magick users this time, it was the creatures in the portals. The magick was combatting each other, stirring into an unchecked hurricane. The other portals were on the verge of breaking through the shield, but he could not focus on them. His head felt ready to explode.

"Eli?" Daniel whispered, his voice dripping with concern as he held him tighter.

"Too loud," he murmured.

Daniel stared down at Eli in confusion. What was too loud? It dawned on him when he saw the portals flicker, trying to fight Alexis's spells. Spotting her magick pouch on Eli's hip, he pulled it off him. With one arm, he held Eli and the staff, with the other he threw the pouch down to his daughter. "Alexis, heads up!" he yelled.

She slowed its descent and caught the pouch in her outstretched hand.

Keeping an arm around Eli, he called upon Anthony's magick circle. "For just one night, combine our power to its former might," he chanted softly, praying to whatever god was willing to heed his plea.

He hugged Eli's half-conscious form to his chest. There was no way he could do this without Eli.

The power in his chest grew, but it was no longer painful. Both he and Eli began to glow brightly. He could feel Anthony's magick platform spinning around them. It was the most exciting warm feeling.

"What once was done, now undo," he whispered. "Return us to the form once true."

The moon was completely overlapping the sun now and, in a sense, Daniel now overlapped Eli. When he opened his eyes, Eli was no longer in his arms, rather he felt the youth somewhere inside him. Their bodies and minds joined as one. He no longer thought of himself as Daniel Dion, but as Anthony Sinclair.

Even his clothing had changed. He no longer wore his trench coat or slacks, but Anthony's long ceremonial robes. His hair, once short and auburn brown, was now long and black like Eli's and he had no doubt that even his eyes matched the youth's now. All was as it should be.

The magick came to him easily as did the knowledge of what must be done. "Alexis, get down," he called, descending to the altar. Everyone stepped back in a mixture of confusion and awe. His feet touched the smooth stone surface and he stood tall, his staff held slightly in front of him.

"Powers of the Divine, hear my plea," he chanted. "Do not allow these beings within the folds of our world. Allow me the strength to lock these gates for all eternity. I, Anthony Sinclair, child of the Sun and Moon, summon thee."

His staff came down hard on the stone altar. There was an earthshattering crack that resounded across the plains, followed by misty tendrils of magick that lashed out at each gateway. One by one, the portals flickered and glowed brightly before turning black and fading into the nothingness from which they were born. Anthony continued to stand in the center, chanting in ancient Latin. Again, the portals glowed, but this time a fiery red shield overlapped each before truly vanishing from all existence.

Anthony let out a sigh of relief.

It was finally done.

The portals were closed.

Not even the most-gifted magician could call upon them now. He held onto his staff as his knees buckled. It had taken far more magick than he had thought he would. He felt beat and exhausted.

The world swam before his eyes and the next thing he knew he was falling.

Chapter Thirty-eight

Arms were all around him. Someone, Alexis it sounded like, was calling his name. Opening his eyes, he smiled tiredly at his daughter's worried face. "Hi, honey."

The worry disappeared, replaced by a huge, relieved smile.

"Dad! You're okay!" she cried, wrapping her arms around his neck.

Daniel smiled, wrapping his own arms around her slim frame. "I'm fine, honey," he whispered into her hair, relieved to see everyone was alright.

With both his children's help, he sat up and began searching for Eli. The youth wasn't far. He was lying in Selena's lap, dazed, and confused. Crawling over to him, Daniel gently pulled him into a sitting position against him.

Eli stared up at him. "Dan? Is it really you? Wha—what happened? We…Anthony…"

Eli never thought they could combine their souls, not that Daniel had thought it truly possible either. "It's okay, Eli. I'll explain later."

The young man sat up straighter and looked around. Many of the other magick users had drifted back inside to see the extent of the damage and retrieve their dead. Luckily, it was nowhere near as bad as everyone had feared it would be. Only four of the eleven guards had been killed.

"Can you stand?" Selena asked, helping Eli to his feet.

Scott placed one of Daniel's arms over his shoulders and helped him to his feet as well.

Nathaniel, Miao, and the familiars flanked them, keeping everyone but their group at bay. Duncan Porter was desperately trying to get past Cleo to Eli, but Sif growled a warning to the warlock to stay back.

"Cleo, let him through," Eli gently ordered even as Selena shook her head.

"No, Eli. When you're stronger, he can visit. We're going home," she spoke soothingly, as if talking to a small child. She began forcefully walking to other way, holding his hand tightly.

"No wait! Selena, you don't understand!"

Daniel stepped into Eli's line of vision, completely blocking his view of Duncan. "Eli, hush…it's alright. Duncan can come with us. Alright?" The four Guardians stared at him as if he had lost his mind.

"What?" Nathaniel demanded even as Selena agreed. "Dan, that man murdered Anthony's sister! Abducted Eli not once, but twice! How can you trust him not to do the same the moment he's alone with Eli? What about Alexis and Miao? Are you willing to risk their lives simply because Eli is confused?"

Eli's eyes looked hurt by his words. He looked from Nathaniel to Daniel, waiting for the final decision.

Richard Sinclair stepped up next to them. "Are you two alright?" he asked, placing a hand on Eli's shoulder.

Eli nodded, staring down at his feet.

The young man's reaction caught Daniel by surprise. Eli had an odd submissive look. He wrapped an arm around Eli's shoulders and drew him away from Richard. Selena had told him Richard and Eli didn't get along, that Richard had even disciplined Eli on several occasions but had never truly harmed him. Eli was merely frightened of almost everyone now. "We're good," Daniel said with a smile. "More than ready to go home, eh, Eli?"

"Home…" Eli blinked as if the concept had escaped him since being captured. "Ravenwood?"

"Of course."

"No!" a man boomed.

Instinctively, Daniel pulled Eli behind him, using his own body as a shield. He would not let Henry Griphan or anyone hurt him again.

The man stormed up to him, but was not Griphan, nor anyone he knew. He was dressed in a High Priest's robes and was seeping magick. He was literally pushing it at Daniel as if trying to prove who was stronger. Daniel stood his ground, not allowing the magick to bother him. He knew, if he had to, he could easily beat the man with the force of his aura alone.

"Elijah Hawke is to return to London for questioning. His magick is obviously not under proper control."

Richard frowned. "Oh, shut up, William. Eli is a Sinclair. He is our concern, not yours."

"I am—"

"The new leader of the High Council, and no match against any Sinclair. Do you honestly think your followers will be suicidal enough to follow you into battle against us?"

The magician looked at the gathered magick users who merely shook their heads, many walking away, dismissing his claims over Eli. The battle to contain the portals had taken its toll on all of them.

None looked in shape for another battle.

"Go home, William."

Grumbling under his breath, the high priest stomped off. He knew better than to fight the Sinclairs.

Daniel sighed in relief and smiled at Richard. "Thank you."

"Don't. It took me a long time to trust Eli enough to take care of himself." He smiled at the youth. "If I had my way, he never would have left the family. Mae could be very stubborn and it's that strength that now flows within him."

Daniel gave a small laugh at Eli's stunned expression. He was about to pull the young man back around and ensure him he was safe when Eli was ripped from his hands. He spun around in shock as Eli's cry cut short.

Henry had a hand around Eli's throat and a gun, one Nathaniel must not have found, aimed at his head. Eli's eyes were wide with fear and his bottom lip trembled slightly. He stood perfectly still against the large man. This was not a situation for magick.

"He's my grandson!" Henry bellowed, his gray eyes bright with insanity. "You can't have him. He's mine! You have your own family!"

The man was shaking with such fury that Daniel feared he might accidentally crush Eli's throat as he raved. He seemed to have little control of himself. Daniel raised his hands, showing he was unarmed, except for the totem. "Hey, Henry, look, it's okay. I'm not trying to take Eli away from you. I just want to make sure he's alright. Okay? I'll personally drive him back to your cabin. How does that sound?"

For a moment, Henry seemed to think about it. He let go of Eli's throat and hugged him possessively. "He's all I have left," he whispered. "He's mine." His gaze roamed to Selena. "She's mine, too."

"I know, Henry, but they're very tired. They need to rest a few days. Can you give me a few days to make sure Eli's alright?" Daniel urged gently. He didn't want to anger the big man.

"Days?"

Pulling up his sleeve, he offered Henry his bare arm. "You can feed from me to hold you over."

Henry's eyes flickered from his arm to his face. "You'll let me feed?"

"Yes. Just let me have Eli for a few hours."

"You'll bring him back?"

"You have my word of honor."

His gray eyes shone as Daniel stepped up to him. He shoved Eli into Selena's arms and grabbed Daniel roughly around the waist. He drew Daniel against the length of his body and held the proffered arm to his mouth.

"Dan, no!" Eli screamed as Selena and Miao held him back. "Don't do this!"

"Dad?" Alexis pleaded in fear. She clung to her brother's arm as Henry latched himself to Daniel's arm.

"Ugh…" Daniel grunted as Henry bit into his forearm. He never thought Henry would actually bite him. He tried to pull away, only to be crushed against the larger man by one powerful arm. His head began to feel fuzzy and he was forced to lean his head against the broad chest to keep from throwing up. "Stop," he whispered as his throat began to fill dry.

Stay calm, Duncan's voice whispered in his mind.

He opened his eyes in time to see the warlock share a look with Scott. He barely had a chance to consider the look when Scott came charging at him. He was thrown to the ground, his son covering him as Duncan attacked Henry from the other side.

"Run!" Duncan ordered, fighting Henry for the gun.

Daniel didn't even have a chance to think before Scott hauled him to his feet and began pulling him away from the two. They broke into a run to get to the other. His arm stung, but it was something he could ignore for the moment.

Eli tried to fight Selena and Miao off him in order to help Duncan. Alexis wrapped an arm around his waist and tried to help drag him to the waiting SUV. Even Richard seemed unable to hold him back. Eli kicked and screamed, fighting with all his might until a gunshot echoed through the plains.

Everyone feel silent. An eerie stillness fell upon them. Eli's eyes grew wide and tears began to slide down his cheeks. "Duncan?" he breathed.

Daniel froze next to him. Indeed, the magick they felt from Duncan seemed to be gone. Was he dead? It didn't seem possible, not after all this time.

"No! Duncan!" Eli wailed, fighting more than ever to break free of his friends. He was frantic, completely terrified of losing his former rival.

"Eli, we've got to go," Daniel said sternly. Eli was on the verge of throwing all four people off him.

"No, no! Let me go!"

He grabbed the Eli's chin. "We can't stay."

When Eli continued to struggle, Daniel raised his hand to his forehead and chanted softly. It shouldn't have worked. He had never had the power before. Eli's eyes rolled into his head and he slumped forward into Daniel's arms. He was sound asleep. Ignoring his bad arm, Daniel picked him up and held him protectively against his chest. It would be easy now that he was unconscious. Together with the Sinclairs, they tore out of the Salisbury Plains and headed northeast to Cambridge. Eli slept the whole way.

Duncan wrestled to keep the gun pointed away from him, but Henry's superior strength was proving to be far too much for him. Once again, the gun aimed between his eyes.

"You let him go!" Henry screamed, his eyes wild. "You let them take my grandson!"

"He would have died if you continued to feed from him. He almost did!"

There was no getting through to Henry. Not any more. Whatever shred of humanity he had left was now gone with the wind. In the distance, they could still hear Eli fighting his friends, trying desperately to get to Duncan. To help him. Duncan only prayed Daniel found a way to get him to safety.

Henry pushed the barrel of the gun against his forehead, his finger slowly squeezing back on the trigger.

It was now or never, Duncan realized in horror. He had to do it now or die. If he died, Eli would never be safe from Henry. He made complete eye contact with Henry, silently hating himself for what he must do to survive and ensure Eli's well being. "The eyes are the window to the soul," he said softly. "What was yours is now mine." Henry's eyes widened, but it was too late now.

The gunshot thundered throughout the land.

Blinking, Duncan fell back. Beneath him, lay the body he had become so accustomed to. He half-cried at the sight of those dead blue eyes staring up at him. He had loved them so much. He had loved living in that body. The soul transfer had happened just in time, but he had lost so much in the exchange. He had lost the one true friend he had always had. Then again, he had lost Henry some time back.

Choking back a sob, he threw the gun away and wept into his hands. He didn't bother fighting when the Sinclairs arrested him for the murder of Michael Sinclair. They didn't know of the soul transfer.

Not that they or anyone else would ever understand why.

Chapter Thirty-nine

Warmth. Blessed warmth. Eli snuggled under the covers more. He knew without opening his eyes that he was in his room.

The familiar sense of Raven filled him. His former self was everywhere. The pillows, the sheets, even the comforter, all smelled of Anthony, even after all these years. It was a scent that would forever remain, and it felt so much like home.

He smiled at the warmth against his back. Duncan, he thought, feeling the calming magick fill him. Good, they had gone back for him. He had not died when the gunshot went off. Henry must have.

He rolled over, ready to tease the older man for his foolhardy attack of Henry as well as thank him for saving Daniel. He froze when he saw the man lying next to him. It wasn't Duncan Porter, but Daniel Dion.

The grown man was laying next to him in a t-shirt and jogging pants. His left bicep was bandaged and his right shoulder had a nasty bruise that looked rather serious. There was nothing sexual in the way he laid next to Eli. It fatherly, and appeared he was using his magick to keep Eli calm as Duncan had done many times alone. He looked exhausted and Eli realized the last few days had been the most he had ever used his magick.

Eli watched his steady breathing for a moment. It seemed odd how Daniel would be here caring for him rather than his own children. He wasn't really hurt, a little confused perhaps, but not physically hurt. Surely, Alexis needed Daniel more. He sighed inwardly. Perhaps Duncan was dead and Daniel was just here to comfort him. After all, it had been Daniel's magick that subdued him. His chest knotted as that thought played through his mind. No, it wasn't possible. Not after so many years. Duncan simply wouldn't die after all this time, not now that they were finally friends.

Yet there was still a sense of Porter's magick in the air. Faint and somehow different, but still Duncan's. The part that was Sinclair seemed missing as if torn away. Now there was Duncan's magick and something else. Where was it coming from?

Carefully moving Daniel's arm off him, Eli climbed out of bed, fetched his glasses, and silently left the room. The hall was dark. Everyone had to be asleep. Duncan had to be there somewhere. His presence was so strong in Eli's mind.

The old dungeons in the bowels of the mansion. If they knew he was truly Duncan Porter and not Michael Sinclair that was where Richard would take him. It was the one place no one could use magick. The wards within each cell prevented it.

Nathaniel sat up with a start. Eli was awake. He felt the young man's aura pass by his and Scott's room. He glanced at the clock. 3:47 AM. What was he doing up at such an hour? Curious, he shook Scott awake.

The larger man rolled over with a grunt but refused to open his eyes.

"Scott, wake up. Eli's wandering the mansion."

"So?" came Scott's muffled response under a mound of covers.

The patter of rain bounced off the windows. It had been raining half the night as if the sky itself was mourning over those they had lost that day. It was nothing new for it to rain whenever a magick user passed on, but for four in one day, the land wept for hours, even days. "He sleepwalks, Scott, and it's been raining all night. I don't want him wandering outside."

Scott groaned and peered up at his love. "He knows this place like the back of his hand."

"Doesn't matter. You heard the stories Richard told your father."

"What about Selena?" Scott yawned, reluctant to get up. He slowly sat up.

"Patrolling." Pulling on his trousers, Nathaniel went to the door.

"Okay, okay. I'm coming."

Where was it? The door to the dungeon seemed to be missing. He searched along the wall where he knew the hidden passage was located, but could not find the button. It had to be there. It had been over fifty years since he, or rather Anthony, had used it. Perhaps Jonathan Sinclair or maybe even Richard had changed it. Maybe there was another way. There had to be.

He ran his hands over the smooth surface, looking for that little piece of imperfection that you could not see with your eyes. He found none. Desperation began to fill him. He knew Duncan was close. He could feel it. A hand fell on his shoulder, scaring him half to death.

"Eli?"

His mind must have been playing tricks on him. The man's height and broad shoulders instantly reminded him of Henry in his young form. It didn't help that he completely cloaked himself in shadow. Terrified, Eli pulled his arm back and ran blindly away from him. He would never let anyone feed from him again.

"Eli, wait!" the man called, running after him.

Damn, damn, damn! He had to find Duncan fast. Having a power-hungry vampire after him was not part of the plan. He was getting closer to Duncan. It was almost as if he was standing on top of him. If only he could find away to get to him. He almost screamed when his pursuer grabbed him from behind. He kicked and struggled only to have a large hand cover his mouth.

"Shh…It's okay, it's me, Scott," the man whispered very close to his ear.

Taking a deep breath, Eli slowly turned around and took a good look at his pursuer. "Scott?"

"Hey, sorry I scared you, but Nate was worried."

Feeling giddy, Eli threw his arms around Scott's waist and buried his face in the older man's shoulder. "I thought you were Henry.

Where's Duncan? They took him to the dungeon, right?"

"Eli," Scott began very carefully. "Duncan's gone."

Eli froze in shock. "No…"

"I'm sorry, but he died. Henry shot him."

"No!" He tried, pulling away only to be held tightly. "No, that's not possible! I can feel him. He's here! I can feel him!"

Scott only shook his head, a look of pity covering his face.

Frost quickly approached them from behind. "Eli, it's true," he said softly, taking him from Scott's arms.

"No…I can feel him." He wanted to fight them, prove that Duncan was hidden in the dungeons, but he was shaking too hard to do anything more than cling to Frost.

"Come with us."

Eli stared at him for a moment. He didn't like the sound of his friend's words. After throwing on a trench coat, he followed Frost into the pouring rain to the Sinclair chapel, a place of worship for the Catholic magick family. All the lights were lit on the first floor. A cold chill ran up the length of Eli's spine as he stepped inside. He didn't want to be there. He didn't want to see what Frost had to show him. At the sight of the black polished coffin on the altar his knees almost buckled.

"Eli?" Frost asked. He held him until his was strong enough to continue.

Hesitantly, Eli approached the coffin and peered down at the body. A strangled cry escaped his lips. Inside, lying peaceful as an angel was Duncan Porter, or rather Michael Sinclair's body. Soft red cushioning lined the inside, complimenting the youth's tanned features. His long hair brushed back in waves around his face and over his shoulders. He didn't look dead, only in a sound sleep. One from which he would never wake.

"Duncan," Eli breathed, leaning over the coffin. He brushed back a stray strand of hair, his fingers grazing over the bullet wound that was hidden by makeup.

Yet something didn't feel right. The fading magick the body was still emanating was no longer Duncan's. It was purely Sinclair with a touch of Henry's aura.

Eli's eyes widened. It wasn't possible. Duncan's soul had not passed on in this body. Henry's did. That meant somewhere, somehow, Duncan was still alive. He had switched bodies again.

"Michael's parents will be here tomorrow to claim the body," Frost said softly, placing a hand on his shoulder.

Claiming the body? Eli had come to love that body. It was Duncan's, not Michael's. Yet Henry was the one to die in it. Shaking his head, he tried to stop the headache that was mounting against him.

"Eli?"

He gazed up to see Daniel walking down the aisle. He looked concerned and more than a little wet. Eli nodded to him before turning back to the body. He closed his eyes as he brushed his lips over the body's forehead, a tear rolling down his cheek and onto it.

"Goodbye, Grandpa," he whispered, not wanting any of his friends to know the truth. How would they react to Duncan Porter being in Henry's body?

Daniel wrapped his arms around him. "I'm sorry about your friend," he whispered.

Eli nodded. He turned slowly in the man's arms and hugged him tightly. "Dad."

Daniel's eyes widened for only a moment, but he held Eli tightly.

"Everything's going to be okay, son."

Daniel stayed at Eli's side for the next few days, rarely leaving him for more than a minute or two. Eli greatly appreciated it. He needed the kind aura of protection next to him as he was questioned continually again by the Sinclairs.

"Tell us again, Eli, where were you?" Richard asked, a video recorder aimed solely at Eli's face.

Eli sighed. After three hours of explaining everything that had happened in the last few weeks that had actually turned out to be three and a half days, he was getting tired of the same questions. He had already told the story twice yet now they wanted him to change it for Michael's parents. They did not want the Canadian Sinclair family to know that their son had switched bodies with Duncan Porter and then committed suicide.

"I don't know what else to say," Eli admitted. He looked up at Richard in frustration. "What do you want me to say? That Henry kidnapped Michael and me for food? Or to inherit the fortune of our two families? Then it would be completely Henry's fault. I don't want his family viewing him as some monster, no matter what he did. He did raise me."

Richard motioned for the camera to be turned off. "Eli, Michael's parents are downstairs. They'll never believe what really happened."

"That's your problem. All I want is to go home and forget all this insanity." He stood and glared at the elder. "Tell them whatever you like, but I'm sore, tired, and hungry. If you don't mind, I'd like to spend some time with my friends."

Richard stopped him at the door. "Michael's parents will most likely wish to speak with you. You need to have your story straight."

"If that happens, I'll tell them the truth."

Richard furrowed his brows in doubt.

"The soul within that body was gentle and loving. He saved my life and in that I owe him."

Richard nodded in satisfaction. "Go eat, Lord Hawke. We'll talk again later."

Daniel loyally followed Eli into the vast corridor. Eli walked ahead of him, not wishing to discuss the meeting. He knew Daniel was worried, could feel his magick brushing against his own in search of answers, but Eli kept his shields up. Finally, Daniel caught his arm and made him stop.

"Eli, slow down."

Surprised, Eli spun around and stared up at him.

"Are you okay?"

"Define *okay*."

Daniel pulled back. Eli was tense, still fighting the stress of the last few days, or weeks in Eli's case. There were tears that had yet to shed. Tears that he refused to reveal to anyone. He really must have formed a bond with Duncan Porter.

"Eli, you know it was only Duncan's magick, right? He used a calming spell on you. I know you care for him, but—"

"You don't know anything!" Eli suddenly growled, pulling away. He turned away.

Daniel was taken aback by the sudden outburst. He hesitated before placing his hand on Eli's shoulder.

"I can still feel him," Eli said in a small, calmer voice. "He's alive."

"Eli." He slowly turned the young man around to face him. "What do you feel for Duncan?"

"I…I don't know. Not love, well, not as if I'm in love with him or anything, but a friendship, I suppose, that I never had before. An odd form of complete understanding."

"How did you feel when you heard the gun shot?"

"Terrified he was dead."

"And when you saw the body?"

"Torn in two. I wanted so much for him to open his eyes and say it was all some crude joke. The funny thing is, I didn't sense Duncan in that body. He wasn't there." His eyes were pleading. "I'm not going crazy, am I? He can still be alive. What if he took Henry's body?"

"Perhaps. How do you feel about that?"

"I don't know." Those unshed tears began to flow down his flushed cheeks. "I just don't know. I must be losing it."

"No, Eli, you are perfectly fine. Just let it out." He pulled Eli into his arms and let him cry. It was what he needed most. "Let it all out."

By the time Eli stopped sobbing, they were in the drawing room. Eli would do anything but sit though. He was pacing back and forth, his dark eyes in deep thought.

He had returned to using glamour to hide his eyes, not really telling Daniel why. Daniel had never seen eyes quite like them, except in Selena's tri-coloured red ones. Eli would frown, glance at the floor, then look at Daniel. He paced for nearly twenty minutes before standing in front of Daniel with a puzzled look.

"Why do I still sense him?"

"Why don't you sit down and eat?" Daniel countered. "You may just be overly sensitive right now." Daniel shook his head as Eli continued his endless pacing. "I'm sure Miao and Alexis would like to spend some time with you."

It made Eli stop. His shoulders slumped as he turned around. "Yeah, I know. I should, but…oh, Daniel, I can't stop thinking about him."

Daniel sighed. This was no good. Eli was going to drive himself insane if he didn't find out what truly happened to Duncan. He had little choice. Standing, he patted Eli's shoulder. "I'll be back in a moment."

For a moment, it looked as if Eli was going to cling to him rather than letting him leave the room. It took a moment for the young man to ground himself. He gave a small nod and turned to the fireplace. A fire roared to life instantly, warming Eli's ice-cold hands. The cold was psychological, not physical, his hands only cold because that was how he felt inside. He stayed close to the fire as if it would make him feel better.

Daniel made his way to the back of the large house. Eli would be fine on his own for a few minutes. His hand slid along the paneled wall until he found the imperfection that indicated the opening for the basement passage. He pushed it open and stepped into the dimly lit staircase. He passed the main basement to the sub-basement. It was damp and stank of moist soil. A shiver ran up his spine. Instantly, he hated this place. It was full of death, old death, from back it the days of war. How many rival magick users had died behind these walls, he wondered. He had to continue forth.

Light shone brightly at the end of the steep staircase. He was never so thankful to see such light. How did Anthony ever handle coming down here? It was spookier than any fun house he had ever visited in his youth.

"Mr. Dion?"

He jumped at the sudden voice. Holding his chest, he let out the breath he had not known he was holding.

"What are you doing down here? It can be dangerous," said a guard, walking up to him. "Sir, are you alright?"

He nodded and took slow, deep breaths, and instantly regretted it. The air was too stale. "Yes, yes. You just scared me." He sighed, letting himself relax. "I need to speak to the prisoner."

"I need to clear it with Lord Sinclair."

Anthony stirred within Daniel and before he knew what he was doing, he raised his hand in front of the guard's face and cast a small spell. The man sank to the rocky floor, deep in sleep.

Stepping past him, he went to the dungeons. Henry, or rather Duncan in Henry's body, was sitting on a bench. His head was in his hands. He looked terrible. His large body trembled as if he were coming down from the largest high in his life. The energy Henry had taken from his victims was draining away, leaving Duncan trapped in an addict's body. Grasping the thick metal bars, Daniel stared at the hunched-over figure. Pity filled him. No human should suffer like that.

"Duncan?" Anthony's voice asked.

Henry's gray eyes were swollen and teary as he gazed up at him.

"Is he okay?" Duncan whispered in a hoarse voice.

"Eli is alright. Are you?"

Wiping his eyes with the back of his sleeve, Duncan nodded. "I will be. He's been pacing so much, trying to locate me that I've developed a headache."

Daniel-Anthony was silent for a moment. "Eli has been very worried about you."

The warlock shook his head. "I don't want him to see me like this. What Henry took is now unstable. I may hurt him."

"I'm sure you can control yourself."

Duncan shook his head. "Even if I could, how am I to get to him?"

There was a moment of silence before Daniel pulled a key he had swiped from the guard. Duncan stared at him, flabbergasted.

"If you harm him...or so much as touch him inappropriately...I won't hesitate finishing was Henry started," he warned. He quietly unlocked the old metal door, cautious to make as little noise as possible. The last thing he needed was a guard to find him freeing the prisoner.

"You sure you don't want to eat?" Alexis asked, sitting across from Eli. A bowl of fruit sat on the marble and glass coffee table between them. "Tea? Juice? Anything?"

He smiled. "No. Thank you." Alexis was persistent to make him comfortable. He hated seeing her worried. Even the familiars were overly concerned, as if having him home was not enough. Sif sat beside Alexis while Cleo curled up on Eli's lap. Miao sat on Alexis's other side, fingering the video camera he had brought for their summer trip.

According to Alexis, they had been wandering through Sinclair mansion recording everything they could find on Anthony's past. Miao had teased that Melissa would end up doing a documentary on the *Life and Times of Anthony Sinclair*. Melissa would most likely have Eli do a commentary. It actually sounded like fun. If Eli were in a better mood, he would have taken them to some of Anthony's favourite spots.

"Well, do you want to do anything? Go swimming? Hike?" Alexis continued.

"Help us with Mel's newest movie?" Miao threw in, holding up the camcorder.

Eli chuckled. They were trying so hard. "Maybe later."

"You can't stay inside all day. It's beautiful out," Alexis insisted.

"I won't stay in all day. I'm just getting myself grounded. After weeks—days...whatever, of being fed upon by Henry and all the training...it's just nice to be back. I promise, in a day or two I'll be back to normal."

"You sure?" Miao asked in concern.

"Yes, Miao, I'm sure."

Alexis looked past him, her eyes widening for a moment. She quickly recovered. "Yeah, okay. Well, we're going outside to…uh…film a little more. You take care." She pulled Miao to his feet and out of the room.

Surprised, Eli followed them to the large archway. His breath caught in his throat. Henry stood in the archway next to a smiling Daniel. That smile was one of Anthony's. It spoke volumes only Eli could understand. His gaze turned back to the larger man that had once been his grandfather. "Duncan?" he whispered, not sure if he was dreaming.

The big man smiled shyly. "Hi…Eli."

Eli couldn't move. It didn't seem real. He had to be dreaming. He glanced at Daniel and then unsure what else to do or say, turned back to the roaring fire. As much as he wanted to believe it was Duncan, even sensing him, he just couldn't. Not in that body.

"Daniel?" he whispered softly.

"It's alright, Eli," Daniel answered.

Those massive arms that cradled him as a child, and abused him only days ago, wrapped around him. He was gently pulled against the much larger body as a pair of lips brushed against the top of his head. The tears resurfaced immediately. He hugged those arms and let his emotions overwhelm him.

"Shh… Hey, come on, I didn't scare you that much, did I?" Duncan's voice overlapped Henry's. "Where were you?"

"A little detained. I'm here now." He kissed the side of Eli's head. "I'm so sorry I scared you, Raven." He turned Eli around and cupped his cheeks.

It was a long look up, far more-so than it had been when Duncan was in Michael's body. He took a deep breath and let it out slowly. "The Sinclairs are asking so many questions. I don't know what to tell them. Michael's parents are here."

"I know. Eli, I need your help one last time."

"With what?"

His eyes were sad, almost desperate, but he was reluctant to ask straight forward. "I think this will help us both in the long run."

"What is it? I'll help you any way I can."

Duncan chewed his bottom lip for a moment. "I want you to open the gate to the Land of the Dead."

Chapter Forty

"What? No!"

Eli broke free of Duncan and stormed to the other side of the room. He couldn't believe it. How could he ask such a favor? He spun around and glared at him. "After everything that happened yesterday, you want me to do it again?"

He could hold back the anger that he felt. The portals were all that Duncan cared about. It hurt but now Eli knew the truth. He folded his arms across his chest. Duncan didn't care about him.

Never had. It was all a ploy to get him to do what he wanted.

"Eli, no. You don't understand," Duncan pleaded.

He moved away as Duncan went to him. He didn't even want to look at the warlock. He was sick and tired of all his games. He just wanted to go back to Ravenwood and leave all this behind him. He inhaled sharply as Duncan cornered him next to a wall-length scenic painting. He gazed upward in slight fear as Duncan grabbed his upper arms.

"I don't want you to open it in the real realm, but in the astral realm. It doesn't take as much power."

"I can't believe that's all you care about!" He tried to pull away, but Duncan now had Henry's strength. He could break his arms and it would be an accident only because he did not know his own strength now. "Let go! Dan!"

He looked toward the archway for help, but Daniel was no longer there. He had vanished.

Duncan stooped down until they were nearly the same height. "I'm not here to cause you harm, but to give you a gift. For that, I need to get into the Land of the Dead. Please help me."

Eli struggled. "No!"

"Then please forgive me."

Eli's eyes widened in horror. Duncan's hands moved to either side of his face. His fingers stroked Eli's temples tenderly for a moment before the flow of magick nudged its way into Eli's mind. At first, he fought, a part of him terrified that Duncan would slash at his mind as he had months earlier. This time was different, however. Rather than trying to force his way in, Duncan followed Eli to the depths of his subconsciousness.

Don't fight him, Eli. He won't hurt you, Anthony's voice whispered. *He won't let anything happen to you.*

It took a moment for Eli to relax. Anthony's words were reassuring, but Eli still had his doubts. What was so important about the Land of the Dead? He finally gave in, due to his own curiosity. If Anthony was so certain Duncan's intentions were good, then by hell he'd open the blasted portal, Eli thought rashly. Not that he liked being double-teamed by his past self and former rival.

He let Duncan in his mind and onto the astral realm. They sat at the graveyard much as he had with Daniel the day before. The day was as it always was, peaceful and perfect in its serenity. The portal flickered in and out of life several yards ahead of them as it had for as long as Eli could remember.

"That is the doorway to the realm of the Dead," Eli said, studying Duncan carefully as he sat on his usual perch. The warlock was no longer in Henry's form, nor Michael's. Instead, he was in his own body, much younger than when they had met in Ravenwood that past March. No, this was how Anthony had last seen him before he had passed on. Duncan donned the robes of his office and stood proudly, if not a little confused, beside him.

"That's the opening?"

"Yes."

Duncan held out his hand. "Come with me?"

Eli shook his head. "We'll be swarmed."

"Not if Raven guards the gate. I'll protect you."

Staring at the proffered hand for a long period, Eli wasn't sure what to do. Anthony insisted he could trust him, but what if Duncan betrayed him at the last moment? He did care for Duncan, but he really didn't know if he could ever completely trust him. Maybe it was because he was now in his own body rather than Michael's. There was no Sinclair magick in him to make Eli feel safe.

Duncan took his right hand and kissed his knuckles like a servant adoring his lord. "I would never allow any harm to befall you, Eli. I swear on my honor."

"There is nothing to fear, Eli." Anthony's hand fell upon his shoulder.

Looking up, Eli saw his former self smile reassuringly. "I'll be right beside you." With a sigh, Eli nodded.

* * *

"What the—" Nathaniel cried, stepping into the drawing room. Rage took hold of him at the sight of Eli being pinned to the far wall by Henry Griphan. "Get away from him!"

With a growl, he stormed into the room, followed closely by Scott. They were practically on top of Henry when a shield forced them to stop. Frustrated and ready to blow, Nathaniel called his magick bow into existence and aimed at the big man, fully ignoring the trance-like state both he and Eli were in. Pulling back on the string, he prepared to kill Raven's former best friend.

"Stop!"

The bow vanished from his hands just as he was about to let the arrow fly. Enraged, he stared at Daniel in disbelief.

"He's not hurting Eli. They're just finishing business."

"Dad, you've got to be kidding! Henry almost killed Eli with his constant feedings. You saw the gunshot wound across his arm," Scott pleaded, gesturing to the big man. "He could have killed you."

"Yes, Scott, but that's not Henry." A mysterious smile crossed his lips.

Nathaniel knew instantly Anthony had everything under control.

"That's Duncan Porter."

That didn't necessarily mean it was a good thing.

* * *

The Land of the Dead was exactly as Eli remembered it. Colourful orbs danced all over the place, some taking human form as they neared him and Duncan, only to quickly change shape once more and continue their eternal waltz. Duncan's magick kept the spirits from swarming them. It was also calling out to the spirits he was looking for.

Eli stayed close to Anthony, refusing to leave his side in case Duncan suddenly changed his mind and turned on them. It wasn't so much he didn't trust Duncan, but feared what Henry's insanity may have done to him while he was trapped in that body.

A bubbly little violet orb came speeding out of nowhere. It danced before them before turning into a small ghost child. A five-year-old with long black hair in little ringlets and big green eyes stared up at them.

Eli couldn't help but smile. She was adorable in her long purple nightie. She looked just like—

"Sara!" Duncan cried in glee. He knelt down and threw his arms wide open.

The child instantly ran into his arms. "Papa!"

This was Sara Porter? She was only a child. When Eli had met Dominique, she was in her early forties. How was it possible for her to be so young here?

"She died, truly died, when she was a mere child. Dominique's spirit claimed her at this age, making it impossible for her to mature. She literally died at the age of five," Daniel explained.

Eli looked up at him. "Not a reincarnation? Not like you and me?"

Anthony shook his head. "No. You and Daniel have free will. I am simply what you once were. Your past. Your guide in this time. The magick you possess you would have with or without me awakening."

Leaning into him, Eli watched Duncan play with his lost daughter with a smile. "I'm glad you awoke. If it weren't for you, I would never have met Alexis and the gang."

"You may never have suffered either. I'm sorry, Eli."

"Hmm...I'm not. Don't get me wrong, I hate being fed upon, and beaten, and all the battles, but sometime, just sometimes..." He waved toward Duncan and Sara. "...some of it is actually worth it."

Anthony must have thought Eli was losing his mind, or maybe the trauma had finally taken a hold of him. He stared down worriedly at Eli, but he only smiled at the reunited family. There were times when all the past pain no longer mattered. Only the present.

It was a topaz and an emerald orb that drew his attention away from the father and daughter. Eli gazed at the two newcomers suspiciously. They looked familiar in an odd way, but it wasn't possible. It had been so long. He looked back at Anthony, hoping for answers, but the sorcerer only gave an enigmatic smile. Confused, Eli watched as the two orbs slowly morphed into a man and woman.

Eli's mouth suddenly felt dry as he stared at them. The woman was thin and relatively short, only five foot, two inches. She wore a richly coloured emerald gown, one Eli knew for a fact she had made herself out of the finest silk in all of Spain. Her long black hair was up in a loose bun-ponytail. Her brown eyes, as dark as chocolate, sparkled at the sight of Eli.

The man was at least a head taller than the woman was and wore an expensive black tuxedo. His soft amber-brown eyes held heartfelt laughter. They looked exactly as they did the day they died. The night of their anniversary.

Eli's heart swelled at the sight of them. He remembered that night as if it was yesterday.

* * *

"You look pretty, Mama," a six-year-old Eli declared, bouncing into his parents' room. He held his stuff Tigger backpack already to go to his grandmother's house for the night.

Suzanna Hawke smiled, placing the last pin in her hair. "Thank you, sweetie." She picked him up and held him on her lap. She teasingly rubbed his nose with hers. "Nose kiss?"

He giggled. "Mum!"

"You two ready?" Ian Hawke asked, fixing his tie in the doorway.

"Do you have to go out tonight?" Eli asked for the umpteenth time.

His father scooped him out of his mother's arms. "You're so persistent, squirt. Miss us already?"

"No…my tummy feels funny. Can't you stay home and take care of me?"

He laughed. "What did we do to have such a beautiful, smart, sneaky little boy like you? And one with such amazing blue eyes?" He hugged Eli tightly.

"Oh, I love you so much, kiddo. You always remember that."

"I love you, too, Da."

To see them again was like a dream come true. Biting his lip, he left Anthony to go to them. "Mama? Papa?" he whispered in disbelief. It had been so long since he had last seen them. He cried out for joy when he was able to wrap his arms around them once more. They were real. They were really there.

"Hi, baby," Sue whispered, hugging him tightly.

He could even smell her perfume and the tangy smell of her shampoo.

"You've grown!" Ian teased, pushing Eli's head back just enough to get a good look at him. "I like your hair. You take after your mother."

He blushed slightly at his father's comment. Everyone said he took after his mother in his features. His father for his height. "I've missed you," he half-laughed, half-sob.

"We've missed you, too, sweetheart," his mother said, kissing his cheek. "And as much as we would love for you to stay—"

"I know, Mum, I know." He buried his face in her hair, hoping to imprint her scent on him forever. "Just for now let me hold you. Both of you."

* * *

"Hmm…" Eli opened his eyes slowly. It took effort, but he was able to focus once more on the real world. Duncan was still leaning above him, his hands holding the wall as he tried to bring himself back. His face twisted in anguish and Eli almost wished neither of them had had to return. However, they were still alive. They could not survive in the other realm for long. He reached up and wiped the tears away from Duncan's face. Was it his imagination or did Duncan appear older? "Duncan?"

Duncan opened his eyes and gazed down at him in sorrow. He gave a hiccupped sob before falling to his knees and hugging Eli's waist for dear life. His tears soaked Eli's t-shirt as he buried his face against Eli's chest.

Smiling understandingly, he wrapped his arms around the man's broad shoulders. "It's okay, Duncan. Mum and Da will take good care of her. She'll be waiting for you."

It was the right thing to say. Duncan quickly calmed himself and sniffled. He wiped his nose with his sleeve, something he seemed to be doing a lot lately, and gave a teary smile. "Thank you, Eli."

"Would someone kindly explain what the hell is going on?" Frost snapped.

For the first time, Eli realized they were no longer alone. He looked around, not completely surprised by those in the room. Daniel stood by the door, smiling like a proud father. Scott was next to Frost, staring at the in utter confusion. Frost's anger was undeniable. He was fuming.

Concerned for his friend, Eli went to move around Duncan only to learn that the warlock's weight had been the only thing to keep him standing. He fell to his knees with a surprised cry. Before he could say or do anything, everyone swarmed around him to make sure he was alright. So many worried faces only made him giddy and to their surprised faces, he burst into laughter.

Frost definitely thought he was insane. "Eli?"

He was finding it difficult to stop laughing. It felt so good just to laugh. "I'm fine, I'm fine. Just need to get my bearings."

"Damn it, kid. You scared us to death!" Scott growled, swatting his shoulder, but he smiled.

"Sorry, Scott." He stared up at Frost, even as Duncan helped him to his feet. "Frost?"

He looked incredibly upset at Duncan even touching him, especially since the big man had his arms around him in a more than friendly manner.

"We need to talk," Frost growled, grabbing Eli's hand, and pulling him away from Duncan.

Eli didn't have time to hesitate before he found himself dragged to one of the large libraries.

Frost locked the door and sighed, leaning against it. "Eli, do you have any idea what happened to me and Nathan?"

It was an odd question, completely off topic and not explaining Frost's hate of Duncan. Eli raised a brow, hoping for a simple answer. His head hurt too much for games. "No."

"We merged."

His huge smile filled Eli's face with surprise and glee. "You did? That's great! Fr-Nathaniel! I'm so happy for you. I wish I was there for you."

"No, you wouldn't have," the faery being sneered, walking up to him. "We—I was nearly killed. Had our minds not merged when they did, I would have never been able to access my powers in Nathan's form."

"You were trying to save me. Henry's men—"

"Tried to capture us. Daniel suffered when you suffered. Selena's neck is still healing, but it's going to scar, and you're treating Porter like your new best friend. What gives?"

"It's a long story."

"Tell me."

Eli stared at his feet. They seemed a long way down.

"Do you know what I think?"

He shook his head. He didn't want to know what Nathaniel thought of the matter.

"I think Porter had Henry kidnap you. Then inside Porter's shields, he placed a spell on you, maybe a love spell or a calming spell. I don't know."

Nathaniel circled him while he talked, like a lion around its prey.

"Time was slowed down. A few weeks from what Daniel's told us, but even in that amount of time, I can't believe you would have fallen in love with that man."

"We're not in love. We're just friends."

"Friends?"

"Yes."

"You kissed him at Stonehenge."

"So?"

"So?"

Eli stepped back when the angelic being's fist clenched together. He would never strike him, would he?

"Eli, he's using you! He's playing with your emotions. Damn it, can't you see that?"

Eli tried to stay calm. Nathaniel had a right to be angry. So much had happened in such a short amount of time. That and everything Duncan had put them through months earlier was enough to make anyone leery. Nevertheless, he had no idea what had happened behind the castle walls, how Duncan had risked his own life for Eli.

"I know, Nathaniel, but it is my decision. You don't know how much Duncan put on the line for me." He took Nathaniel's arms and gently massaged them as Anthony used to. "Had he not made Henry feed from him instead of me, I may have died long before I opened the portals. Had he not fought Henry, we all might have died. I do care for him, Nate, but he was my only friend there and Henry abused him just as much as me. It's hard to explain. We just developed a bond."

"A bond?"

"Yes. Things have changed. Even Anthony forgives him." Those beautiful eyes were confused and hurt and they had a right. He would never understand the bond he and Duncan had formed. Very few ever would. Giving him a sympathetic smile, Eli hugged the silvery being. Nathaniel didn't hesitate to embrace him in return. It was good to be with family again.

Chapter Forty-one

The family church was built at the beginning of the medieval era. It had been the Sinclairs' only hope from being convicted of witchcraft in those dark ages. It saved many families and friends by declaring Christianity. They were one of the first families of Christian witches in England, survived by the blessings of the church. The church saved them from being burned at the stake by declaring they were healers and seers, prophets of the Lord. It was a place of many happy and sad occasions.

Today was a mixture of both.

Even though Michael's body was to return to Quebec, Canada with his parents, the Sinclairs were holding a requiem for him. The church was decorated with numerous summer flowers and colourful flags representing both countries and the family shield.

Michael's body lay on the altar. An earthenware bowl with a silver cord tied to it, laid next to the body with a silver hammer meant to break it at the end of the ceremony.

Eli sat between Daniel and Selena, silently watching as the ritual began. This wasn't the first time he had watched The Legend of the Descent of the Goddess. Richard, the high priest of the family, and the high priestess were performing it. Nudity didn't bother Eli, it was common practice in some covens, but he could not suppress a smirk when Alexis and Miao gasped. It was their first time. His only regret was that Duncan could not be with them.

Duncan had to stay outside the church or in the manor as to not upset Michael's parents. Not that either Chris or Lynda knew who killed their son. As far as they knew, his killer was dead. In some senses, it was true. Henry's body was rapidly aging now that they were in the real world. Duncan explained that Henry had fed too much and now his body needed a magickal fix every day. However, he refused to feed from Eli, or anyone. He would not become like Henry. Now Duncan was in his mid-forties. In another day or two, he would be in his eighties once more. If only Duncan would just take a little magick from him, Eli thought miserably.

Taking a sip from the glass of wine the high priest and priestess had consecrated, Eli ate the little slice of cake, giving a small prayer for Michael's soul. Together with the rest of the Sinclair family, he and his friends followed the priest and priestess to a stream where the shattered bowl was thrown in.

"Return to the elements from whence thou came," they said in unison.

On the walk back to the manor, Daniel wrapped an arm around his shoulders. "How are you holding up?"

Eli gave a small smile. "Hmm…tired. I spent half the day with Chris and Lynda. You wouldn't believe the stories they told me."

"Yeah?"

Eli grinned. "He was the captain of his football team. I thought they were talking about soccer, but they really meant football. Apparently, he wanted to travel to England and learn of his heritage before college this fall. He graduated with honors in January."

"Wow." Daniel scratched his arm where the bandage still bothered him. "So, what happened?"

"No one knows. Duncan said he was depressed. The *Sight* was too much for him. I'm guessing he was a seer amongst other things."

Possible. It can be overwhelming."

Glancing up at the huge mansion, Eli spotted Duncan standing at a bay window. It was already getting late and almost all of the first and second floor lights were on in the house. "I think I'm going to check on Duncan before I go to bed. He didn't look well."

"Sure. Take it easy."

Duncan sat in the library at one of the window seats. He had aged considerably in the short time Eli was gone. A kind smile came to the man's lips as Eli sat next to him and brushed a hand through his short graying hair.

"How's everyone doing?" Duncan asked, glancing at the Sinclairs outside. Soft music played down the hall.

"They're still celebrating. His parents are still very emotional. Understandable."

Duncan nodded. "What about your friends? How did they take to the ritual?"

Eli grinned widely. "When the high priest and priestess stripped, they went pale. Scott covered Alexis's eyes while Nathaniel kept Miao from filming it."

Duncan laughed and ruffled his hair. "And you didn't blush?"

"Well…"

"We'll get you up performing one of these days." Reaching for his cane, he pushed himself to his feet.

Eli got up and helped him. "I doubt it. How do you feel?"

"Tired, my boy. Very tired."

Eli helped him up the stairs to one of the former servant chambers. Richard refused to let Duncan stay anywhere near the rest of the household. Fear of what the warlock may try next kept the family on their toes. However, Eli refused to stay away and Richard constantly chastised him for it. Duncan was his friend. He was not going to abandon him now.

He helped Duncan change for bed. It seemed he was having trouble with Henry's fake leg. His balance was off and getting worse by the moment. He was literally aging before Eli's very eyes. He was also unable to hold down food now. His systems were simply unable to cope with the sudden increase in age. He was dying. "Duncan, you look horrible," Eli murmured, as he took his suit jacket off.

"You're so sweet."

"I'm serious," Eli snapped. He took Duncan's cheeks in his hands and looked him in the eyes. It hurt to see him like this, not when his magick could heal him. "Feed," he urged in a soft whisper. He gently pulled Duncan's head to his bare neck.

For a moment, the parched lips grazed his smooth flesh. Eli closed his eyes, expecting the pull of magick. He knew Duncan would be gentle. He would never hurt him no matter how thirsty he was. His eyes opened when Duncan placed a gentle kiss on his neck and pulled back. He looked up at the aging man in confusion. "You are sweet, Eli, but I can't do that to you."

"I want you to."

"No, Eli. I love you far too much to do that to you." He cupped Eli's cheek and gave him a soft kiss on his forehead, then nose, then briefly kissed his lips. He pulled the youth into an embrace. "Your doctor friend says it's my heart. The stress is too much for it."

"Then—"

"Magick cannot save me."

Eli buried his face in Duncan's cotton nightshirt. "I don't want to lose you. Maybe Scott's wrong."

Duncan laid back, his eyes closing briefly as he rested against the fluffy pillows. "No. I can feel it. My time has finally come." He reached up and wiped the tear that made its way down Eli's cheek.

"Lay with me for a while, please?"

Eli gave a comforting smile. He took off his glasses and lay next to Duncan, his head resting against his chest. As long as he could hear Duncan's heartbeat, everything would be alright. He knew that wasn't true. He could see the big man's colourful aura fading. It looked sickly. There wasn't much time left. They would be lucky if he survived the night. For Eli, sleep was next to possible.

Early the next morning, far too early to get up, Duncan took a turn for the worse. His aura flickered in and out of existence. His breathing became shallow as he tried to draw in enough air for his lungs. He did not appear in pain, only fighting for a few last moments of life. Eli lay away next to him, watching as his chest rose and fell. He would not sleep, not while Duncan was like this. He could not fight the tears that rolled down his cheeks onto Duncan's chest.

"What's wrong?" Duncan whispered. His gaze turned to Eli.

He was so old now, in such a short amount of time, it was hard to believe whom he was laying next to. Eli wiped away his tears and tried to put on a brave face. "No—nothing."

Duncan smiled weakly. "Don't cry. Sara is still waiting for me."

It brought a tiny smile to Eli. "Yeah, she is."

"Be happy for me."

The tear refused to stay at bay. "I am."

Then he was gone, like someone turning off a light switch. His chest no longer rose or fell, his last breath escaping into the night. The magick slowly left the still body to join that of another realm, another time. Duncan's musical laughter filled Eli's mind with words of reassurance.   Eli fell asleep with a soft smile that was not to be disturbed for many hours.

Chapter Forty-two

They returned to Henry's cabin for Duncan and Henry's funerals. Although one body, they paid respect to both. At least Eli and his Guardians did, as well as Daniel. The others merely attended for moral support. They followed Henry's last will and had him cremated, his ashes buried next to his wife, Dorothy Griphan, whom he held in his heart right to the day he died. She was the cause of his insanity, his quest to bring her back to life. It was only right that he now lay next to her.

Aaliyah laughed as she and Daniel watched the teens from their seat under a large birch tree. Neither had expected Eli to recover so quickly, although Daniel was certain Eli was merely acting for their benefit, but the laughter was real. It was a sight he was happy to see. Straightening the letter Duncan had left him, he began reading it again. It was such a strange goodbye.

"Did you tell him, yet?" Aaliyah asked, casually rubbing her swollen belly.

"Not yet."

In his hands was the letter of a lifetime—for Eli at least.

In Henry's handwriting, Duncan had signed sole custody of Eli to Daniel until the young man was twenty. It didn't mean Eli had to move in with the Dion family. That was his choice.

He was eighteen, a legal adult in Canada.

It just meant he was Eli's trustee and, in a way, foster parent. Daniel was honored to play such a role in the young man's life, even if it was for just one year.

His family was getting larger by the moment. Eli was family, he always would be whether or not Daniel had custody. He loved Eli like a son as he did all the Guardians. They had been and always would be family.

His fingers ran over Henry's journal that had mysteriously appeared in a package at the front door. Henry had many secrets he had never told anyone.

They were now Eli's to discover.

There was far more happening around them than met the eye.

About the Author

Canadian born and raised, M.J. Spickett has a long history of writing, both as a novelist and freelance journalist. However, her primary focus is to write primarily urban fantasy, erotic paranormal thrillers, young adult fiction. In recent years, she had branched out to write screenplays with the hope of one day turning her novels into film. When not writing, M.J. enjoys traveling and research. Often times, family vacations turn into exciting road trips to find new, exciting locations and experiences to feature in an upcoming novel.

To become an ARC reader and join our newsletter for chances to win swag and/or gift cards visit:

www.mjspickett.ca

www.ingramcontent.com/pod-product-compliance
Lightning Source LLC
Chambersburg PA
CBHW030546020726
47494CB00005B/1498